potency

POTENCY

Wendy Clarke graduated from St Anne's College, Oxford in 1983 and took a PGCE at the University of Birmingham three years later. She has worked variously as a policewoman, biology teacher and research assistant. More recently her interests have turned to homœopathy and natural healing. Her first novel, *Baudelaire's Desire*, was published in 1999 by Citron Press. She is married with one daughter and lives in Devon.

potency

a novel by
Wendy Clarke

protean press

Copyright © Wendy Clarke 2003

The right of Wendy Clarke to be identified
as author of this work has been asserted by her in accordance
with the Copyright, Designs and Patents Act 1988.

First published 2003

All rights reserved.
No part of this publication may be reproduced or transmitted in
any form or by any means, electronic or mechanical, including
photocopy, recording, or any information storage and retieval system,
without permission in writing from the publisher.
Cover images - Wendy Clarke
Suza Scalora - Getty Images

Published by Protean Press
PO Box 141
Totnes, Devon TQ9 6XJ

ISBN 0-9545986-0-1

A CIP catalogue record for this book is available
from the British Library

Produced by Creative Media Ltd
35 Woodland Park, Paignton, TQ3 2ST
Printed by Ashford Colour Press Ltd

For
Vernon
and
Felicity

ACKNOWLEDGEMENTS

My thanks to:

- Nicholas Burton-Taylor and Misha Norland for guidance on the homœopathy, and Marcus Christo for information on the Travelling Homœopaths' Collective.

- Mark Gibbons and Robert Coram for extended loan of photography books; Ian Allenden (Powerstock/Zefa); Michelle Kenny (Association of Photographers); Stewart Gibson (Bureau of Freelance Photographers); Nick Johnston-Jones for advice on advertising; Oliver Hurd-Thomas for his talk on Soul Portraits.

- David Hawkins, for showing a non-birder round Farmoor; Jeremy James for his demonstration of the Larsen trap; the RSPB for its impromptu Christmas quiz on Oxford rarities; Emma Wilding of Berkshire, Buckinghamshire and Oxfordshire Wildlife Trust.

- Vernon Clarke, Ted Foulkes and Geoffrey Negus for assisting with legal points.

- Dr John Whitehead and Mr David Footitt for providing information on medical issues; Lorraine Hutchinson-Gale and Sue Regan for answering the steady trickle of nursing queries.

- Judy Hempstead, whose musical ear is more finely tuned than my own; Bob Cooper, Mark Williams and Merle Esson for background on Oxford; Gary Essex for advising on Tewkesbury's Medieval Fayre; my parents and the Spanish National Tourist Office for additional detail regarding Tenerife; Barry Collacott for his help with the police.

- Misha Norland, Vernon Clarke, Barry Collacott, Lorraine Hutchinson-Gale, Kate Mount, Gordon Waterhouse and Marcus Christo for reading all or parts of the manuscript.
If any inaccuracies remain they are my responsibility entirely.

1

Karin Shilan had no problem with chocolate. Or her weight, or her consumption of Chardonnay and caffeine, which was virtually nil. In fact, when she announced her New Year's resolution she had every intention of keeping it. She had no idea that she would be substituting another so shortly afterwards, or that the second would change the course of their lives forever.

In the early hours of New Year's Day, the taxi from Summertown swung through the gateway into the drive. Gravel spat against the terracotta edging tiles, and the beam from the headlamps shrank to a bright pool on the brick façade.

While she settled the fare and waited in the back seat for her change, Brendan got out. He instinctively withdrew a hand from his pocket and shrugged up the collar of his navy overcoat as he crunched across the gravel towards the house. Karin watched him pause and squint into the headlights like a stage vampire, his skin bleached and mouth down-turned, his eyes squeezed to slits against the glare. Either side of him the dormant branches of the wistaria wound, bare and desiccated, into the darkness.

She thanked the driver and joined Brendan in front of the car. She pulled her keys from the pocket of her synthetic fur coat and inclined into the beam of one of the headlights to pick through them. The taxi's radio crackled over the churring of the engine, then the engine note rose and the headlamps began to pull away towards the road.

For a second she regarded her husband. He seemed fixated by the receding lights, his arms plunged rigidly into the depths of his pockets. She breathed in the gently settling shadows and the winter air prickled her nostrils with ice. Wrinkling her nose, she took a step towards him. She swung her arm, heavy in its plush muff of fur, across his shoulders. They turned in unison and swayed, like a weary bear, up the front steps.

'You seem very pensive all of a sudden,' she said as the door gave way under the key. 'Or have you just slipped past the pleasant stage of intoxication without my noticing?'

'No, no,' he murmured. 'I couldn't be more perfectly inebriated.'

'It's Leon, then. God, does the man never stop?'

She switched on the lights, kicked off her flat, strappy sandals behind the door and padded up the hall. To her left, the white panelled door of her consulting-room stood half-open. She studied the rectangle of darkness briefly, then reached for the lacquered brass knob and pulled the door shut, turning the knob very steadily till the catch engaged without a sound in the door-frame.

'So, where was I during the latest spat?'

'Out in the kitchen, I think, concocting some more punch. Which, in view of the drinks he'd already mixed, was probably not a good idea.' Brendan pressed the front door shut with his heel, arched his shoulders and let his overcoat slide down his burgundy shirt-sleeves. He twisted to catch it by the collar and trailed it across to the foot of the stairs. 'How does it feel to be past your sell-by date, that was his opener. He should know. That's the one thing we have in common, though most agree my shelf-life has been considerably longer than his.'

'Brendan, you're hardly pushing up the daisies.'

'Oh no, when you've reached the top of the tree and got to my twilight years the only thing left is to jump, apparently. Make room for new blood. Not likely, I told him. Not when all that's climbing up behind is a prick-driven monkey.'

He bundled his coat behind the mahogany egg of the newel post, then extended an arm towards her. She meekly presented her back. He helped her off with her voluminous pelt and draped it over his coat, perfunctorily re-distributing the weight when both threatened to slide.

'Fortunately Rose had the wit to stick a joint in him at that point, and I went outside to cool off. We patched it up. Or Leon got so stoned he forgot about it. And you were obviously enjoying yourself.'

She waved her hand in a mock slapping gesture in front of his face, and went into the kitchen.

'Drink?'

'Coffee. Thanks. Instant will be fine.'

She told him she would bring it through to the sitting-room, but he appeared in the kitchen even before the kettle had boiled. He paced up and down the other side of the refectory table, worrying at his upper lip with his finger and thumb.

'What Leon said. You don't think he's right?'

'No!' She spooned some ground coffee from a tin into the cafetière and half-filled it with hot water from the kettle. 'I'm making you some proper stuff, seeing it's New Year's Eve.'

'New Year's Day.'

'*Our* New Year's Eve,' she said, fitting on the lid of the cafetière. 'And don't you dare go handing in your resignation. You're so sensitive lately. God, I'd love to give Leo a dose of Tuberculinum. Can't you get him to come and see me?'

'Invite the man to be alone in the house with you?' He snorted. 'There's nothing wrong with Leo that an emasculator wouldn't correct in minutes. Did he get that New Year's kiss he was angling for?'

'Only on the cheek. He called it an *amuse-gueule*.' She opened the larder door and leaned inside. 'Now, what shall I have?'

'There's a bottle of your sparkling apple stuff next door,' he said. 'I'll open it, shall I?'

She set the cafetière on a tray with a mug and the box of mints one of her clients had given them for Christmas. As an afterthought she removed the smoked salmon from the refrigerator, laid it on the work-top and helped herself to a few slices straight from the pack, prying them from the greasy orange slab with her fingers.

The early-morning silence thrummed in her ears. Or maybe it was the lingering echo of Leon's New Year's Eve celebrations.

Leon, Brendan's most colourful colleague, was the only don she knew who insisted on red light bulbs at his parties. In their sleazy obscurity he threw together other Fellows from Oriel College, most of the research group from the Physiology Department, his hippy neighbours, squash comrades and wine club buffs, and ever-changing strings of post-grad students, who were usually female and attractive. Not forgetting Brendan and herself. The protégée that got away.

The research team's Christmas social had done nothing to cover Leon's intentions with glory. Not altogether sober before his arrival at the White Hart, he had quickly offered her a corner seat, then sat diagonally across the chair next to her, gathered her hands in his and looked straight into her eyes.

'Karin, marry me.'

She knew that Brendan would be watching from further up the table, and that Leon knew and didn't care. She excused herself, and Leo made a gesture of adjusting his chair to let her pass in front of him. He did not significantly change its position, however, so that despite drawing herself up she could not avoid brushing against his thighs.

When she came out of the Ladies', Brendan was leaning against the wall in the passage, his arms folded.

'You two look very animated in the corner. Having fun?'

'Don't. I'm trying very hard not to be rude to him.'

'No doubt he isn't returning the compliment. Has he told you he loves you yet?'

'He has been drinking, yes.'

'Christ!' Brendan leaned over and peered through the doorway back into the minstrels' gallery. 'Look at him, posing with the creased, bohemian linens. Isn't he magnificent? Even the rats go into lordosis for him. And that's just the males.'

She laughed and pulled him away. 'Stop it, Bren. He's seen you.'

'He still thinks he'd be wearing the wedding band if I hadn't got in first with the ball tickets. Seriously. He lusts after my chair. He definitely lusts after you. And he still keeps that blasted photo on his desk.'

Yes, she reminded her husband, when Leo was best man at their wedding. 'Anyway,' she teased, 'it would be even more insulting to be ignored by him. It's hardly a privilege to suffer his attentions. He's an eternal flirt. Too crazy to take seriously.'

'Too good-looking to shrug off?'

'It's just a game.'

Leon appeared round the corner, feigning scandal.

'Then let him play it with someone else,' Brendan whispered, not looking at him.

She cupped her husband's shoulders, walked him against the wall and kissed him on the mouth.

'Hey, season of goodwill,' Leon protested, raising his hands. 'Hey, I don't suppose there's any chance —'

'Sure, I'll leave her entirely to you,' Brendan said. 'In my Will.'

When she carried the coffee into the sitting-room, Brendan was at the sideboard, opening an elongated emerald bottle. She set the tray down beside the decanters.

'I can't help thinking you should be toasting the New Year with something a little more meritorious than this,' he said. 'Disgusting stuff.' He poured the fizzing yellow liquid into a couple of champagne glasses. 'No matter. I can have a little cognac with my coffee to make up for it.' He handed her a glass. 'Here's to us.'

They clinked glasses and their eyes met over the rims.

'I'm making a resolution,' she said.

'Oh? So am I. You first.'

She grinned and twisted to and fro, clutching her glass with both hands. 'To quit worshipping at the altar of homœopathy... To integrate it into my life without making it my life... Not to talk shop at table... Oh, and to have more meals together in the first place. To take up a new hobby, maybe one we can share.' She broke off her citations to catch his eye again. 'In short, Brendan, to make sure we spend more time together.'

'Are you quite sure that's enough?'

'You were right to complain.' She emptied her glass. 'And I'm sorry, and I'm going to fix it.'

He pushed his glass on to the sideboard and opened his arms to her. She stepped into the welcoming semicircle they made, and he drew her into a hug.

'I'm proud of you. I'll never stop loving you, Karin.'

'That'll do me.' She sniffed his breath. 'You smell delectable.' She put her glass beside his and picked up the Louis XIII bottle from the silver tray where it had stood with several other, more traditional decanters. It was a plump, amber disc with distinctive tweaked glass spines running down its shoulders, and the neck and stopper resembled the top of a crystal mace. She took out the stopper and sniffed it. 'It's this brandy! You've been swigging it in here on the sly.'

'*This brandy* is a pure, Grande Champagne cognac.'

'So why did your mad uncle send it for an eighth anniversary present? Eight is supposed to be bronze. My parents didn't even give us a card.' She replaced the stopper and put the bottle back. 'Anyway, it tastes like something you might want to put in a fuel tank.'

He exhaled over her face. 'Better stick to the angels' share then.'

'I'd prefer a kiss.' She raised her face, but he pulled back. 'What is it?'

'I'm happy with you. I just want you to know.'

'Then kiss me, you happy bastard!'

She lunged for his mouth, laughing, but he caught her by the upper arms.

'There's something I have to say. For both our sakes I'd rather we dealt with it openly. I – was seeing someone else last year. Last autumn.'

She tensed. His response was to tighten his grip, but she braced herself like a cat. His eyes seemed to be swimming in her face. The tension flowed out of her muscles, sickness circulated in her blood vessels. She shoved him away with a violent shrug, which overbalanced her and made her step backwards.

He raised his hands in surrender. 'It's over,' he said. 'It is over. I know it sounds trite, but it was the worst and most foolish thing I've ever done. I could pretend it never happened, but it did. Karin -'

'Don't touch me!' She threw up her arms. 'Get away from me.'

He crossed the room and stood meekly in the centre of the hearth rug. She paced up and down by the sideboard.

'And you criticise Leon? How can you?' She turned on him. 'How dare you? He goes round with "Sleep with me" tattooed on his forehead, and you want to play Mr Butter-Wouldn't-Melt. Okay, okay.' She resumed her striding. 'Shit, so this is what people write about in the magazines. Welcome to the modern world, Karin, to how-it-really-is. Seeing someone else?' She screamed at him. '*Seeing someone else* means not a one-night stand, Brendan.'

'It lasted – six weeks? A couple of months? We didn't meet on a regular basis. A dozen times, if that. I'll tell you anything you want to know. But what I want you to know is that I went into it looking for someone to fall in love with and it didn't happen because I found I still loved you. Even when things were pretty shit at home, frankly. I should have known, but I didn't.'

She circled the room and trailed, barefoot and hunched, round to the fire-place. He made a move towards her.

'Stay on the mat!'

The cat leapt off the sofa and disappeared through the door in a white streak, his body low and his ears flattened to an arrow-head.

She crooked her arms across her chest. 'You went looking to fall in love. That's a brave statement from someone in your position.'

'I'd lost my wife to the celestial skies of complementary medicine, remember?' He struck his hand to his forehead. 'Of course you can't, because you didn't notice wafting away in the first place.'

'Fuck off.'

'Oh no, honesty in every quarter. I supported you all the way with your career change: your course, all four years of it, then setting up your own practice with the tribulations that brought. Then suddenly it's not just practising, you're off to conferences and seminars and post-grad courses – as if you hadn't done enough already – wacko provings, all of which I've had to live through. And as if that's not sufficient, you start running courses and teaching and wheeling students in here.'

'And you don't?'

'Yours seem to bring bottles of wine and stay for hours, laughing their heads off behind closed doors.' He prowled up and down the mat, like a zoo animal in an invisible cage. 'I've got a lot of time for homœopathy, if you haven't already noticed. I don't understand it. It seems to work so I accept it. But how do you think I used to feel when you came back from college weekends with your scintillating colleagues? You're a rising star, Karin. I'm just a boring academic with nowhere else to go. A boring *old* academic if you listen to Leon.' He halted and turned to her. 'Where were you when Dad died?'

'You've lost me,' she said sullenly.

'Too right. You attend the funeral, but are you really with me? No, you're psyching yourself up for that *Women In Homœopathy* conference. I arrange a surprise trip to the theatre and you don't arrive home till nine because you've arranged a home visit and not put it in the diary. And it goes on.' He made her an off-handed salute. 'Nothing but the best for your patients. Perhaps I should have made an appointment? You're so busy "perceiving what has to be healed," you can't see the sickest relationship of all. I try and tell you and you don't hear till too late. You don't hear me, you don't see me. What kind of therapist are you?'

Confusion, entreaty, accusation, disbelief. She heard them all. She fixed him with eyes that were momentarily unguarded, pained with both his hurt and her own realisation.

'What kind? A human one. Flawed, but faithful.'

He sank on to the rug, like a toddler collapsing under his own weight. His shoulders were shaking. He covered his face.

Karin stared down at him. 'Who is she? No, do I want to know who she is?'

'She's older than you.' His fingers peeled away from his face and dropped to his thighs. 'She's not beautiful.'

'But she has the mind of Galileo.'

'She organises some sort of Play Scheme set-up for some

charity. I don't know the details. I met her in a café in town. The place was full, and I sat next to her because there were no other seats free.'

'Thus far, she seems to have to have little to recommend her. Or was the chief allure to be found between the sheets?'

'She's not as lithe as you, or as well preserved. But she was comfortable and she was fun. And above all she showed some interest in me when you'd forgotten I existed. That's all there was to it. I don't even recall when it started. October? November?'

She nodded to herself. 'You were distant. Where did you meet?'

'She has a house in Jericho. Don't you want to know who she is?'

'No. I don't know. Her first name.'

'Sally.'

She let herself fall on to the sofa and lay, inelegant and semi-recumbent, across a cushion with one foot on the seat and the skirt of her green velvet dress gaping.

'If you'd found this new love you were after, instead of the respite care you seem to have ended up with, you'd have left me, wouldn't you. I hate you for this.'

'I didn't take the easy way out, telling you.'

She twisted her head to look at him. 'Oh, hooray! Martyrdom to boot. And when did you finish it?'

'I don't know,' he said, wearily. 'Early December? Before the end of Michaelmas.'

'How did she take it?'

'You haven't had any strange calls or letters, have you?'

'No.'

'Then that's how she took it.'

Karin rested her left hand on the arm of the sofa and slid her fingers up and down the upholstery. She made an exclamation of annoyance and sat up, tugging at her wedding ring. Brendan leapt to his feet and stepped off the rug, reaching for her as though he were drowning.

'Karin – no! I've risked losing your love completely to try

and work this out.'

'Wrong. You lost it when you went and screwed someone else. I don't suppose you bothered to take yours off, did you?' she snapped, angered further when the ring stuck at her knuckle. She got up, wrenching at it. 'Down my throat you ram months of deceit, sugared with nothing but a lame apology, and in return I give you hope on a plate with the offer of seconds. Is that the deal? Sorry, there are plenty of places I can go where I don't have to listen to this.'

She walked towards the open doorway. He dug his fingers into his thighs and shifted from foot to foot beside the rug.

'Okay, I'm not going to be patronising and say I understand how you feel. I've been a shit, so leave if you want, think things over. Or I'll go, if you prefer. Just don't leave forever. I don't want anyone else.'

Her finger had swollen with her clumsy efforts to free herself of the ring, and it was beginning to hurt. She made a fist with the hand, and absently clenched and released her fingers.

'I was only thinking how much happier you'd been recently,' she said into the hall. 'Ironic, isn't it. I noticed the difference.' She turned and took a few steps back into the room. 'How do you know *I* don't want anyone else? How do *I* know?'

He hesitated. 'I think underneath all this you might still care for me.'

'Might I?'

'I don't mean now. Maybe not for a long time.'

'Shall I show you how much I care, Brendan? This much!' She seized the Louis XIII by the neck and sent it spinning towards the chimney-breast. 'And this much!'

She grabbed the cafetière and hurled that, modifying her aim slightly to the left. Brendan ducked, his hands over his head. The crystal exploded in the recess to the right of the chimney-breast and sent out a shower of shards, flashing briefly like a chandelier in the light of the wall-lamp. The cognac streamed in pale claws down the wall-paper. The cafetière hit its mark, shattering the huge, gilt-framed mirror that sat over the mantelpiece. Silver and black tears cascaded from the hole, and the air stank of opulence and loss. That night the angels would have more than their share.

Brendan watched the pale blue hearth rug wicking the coffee out of the cafetière. She heard him follow her, at a distance, to the kitchen, where she yanked open the utensil drawer and rooted out an old toffee hammer. She pushed past him into the dining-room. With mechanical composure she scanned the walls, then strode up to the two photographs of herself and Brendan on the dresser and dashed the glass with two smart raps from the hammer. She repeated the exercise in her office, the sitting-room, the hall and up the stairs, in their bedroom and finally on the landing. The only one left intact was the ball photo. She didn't want to step over the threshold of his study. Anyway, such an act would have been an overkill for two small faces specked amongst a couple of hundred.

With cold, numb hands she returned to the bedroom and flung a few clothes and washing essentials into an overnight bag. Down the stairs her unsteady legs lent the impression of greater weight to her steps, the illusion of resolve and confidence. The black, cylindrical bag bounced on her hip, its shoulder-strap slashed across the green velvet dress like an ammunition belt.

Brendan was waiting by the front door, her coat hanging in luxurious folds from his hands. As she approached he lifted it towards her.

'Thanks, I'd rather freeze.'

She worked her feet into the sandals, unfastened the door and bundled the bag round it as soon as the gap allowed.

'Karin!'

His voice was thin with impotence, and he did not try to stop her. She dragged up the floor bolts of the garage to the side of the drive and strode open the pair of old wooden doors. From the top step she felt his eyes on her, noting the abruptness and exaggeration of her movements, the determined slicing of her bare limbs through the cold.

'Karin!'

She threw her bag on to the front passenger seat and slid behind the steering-wheel. The tears began to well as she niggled the key blindly in the ignition. He was running down the steps.

'Karin, where are you going?'

The engine started.

2

Karin turned north, retracing the taxi journey. The streets were almost deserted. The cold bolted through her shoulders as she drove, and the air fluttered unevenly between her chattering teeth. Twice she tried the heater, but the temperature gauge had scarcely risen from the blue.

By the time she reached Summertown the anaesthetic of the cold had begun to wear off, and peaks of anger pulsed through the numbness. She decelerated to give herself thinking time. Her thoughts seemed to turn over so slowly, abnormally slowly, possibilities clunking through their consequences. After a hesitation her foot pressed down once again on the accelerator. She left Oxford behind her and took the road to Banbury.

A light was showing through the glass panel above the front door, and round the edges of the curtains she saw crinkles of flashing blue light. She rang the bell. Nothing happened. She rang a second time and heard ill-humoured muttering. Presently footsteps lumbered down the hall. The door opened a hand's width and an accusing face appeared in the gap.

'Karin? Oh, thought you had a party! Come in, come in. Happy New Year.' The door opened wider and Zoe Seymour pulled at her lower eyelids with her fingers, showing fleshy, dimpled knuckles. 'Has my clock stopped?'

'I need somewhere to stay.'

Zo paused. 'I see.' The words rolled slowly round her mouth as though she were tasting them. 'Jesus.'

She pressed herself against the cream glossed Anaglypta. Karin squeezed past into the porch and Zo followed her inside.

She took Karin's bag from her, frowning when she accidentally touched Karin's bare arm, and deposited the bag at the foot of the stairs. A crack of gunfire rang out from the direction of the front room.

'I'll fetch a couple of blankets. You go in.' Zo indicated the door with a sleepy wave of her hand. 'I think I sense a large alcoholic drink in the offing.'

Karin was incapable of remaining on a chair, but she accepted a shot of whisky from the bottle on the coffee-table. Periodically she sniffed at the tumbler as she circled the cane table, keeping Zo's blue and red tartan blanket pinned across her chest with her free hand.

'The worst thing,' she muttered, 'is that you don't seem surprised. You're not fucking surprised. Are you?'

'No,' Zo said quietly. 'But even in a throwaway world no one wants to be betrayed. I'm very, very sorry.'

Karin stopped in her tracks. 'Could I make a phone call?'

'What, now? It's barely seven.'

'Please, I have to.

Zo levered herself up from the sofa, somnolent and larval in her cream chenille kaftan.

'Sure. I'll disappear upstairs.' She squeezed Karin on the shoulder as she went out. 'Good luck.'

The phone rang three times and switched to a recorded message. Karin paced back and forth in front of the gas-fire with Zo's cordless phone pressed to her ear, and waited for the beep.

'I know you're there. It's Karin. I guess you're drunk, and I know you've only had a couple of hours' sleep, but please pick up. Don't try dialling me back here.' The tape carried on running. '*Leon!* Wake up, it's urgent! Please, pick up the phone.'

She heard a scrabbling, followed by the steady sound of plastic dragging across a hard surface.

'Sorry... Still in bed. Party, remember?' Leon spoke with a drunkard's precision, his voice gravelly from a combination of smoke, alcohol poisoning and fatigue. 'What's up? Karin? You still there?'

She stopped her pacing. She bit her knuckle and smiled to

herself. 'Your voice is quite sexy when you're half-cut. But I guess that's not news.'

There was silence down the line.

'I take it you've still got company, Leon?'

'Five or six bodies littered about the place. Or there were at three this morning. Some may have crawled off by now.'

'You?'

'Hah!' He checked himself. 'Well,' he began in a more thoughtful tone, 'strange as it may seem after playing a mean Dionysius all night, I did indeed find myself alone when I retired.'

'No Rose?'

'Hoofed it. Ages ago, before you and Brendan. Apparently it was the frequency with which she caught me looking at you.'

He laughed to himself and sighed, sleepy and cat-like. She thought she could hear his body moving across the sheets.

'Leon – ?'

He did not respond. The silence lacked the emptiness of an unattended line or a genuine hesitation. No, he'd made a conscious decision not to reply. Clever. Clever, even when drunk. Not to mention good-looking and fond of her, alone and only fifteen minutes away, and it would be so easy – that was to say, not impossible –

She twisted her lower lip between her teeth. 'Leon – is Brendan there? It's just that he's disappeared. I suppose he could have gone for a walk. But I wondered whether he'd driven over to your place, you know-'

'Oh, has he forgiven me? I gather I was rather overbearing.' Leon swallowed something in a succession of noisy gulps. 'Well, to my knowledge he isn't here. Which means precisely nothing. I love him really. I suppose I should give him a call. In the meantime –'

'Tomorrow, maybe. You catch up on your hair of the dog. And the cleaning.'

'Well, if the old man doesn't materialise...'

She thanked him for the offer.

Zo's fingers appeared round the edge of the door, followed by half of her face and mousy, pudding-basin bob.

'I cannot believe you nearly did that. I thought you were doing the decent thing.'

'Strangely enough, retaliation with an amorous, brainy hunk who happens to be one of Brendan's colleagues seemed a more attractive prospect. What about being upstairs out of earshot?'

'All that blarney about him going out...' Zo ducked behind the door again and her voice took on the echo of the kitchen. 'You could have stopped off in Summertown last night, Karin. You know,' she began again when they faced each other over the breakfast table, 'struck while the iron was hot?'

From the plate in front of her, Karin picked up one of Zo's vegetarian bacon sandwiches. She bit into it, fixating Zo with the faintest hint of amusement as she tore through the bacon with her teeth.

'Oh - my - God!' Zo's voice gathered volume until it reached a pitch of manic delight. 'What made you change your mind?'

'Party,' Karin mumbled through the bread. 'Too public. I didn't want to make a complete fool of myself.'

'Oh, my God...'

'Well, why shouldn't I? It would serve Brendan bloody well right.' She replaced the half-eaten sandwich on her plate and wiped some ketchup from her lips with the back of a finger. 'Leon finds me attractive. He likes me.'

'He worships you,' Zo corrected. 'You're his unattainable ideal. Present yourself on his doorstep, naked but for a gold lamé ribbon, and he won't have a clue what to do with you.'

'I think he'd figure it out.'

'Then why are you still using the conditional?' Zo said flatly. 'You've rung him up, whetted his appetite. Why don't you get round there, do the deed. Shag him and have done with it.'

Karin reached for her mug of lemon verbena tea. 'I can't.'

'Can't?'

'I should be able to. I want to.'

'So? If Brendan deserves it?'

'I *know* Leon. I've known him too long. I had –' She gazed along the grey wand of the strip light. 'Let's just say I had an acute attack of misgivings. Discretion, call it. Even Brendan managed to leap the gulf between town and gown for his infidelity.'

Zo hesitated. 'He left a message on the answer-phone. A couple of hours ago. I didn't think it was terribly good timing earlier...'

Karin closed her eyes and waited.

'Karin, why don't you phone him...'

The call went unanswered, in spite of which – or maybe because of it - she returned home. She'd made the right decision with Leon. He played the seduction game so well he could win when he was canned. He would have picked her up and eaten her alive, moist and defenceless, like an oyster, and thrown away the shell. Another pearl for his University necklace collection.

Brendan's car stood in the drive, but the house was empty. It smelt stale and sad, a place to be visited and left. On the carpet just inside the front door she found a message, written, she noted with a spark of irritation, on a compliment slip he'd removed from her desk:

9.15am

Dear Karin,

Going for a walk, just round the University Parks. After last night I need to clear my head. Left messages everywhere I could think of. I'll be home at 10.30. Please, please wait.

The last three words had been individually underlined.

She checked her watch: a quarter to ten; she must just have missed him when she rang. Ruskin emerged from the sitting-room and came to greet her. She put the note on the hall-table and picked him up, kissing his head and ruffling his long white fur to distract her from the grieving ache in her chest.

With a frown she studied the hall carpet. She pushed open the dining-room door with her foot and checked there too, but it appeared Brendan had already swept away the glass.

She put Ruskin down and left him to stroll upstairs after her. She dragged two suitcases from the cupboard on the landing, packed the larger one with extra clothes and stood them both at the head of the stairs. Then she retraced her steps down the landing towards his study; he wasn't there. He would never know.

The door made its familiar sequence of squeals under her fingertips. It sounded so loud when it cut the stillness, betraying her presence like the Giant's harp. Her heart hammered in her chest, as though in leaving she had relinquished any further right to the house. But she had to see it, the ball photo; it was the only picture of them she'd left undamaged, and, therefore, the only one capable of affording any kind of hope.

Above the CDs and tapes lined up against the wall behind his desk, a swarm of moon-like faces grinned out from the large, silver-plated frame. The picture was bordered on three sides by the walls of Pembroke's Old Quad, studded with their window boxes of petunias and trailing, scarlet pelargoniums. Within the honeyed stonework the guests had grouped in a ragged circle. The formality of the dinner jackets was relieved by the occasional, thrusting cleavage and, round the edges, drifts of colourful gowns. A couple of hands were blurred in some lost salutation and, at the back, another attention-seeker had pogoed his moment of glory to a soft smudge of cream and black.

She and Brendan, only their heads and necks visible, stood somewhere near the centre. She needed to study the picture carefully to find them. She'd still been wearing her hair piled high then, and Brendan was baring his teeth, chill and impatience having set in at the length of time the photographer spent over the shot.

Her gaze touched on the neighbouring picture. She blinked it away, broke across to the window, replaced it with the view of the garden. *The swing.* She could just make it out from the study window, hanging from the chestnut at the bottom of the garden. She'd pointed it out the very first time she'd visited the house, nine years ago. Their first date. The taxi had just dropped them off after the ball. It was a clear June morning, not yet seven o'clock, and Brendan was delighted to amble round after her, impressing her with the garden. He'd shown her the vine in the original lean-to conservatory, pressing its growth into the condensation on the glass and sporting pin-head clusters of new green grapes. Everything was moist and lush.

'The swing? It's always been there,' he told her as they stood side by side in front of the conservatory. 'My nephews and nieces adore it. The ropes rotted so we replaced them with chains looped over old car tyres. But the seat is original.'

She slipped off her high-heels and set off down the brick path across the lawn, the shoes hooked from her fingers and her cloak flowing, blood-red, almost black behind her. Brendan followed slowly, his hands in his trouser pockets.

Where the path petered out under the chestnut and became dusty soil, she brushed off her feet and wriggled them back into her shoes.

'Nice and wide,' she said, patting the swing seat. She grasped a handful of her cape and evening dress, hitched them up a little, then lowered herself on to the slab of grey wood and tested her weight. 'And it seems solid enough.' She wrapped her fingers round the chains, pushed back against her feet and let herself swing passively, her legs dangling and her swollen feet pointing inwards. The moving air pulled on the hem and loose hood of her cape. 'God, this is lovely, Brendan. And it's in the sun. I need to soak up some heat.'

Brendan stood hunch-shouldered on the edge of the sunlight, his bow-tie draped round his neck, his jacket and the top few buttons of his dress-shirt undone. With the sun in her eyes, the detail of his face was lost to her.

'Did you know,' she announced, as the swing began to slow, 'that with the high walls and the way your neighbours have planted their trees, you can't be seen from here?'

'So the children tell me.'

'I love your garden.' She leaned back, supporting her weight against the chains, and gazed up into the patchwork of green, fish-shaped leaves. 'And your house,' she added. 'But especially the garden.'

'I'm glad, because you look quite at home in it.'

He stepped forward, took hold of the two chains above her hands and brought the swing to a halt. He knelt on the earth in front of her and smoothed her calves lightly, almost reverently through the dress fabric. It was a silk-viscose dévoré decorated with thin velvet flowers and leaves of the same dark red.

'You look beautiful. Noble. Gothic.'

She cupped her hands in her lap and picked at her fingers. 'It's the dress.'

'It's not the dress.' He raised his head and smiled at her. 'I was proud to be out with you last night. I can't remember what anybody else was wearing. God, that must mean I spent the whole time staring.'

'I don't recall being offended.'

'Leon says he's booked you for next year.'

'Does that mean he'll be inviting me as well?'

'I told him you're giving me first refusal.'

'I see. This all seems very slick.' Her brow furrowed suddenly. 'Brendan, have you been out with many students?'

'Ah, because I'm surrounded by a constant tide of intelligent and available young women...' He sat back on his heels, pressed his hands together and drew his fingers down over his nose until they rested on his lips. He angled his fingers forward. 'It's – just over two years now. Watching someone you love, die – Yes, I did go out with a student just after Christmas. It lasted a couple of weeks. Mutually unsatisfactory. Since then, no one. Till now.'

'I'm a student.'

'A mature student, there's a difference. Above all, you're you. If what you mean is, do I make a habit of this kind of thing, the answer is no.'

'I'm sorry.' She held out her hands, and he took them. 'You've spilt red wine down your front.'

'You dropped port down yours.'

'Ha!' She released his hands and jumped up from the swing. 'You have a go.'

'Me?'

'Why not you?'

He dusted down his trousers and took her place on the seat. She watched the supporting branch as he sat down.

'It seems to bear your weight.'

'Karin, an elephant could sit on this. Two, probably.'

'Is that so?'

She reached behind her back and unfastened the zip, her eyes not leaving his.

'Believe me,' he murmured, transfixed, as the sheer red fabric slid to earth, 'it's not the dress. It is not the dress.'

She slipped off her wine-red underwear and dropped it with an almost careless gesture on to the dress. Taking her weight on the chains, she stepped over his thighs and lowered herself on to his lap, facing him. She undid two more of his shirt buttons, then plucked the bow-tie from his neck and tossed it into the nearby swathe of Bergenias.

'Are you sure about this?'

'No.'

'Karin —'

'In front of you sits a woman naked but for a hooded cape. So, Brendan, is that really the question to be asking?'

And she put her palms to his temples and kissed him on the lips until he made up his mind.

She would never forget his howl as he crashed to earth not five minutes later, dragging her down with him under a balloon of taffeta. He clenched his teeth and ground his head back and forth in the dust.

'God!' she cried. 'What's wrong? Not your heart?'

'Cramp! Christ, cramp in my calf. Swing was too close to the ground...'

She stretched his legs and flexed and extended his foot. She hushed his abandoned groaning with words of comfort that turned to laughter about the liberation, limits and survival instincts that attended airborne love. Afterwards they repaired to the luxury of his bed with a box of Belgian chocolates and two bowls of muesli. There they had stayed all day, exploring each other with words and caresses, making love and melting chocolate on to the sheets.

Why had she approached him on that first date? She was hardly promiscuous. In fact her caution had frustrated more than a few lusty suitors. Intuition, maybe. After all, it was impossible to spend nine hours with a man at an Oxford ball and fail to discover whether one could – and should - fall in love with him. They'd got drunk, with alcohol and with fatigue, danced with less elegance and less restraint than was their custom. They had both seen each other drop food and stumble against strangers. They'd managed to indulge their respective musical tastes without incurring boredom or resentment. In short, they were sober enough to make the survivors' photo, and sufficiently in love to smile well before the request was yelled across the crowd.

The ferocity of the tears caught her off-guard. They welled in a snorting cough, and the view from the window instantly washed to a blur. Clapping her hand over her mouth in an attempt to stop up the sobbing, she blundered back on to the landing. She collected the cases, carried them downstairs, bumping against her knees, and left them just outside her consulting-room. She pushed through the door into the kitchen and ripped a sheet of paper towel from the holder to blow her nose. As an afterthought she picked up the kettle from the work-top and tested its weight: heavy enough, and she desperately needed a drink.

She clumped the kettle on to the hob of the Alpha and sank on to the bench to wait. The muesli box sat on the table, its cardboard flaps pricked up like ears. Brendan had left his breakfast bowl and spoon beside it, with a sprinkling of stray oat-flakes. A thin halo of milk had already formed around the base of the dish.

Prodding the bowl further away, she got up and scooped a mug out of the drainer. She dropped a tea bag into her mug, poured in a rush of hot water from the kettle and dunked the tea bag up and down on its string. She carried the tea through to her calm, uncluttered consulting-room and put it on the desk while she gathered her laptop, files, remedies and an armful of reference books into the smaller of the suitcases. She zipped it up and sat at the desk, sipping the tepid tea as her eyes travelled the high, ornate track of the picture rail. Alone in the house, it was easier to swap anger for sadness, easier to feel pain than aggression. And easy to hanker after the past.

Five years ago she had returned from the last college weekend of her second year to find the small guest bedroom wrecked, emptied of its twin beds and furniture, the carpet littered with boxes, and the walls blank and scarred where pictures had once hung. Brendan came in then, his cheeks blue with weekend stubble, his shorts and T-shirt grubby and smelling of sweat.

'What are you doing?' she cried. 'Where are the beds?'

'Sold.'

'What?'

'And the wardrobe, and the dressing-table. One of my post-grads picked them up this afternoon. Has Karin Shilan, homœopath, seen her new consulting-room yet?'

She rested her hand on her hip. 'Brendan –'

'Well, you're entering your first supervision year in a couple of months. You'll need somewhere decent to interrogate your patients. I was kicking my heels while you were away in Devon, so I thought I might as well get on and deconstruct my study.' He held up his hand to silence her protests. 'Yesterday I plundered two decades of accumulated bum fodder on your account. You are serious about practising?'

'Yes. I was going to convert this guest room –'

He jerked his head towards the door. 'You can't drag your arthritic old ladies up here. Where's your sense of professionalism? My old study is perfect. Light, airy, near the front door, near the loo. Plenty of space for fractious kids to play.'

'Brendan...' She encircled herself with his grimy hands, which he linked and rested in the hollow of her spine. 'Thank you. But you'll find this too small.'

'Since when did I need a home lecture theatre?' he'd demanded. 'This will suit me fine.'

The following week she had over-painted the mushroom walls of his study with yellow, and broken up the carpet with rugs, and the walls with prints and homœopathy posters and wall-hangings. That was Brendan all over. The golden boy had insisted. Gold was his metal, and his remedy frequently turned out to be Aurum. Upstairs she had a whole tangle of fine gold jewellery he had bought her before realising that she actually preferred ethnic copper and brass.

She placed the note back on the carpet in the exact position she had found it, and left the house at ten fifteen.

'But the golden boy forgot the golden rule,' she mused, when Zo persuaded her to go for a walk round Otmoor that afternoon.

The golden rule - *do to others as you would have them do to you*.

'You seem a bit calmer anyway,' Zo ventured. 'I think I'm right in assuming it's not the countryside or the numbing effect of the company?'

Karin smiled. 'I couldn't face him this morning. I feel guilty as hell. But I've decided the marriage isn't beyond redemption. Provisionally. I'm working on it.' She kicked over a puddle with the sole of her trainer. 'How would you feel if I booked a last-minute holiday?' she said tentatively. 'Abroad, I was thinking. A week, maybe ten days? Somewhere warm.'

'Sounds good to me. I'll locum for you, no problem.'

'I'll re-arrange what appointments I can. The first week's pretty quiet anyway.'

'Trust me,' said Zo. 'You'll be able to take stock far better away from this place. God, it's dreary at this time of year.'

By the time she rang Brendan on Friday evening and arranged to meet him at home on Monday night, the heat of her anger had dissipated. What remained had grown cooler, harder and brittle.

'I'd love to see you, of course I would,' he said. 'If you like, we could go for a drink –'

'I don't think –'

'Or we could stay in. I'm happy to do anything. Whatever you want.'

He met her at the door that Monday at eight, wearing his

black corduroy trousers and a grey, chunky-knit pullover. It was a combination he knew she favoured, and he was also holding the cat. She extracted the cat from his arms without returning his smile.

'You look –'

'No, I don't,' she said.

She squeezed past him into the hall and went into the kitchen. It smelled of citrus cream cleaner. She could almost hear the delighted chatter going on in his head behind her, and on her back she sensed his smile and his hopefulness. She pulled out a bench and sat, half-turned to him, caressing the cat about the head.

'This is tidy.'

'Only just done it, to be honest. Can I get you something to drink?'

'Tea, please.'

He pressed his hands palm to palm, then parted them again suddenly. 'Food, what about food?'

'I've eaten, thanks.'

'Sure?'

'I'm fine.'

He turned to the Alpha, grabbed the kettle from the hob and filled it from the water filter. He was a knot of energy, of exuberance checked for fear it might cause offence. He stood the kettle back on the hob, set out the mugs and leaned against the unit, his fingers gripped round the edge of the oak work-top.

'How have you been?'

'As you see,' she said. 'You?'

'Can't say too much, can I?' He lowered himself to his haunches and chucked the cat under the chin. 'Missing you. Aren't we, Rus? Glad to see you again.'

'Brendan, I'm going away tomorrow.' She fluffed the cat's fur harder and faster. 'I've got a flight to Tenerife, Puerto de la Cruz. Just for ten days. A break.'

The kettle began a half-hearted whistle from the hob, but she didn't raise her voice.

'And during my stay there, I'm going to be sleeping with

someone else.'

His fingers retracted from the cat's chin. His larynx bobbed in his throat. He got up and walked to the far end of the refectory table, paused at the corner to look at her, then took a few more steps to the next corner.

'Do I know him?'

'No.'

'Who, then?'

'No one we know.'

'You're going to pick someone up?'

'I won't be looking for a relationship, if that's what you mean.'

He ran his tongue inside his lower gum, his lips parted. 'I understand your reaction,' he said. 'Though I've never thought of you as the vengeful type.'

'I never thought of you as the unfaithful type,' she countered, absorbing herself with the cat. 'Anyway, I'm not doing it for revenge. Do you hear bitterness in my voice? Vindictiveness? Triumph? No, if I'd screwed Leo the morning after the party, that would have been revenge. This is different; I want to do what you did. I want to lower myself as you did, make myself like you, and then, when I'm no better, who knows? Maybe we can make a new start.'

'Karin, Christ! Why are you telling me this?'

She considered. 'I thought so highly of you. It never even occurred to me that you could stoop so low. And now I feel I'll always have this power over you. The relationship has tipped so far out of balance I can't pull you back up.'

'You can! Yes, you can!' He ran to her. The cat leapt out of her lap and darted under the table as Brendan dropped to his knees. 'You can forgive me. That's what forgiveness is.'

'You can explain to me a thousand times what it is, but I don't know it, Brendan, I can't *feel* it. *Similia similibus curentur. Let like be treated with like.* I can't see any other way.'

He stared at her. 'I don't get it. Sorry, I'm missing something here. You're going to screw some complete stranger for my benefit?'

She refused to be deflected. 'We talked about it at the beginning of my course, remember? How in Hahnemann's time they used to stick frozen sauerkraut on frostbite? Think about it. If you hit your finger with a hammer, what do you instinctively do to take away the pain?'

'Jesus...' He shrugged, incredulous. 'Hell, I don't know. Apply pressure?'

'Right, like a remedy producing a set of symptoms in a healthy person can cure similar ones in a sick person. *Similia similibus curentur*, the Law of Similars.' She sat up straighter. 'You understand the principle perfectly.'

The kettle was emitting its maximum and most penetrating whistle. A concentrated ray of steam jetted from its spout.

'Shut the fuck *up*!' Brendan got to his feet, seized the handle and dashed the whole thing on to its side in the sink. He turned on her. 'You didn't have to say this now. You knew I'd be looking forward to seeing you. If you had to exact your pound of flesh, couldn't you at least have done it without a preview?'

'We said no secrets.'

'You could have told me afterwards, but no, you drop the bombshell the day before you fly. How am I supposed to get through the next ten days, imagining, hour by hour, what you could be up to with some other man? Or are you going to phone me to put me out of my misery? Maybe one isn't enough. And how many times do you have to do it, Karin, the same number as Sally and I? Do you want me to work that one out for you?'

'Getting quits isn't the point. The point is similarity.'

'Similarity, shit! Have you told Zoe?'

'Why should I?'

'You tell her a lot. I daresay you told her about me. Think she'd approve? I wonder what she'd say, Karin?'

'Sex is no big deal till it goes wrong. It's what she always says. And she knows better than to interfere.'

He sighed, a hard, desperate sound that that caused his head to drop as the air escaped his lungs.

'Well, I'm surprised you bothered to go abroad for it. Wouldn't a college student have done? A cosy little one-nighter at some conference? Or is that too close to home? Too close to homœopathy, perhaps I should say? Prejudicial to your standing in the homœopathic community?'

He raised his eyebrows at her, but could draw no reply. She merely walked out of the kitchen. He followed her to the front door.

'Please, I'm sorry. Is there nothing that will make you consider changing your mind?'

She shook her head.

'Then promise me you'll come home to us when it's over. And you'll tell me about it, so we can lay the ghosts to rest for good.'

She nodded.

'And don't send a card.'

You could never erase history. At best you could obliterate, or at least minimise its effects on the present. People had been trying for as long as they'd had the wit to remember. The goal never changed. Only the motive and the method varied. Her motive was laudable: the restoration of the marriage to firm and level foundations. From that it could be re-built, stronger, better, with the care and deliberation it deserved. They would appreciate what they had rather than lament what they lacked, and neither would take the other for granted again. Ever. Ice for frostbite. Infidelity for infidelity.

She gave him a tight smile.

'No card.'

3

When you wanted to sleep with a man, it was amazing how many male faces suddenly bobbed to the surface of the human soup.

The plane hauled steeply away from Gatwick. The landscape shrank to a tissue of fields and then green cells, wiped out by drifts of stratus. England had ended and the quest was beginning.

'First visit?' inquired the man in the next seat. 'Or is it your fifth? It tends to be one or the other.'

Right first time, she told him. 'You?'

'Fifth. I alighted on it as a non-bankrupting way to avoid the post-Christmas misery. You know, the long faces and the bills and relentless furniture promotions. And dark mornings.'

She laughed. He might have been a little younger than herself, but both his shirtsleeves and his trousers had razor creases, and he was wearing a dark tie with a pin.

'Are you a golfer?'

'Can't stand the game.' He laid his biro on the last page of the letter he'd been writing in a pad on the tray. 'Well, I might slot in two or three rounds over the week. I'm just an addict. Do you play?'

'With an infrequency matched by a considerable lack of talent.'

'But you're brilliant at crazy golf?'

She stared at him. 'Actually, yes.'

They exchanged names. He was called Matt.

'So, Karin, are you heading for Veronica's?'

'Puerto de la Cruz.'

'Damn!' The tray gave a little under the pressure of his fist. 'Los Cristianos, me. Sun guaranteed, though sunshine's inversely proportional to culture down south; about the only two unhappy bedfellows. Oh, that's a shame.'

But it was to her enormous relief when they parted in the coach-park outside Reina Sofía airport.

'Are you hiring a car?' he called after her.

She had already planted her foot on the second stair of the coach, and did not remove it.

'I haven't booked one, no.'

'Just a thought. Well, if you change your mind and come south to take in the wildlife, I'm at the Paradise Park.'

She nodded and wondered if he realised she had not the slightest intention of looking him up. He would not be the first man in the world to mistake a benevolent smile for sexual interest.

She ascended the last few stairs into the shadows of the coach, found a place next to a window and arranged her kilim rucksack on the seat beside her. Another noisy gaggle of passengers arrived, wrestled their belongings on to the overhead shelves and settled into the seats round her. Cheap carriers crinkled and water plashed in plastic bottles. Below, suitcases and hold-alls thudded rhythmically into the luggage store.

She rested her forehead against the glass and watched Matt, now sporting a beige sunhat, as he towed his wheeled case away in the direction of another waiting coach. She had warmed to his mild manner and his humour. He had shown himself to be genuine, possibly honourable, and not in the least attractive, which was no doubt the reason she'd liked him so much. But the man-next-door did not necessarily make a lover. She remembered the letter he'd just signed off in the plane, something about Legoland in the spring and then *Lots of love, Daddy*. She wanted more than a wiggle in the dark with a lonely divorcee on his golfing holiday. There had to be some reciprocal engagement. The holiday hardly promised to be a distilled pursuit of hedonism, but neither did she intend it to become a feat of endurance. The sex was a mission, not a favour.

The Lover had to be attractive, she decided, but not loutish, and not so charming that he never needed to reach for the suntan lotion. He had to appreciate her without inciting her to display acres of naked flesh or fake her chest with pneumatic bras. He had to be alive to the possibilities of sex without walking as though he had a permanent erection, happy to approach an encounter with subtle anticipation and relish the smouldering of the sexual fuse. And sex, when it occurred, should take place in a mutually agreed, mutually satisfying fashion. She would not, at the age of thirty-five, be welded to some hasty José's car bonnet. The act would intend nothing more than shared pleasure with no further obligation, declaration or involvement. And the rules, if not intuited, would have to be voiced and accepted without reserve.

One-night stands were supposed to be easy.

*

She watched him lean forward and exchange one pair of tongs for another. He hooked up slices of cold meat and then charcuterie, laying them in generous portions on the waiting plates. He stood about her height, and had wavy hair and bold Latin looks set off by a pleasingly understated moustache. And he was a possibility. Unless he had a wife; a married man was taboo. She put him in his late-twenties. He could be married with three kids.

The queue advanced along the buffet table. Just in front of her, a large, middle-aged woman with limp dugs held out her plate. The woman giggled. She adjusted the straps of her halter-neck and reclaimed her filled plate, tossing her head like a mare.

'*Guten Abend.*'

His eyes were too dark for Karin to question his sincerity, but the smile appeared light and open. She waited for the guilt, but none came. Her guilt had a price-tag, and Brendan had unwittingly paid it. The Lover might now have a face.

'*Buenas noches,*' she said firmly. '*Y soy inglesa.*'

'English?' His eyes darted to the party that had just filed past. 'I think you are with those.'

'*No, estoy sola.*'

Availability. Availability in flashing pink neon. Heat erupted on her cheeks, and she lowered her eyes.

'So, what do you like, Miss? *Éste?*' He motioned to the roast beef, then to the pork. '*Éste?*'

'*Quisiera...*'

'*Cuál? Éste?*' The tongs swung to the chicken and clicked open and shut a few times. '*O éste? O jamón de Tenerife?*'

She smiled harder to stop herself laughing.

'*O chorizo? O salami de Milano? Mira...*' He held out his hand for her plate. '*Un poco de todo.* No difficult decision. Something of everything!'

She didn't care. She just wanted to watch the lean, deft hands at work, with their artistic fingers and neat nails.

He presented the plate back to her with a slight bow. '*Buen provecho...*'

She thanked him, took a couple of spoonfuls of salad and some salt-skinned potatoes, and sat at a table in direct view of the serving area. She observed only when he was occupied, though he once caught her out. He made an almost imperceptible nod and revealed a slash of white teeth.

Back in her room she kicked off her sandals into the *en suite* and crossed the cool cream tiles. The room was spacious enough, its décor somewhat clinical, and the identical white coverlets of the twin beds looked as though they had been ironed to the mattress.

She sat on the edge of the nearer bed, swung up her feet and lowered herself on to the immaculate covers. How to proceed from idea to execution? Some women seemed to conjoin the two, without effort, without a second thought. Desire. Seduction. It just happened. It would be happening that very evening in the nightclubs between the dancing, the easy banter and cocktails.

For a moment she remained still, laid out on the cover like an offering. A mosquito, equally motionless, hung on the ceiling near one of the light-fittings. Nightclubs were a sordid affair for solitary women of her years. She might be approached by a youth half her age, and – worse – might now be old enough to be his mother.

Shuddering, she picked up the winter issue of *The Homœopath* from the bedside table. She scanned the Contents, turned to a case study on ankylosing spondylitis, and imagined the waiter, shirtless, at the foot of the bed. His torso would be sharp against the white walls, his muscles defined by subtle shadows. English ice would melt before Spanish fire. She would be a curiosity, combining the exoticism of the foreigner and the black hair of the Latin with pale skin and blue eyes. She would be the ultimate sacrifice. *Take this and eat it: this is my body, which will be given up for you.* Brendan, for you.

She pushed her heels apart in a smooth arc until her feet dropped either side of the bed. At the end of the day, one movement was all that was required of her. Synchronised swimmers did it all the time, opening, closing, scissoring into the kaleidoscopically changing forms of suns and stars and buds bursting into bloom. One movement; one man would do the rest, and feel pleased with himself at the end of it.

A waiter, though. A waiter, for goodness' sake. But did it matter? Even Einstein served time as a third-class patent officer. And the Lover was young enough to be very picky when each week brought a fresh and cosmopolitan tide of youth to his doorstep.

On Friday he had switched to the hot dishes.

'Beef stroganoff,' he said, pointing. 'Chicken curry here and, from Canaries, marinated chops. Also from Canaries we have grilled *vieja*. *Vieja?* Widow fish. She is very good. And we have rabbits in *salmorejo*.' He lifted the lid of a deep rectangular tray in the heated cabinet to reveal a mass of little carcasses with bones protruding through a thick, red gravy. 'The sauce is full of sweet and hot peppers. *Salmorejo*, very spicy. Very local.'

Just then the other waiter leaned forward. He touched the Lover's arm and addressed him with great speed, watching her all the while. The Lover jerked his head and made some riposte, and his colleague returned to his patch, grinning.

'What was that about?'

'He said if you wear those black trousers and white blouse in here, the guests will think you are a waiter.'

'Oh.' She looked down at herself. 'And what did you say?'

He shrugged.

'*Sí, sí!*' called the other *camarero*. 'Jesús says you are too beautiful to be waiter.'

The surge of heat into her cheeks was immediate and almost painful. Neither of them looked at each other as the plate passed between their hands.

'Rabbit, then,' she said. '*Por favor.*'

'Not rabbit. For you, *conejo*.' He laid a nest of thighs in her plate and spooned the sauce over them. '*Cómo se llama?*'

'Karin.'

'There is a discothèque, Karin. Here, downstairs. You can dance tonight. Do you like to dance?'

'I – Yes, maybe I'll look in.'

'But not too early. Later. There is more atmosphere.'

Leaving the buffet table was like walking on sponges soaked in alcohol. She sat down, her limbs cold and shaky. She had received the green light; the Lover, if she wanted him, was hers. Moreover he had been Christened, and things boded well: she was going to be sleeping with Jesus.

After her shower that evening she lay on the bed. Confidence and doubt ebbed and flowed through her mind, and the doubt wore Brendan's face. The novelty of the past few days had pushed him easily into the background, like a forgotten pet. And now he came to her with beaten-up familiarity rather than fondness. She was still too bitter for fondness. Would she think of him, she wondered, at the moment another man entered her? She bit the side of her mouth. Had he spared a thought for her as he'd betrayed her with Sally, or had the added excitement of the forbidden and the lure of the gene pool eclipsed loyalty altogether? She leaned over and tucked a condom under the pillow.

*

Five teenagers, periodically bathed in whorls of coloured lights, huddled on the dance-floor round a pile of tiny handbags.

She found a seat in the darkness and occupied her fingers with her hi-ball of mineral water. In England she felt at ease anywhere. Now she had forsaken her homeland and wedding ring, the self-possession had deserted her. All the time the passe-partout had been Brendan, and she'd worn the confidence of their relationship like an old thermal vest. She touched the glass to her cheek and the icy condensation numbed her skin.

A few more people entered, a mixed group of men and girls who ploughed straight on to the dance-floor. She pushed the glass on the table, fell in to their slipstream and positioned herself exactly between the two groups. Her skirts flowed with every movement. The side-splits took their first breath and, when she turned, the puritan bodice became a plunging back laced with fine purple straps.

The teenagers stopped talking and watched her with steady, sidelong glances, their dancing less vigorous. She just smiled into the noise and light. She couldn't see him. She didn't even look.

When the record ended she walked off the floor, her head high. Approval bubbled from the cluster of beaming men near the bar. Jesús stepped from amongst them. He was still in his waiting clothes, but he had lost the tie and undone three or four shirt buttons. He blocked her path.

'*Eh!* Karin...' He took a draught from his beer glass, and a line of smoke streamed from the cigarette he held in the same hand. 'You dance very good. I watched you. Very *well*,' he grinned. 'Please, let me buy you a drink. Have you tried Canary rum?'

'No –'

He patted her twice on the waist and turned to the bar.

'*Salud!*' she said, when he passed her the tumbler.

'*Salud!*'

He raised his beer glass. She sipped the dark spirit and sucked it through her teeth. It seared the tip of her tongue and the heat flared up the sides of her mouth. He finished his beer and she swallowed down the liquor. He took her empty glass and stood them both on a nearby table.

She touched his arm. 'Would you like to dance?'

'Sure.'

He took a drag on his half-smoked cigarette and turned back to the table. He twisted the cigarette on its end in the ash-tray, then increased the pressure until it creased in two.

The floor was filling up. She went ahead, threading herself between the gyrating bodies while he shouldered awkwardly after her to the space she had created. He left a good distance between them, a surprising distance, and began moving from foot to foot with the rhythm, his mouth fixed in a grin. Soon his eyes left hers and settled on the sway of her skirts.

Towards the end of the track he took a few steps closer, in time with the music. He put his arms round her, and his hands clasped in the small of her back. She linked hers round him in return. They were close enough for their bellies to graze when they mistimed a beat, and she could feel his arousal. Presently his fingers parted and slid to her hips, and he muttered something to himself in Spanish. She could have kissed him.

She reached behind her, grasped his hand and led him off the floor. When she stopped he slid his arm round her and smoothed her waist.

'What is wrong?'

'Can we go?'

He ushered her through the double doors into the passage at the foot of the stairs. 'Are you all right?'

'The music's too loud.'

'It is loud. Okay, would you like to drive, or take a walk?'

'I don't want to go too far from the hotel...'

'There is the roof terrace.'

'Is it open at this hour?'

'The lights may be off, but we can still go there. You have a magical panorama over Puerto, and it's a fine place to gaze at the stars on a clear night. And, of course, it's quiet.'

After the disco she welcomed a quiet place. A walk on the rooftop would make a suitable, mellowing prelude to her invitation.

Jesús pressed the call button and, arm in arm, they took the lift to the fifth floor and walked the last flight of stairs. The blackness beyond the terrace door forced them to stop for their eyes to adjust, and from the void formed the pale block of the bar and the stripes of the white plastic sun-loungers round the roof-top pool.

She took a deep breath, threw her arms in the air and spun herself round three or four times.

'Jesús, this is wonderful!' She ran to the railings. 'Look at the town...'

'You are much more beautiful.'

He rested his hands on the railings either side of her back, and she turned to face him.

'May I kiss you?'

'May you kiss me? Yes, I hope.'

He drew her away from the edge. They turned, rocking through the steps of some lazy, timeless dance, and the embrace grew more and more fervent until she could hear his breathing.

Suddenly he reached out with his left hand and she heard a sharp crack from the concrete. She pulled away.

'What's that?'

He touched his shoe against a flat rectangular shape on the terrace floor, and nudged it parallel to the wall of the bar.

'A mattress. They are piled here for the night, from the sunbeds. Karin –'

He took her by the shoulders and pressed her to the bar wall. She felt a hand insinuate itself under the folds of her dress, and he kissed her again hard. His left hand closed over her breast and squeezed so roughly that she yelped.

'Hey! There's no rush –'

'Feel!' He pulled her from the wall with such force that she fell into him, and he drew her buttocks to his groin. 'There, now you feel. The mattress is good–'

'Jesus, this is too quick –'

'No problem.'

He reached into his trouser pocket and held up a small square packet. She twisted free of his other arm and backed off. He took a step after her, his palms upturned in appeal.

'You are beautiful. Look how you make me. I cannot help desiring you. Look!' He fumbled with the zip of his fly. 'I crave for your body, Karin. I crave for you.'

For a moment she stared, then she fled for the crack of light behind the terrace door. With a crash she threw the door open against the wall and tore down the stairs.

'Karin!'

Down more and more stairs she ran, deafened by her own breathing, spinning her shoulder against the wall as she took the corner into the next flight and hitting her flank on the rail. Behind her his heavy steps took the stairs two or three at a time.

When the third floor sign came into view she raced along to her room, grabbed the key-card from the top of the architrave and shoved it into the lock. She threw herself inside, slammed the door and twisted the brass button to lock it from inside. She shut herself in the bathroom and locked that. She pulled off her sandals and sat, panting, on the lid of the toilet with her knees drawn into her arms. What had she expected? Something, anything better than this. She wanted to go home, *be* home, hold the cat, turn the clocks back. The man in her imaginings appeared to order, like a hologram. He obeyed her thoughts, he acted on her terms. Free will was a loose cannon, and victimisation was definitely not in the rules. Bastard. Craved for her body? The shit had eaten a dictionary.

Leaning forward, she grasped the sides of the sink and hauled herself to her feet. Her stomach lurched. Over the white porcelain she retched twice, the guilt of a woman who had not pandered, and the simultaneous degradation of one who had.

Slowly she raised her right arm in front of the mirror: the side-seam of her dress gaped with ragged loops of stitching visible. She smacked her hand against the glass. Had simple decency fallen from grace too? Even Sally ran play-schemes and mothered small children. Matt wasn't the right man, nor Jesús; the right man was seven hours away, sweating beads of shame in an overheated kitchen in Oxford. All she had to do was lower herself a little. No one could deny Jesús' good looks, and there would have been no repercussions beyond the next transfer from Reina Sofía. But sleeping with Jesús would have made her worse than Brendan could ever have been.

If Reception had rung to say there was a taxi idling outside, and a ticket to London waiting at the airport, she could have left her justice in the foil packet under the pillow and run straight into the street. Only she knew she would have left her pride behind, like Cinderella's slipper, on the stairs.

4

Behind her, she heard the damp, distant roar of a car. She stuck out her arm and turned, backing down the side of the road in small, awkward steps that disrupted her normal rhythm.

It was a white car, travelling fast, its headlamps sallow in the mist. Desperately she jerked her thumb, blew the drip from the end of her nose and forced a smile through the strings of her wet hair. This car had to stop. It was the first she'd seen in almost an hour.

The wraith-grey driver glanced across at her. She stopped thumbing and frantically waved her arms. The car sailed past without even decelerating.

'Moron!' she yelled at the tail-lights. 'What do you expect on top of a mountain? Bloody *up Spain!*'

She stopped walking, let her head drop and pinned her hands round her ribcage. The bones heaved against her fingers. How much longer before darkness settled, she wondered, before the temperature really started to fall? She'd left Puerto de la Cruz just for a day's hike, to exercise her body and exorcise her mind. Bivvying for the night on a Spanish mountain in early January had not formed part of the programme. Going on her recent track record with providence they'd find her body in a foetal huddle, her face with all the pointless serenity of a dead saint.

She eased the rucksack from her back, flexed her shoulders and picked the clinging patch of sweat-shirt away from her skin. Saturday had started so full of promise. She'd taken a bus to Punta del Hidalgo on the north-eastern coast, then quit the town on foot and set off for the remote village of Chinamada. Between the side of the mountain and the tail of the opposite ridge, the houses and high-rise hotels of Punta del Hidalgo had gradually reduced to a smattering of white flakes, and the sea fused with the sky in a gamut of fading greys. Ahead, mountains erupted from the horizon like the cusps of vast volcanic teeth.

The night had tormented her with repeated clips of Jesús, dashing as a film star, and twice as callous. For him, she had been little more than a Friday without a shag, a state of affairs he would no doubt rectify that evening. Against the immutable majesty of the Anaga mountains, however, he began to shrivel to a triviality, spent and impotent.

Her feet resounded in a hypnotic rhythm on the damp earth and stirred the scent of aromatic herbs. The sun filtered through occasional gaps in the cloud, throwing up the ridges and hollows of the mountainside. A cover of low-growing vegetation softened their forbidding aspect and gave them an attractive but incongruous woolliness reminiscent of the hills in her brother's old train lay-out. Far in the distance, the opposite side of the ravine was criss-crossed with tracks and incised with hundreds of tiny, bright green terraces. Once they must have been cultivated, but now they rimmed the hillsides like the tide-marks of a vanished lake.

At last her path levelled at the foot of some terraces still in use, their bare but furrowed soil shored up by walls of boulders. Below the path a dense growth of cacti tumbled down the slope. Spiders squatted in dusty labyrinths slung between the fat green stems.

Above the terraces she caught her first sight of Chinamada's habitations, nestled in line along a ledge under the rock face. *In* the rock face, for the tiny, startling white façades disappeared straight into the mountain.

After picking her way up the last, rocky section of the path she stopped to stare at the immaculate windows and doors, some painted, some stained, some with a number nailed above the lintel. Pots of red geraniums sat in rows along the front walls and window sills, and one outside wall supported a family of finches in a cane birdcage. Solar panels reclined here and there, like giant washboards, against the rocks. A line of washing hung, becalmed.

She took a couple of photographs of the troglodyte dwellings, then followed the track to a road, a proper road and - a village hall, a modern village hall with a large, crazy-paved square enclosed by walls of peach-painted cement... A village hall on top of a scarcely inhabited mountain ridge! And beyond the plaza lay a spacious - and completely empty - parking area, and the first curl of tarmac that linked Chinamada to civilisation...The embrace of modernity and convenience had pressed itself on the face of Chinamada like a Judas kiss.

Leaving the village behind, she forked right off the road as soon as her route allowed, and the black umbilical cord wound away out of sight down the valley. Further along the trail she untied the sweat-shirt from her waist, laid it over the vegetation at the side of the path and settled down to a late lunch. Once, not so long ago, everything must have reached the hamlet on the backs of mules or the broad shoulders of its inhabitants. Walkers, she'd read, had trekked there in dozens, attracted by its unspoilt beauty and isolation; now tourists could drive there on their circular tour and wonder why they'd bothered. Yet another slice of perfection betrayed without a thought for the consequences.

She finished a cheese sandwich and an apple, and launched the core high over the precipitous side of the *barranco* before her. It arched and vanished silently into the scrub.

The air was mild and moist, redolent of a lingering autumn or an early herald of spring. She leaned into the cushion of plants at her back, admiring the large, orange, bell-shaped flowers that scrambled over the banks.

Awareness returned, of icy arms and a cadaverous chill in her chest. She opened her eyes to find a curtain of mist over the *barranco*. She jerked her watch to her face, her dark hairs spiking from the gooseflesh of her forearm: twenty to five? She'd been asleep for almost an hour.

'Shit!'

With shaking fingers, she unzipped the front pocket of the rucksack and snatched out the bus timetable. She flattened it on the track and knelt over the schedule of departures, pinning the paper to the earth with her elbows. Four forty-five from Las Carboneras, five o'clock from Taborno. Ten minutes or so later from the roadside stop at Las Escaleras, the end of her walk.

She slapped the walk plan on the timetable. Maybe, by taking that branching trail off the route – no, she could forget Las Carboneras. An alternative would be to jog back to Chinamada and beg a lift in the car park, if there were any cars; it might be a waste of valuable time. Perhaps she should keep to her planned path and run to Las Escaleras? Would she make it even then? Her heart knocked in her chest. She had to; it was the last bus of the day, the last bus out of the mountains.

She stuffed the two sheets into the top of the rucksack, pulled on her sweat-shirt and set off at a run, swinging the bag against her shoulder. The sweat-shirt clung, cool and sticky, to her arms. The air was colder in her mouth now the cloud had rolled up, and seemed thick and porridgy with moisture.

Surrounded by mist, she had no way of gauging her progress. Her trainers pounded the earth in time with her breathing, and scoured the loose stones. She ran, checked the watch, ran, walked, checked her watch and broke back into a trot. Her waterproof rustled inside the rucksack behind her. The zips jingled and the remains of the water whipped up and dripped eerily inside the bottle. Nothing else moved in the stillness.

When the watch showed ten past five, hope, too, receded into the mist. She threw back her head and came to a halt, arms swinging. What she could see of the earth and rock and greenery glazed beyond tears. Conserving her energy and walking now seemed the best option.

Eventually wax-myrtles and tree-heath appeared, dripping with dampness at the sides of the path. The path zigzagged upward, and at last she'd climbed the stone steps on to the road that marked the end of the journey. It was as silent and shrouded as the trail from Chinamada, and from there beckoned an uphill hike of well over three kilometres to the main road. She'd arrived there forty minutes later without sight of a single vehicle.

Glancing up and down the empty road, she swung the rucksack back on to her shoulder and resumed walking. Maybe there would be a bus from another company, or a stray coach tour on its way home. And the Cruz del Carmen viewpoint was only half a kilometre away. Perhaps a café would still be open, or some dreamy sightseer lagging in the car park. Who was she kidding? The tourists would have turned tail when the mist claimed the *miradores*, and few locals would be driving to La Laguna or Santa Cruz at that time of day. And if she did get a lift the driver would probably reveal himself to be John the Baptist or Mengele.

She smeared the most annoying strands of hair, sodden from the humidity and exertion, away from her face. Saturday had begun so well and now it looked to be heading the way of Friday. Only worse. This had to be the stuff of the pitiful, daily column-fillers in the papers. People met their deaths through such freak turns of events as these, people who had every expectation of surviving, yet somehow managed to die against all the odds.

The hiss of another vehicle sounded on the bend behind her, and a burst of desperate energy smothered her doubts. She swung up her arms, waving, and the little red Opel veered wide across both lanes to avoid her. Her arms flopped to her thighs. Suddenly the brake lights lit, and the car slewed sharply across to the near-side. She stared at it for a moment before breaking into a run. The steamy passenger window was already winding down.

'La Laguna?' she panted.

'La Laguna's good.'

Male, and he sounded English. He flicked the catch on the passenger door. He looked reasonably decent: in his early forties, messy brown hair. He could have done with a shave. She didn't notice the details. She had a penknife in her bag anyway. What mattered were the wheels.

She bundled herself inside and dropped her bag between her knees. The car pulled back on to the road.

'Where have you walked from?'

She told him. 'My reward was going to be the scenic drive back past all these *miradores*. Cloud permitting.'

'And is that the end of the line, La Laguna?'

'Unless you're going to Puerto de la Cruz.'

'Puerto?' His scruffy face grinned at her. 'Well, in that case I can drop you right on your doorstep! Where are you staying?'

'At the San Felipe. On the sea-front.' She paused, still guarded. 'You?'

'Up the hill. The Parque San Antonio.'

The next few minutes passed in complete silence as she watched the intermittent wipers clear the windscreen.

'I've seen you before, haven't I,' she announced, her voice curt. 'Wednesday lunch-time, the *Café de Paris*.' Still she refused to look at him. 'You were with a Spanish girl. And later you arrived at the beach, just as I was packing. I watched you stroll down to the breakwater. It was late; everyone else was leaving. And I saw this girl peel off every stitch of clothing until she was stark naked.'

'Ah.'

'And you began photographing her with a camera the size of a dog.'

He seemed to let this observation sink in for a moment. 'Green and purple dress,' he said.

She turned sharply.

'I thought so,' he said. 'With the wet hair I wasn't sure.'

'You're a photographer?'

'In a manner of speaking.'

'A glamour photographer?'

He laughed. 'No, I'm a stuffed shirt. Photographer, yes, in my dreams. Of glamour, no. The girl was, well, just a pretty face with a good figure. I asked if she'd model.'

'So photographing naked and amenable young girls is your hobby?'

He sighed. 'I happen to find the human body beautiful. Nudes are what I do best. Actually she's twenty-two with a three-year-old son at home with her mother. And I paid her.'

'Do you always pay?'

The car swerved into the entrance of the *mirador*, and came to a standstill so sudden that they both lurched forward. He flung off his seat-belt and got out, leaving the door gaping. He strode to the rear of the car and threw up the hatchback, his face set, shifting objects around inside with quick, sharp movements.

Before she could slip out, the hatchback banged shut, rocking the suspension. Grit rasped on the tarmac behind her and he opened her door.

'See this?' He waved a large, flat, bottle-green book at her. 'I'd like you to have a look at it. Go on, take it. I'll be over there.

And you might like to know the keys are in the ignition.'

She accepted the book in silence, like an undeserved gift of chocolates, and watched him walk off with his hands in his pockets towards the viewing area. He was wearing caramel brown trousers and a light blue shirt with the cuffs turned up. He held his head high despite the drizzle, and moved with a fluid briskness that could have been arrogance, vexation or natural grace. He didn't look back.

There seemed little point in driving off and deserting a man who had deliberately left her the keys. She pulled both doors shut and sat with the book over her knees. She saw now that it was an album with covers of imitation leather. With one finger she rubbed a tiny viewing hole in the condensation that had misted her window and watched him out of sight, a faint blue smudge fading in the greyness. Wiping away the wetness against her trousers, she used the same finger to hook open the cover.

In the middle of the first page, stark against the black background, was a white paper sticker with a name and address printed in italics: *Roy Meredith. Southampton, Hants.* Roy Meredith. She turned the first page.

She left the album on the seat, switched off the headlights and made her way across the parking area to the *mirador*. He was standing at the balustrade beyond the stone benches, staring out into the cloud that concealed the view.

A good way behind him she stopped and waited, her fists clenched against the cold; he didn't appear to have heard her. She reached out with the toe of her right trainer, rolled a small stone towards her and then scraped it hard with the sole against the paving stones. He moved his head, then checked it. Finally he turned, his hands still in his pockets, his hair flatter and spiked like hers, the damp sleeves of his shirt collapsed against his arms. He stared at his feet for a while before raising his eyes. Strange eyes, the colour of reen-water after days of rain, muddy and difficult to read. She searched them for anger, slight, self-righteousness, vanity, but saw none, not even the cool armour of disdain.

'They're beautiful,' she said. 'They are beautiful. Works of art. Please accept my apology. I take back everything I said. And thought.'

'I don't deal in sleaze.'

She shrugged. 'I've had a rough time with men recently. Sorry, it's left me over-sensitive. *In*sensitive, depending which way you look at it.'

He smiled, shaking his head. With a casual flick of his fingers he dismissed her guilt and high-handedness into the mist. He took a few slow steps back in the direction of the car, and she fell in alongside him.

'It's a nice name, Roy,' she said. 'Unusual these days. A strong name.'

He looked at her with a quizzical expression.

'The album,' she said.

'Ah yes. And you?'

'Karin.'

They arrived back at the car. As they climbed in, the two slamming doors exploded the silence like gunshots. She handed him some tissues from the rucksack to clear the windscreen.

'So, what were you doing in the Anaga Mountains? Walking? More nudes?'

'Clouds,' he said, zigzagging swipes of landscape through the condensation. 'El Bailadero's renowned. I'm not generally into landscapes, but clouds can be interesting.'

She rubbed her palm with her thumb. 'You do nudes and the occasional cloud. Your work is brilliant, but you say you're not a photographer, and you call yourself a stuffed shirt.'

'I'm a solicitor.' He started the engine, switched on the lights and pulled back on to the road. 'Twenty-one years I've been in practice, all with the same firm, which is, I suppose, as good - and bad – as any decent-sized provincial firm. Equity partner for fifteen years, head of department. Doer of any number of administrative tasks no one else was fool enough to take on. For some reason it's unbelievably easy in business to disappear up the exhaust-pipe of your own ego. I couldn't even see there was a life to get, and the one I had, I screwed up mighty successfully.'

'Children?'

'Two step-daughters, eleven and thirteen. Their mother took them to Scotland to live three years ago.'

'I'm sorry.'

'I think she was sorry once.' He lapsed into silence. 'Still, I've always loved photography,' he said at last. 'And it's hardly a decision that will make me rich, but who cares? I've made the switch to salaried partner. In fact I'm starting to look for premises. And there should be the chance of some legal work on a consultancy basis to keep the wolf from the door. Exhibition work, that's my dream. Till then, portraits, weddings. Pets. Whatever it takes. What's yours?'

'My dream? Hah, which one?' She let her head roll against the headrest. To love, and be loved perfectly... Too saccharine. For a flawless balance between work and home-life. Too telling. To find the perfect remedy first time, every time. Too complicated. To forgive and be forgiven... Too sad. 'God,' she said slowly, 'I'll depress myself if I reel off all the dreams I've failed to achieve. But I wouldn't be surprised if you made it.'

'What?'

'As a photographer. You're doing all the right things.' She turned her face to him, her hair still scrunched against the headrest. 'And you really want it to happen, don't you.'

'Yes, I do. Thanks.' He seemed genuinely moved. 'Thank you.'

*

Las Mercedes, Las Canteras, La Laguna, even the motorway, one by one they merged into the dusk until at last the car veered off down the hill towards Puerto de la Cruz.

'I thought you told me you were at the Parque San Antonio?' she said suddenly.

'I am.'

She twisted round in her seat. 'Didn't we just pass it?'

'After bringing you this far,' he said, 'did you think I'd dump you on the outskirts?'

*

When she bent to say goodbye through the open door, he extended his hand. She leaned inside to shake it, a curious, rather formal conclusion after the conversation they had exchanged on the journey.

'What's your surname, Karin?'

She withdrew her hand.

'You know mine,' he reminded her.

'Karin,' she said. 'It's just Karin.'

She slammed the door and ran up the cream marble steps before turning to wave. He was looking at her, leaning forward in his seat. He didn't return the gesture. Only when her upper arm had dropped did he raise his hand in a smooth, brief farewell. As he lowered it again he pulled up on the hand-brake and the car moved away towards the Avenida.

She remained on the top step, one hand still frozen in a claw, the other dangling her rucksack. She watched the car safely out of sight, then descended the steps and walked off in the opposite direction, back to her hotel.

*

Roy Meredith: he was kind and amusing. She thought about him that night when she lay in bed, warm, bathed, fed and alone. And he was different. She had known the moment he left her, damp and panicky, on the pavement outside the San Felipe. She had suspected before he left her. He made her so relaxed that she felt nervous again.

On Sunday she pottered about the resort. She remembered how the same tuft of hair fell a dozen times across his right eye, and how each time he would run two fingers along his eyebrow and then tuck the hair upwards without a trace of irritation, as though it were a habit of long-standing. She didn't find him unattractive either, his mild features rendered all the more intriguing for the suspicion of a broken nose.

It could end up another fiasco, she thought on Sunday evening as she sat on the stool and stared at herself in the dressing-table mirror. But he photographed naked women, therefore he had to be capable of professional self-control, whether innate or acquired. And on the journey home he had shown not a hint of impropriety towards her. Though he'd marked the dress she'd been wearing at the café, and she didn't recall him looking at her once.

She pulled the complimentary hotel stationery from the wallet on the dressing-table and removed a sheet of headed paper. She folded down the hotel logo, cut it off, painstakingly, with nail scissors, and scribbled a brief note on the piece remaining. After folding the paper twice, she wrote his name on it, then walked to the Parque San Antonio and left the note at the reception desk.

5

Though clouds still crowded the sky on Monday, the air was mild. She arrived at the Columbus Plaza on the Plaza del Charco just before half-past eleven. Roy, clean-shaven this time, waved from a table outside. He folded up his newspaper, pushed it on to the red and white checked table cover and stood to greet her. The waiter appeared almost immediately and Roy ordered her a lemon tea, and a beer for himself in heavily accented Spanish.

'Thanks for coming,' she said.

'How could I resist investigating "something I would like to discuss?" Particularly after my dismissal on Saturday.'

'I was weary.'

'Weary? Wary?'

She smiled. 'Both. Notwithstanding, I've decided I'd like you to take some photos of me. I'll pay, of course. I'll leave you my home address and you can forward them.'

'My pleasure.'

'I mean nude.'

His hand, outstretched to grasp his beer glass, froze for a second. He brought the glass to his lips, took a couple of mouthfuls of the yellow liquid and set the glass back on the table. His eyes returned to hers.

'Have you taken your clothes off for the camera before? Modelled for life-classes, anything like that?'

She shook her head.

'Do you do a lot of photography?'

'I can't say I do. I take quite a lot of photos. Well,' she reflected, 'I used to. This last year, eighteen months, I don't seem to have taken many at all. Too busy, I suppose.'

'Would you excuse me for a moment?'

He scraped back the chair and disappeared into the café. She extracted the limp lemon slice from the bottom of her glass, bit through the pith and chewed out the tepid, acid flesh.

She stared out across the Plaza del Charco, the branches of its tall palms playing restlessly in the breeze. In the centre of the square an elderly woman holding a camera called instructions to a child with a dog, waving them into a suitable position on the wall at the base of the fountain. Two jets sprayed thin, dotted lines of water into the pool either side of them, and a lush plant with huge, heart-shaped leaves mounded above the small, fidgeting figures.

Why hadn't she taken more photos that past year? She loved to catch Brendan on film, or ask friends, or even complete strangers to photograph the two of them together, arm in arm. Of late, the camera had been forgotten more often than not. Occasionally she had neglected to take it, but mostly she had forgotten. And those photographs that had been taken and developed she had posted into a drawer and not arranged in the album according to her custom. It coincided perfectly, she saw that now, with their estrangement. When they had been veering, on that subtle undercurrent, ever nearer to the rocks, photographs had been the first victims to be jettisoned. Her fear of witnessing the truth had exceeded her wish to validate an illusion. *The camera never lies*. She remembered the snaps taken by Leon at Westonbirt arboretum in the autumn, of smiles under strain, and closeness neither as close nor as genuine as it should have been. And the shot under the acer of Leon with his arm round her when she was humouring him: they looked the better couple. Leon had presented them with an enlargement. Later Brendan had torn it up.

Roy came back. He sat down and rested his elbows on the table, cupping his left hand in the right and rubbing the pad of one thumb back and forth across the nail of the other.

'I'll take them.'

'That's wonderful! So, where do you think we should do them?'

He stopped fiddling with his fingers and caught her eye. 'Why do you want to be photographed nude?'

'I – just want to be seen for who, and what I really am. I think it would be a privilege.'

'I can't disagree with that. But who *are* you? What image do you want to project? You as you feel you truly are, you as you would like to believe you are? Or as you would like the world to perceive you?'

'Well, I don't want to be photographed scrunched up in a shopping trolley.'

'Listen, Karin. People go for studio portraits in clothes so smart they've only ever worn them once, and they end up sitting like ramrods against a background of clouded brown or muzzy blue... If you want the pictures, I'll do them, but it will be a far more rewarding experience if you call the shots. Unless, of course, you want to present yourself as a victim.'

'No!'

'Then you must be the one making the creative decisions. What about the location? If you want a landscape background, there's everything here.' He raised his arm and made brisk sweeping gestures, as though leading an orchestra through a particularly vigorous interlude. 'Sea, moonscape, volcano. Tertiary forest. Sub-tropical paradise. And what sort of lighting? Pale dawn? A glowing sunset? Cloud? Mist? Then there's your hair and your make-up. Any jewellery or other props you might need to support the image or mood...'

'I just want a few photos...' she said lamely.

'But this is the stuff photos are made of.' He slid further

down the seat and clasped his hands behind his neck, faintly shaking his head. 'You must really know the image you want to create. Do you want to be taken coming up out of the sea holding lanterns, and make a statement? Or blend with nature? Or be in nature but not blending with it – amongst rocks or cacti or something; a study of shape and form?' He reached for his glass and finished the rest of his beer. 'You're looking daunted, Karin. Are you sure you want to go ahead? Would you like to think it over?'

She opened her mouth to reply, and at the last moment averted her eyes. 'I must be mad,' she grinned. 'No, I'll do it.'

They arranged the shoot for Thursday, which gave her two days in which to decide on her requirements and to prepare any props. She was to send word as soon as she had chosen a location so that he could visit in advance to check out the lighting and gain a feel of the place for himself.

The waiter collected up the glasses and bottle and clattered them on to a metal tray.

'In fact,' Roy said, 'it's almost half-past twelve. We could have lunch. If you're still mad enough.'

Who was she? The reflection in the dressing-table mirror stared back at her, serene and naked on the stool, and gave nothing away.

Who was she? The image she needed to create was not that of herself laid bare, fearful, wounded and mistrustful, but one she would wish him to accept as her inner image. Something to disturb and provoke. A credible fantasy that a man would like to discover in a woman.

'Your work,' she'd asked him over the *tapas*, 'do you see it as sexual?'

'The finished product, or the process of making it?'

'Either. Both.'

He'd chewed up an olive. 'When all's said and done, most of my subjects are naked women. My pictures have to be sexual to a greater or lesser extent. With abstracts or studies there's more detachment, but the human body never entirely loses its sensuality. The sexuality I prefer to keep subtle. Were you offended?'

'I expected to be.'

'Well, if you create a subtext of sexual tension it's inevitable the erotic comes to the fore. But only a vulgar presentation of the body destroys its dignity. As for being behind the camera... Well, I'm clothed, they're not. The camera is an eye, prying on what should eventually appear as a private and intimate scene, but there's also a brain behind it. I'm not saying I'm impervious, but one does get taken up with the technical details, the lighting, the reflectors, composition. Pose. Reducing the impact of the models' physical defects, because they all have them.'

'Have you had affairs with your models?'

'Wow...' He laughed and helped himself to a couple more olives. As he bit into one, a spurt of brine ran over his lower lip and he scooped up the drip with a finger. 'I got involved with two, just after my wife left. Futile attempts at reassurance, I'm afraid. So yes, I pander to society's obsession with image. Peddling physical beauty is my goal. But in the absence of compatiblity, models are strictly business.'

When they parted, he placed his hands on her upper arms.

'If you change your mind, want to pull out or be clothed or approach anything from a different angle, just let me know. You won't be letting anyone down. You need to feel confident.'

She'd muttered her thanks, her gaze fixed on his watch. It was the first time he'd stood so close, the first time he'd touched anything other than her hand. And it was the first time she'd felt so naked when dressed.

A photographer of nudes... This should have been simple, she told herself. But it had metamorphosed into a project, an entire campaign. Worse, he was forcing her to take a good look at herself, body and soul, before he ever got near.

She sat up straight and scrutinised her breasts. Could the right one be very slightly larger than the left? Would the camera notice? Would Roy? Her chest could have done with being ampler. On the other hand, some women's breasts had turned to onions in a pair of tights by the time they hit thirty-five.

And at least hers weren't fakes; some models' contained more saline than a rock pool.

She got to her feet. Aesthetically, her waist would have benefited by being a shade narrower, and her hips correspondingly larger. She frowned. She had height on her side, but her athleticism teetered on the brink of masculinity. The curves were there; they just weren't curved enough. Kinks instead of ox-bows, and mandarins instead of melons.

She crossed the room, drew the nets clear of the sliding window, and pressed herself against the glass. Confidence, it had to be the key to everything. Her chosen image must exude it from every pore. Confidence, independence and power.

She perched on the stool again, pulled her hair into a pony-tail and coiled it into a bun which she pressed with both hands to the back of her head. She smiled at her reflection. Very elegant; a new take on advertising for coffee or after-dinner mints. No, elegance smacked of manufactured inaccessibility; it missed the point. And the pose looked over-done. She needed grace, grace and wildness. And sexiness, of course, to be implied without blatant or gratuitous exhibitionism. Woman as the untamed and self-contained inhabitant of a world complete without man. Perverse. Aloof. The vision began to condense into reality.

She leaned over and plucked the guide-book off the bed, then threw it back on to the covers; she didn't need to look for backdrops. The setting was obvious now: grand, harsh, inhospitable, but full of beauty, a place ancient and untouched but for the feet of tourists. Only one place would do.

*

'I can see this promises to be an interesting shoot.'

Roy eyed the spear, but she walked down the steps of the San Felipe as though it were no more remarkable than an umbrella.

'Hey, that's awfully realistic. Can I see?'

She passed it to him. 'It's a broom handle. I bought the knife in a tackle shop and tied it to the stick, then bound the dark green ribbon over the string. Those three gold studs underneath are bottle tops. Then I just strung on the longer brown and yellow ribbons.'

'And a couple of seagull feathers, by the looks of things.'

'I found them on the beach.' She swung her rucksack and carrier through the passenger door and on to the back seat. 'Look, do you mind if we get in, Roy. Those people are staring.'

They took the road to La Orotava, and wound the long bends up the valley towards the dark forest of pines.

He inquired how she was feeling.

'Well, I've been trailing about naked in my room, trying to accustom myself to the novelty. And I've been practising various poses and expressions in the mirror. Not that either exercise will prepare me for baring my soul in the middle of Las Cañadas.'

'Speaking of which,' said Roy, 'I did the recce. The locations with the most artistic merit are perpetually swarming with tourists, I have to say. It might have helped if you'd revealed your peg, though I assume the spear is a heavy clue.'

'I want,' she said, teasing her fingers through her damp hair, 'to be a fighting spirit set in a mystical landscape.'

'The warrior woman?'

'To be approached with caution. Definitely.'

Teide vanished, masked by the pines and gathering cloud. She had studied the volcano several times that week through the dining-room window. On a clear day the stark, forested ridge to the west swept the eye upward to Teide's distant grey cone and neat fondant snow-cap. Dominant, dormant, it watched over the island, a testament to its violent past.

At last they emerged above the cloud layer into scalding white sunshine and blue skies, and the cloud stretched away below, pale and flat, like a second sea.

She recalled a question. 'The eyes! In almost every picture of your portfolio, the eyes are averted – that's if the models are facing you at all. Is there something I should know about the eyes?'

He sighed. 'Traditionally, the nude found greatest acceptance as art when the emotion was played down. The old return to Eden, you know the kind of thing. Even now nudes tend to be mood images rather than representations of the individual. Once a model's personality makes its mark, the image is lost, you see. Personality comes from body language, the face and, above all, the eyes. Once there's eye contact between model and camera, there's a direct avenue for communication. Personal expression to the viewer of the picture.'

'And if the model is deliberately talking to the viewer?'

'What you end up with then is a portrait.'

'So, what should I do? Where should I look?'

'Wherever you like is the simple answer. These are *your* pictures, Karin.'

She picked at the cuticle of one of her copper-varnished nails. 'I'm going to make a prat of myself.'

'You won't.'

'Roy, I'm bloody terrified.'

'I happen to prefer working with inexperienced models.'

She studied the side of his face, watching for deception. 'Do you?'

'Professionals give you whatever expression you ask for. They're easier to work with, but there's less manufacture from an amateur, less guile. More art.'

'I'm not twenty-two any more,' she said flatly.

'If I thought it was going to be a bad idea for you – or for me – I'd have told you so before now.'

'Would you?'

He turned his head from the road to look at her. 'Yes.'

As they left the cloud and the trees behind, new panoramas evolved out of the dust and the sunshine. They stopped for a snack in a restaurant at El Portillo before finally crossing what looked to be the rim of a huge crater. The floor of the ancient volcanic landscape, strewn with boulders and sculpted crusts of lava, stretched away, pale, into the distance. Its spawn of younger volcanoes reared above on the northern edge in colours of cream and stale coffee, and clusters of coaches marked out the gnarled pillars of Los Roques and the base of Teide's *teleférico*.

'I guess you've already been up?' she said, tapping her nail on the window. 'I came here on an organised trip last week, but the lift was closed. Too windy.'

'Well, it's running today. If you wanted –'

'No,' she said. '*This* is what I want.'

'I've taken the car as far as I can,' said Roy. 'I'm afraid we're going to have to hike some way into the mountains now to find a little privacy.'

He got out and began to sort his equipment bags in the boot. A brown bottle flashed from behind and bounced on the driver's seat. She picked it up.

'Baby oil?'

'To give your skin a bit of texture. A *soupçon*, please. We're not frying chips. So just the make-up here, perhaps, and we'll take the rest with us. Sorry it's so basic.'

They climbed for almost half an hour, up into the dusty ochre mountains of the caldera, until he reached a savage configuration of rocks compatible with the position of the sun. He set up, chatting constantly, while she stripped to nothing behind a rock. She tied a green, yellow and brown speckled sarong round her hips, firmly looping the ends, then put on a necklace of patterned clay beads, a metal armlet and several ethnic bangles. Shaking her hair free of its pony-tail, she whipped it forward and back a couple of times. She hadn't brushed it since washing it, and it had dried to a wool of soft, loose coils.

The air was unmoving, the sun hot on her shoulders. Every sound seemed amplified, the grit, Roy's voice, her bracelets. She rested her hands on the rock and watched him over the top.

'I'll do some black and white, and some colour,' he said, slipping the strap of the camera over his head, 'and later some infra-red, which, I think, will be ideally suited to your theme.'

'Why's there a sheet over that rock?'

'It's a reflector, Karin. So your unlit side doesn't vanish into shadow.'

'I see. I don't want to do any pointless or farcical poses.'

'You won't have to. Well, this is it...'

She swallowed hard, caught the bottom end of her spear against a spur of rock and dropped it with a wooden clatter.

Where was Mata Hari now, and Mae West, and Marilyn Munroe? With the exception of Brendan, no man had seen her naked for a decade. Swimming costumes counted for nothing. Even bikinis didn't compare with unveiling before a camera. The lens loomed, neither as negligent as the human eye, nor as diplomatic.

'What about,' he said, 'if we start off with some shots from the back? Maybe a few silhouettes. How does that sound?'

'I think I'd like to do some silhouettes,' she said.

*

Forty minutes later they broke for some mineral water and slightly flattened slices of almond tart Roy had brought along in his equipment bag. They decamped to the second location, she in her trainers and wrapped in the reflector sheet.

The posing became easier. She grew used to his stream of gentle patter while he changed a lens or a film. He would walk up to her and straighten her armlet, or re-position an unruly strand of hair, picking at the tiniest details with a photographer's critical eye while he praised her efforts and made suggestions.

'This,' he said, 'is what I've been waiting for.'

It was late afternoon when they arrived at the great, sculpted tusks of Los Roques. All day the rocks had been flecked with anoraks, crawling like garishly-coloured mites across the pink, mauve and orange stone. But now the movement of cars had slowed and the coaches were gone.

They stood, both clothed, on the viewing-platform near the foot of the rocks. They shielded their eyes and scanned the Ucanca plain with its expanse of dark, chocolatey lava and sandy plateau.

'Mono infra-red,' he murmured. He pointed down at some

pale crags of rock that rose like an island from the sea of sand. 'I want some wide-angle shots over the lake bed, with those rocks as a back-drop. The sun's still bright and the infra-red will enhance the mythical quality you're aiming for. Fantastic!' He bundled his tripod against his shoulder, climbed over the wall and set off down the slope, picking his way among the bumps of vegetation and the scree of loose orange and grey stones. 'Come on, Karin. Kit off! These will be the best shots of the day.'

She grasped the spear at an angle across her torso, her right wrist just masking her breast. He had fixed the camera on a tripod, and was playing round with some coloured filters and another camera, which he seemed to be using to assess her poses.

'Okay,' he said, hovering behind the tripod, 'just for a few frames I want you to look at me.'

'I can't.'

'I can't even see through this filter, Karin. Just keep in your mind who you are. Who are you? Give me a name.'

'Boudicca.'

'Boudicca didn't whisper.'

'Boudicca!'

'Brilliant!' The shutter clicked and Roy adjusted the camera. 'And again, Boudicca. Right, and who else are you?'

'Emmeline Pankhurst!'

'That's right, you show me.' Click, click, click. 'And who else? Look just to your right of the camera now. Who else?'

'The queen of the Amazons.'

'Queen who? Don't you have a name?'

'Penthesilea!'

'Good!' Click, click, click. 'Now look out across the plain, Penthesilea. It's all yours.' Click, click, click. 'What are you looking at?'

No reply.

'There's something over there in the distance and you want it, want to make it yours. What is it?'

'A man.'
'A man? That's no good to me. What man?'
'Achilles!'
'What's his weakness, Penthesilea?'
'*I* am his weakness!'
Click, click, click.

*

'I know it's been a long day,' he said on the journey home, 'and you're probably sick of the sight and sound of me. But would you care to join me for dinner at the San Antonio?'

'Yes!' The word hit her ears like an over-enthusiastic yelp. 'I mean, I'd love to. If you're sure.'

*

She held the saucer high, just in front of her chest. She took frequent sips from the broad white cup, each time extending her neck slightly, her eyes staring beyond the rim to the vase of orange and purple flowers on the coffee table. Cranes, yes, they resembled the heads of cranes.

'Hey...' Roy leaned forward in his armchair. 'Are you okay?'

'Fine.' She rattled the cup back on to the saucer and placed it, in one fluid motion, on the table. 'Yes, I'm fine.' She pulled a face. 'Remembered I've got to make a phone call, that's all.'

'No problem. I'll chill out here with the Birds of Paradise.' From the vase he plucked one of the flowers and tapped its mauve beak in the palm of his hand. 'You can use the phone in my room, if you like.'

'No! Thanks.'

She slid off the seat and picked her way round the islands of seats towards the Reception area.

The line clicked and whirred inside the ear-piece while she dabbed in the number. She tucked the receiver even closer to her neck.

'Be there,' she breathed. '*Be there.*'

'You have reached Brendan and –'
'Damn!'
It was her own voice.
'Sorry we can't take your call right now, but –'
'Shit. Shit!'

She slammed down the re-dial button and immediately released it. A different number, the phone in his study. Maybe he'd be there.

This time the line was answered. She could have broken into laughter. Her whole face seemed to stretch with her smile.

'Brendan?'

There came a pause.

'Hold on. He's just gone downstairs.'

Female. The voice was female.

The receiver seemed to drift from her ear, her breath panted unevenly over her lips.

'Who shall I say is calling?' the voice inquired distantly.

Karin put a hand on the wall to steady herself and brought the receiver back to her face. 'Are you his wife?'

A snuffle of amusement. 'No.'

'Who is this?'

'My name is Sally.'

Her eyes snapped shut. She fumbled with her free hand over the telephone apparatus and depressed the lever that cut the call. Her heart felt as though it were being drawn out through her back.

Everything in the lounge looked so glossy. She could have been walking into a photograph. Cocktail music bonged softly in the background, music she hated.

'Get through all right?' said Roy.

'Yes. It's my great-uncle's eightieth birthday. You know, I'd promised.' She pinched the corner of her lip so hard with her canines that she wondered if it might bleed. She checked it with a finger and flopped back into her chair opposite him. 'Roy, I know you must be worn-out, so I probably shouldn't ask –'

'Since when did you let that stop you?' He opened his arms.

'Fire away!'

'Well, I wondered if you might take a few more photos of me this evening. But indoors.'

His lips parted and the saliva shone on the curve of his lower lip. He sat back in his seat.

'What, somewhere like here, you mean? More contemporary?'

'No, not here,' she said. 'Still nude. In your room, I was thinking. If you have no objection.'

6

She knew he'd be there, waiting. She had the key singled out in her pocket, but at the last moment she reached for the bell.

Within seconds the door was snatched open. Its arc came to an equally abrupt halt. Brendan looked stiffly down at her, his thumb hooked round the edge of the door. He swallowed and his lower lip rounded with suspicion. Without a word he took a step back into the hall and folded his arms.

He was dressed entirely in grey. He looked grey. The shadows at the corners of his nose cut deeper and darker than before, like mirrored scythes. Pockets swelled under his eyes, and his eyes reflected outrage and fear. Behind him, the Saturday papers lay scattered at the foot of the stairs. One of the sections had been opened on the carpet.

'You were quick,' she said.

'I was just on my way up to my study. Quicker than you, anyway. I thought you were due back early this morning.'

She didn't move from the step. 'I decided to get a few hours' kip at the airport. Then I thought I'd drop in to see your uncle, who insisted on feeding me lunch. And then I did a bit of shopping.' She waited, but he just carried on watching her with his hard eyes. 'I've come home,' she blurted. 'I've kept my word. You said it was what you wanted.' She paused. 'Aren't you even going to invite me in?'

'Laid a vampire, did you?'

He turned on his heel. She stared after him for a second, then seized her case from the step, threw it down on the newspapers and strode into the kitchen after him. She grabbed him by the sleeve of his sweater and swung him to face her.

'You hypocrite! When did she leave, Brendan? Last night? Or is the bed still warm?'

'What on earth are you talking about?'

She flapped her hand at the pair of place-mats on the kitchen table.

'Oh, come on. "Brendan's gone downstairs." "Who shall I say is calling?" Nothing if not confident, I'll give her her due.'

Brendan's head dropped, as though the weight of the recollection were too much.

'Oh, God. I said it had to be you.'

'Fortunately. A well-timed social call, if ever there was one.'

'I ran downstairs to answer it,' he babbled. 'I've been virtually camping by the phone all week in the hope you'd ring. When Sally told me the caller had hung up, I got her to repeat the conversation word for word. I knew it was you. And I knew what you'd be thinking.'

'Too bad.'

She raised her arm to push past him, but he stepped sideways and blocked her path.

'Karin, listen to me. I tried to ring you. I tried dial-back, but the number hadn't been registered. It wasn't her. It was Sally Franklyn, one of my students.'

'Alibi at the ready,' she sneered, inspecting her fingernails. 'You've had two days after all. Almost long enough to slot in another liaison.'

'But it's the truth! She had a problem with her dissertation.'

'So you gave her a damned good sorting out.'

'No! No!' Brendan smacked at the air. 'She's just – Sally Franklyn would answer anybody's phone. She's that kind of person, nothing fazes her. Look, I'll get her to come round. She'll explain. Not that there's anything to tell, unless you want to hear about rat brains and serotonin.'

She walked up the kitchen and stared out of the window.

Abruptly she leaned over and prodded the compost of one of the lemon geraniums on the window-sill. The compost had shrunk, like an overcooked cake, from the edges of the pot. She took a tumbler from the drainer, filled it with cold water and poured a reservoir on to the desiccated fibres. Drips fell like pearls on to the white glossed sill.

'I couldn't disprove it either way, could I,' she murmured. 'Whatever she said.' She turned. 'You haven't watered the plants.'

'Plants! You can't write off my fidelity just because I forget to look after a couple of geraniums.'

She pointed on the window-sill to a small shrub with twisted, olive leaves. 'That's dead.'

He screwed up his eyes and scratched with both hands at his hair-line.

'If the bay is dead, I'm sorry. But it's not the end of the world. I'll buy another.'

'A bigger one? A better one?'

'Whatever.'

'You idiot.'

'Not that much of an idiot. I can see you're trying to deflect the attention from yourself.'

She turned straight back to the sink and stuck the empty tumbler under the tall chrome arch of the tap.

'I have absolutely no intention of launching into that now. I haven't unpacked. I haven't even sat down. Forget it. I've only just set foot through the door.'

'Launching...' Brendan mused with a hard edge of irony behind her. 'Sounds promising: my wife launching herself into the tale of her nefarious sexual exploits. How long do I have to wait?'

She refused to give a time. When she was ready, she told him. *When I'm ready*, that open-ended, unsatisfactory brush-off reminiscent of her mother when she was rattled, or hedging, or both.

The front door slammed.

She studied the two maroon place–mats and coasters that

lay opposite each other on the kitchen table. One of the coasters bore overlapping, shiny rings from the base of a wine glass. Some powdery crumbs the colour of sand had spilled on to the table from the edge of the place-mat where he liked to sit. She licked her index finger, pressed its dampness into the crumbs and curled the finger into her mouth; he had made a crumble of some description, a sweet one. A pudding. A treat.

Absently she brushed the crumbs off the table into the palm of her other hand. She took them to the bin and lifted the lid. It was full. Some sort of escalope languished under a sludge of pale, congealed sauce. Beside it lay a baked potato, its cold skin matt and crumpled, and a lattice of glistening baby carrots, sweetcorn and mangetout. And - a rose. A dark red rose, tightly in bud.

The crumbs dropped from her skin as she reached for the flower and untangled it from the mesh of vegetables. The petals still felt firm and velvety: fresh, then. But the stalk had been broken. Not cleanly cut or snapped in two. Folded, perhaps, once, in the centre, splintering the green and white fibres.

She put the bud to her nose and inhaled, but it smelled of ginger and soy sauce and olive oil, and the spiciness brought a pricking to her eyes.

She carried her case up to the second guest-room. It was for the best, certainly in the short-term. And during his absence her things could be cleared from the marital bedroom. She could work at speed and make as much noise as she needed, and he didn't have to witness or overhear the dismantling of their intimate past.

The moment she set foot in the room she saw them on top of his chest of drawers: the photographs, in their various frames of shesham wood, beads, pewter and brocade, lac and velvet, all the photos of Brendan and herself that had once been on display around the house.

Transfixed, she crept across the room. Those that had been hanging he had propped at the back against the bedroom wall. The rest stood, randomly spaced but parallel, across the antique pine. All the glass had been removed from the frames, though none of the pictures appeared damaged.

The photos had been positioned so that they could be surveyed from the bed: her and Brendan sitting on a tree-stump in the grounds of Blenheim Palace... doing the lambada in some disreputable nightclub on Leon's birthday. A scene under some trees on their wedding day with a posed stare into each other's eyes. Nonetheless, anyone could see they were in love. *In love.*

She sat heavily on the bed. He'd bought her a rose and cooked her a special homecoming meal, only for the clock to tick his expectancy into doubt and disappointment; he had whiled away hours on the bottom stair, awaiting her return. How could she possibly tell him anything?

'Tomorrow,' she announced that evening, when Brendan stuck his head round the sitting-room door.

'In that case, would you mind if I went out?' He sounded almost plaintive. 'Being round you and not –'

She nodded at the television she wasn't watching.

'I thought I'd give Leon a bell,' he went on. 'Perhaps go for a quick drink. Just so you know –'

Just so she knew he wasn't sloping off to Sally...

He returned not long after closing time and went straight to bed. In the morning he knocked on her bedroom door and she pulled the sheet up to her neck. He brought in a mug of green tea on a tray and looked everywhere but at her, his eyes bouncing round the walls like a crane fly. She thanked him for the tea, fell asleep again and did not drink it.

'Karin?' he called later from the landing.

'Mmm?'

'I'm going to church.'

'What?' She wriggled up the bed on her elbows, suddenly awake. 'You haven't set foot in a church since we got married.'

'Yes. Well, I figure I've a lot of catching up to do. I thought I'd try the Chaplaincy.'

'Okay.' Her voice sounded ridiculously high, swooping with irrepressible surprise. 'Yes, okay, then. I'll do a roast, shall I?

We can have it when you come back?'

The kitchen was where it happened. She called him - once – in a flat and controlled voice. She even put the plates on the table quietly, and they ate with the delicacy of strangers, watching the steam rise from the lamb and avoiding the clash of cutlery against china. Brendan ate about a third of his, then rested his fists on the table either side of his plate, the knife and fork standing to attention.

'You promised. Today, Karin. You promised.'

'After lunch.'

'No, not after. Now. You're obviously evading the issue.' He threw his knife and fork with a clatter back on to the plate. 'From your clam-like reluctance I can only assume you turned your talents to man-hunting with success.'

'If you're going to talk like that,' she said, laying her smeared knife and fork on the place-mat, 'you can assume what you like.'

'But you found a man, a suitable man, did you? Or a boy?'

'A man, Brendan. Please.'

'Nice-looking?' He braced his arms against his thighs. 'Younger, no doubt.'

'Younger than you. And attractive rather than good-looking.'

'Tall?'

'For God's sake, about your height. Dark wavy hair, brownish eyes. English. Another tourist.'

'Called?'

'Roy.'

'Roy! Tank-top Man. Zip-up Cardy Man.' He snarled a laugh and folded his arms. 'And did he have a brain as well as a dick?'

'He's a photographer. Interpret that as you please.'

'Was he hairy?'

She banged the flat of her hand on the table. 'Stop it! Whatever you say, you can't demean him any more than you did yourself. Is this what going to Mass does to you? Because I don't like it.'

'Karin, please!' The bench shrieked against the floorboards.

Brendan abruptly stepped over it and lunged round the table, but his outstretched arms flexed before her as though bowing under some hostile emanation. He stopped, palms raised in submission.

'Karin, help me. You can't imagine the men, the scenarios I've visualised in the time you've been away. Yes, I want details. I need the reality. The truth can't be half as bad as my imagination.' He lowered his hands, but his shoulders continued to heave. 'You went to bed with him?'

'Yes.'

He winced. 'How many times?'

'Just the once. We'd been out socially, and yes, he did have a nice body. Hairy, but not outrageously so. We went back to his hotel room.'

'Did you enjoy it?'

'You'd have liked him.'

'Shit.' He leaned over the work-top with his back to her. 'How did you do it?'

'How did we make love?'

'Christ,' he said, thumping his fist on the work-top, 'how did you screw or shag or, Jesus Christ, fuck? *Fuck!* The thought of you with another man turns me on.'

'We didn't, Brendan. Any of those.'

'I don't care what handle you give it. Are you seeing him again?'

'No. And we didn't do anything.'

He went and perched on a stool at the breakfast bar, his legs wide and his arms dangling between them.

'Forgive my stupidity. You voluntarily accompany a man to his room, remove your clothing, presumably, and leap into his bed. And then you deny anything happened. Or did you enjoy it more than you thought you would?' He jumped off the stool and walked round behind her. 'Maybe that was it, eh? Surprised yourself, did you? Got a taste for it? And now you can't admit it, least of all to yourself.' He grasped her by the shoulders and pressed his groin against her back. 'Didn't do it? I don't think so.' He began kneading her skin. 'At least if you found yourself a good lay, have the guts not to deny it.'

She tried to turn to him, but he twisted her forward again.

'The expiation's over. You should be proud so many men want to screw you. Now I can tell them they just might be in with a chance.'

'All right,' she said quietly. 'If that's what you want.'

He released her. He stepped back and she stood to face him, the bench between them like a miniature wall.

'Twice, we did it. Twice. Me on top, then him. That's what you want to hear, isn't it. The truth?'

His eyes hardened. With one hand he snatched up her plate and brought it down in a single, swift movement on the edge of the table. The plate sheared in two, and fragments of china danced briefly in the air before hitting the floor and the table and bench.

He was gone for a couple of hours. When he came back he shut himself in his study for the rest of the day. That evening she approached the door and tapped, like a self-conscious fresher, with the back of her fingernails.

She found him poring over some computer data, his glasses halfway down his nose. The room was in darkness but for the pool of light cast by his old, brown Anglepoise. The lamp seemed to incline conspiratorially towards him.

He ran a finger down a list of figures, then half-turned to her.

'Not quite what I was expecting, these results.'

She shrugged. 'Do you want anything? A drink? It's gone seven. Something to eat?'

'No, thanks.' He plucked off his glasses between thumb and forefinger and polished the lenses with the bottom of his sweater. He guided the glasses back over his ears, moving his head to ease their progress. 'I just need a bit of time, Karin. You know, sulk in my lair for a while. Get things out of my system.' He looked up, frowning slightly. 'I'll be fine.'

He left for the lab just after eight next morning. She saw clients at home till mid-afternoon. The parallel pursuit of their careers made avoidance easy, inevitable. Avoidance of issues, avoidance of each other, she could see the reality all too easily now. Somehow, it seemed, they'd written themselves out of the equation leaving only what they did rather than who they were. They'd been doing it for months, maybe years, subconsciously choosing the easy way out, like electricity following the route of least resistance to earth. They had both acted in error, but each mistake compounded the one before and paved the way for the next. The concerns they must have buried, the thoughts left unvoiced, the good intentions ploughed up in yet another working day or the shopping or hasty housework... Every day they had laid another brick in the wall between them, and when the height of it frightened them they had learned to equate isolation with safety. Either they took a hammer to the wall that week, or they kept to their separate rooms forever.

She arrived home just after six that evening with a boot full of shopping. She could see lights from the back of the house spilling round the doors of the sitting-room and her office. She let herself in and shuffled down the hall, flat-footed under the weight of four bulging carriers. On the threshold of the kitchen she stopped.

'Damn!'

The table could scarcely be seen beneath the white pyramids of yet more carrier bags. Brendan delved into one and pulled out three identical packs of pitta bread.

'Thought I'd be helpful and replenish the stocks. I should have done it last week.'

'Not to worry.' She staggered the last few steps to the table and lowered her bags into two heaps on the floor.

'Are there more?'

'Six or seven.'

'I'll fetch them.'

'No –'

'And then –' He brandished a fresh pineapple at her and thudded it triumphantly on the table as he walked past '- I'm doing dinner.'

She began to unpack, sorting Brendan's duplicated purchases for storage in the freezer or larder. And two eyes stared up at her between the bags. Eyes, a face. Pushing the carriers aside she found a small wooden plaque, painted in pale yellow, creams and browns. She picked it up and ran her thumbs over the surface, which was pleasantly smooth: lacquered or varnished. The almond-shaped face had dark eyes and a pointed beard. And a halo.

Brendan entered in a rush of short, panting steps, his arms rigid under the burden of six carriers. He dumped them on the floorboards and massaged the deep purple and white dents across his fingers.

She held up the plaque. 'What's this?'

'Just an icon. I picked it up in town.'

She pushed it back on the table. 'Right.'

'Karin, I can hear you thinking. It's an aid to prayer, okay? I need something to help focus my thoughts at the moment. Seven years as an altar boy doesn't leave you completely untouched, you know.'

'I had no idea it was as long as seven.'

'I've got my Guild of St Stephen medal to prove it. The liturgy, the ritual... They get in your blood. The upshot was, I embarked five years late on my teenage rebellion and haven't looked back since. So, after a thirty-year sabbatical, I think one little icon is a permissible indulgence.' He rubbed his hands. 'Bangers and mash, I propose, with some onion gravy and steamed veg.'

Karin sniffed. 'Cooking twice in three days? Couldn't we make dinner a co-production?'

'So?' Zo hissed, her eyes already prying up the hall and the stairs. 'How are things?'

It was Tuesday evening, and she had arrived unannounced.

'Why don't you come in?' Karin smiled. 'You can judge for yourself.' She led the way to the kitchen. 'It's Zo, Brendan.'

'Zo!' Brendan straightened from the dishwasher and hooked the door shut with his foot. 'Great to see you again. Take a pew.

Are you hungry? There's some fish pie left.'

'Actually,' Karin interrupted, 'there isn't.'

'Good God, I only put the dish down a couple of minutes ago. My culinary skills go before me, as you can see.' He cast his eyes round the spotless work-tops. 'What can I offer you? Tea? Coffee? A beer?'

'Beer's great.'

'Karin?'

'Nothing at the moment, thanks.'

Zo pulled out the end of the nearest bench and straddled it. Karin stepped over the bench and sat beside her, her elbows resting on the table and her hands cupped between them.

Zo waited till Brendan had disappeared behind the larder door, then turned to Karin, her eyebrows arched in query. Karin held out a hand, palm down, and seesawed it from side to side. Zo shook her head, rebuked her friend with a grin and flashed her an energetic thumbs-up.

Brendan emerged with a couple of bottles in one hand and a brightly coloured clutch of crisp packets in the other. He released the crisps on to the table, stood the bottles on the work-top and levered off the caps with a bottle-opener. He placed a bottle in front of Zo, then fetched a couple of large tumblers from one of the wall-cupboards. Beer in hand, he settled on the bench opposite the women, and pushed a glass across the table.

'Ta.' Zo took a quick swig straight from the bottle. 'So, got your photos back, Kar?'

'Of Tenerife?' Karin said in a clipped voice. 'No.'

'Don't tell me you haven't even bothered taking them in yet.'

'Yes, yes, I'm picking them up at the end of the week. Don't nag.' Karin nodded at the green ceramic vase in the centre of the table. 'Brendan brought me some flowers, look.'

'Lilies. Yeah, very nice,' said Zo, reaching for the crisps. 'Yellow lifts the spirits.'

'Lovely, aren't they. Yes, I thought Karin would like them.' Brendan pressed the lips of the bottle and glass together, tilting them with scientific precision until a smooth, amber stream sluiced down the inside of the glass. He set the bottle on the table and raised his glass. 'You know, the more I look at my wife, the more I wonder what I ever did to deserve her. Isn't she beautiful?'

'Oh, rot,' Karin said fiercely.

'But she's not bad, is she?'

'Sickeningly not bad,' Zo agreed. 'If I were a bloke I'd be dead jealous. Hell, I'm jealous anyway.'

'Well, I'm lucky,' said Brendan, sipping his beer. 'Very lucky.'

7

When Leon Cooper kissed the girl for the penultimate time late that winter morning, she removed his hand from her thigh and squeezed his fingers securely round the head of the gear stick. She peeled her lips from his, not without resistance on his part.

'No?'

'No.'

She shifted her knees away from him so that she faced the windscreen, and wriggled in the seat until she had eased her grey woollen skirt back over her legs.

'Am I to assume that's it?'

'You can assume what you like, Leon.' She swung down the visor and pivoted her head from side to side in the mirror. 'My lips are chapped.'

'You're the one who wanted to do it "right now" in broad daylight. Your suggestion. Remember?'

'So, we've done it.' She put her right arm through the gap between the seats and hooked the straps of a brown leather knapsack from the foot-well behind. She sat the bag in her lap, unbuckled the front pocket, and picked around inside it. 'And it's cold and clammy as hell. And any minute somebody is going to roll down from Psychology and see us sitting here in the middle of the Science Area with the windows steamed over. It's a giveaway.'

He picked the sponge off the dashboard and began

demisting the windows with methodical, horizontal sweeps across the glass.

'They're all too busy working to notice.'

'Yeah. Precisely.' She took a moisturising stick from the pocket, greased her lips, clamped them together and sucked her cheeks into a dentureless reflection in the courtesy mirror. 'And you have precisely thirty minutes before your tutorial, which gives you just enough time to drop me off at college. Shit!'

She slid down the back of the seat. Leon ducked his head slightly, tensed more by her shrillness than the threat of discovery. A slim, solitary male figure in black slacks was walking up the opposite pavement of South Parks Road towards them. He had his hands thrust in his trouser pockets, over which the flaps of a jade jacket were riding up.

'It's Brendan,' he said softly.

'Christ, you know him? Oh, brilliant! Why don't you just wind down the window and hail him?'

'He won't see us. He's on the other side anyway. Are you as stroppy as this in tutorials? You'll probably get a First.'

'Where's he going?' she demanded.

'How should I know? Back where he came from, I presume. Just keep your head down. He won't see.'

'But if it's Physiology or Anatomy, they're right this way, aren't they.' She raised her head, brow tilted backwards and lips parted, just far enough to see over the moulded grey plastic of the dash. 'Look, he's bloody waiting to cross.'

'Physically. Mentally he's miles away.'

'Quite dishy, though. In a concentrated sort of way.'

Leon clenched his teeth. 'In a quietly self-satisfied, slightly smug sort of way, I suppose so.'

'Why isn't he crossing?'

'I told you, he's thinking. He's off on some lecture tour any day. America. Or maybe he's thinking about his wife. Yes, maybe he's thinking about Karin.'

Her head swivelled just fast enough to bolster his ego.

'Returning to the matter in hand...' He rested his fingers with proprietorial confidence on her thigh. 'I'll consider my taxi fare redeemable at your place tonight, until which time I shall contemplate the earthy delights of your sagging, single mattress.'

'Tom complains you make too much noise.'

'Jealousy.' He slid his splayed fingertips as far between her thighs as the fine weave of the skirt allowed him, and looked up at the figure almost facing them on the opposite kerb. 'Any moment now he'll quit dithering and take the first step of the rest of his successful life. And the minor, but very enjoyable scandal of the Provost of Oriel's daughter will go entirely unnoticed.'

'You think?'

He kissed the tip of his finger and touched it to her cheek. 'Mark my words.'

*

Karin had not even had time to take off her raincoat when the doorbell rang that evening. She picked up the cinema listings she had just dropped on the hall table, and took them to the door with her. There were some decent films showing that Friday, ones they'd missed first time round. She couldn't recall the last time they'd been out together, so if she rustled up a quick dinner – Or perhaps they could eat out. Or maybe facing each other across a small table would prove too demanding with no distractions to hand and no easy escape route.

She reached for the door, a claw of nervous excitement squeezing her stomach. Her fingers closed round the catch and twisted. Maybe a take-away, then, a meal-out in disguise, eaten with messy fingers on the hoof. A fish and chip compromise. Side by side in the cinema would be the closest they'd been for weeks. There they could co-exist, reassured by the darkness and the happy requirement for silence, like a pair of testy parrots under a blanket. It would be a start, though, a start. And later, maybe...

When she opened the door, she was already smiling.

'Ms Shilan?'

Her smile caved in. 'Yes?'

There were two of them, side by side in the dark: a short woman with close-set blue eyes, and a man. The policeman gestured to the hallway with his flat hat.

'May we come in?'

8

Karin closed her hands over her nose. 'He's not -?'

'No. No. He's not dead.'

'Thank God!' She turned to the fire-place, the fire-place that Brendan had neatly laid that morning with crumpled newspaper and kindling. She gripped the open edges of her raincoat, pulled downwards on them, turned back into the room. It seemed to wash round her with unfocused, watery currents, like saline.

One of them, the policewoman, got up from the sofa. Karin heard her shoes crushing the carpet, registered the pressure of a hand on her upper arm. She looked down and saw patches of pink eczema between the fingers. She shut her eyes.

'He does have head injuries, however.' The voice spoke close to her shoulder, each word considered, almost discrete of the rest. 'We haven't seen him, so we don't know the medical details. But he is still unconscious.'

'Unconscious?'

'Brendan is in intensive care. I'm very sorry.'

'Still...' Karin echoed, her eyes now wide open. 'What do you mean, *still*?'

The policewoman cast a glance over her shoulder. Inspector Straker nodded.

'We've been trying to locate you since lunch-time. Your husband's lab gave us your address and phone number. One of our colleagues called here straight away. He tried your neighbours, and someone put us on to the Natural Health Centre.'

'But I took the afternoon off,' Karin said wildly. 'Normally I'm there every Friday. *Every* Friday.' She turned to Inspector

75

Straker. 'I went out with a girl-friend, Zoe Seymour.'

Straker got up. 'Well, you don't have a mobile, and unfortunately, the Health Centre had no idea where you'd be or who you'd gone with. Since when we've just kept ringing and dropping in on the off-chance.'

'Wait!' She ran to the black, uncurtained windows, cupped her hands round her eyes and peered down at the drive. 'His car's here.' She swung round. 'He took his push-bike today.'

'He was on foot, yes.' Straker stretched his lips across his teeth and relaxed them again with a tense, short sigh. 'We're not a hundred per cent sure what happened, Ms Shilan. Not yet. The vehicle that hit him didn't remain at the scene.'

'They left?' Karin felt her lips twittering. 'They left him for dead? Do you have any idea -?'

'We have a lead,' the policeman said slowly. 'But until we see the suspect – and her car – we can't give you facts. We don't know the full story ourselves.'

'But the driver was female?'

'So we believe.'

'You know her name, then. Not Sally?'

'I'm not at liberty to comment. Suffice to say, she's reluctant to return home and face the music.'

'Is she local? You can tell me that much, surely.'

The policeman confirmed it was an Oxford address.

'I must see him,' she said, distracted. 'God, I must see him now. Keys. Is it the John Radcliffe?' She patted the pockets of her raincoat and vaguely scanned the room. 'Oh, God. Keys, where did I put them? Hall table, hall table.'

'We'll take you,' Straker offered. 'No, I mean it. I don't think this is a good time for you to be driving.'

She sat in the back of the police car, her handbag in her lap and her remedy case beside her on the seat. Even in the darkness of the January rush-hour people mustered sufficient curiosity to gawp through the windows. There were blatant glances from pedestrians, making their fleeting speculations as they scuttled along the pavements. The motorists investigated the car with more subtlety and self-interest; at the sight of her face leaned to the window, they looked away, reassured.

Guilty, guilty, guilty. Every Friday she worked at the Natural Health Centre, every Friday except the one that really mattered. Once, on her way home from Binsey, she had knocked down a rabbit. It had been dark and the rabbit bolted from nowhere, straight into the path of the car. Something exploded inside her chest. She heard her own shriek and then a soft clunk below the front wheels and the skirl of the tyres. Hurling herself out of the car, she jogged back up the road, dread drumming in her mouth, sure she would find the rabbit bloodied and screaming. She saw it immediately in the red glow of the car's rear lights. Its oval body lay dark and silent. Nothing flexed, nothing twitched. Brendan appeared then with the torch blazing its white beam on to the tarmac. He directed the light with his matter-of-fact, scientific habit straight at the body. Then he hunkered down and examined it more closely.

'Stone dead.'

'Oh, God. Is it?'

She crept closer, expecting its skull to be splintered, its eyeballs extruded from their orbits. But the animal looked perfect, laid out as though asleep.

'Are you sure?' she whispered.

Brendan pointed just below its tail to a wet, black patch on the scoured grey of the tarmac.

'It's pee'd itself. It must have hit its head against the wheel.'

'God… Oh,' she babbled through tears, 'the poor thing. I feel awful.'

He suggested she get back in the car. She heard him cross the road behind her and knew he was shifting the body to the verge.

'You sure you're okay to drive?' he asked, hanging over the top of the open passenger door.

She nodded.

'Would you prefer me to drive?'

She'd nodded.

'Death must have been almost instantaneous,' he'd said

gently, when he had re-appeared the other side of the car. 'At least it was quick.'

She felt her bottom lip curl all over again. The animal's one shot at life, and she'd stepped in like Atropos with her scissors and snipped the thread. And that was a rabbit. How could anyone leave a human being? Leave her husband? The thought seemed to expand through her skull, replicating and dividing, until it filled the entire car to bursting.

In the front passenger seat Inspector Straker brushed his hair several times up his forehead and wound down the window a fraction.

'Your neighbour,' he said, 'gave us one of your business cards. I gather you're a homœopath?'

'That's right.'

She knew the routine. The conversation would sound as fresh as the first day she'd made it, but her mind was already lost in a maze of hospital corridors.

*

Straker held the door for her. She took a step inside and halted, her black case clutched like a shield across her stomach. Her eyes raced between the beds. Where had they put him? Surely there had been some administrative error. In that warm, twilit world, the half-dozen supine bodies looked identical, clones, homogenised by the whisper of death. And none of them passed for her husband.

A nurse touched her elbow and guided her to a bed in a corner of the ward.

All she registered in that first sight of him was the startling orange of the blanket and the tube, a white, corrugated tube. It resembled the waste from the dishwasher, and it was plugged into his throat. Through the second's silence his inert chest erupted and fell with a hush-hush of machinery.

'Ventilation,' the nurse murmured. 'It's standard. I'm sorry.'

Karin lowered her case to the floor, unable to take her eyes from the motionless mannequin they called her husband. He wore a mask of angry flesh, a Hallowe'en mask, his eyes pulling inward like badly sewn button-holes. Another tube, smooth and smaller in diameter, curled into one of his nostrils, and two more converged in the side of his neck. From a dressing amongst his hair, a wire wandered away across the pillow like some godforsaken frontier on a map.

She knelt slowly on the chair at the bed-head. The tears she had contained during the drive dropped freely on to his cheek, and she kissed them over the warm, lifeless skin.

'Brendan,' she whispered. 'It's Karin. Can you hear me?'

She lifted the edge of the covers, seeking his hand. At the sight of the wire she recoiled and the blanket fell, crumpled, on to the sheet. With finger and thumb she drew the covers down his chest and uncovered more pads, more wires, creeping about his body like a high-tech vine. It seemed as though man and machine had fused; bellows worked his lungs, and the beating of his heart was reduced to the quick, green flicker of the monitor.

She replaced the covers, becoming aware of Inspector Straker's brooding presence at the foot of the bed.

'I'm on till ten,' he said. 'I've left my number at the desk if you need to contact me.'

She thanked him. 'Is there no more news of the woman?'

'Still hasn't been back to the house. The neighbours are out, and she's refusing to answer her mobile, usual thing. But the appeal should be broadcast again shortly, and she'll have to go home sometime.' From his jacket pocket he drew her business card and adjusted his square, silver-rimmed glasses to study it. 'Can I reach you at the Natural Health Centre tomorrow if I need to?'

'I don't work weekends,' she said. 'Not any more.'

*

A voice. Distant, the language foreign. Probably foreign. Someone shaking her shoulder.

With a sweep of her fist, she brushed away sleep and the tangled hair from her forehead. She opened her eyes. Sarah, the nurse, smiled into her face.

'You have a visitor, Ms Shilan.'

She had a visitor. *She* had a visitor.

She sat up, but the man striding across the ward was only Leon. She relaxed against the back of the chair. A fitting visitor, Leo. He completed at a stroke the wavering, illusory dreamscape her life had just become.

He stopped at the foot of the bed. His navy track suit hung about him in slack folds, his shoulders rising and falling in an unsteady silhouette against the subdued lighting.

'I rang the hospital,' he said. 'They told me you were still here. I had to come.'

When she rose from the chair he took her by the arms and hugged her, too close and for too long, the side of his cold, waxen face pressed to hers. She did not have the energy to extricate herself, and waited till he parted them. She touched a finger to her cheek and it came away wet.

'Karin, I can't –'

He took a hesitant breath and she watched him force his eyes to the bed. He hid his face in his hands, caging his eyes behind long, bowed fingers.

She sat back on the chair, hidden beneath her crumpled raincoat. She had left that stage hours behind. One by one her emotions had exhausted themselves against the wall of her husband's closed consciousness. Before her eyes he had slipped into the unreality of a situation that excluded her. He had merged not only with his life-support system, but with the whole quirky matter of the hospital landscape. The nurses, androgynous in their loose scrubs, went about their work like white blood cells. Only she and Leon seemed real enough to get up and leave. And if she quit this serene underworld without looking back, maybe Brendan would follow. Didn't the cat die only when the experimenter opened the box to study him? No, her husband had sustained head injuries, and no amount of imagination, light waves, photons or parallel universes could re-package the fact.

She raised her head. She had the visitor, because Brendan

was too passive to receive anything more sentient than drugs and air. She'd become the projection of his consciousness, his interpreter from Limbo, and the last thing she needed right then was a visitor.

Leon uncovered his face. He sniffed and widened his eyes, the sockets swollen around moist, inflamed whites. He pulled up a chair alongside hers and sat down. She watched him change position, seeking a grain of comfort where there was none to be found. He scarcely glanced at Brendan now.

'How long have you been here?'

'The police didn't find me till gone five.' She got up and moved to the window. Outside, the street lamps and the grey of fluorescent tubes pooled and sent a jaundiced aura into the darkness. She pressed her fingers against the cold glass and drew her fingertips into claws. 'Surely the news hasn't reached the Press already? Or did you hear it on the radio?'

'Radio. They were appealing for witnesses.'

The tremor in his voice turned her head. His mouth seemed to be working around silent, unfinished words. He played his fingers round his chin, and avoided her eyes.

'But I knew anyway,' he said. 'Because I saw it.'

Karin shook her head at him, a soft denial that petered out only when he went on talking.

'The woman, she stared at him out of the driver's window. It seemed to last forever. The car had stalled so she started it again, crashed the gears. I managed to take the number. And then she drove off with the engine screaming. By the time I reached him he'd lost consciousness, but he was breathing. I didn't dare move him. I flagged down the next car, used this kid's mobile and called an ambulance. There was nothing more I could do.'

'So?'

He shrugged. 'A crowd was gathering. I stayed till I heard the sirens. We did a runner.'

'Christ, Leo...'

'I know, I know. Wrong place, wrong time, with the wrong

person, okay. Full Blues for moral indiscretion and cowardice. Yeah, the University's more broadminded these days, but the Provost's daughter?' He trailed Karin with miserable eyes back to her seat. 'Then when I heard the radio bulletins I had no option.'

'What about the police?'

'St Aldate's. I've just made a statement.'

She didn't need to ask more; silence, one of the most valuable tools of her profession, became prompt, whip and encouragement in one painless stroke.

'She – Maggie –' he told her haltingly, 'had tucked the car in the side access overlooking South Parks. We're in the front seat, talking. I spot Brendan at the far kerb. He's looking over his shoulder, waiting to cross. It's usually busy there, but for once the road is clear. He doesn't make a move, though.' Leon finally engaged her eyes and held them. 'Karin, I'm sorry. It just looked like - My guess is he was miles away. He stepped straight out.'

She stood in a swift, smooth movement and put a hand to her forehead.

'I'm only telling you what I saw, I swear to God. What we both saw.'

He reached for her other hand, but she snatched it up and it struck her left shoulder in a fist, the blow hard but muffled against her sweater. Through her mesh of long hair she watched him grip the front corners of his seat and rock forward on his arms a couple of times before shifting his weight. He angled his legs away from her and sat up very straight.

For some moments they said nothing, letting the ventilator heave its hard, rhythmic sighs through their silence. At last he nodded toward the case on the floor beside her chair.

'You've brought your remedies.'

He pointed a thumb inquiringly at Brendan. Karin shook her head.

'I don't really know where to start. I've never had to deal with a situation like this before. I suppose you think I'm wasting my time.'

'Karin –'

'The Registrar was quite supportive, actually. It's just there's so little to prescribe on.' She unhooked Brendan's records from the end of the bed and thumbed back through the sheets of paperwork. 'Glasgow Coma Scale, three... Unconscious when the paramedics arrived.... No response... No response...' She leafed through a few more pages, scanning the forms and scribbled notes, and let the papers fall back on to the clipboard. 'Nothing but what's in front of me. I thought I'd try Opium, yet he's under such heavy sedation –'

Tears stung and seeped like albumen along her lower lids as she leaned over and hung the board back on its hook. She enclosed a fist in her other hand, touched it to her lips several times and squeezed her eyes hard shut.

'Maybe when his condition stabilises?' Leon suggested. 'When they feel he's capable of spontaneous breathing I'm sure they'll reduce the drugs.'

She moved, distracted, back to her chair. 'I made up a solution of Opium and dabbed it behind his knee. 10M is the highest I've got.'

'Behind his knee?'

'I don't have much option right now, do I. He can't exactly swallow a tablet. I had to try something. Finn thinks giving the tablet is just a ritual anyway. Not that all homœopaths agree, mind. You know how it is with theories.' She drew her chair as close as she could to the bed-frame and leaned over her husband's face. 'God, how could they?'

Another tear dropped on to his cheek. It started to roll, in a glistening trail, back towards his eye, like he were crying in reverse. She brushed it away and felt for his fingers through the blanket. Gently, hopefully, she squeezed them. When she met no response she released his hand, leaned her left elbow on the bed and stroked his hair in a slow, abstracted rhythm. With each caress of her thumb across his temple she watched the neat hairs spring back into order, alive and defiant.

'How can someone -? It's inhuman.' She smiled to herself. 'Fright and flight is Inspector Straker's considered opinion. Very physiological. Inhuman rather than uncommon, he said.'

Leon stood. 'I must be going. Look, I'll inform the Department and take care of that side of things. You should be getting home too.' He paused. 'Are you sure you'll be all right on your own? You could -'

'I'll be fine.'

'What about transport? Do you need a lift?'

'I've got the car. Thanks.'

He nodded, sucking his lower lip. He made to take a step towards her, but checked himself.

'Did he tell you?' she said suddenly.

'About?'

'If you knew, you wouldn't be asking.'

Leon frowned. 'I'm the thief of dreams, Karin. I don't think he confided in anybody much. Not to my knowledge anyway. Brendan certainly wouldn't tell me anything important these days.' He paused. 'Not if it concerned you. Far too special.'

He pursed his lips into a smile in which she thought she glimpsed a moment's regret. She waited until he disappeared beyond the doors of the ward, then called a taxi.

9

So he'd been daydreaming, she thought as the taxi pulled out of the hospital. Brendan adored his work as a neuroscientist, and specialised in disorders that led to dementia. He lived his work, much as she immersed herself in hers. It was not unusual for him to return home at night vague and witless, his mind still picking over theories and experimental protocols in the lab. Midweek he had been due to fly out to Pittsburgh Medical Center. He was a visual thinker; final plans and checklists, lecture notes and speeches had doubtless been weaving their threads through his mind. Enough clutter to blind him for a few seconds.

She took a bottle of Aconite 10M from her handbag, unscrewed the cap, tapped a tablet into the palm of her hand and then tipped it into her mouth to steady her nerves. Sucking its faint sweetness, she put back the bottle and drew out his gold Patek Philippe. It had been a gift of congratulation from his father ten years ago when Brendan had been appointed Professor of Physiology.

Between thumb and forefinger she tilted its face toward the pulsing streetlights and watched the second hand jerk into the future. Seconds, that was all it had taken. Sarah had brought her the watch from the nursing station just before she left that night. Young Sarah with the unmemorable face. Only the haircut, savage as an army cadet's, stuck in Karin's mind.

'We'd prefer if you could take this home now,' she'd said, pressing the watch into Karin's hand. 'Much too valuable to leave. If you could just sign ...'

Beyond the windows of the taxi, Oxford was cranking itself up for another Friday night's socialising. Headlights shuttled past like beads on hot wire, searing her eyes. Maybe she should have accepted Leon's offer of a lift, she reflected. She liked to think it as well-intentioned as her white lie, but she did not know what to make of the jester when he was no longer joking. Her uncertainty lingered. She called it uncertainty. It could have been fear. He took quite enough pleasure in invading her personal space when Brendan was about, this man who kept smoothing her dress at the party like she were some favoured animal. This man who'd been entertaining the Provost of Oriel's daughter while Brendan dawdled down South Parks Road with his head full of aspirations.

'Summertown, was it?' the cabbie called over his shoulder.

Park Town, she told him.

Pittsburgh Medical Center. His sisters, his uncle. Sir Philip, the Master of Pembroke. Karin snatched up the pen on the breakfast bar in front of her and added the name to her list. She hooked her toes under the foot-rest of the wooden stool, took her weight on her folded arms and pulled the stool further under the breakfast bar. The kitchen was still warm from the stove, her mug of tea cold and untouched.

It was gone eleven: Sir Philip could be informed in the

morning. Pittsburgh – she needed to ascertain the time zone. And wasn't Brendan due to play tennis early next day, weather permitting, with Emrys Clifford?

When Emrys failed to reply she had to leave a message, stilted and broken, on the answer-phone. He returned the call straight away, and she related everything she would have to repeat at least a dozen times more to inform and re-organise the web of their married life.

'My God...' A rattle arose from his chest. 'This is –'

He did not say what, and she did not ask. It was nothing. It was appalling bad luck, just one of those things, poor timing. Fate kicking sand in one's face.

'I must see him,' Emrys insisted. 'When are visiting hours?'

She didn't know. She gave him the hospital number and they parted, his wife, Liz, calling condolences and offers of help from the background.

College...She was due to lecture that weekend. Picking up the telephone receiver again, she verified the Devon number from her notebook and tapped it out. As she waited for the answering-machine to go through its preamble, she scribbled another name on her list and put a tick straight beside it.

'Finn, it's Karin Shilan.' She explained, a little more coherently, about the accident. 'I feel awful about this. Especially at the last minute, but Sunday's too soon. Too soon, and it's too far. I need to be in Oxford. Let me know if you want me to stay with LM potencies and Hepar Sulph. I'll swap for whichever college weekend suits best.'

Next she rang her parents in Western Australia for a dose of equally distant, and fuddled sympathy. It was eight in the morning there and her mother had not yet galvanised herself with coffee. Her mother had worshipped Brendan, until he'd broken the news of his honourable intentions. There had been a brittle Sunday lunch when she made the ambient temperature fall faster than a poltergeist.

'Not that I've anything against him personally,' she opined when Karin demanded an explanation for her volte-face. 'I simply feel that fifteen years is an insurmountable divide.' She pointed a long, arched nail at the frames of crooked smiles on Brendan's dresser. 'He won't want to start another family just when he's regaining his freedom.'

'It's fourteen, actually, and he never lost it because Diana and Brendan didn't have children either. Those are his nephews and nieces, remember? And Netta's more than making up for my wilful refusal to pod.'

'Yes, but think how much cleverer yours and Brendan's would be –'

Brendan backed in then with a tray of champagne in flutes and confirmed without the slightest hint of apology that he and his wife-to-be would not be populating the world with proto-professors.

'In any case,' she told him after her parents had left, 'it's not children they want round them. It's youth. And you know they're dubious about your potency now, don't you.'

Brendan suggested they acquire a couple of kittens and took her to bed to defend his corner. Whether it was his doubtful potency or his predilection for recreational sex, they never found out; that summer, after the wedding, her parents sold up and followed her younger sister and the three grandchildren to Perth.

Zo... She wouldn't be in bed. Karin ticked the name off her list, and pattered out the Banbury phone number. Zoe Seymour, unmarried, unencumbered and, by her own admission, unlikely ever to fall prey to parenthood.

'Can't have you all alone in a crisis,' Zo announced. 'I'll stay tonight and tomorrow and leave Sunday morning. Don't worry about the bed. The sleeping bag's still warm from India. Oh, and I've got your Tenerife photos, by the way. You left them at my place. Give me half an hour.'

After ringing Zo she took refuge in the marital bedroom with its big, familiar bed and the strewn clothes that smelled of him. The room was littered with details of his existence, his recent presence.

She threw herself on the quilt and curled up with Brendan's towelling robe. Inside it her legs niggled restlessly, making the fabric quiver.

On his bedside table, under the blue lamp, lay a couple of substantial literary novels. He always liked to read two or three at once. She picked them up. The titles were new to her; his reading had moved on since she had last kept him company there. Next to the books he had a small black comb in need of a scrub, a couple of issues of *Nature* and a *Punch*, and his cheap battery-operated alarm clock that synthetically ticked away the seconds. In the silence it seemed so pointed, so insistent, violating the room.

She pulled on his big navy robe, crawled off the end of the bed and stood on the dhurrie in front of the chest of drawers. The shrine of photographs looked like a version of the '*Guess Who?*' game his youngest nephews played. She began to howl with ugly, uncontrollable tears. All this, so nearly thrown away. How many photos had he collected there? A dozen? No, she would carry on sleeping in the guest-room. The darkness played tricks when she closed her eyes. She could not bear all those photographs peering down at her from the darkness, the happy faces. The reminders.

*

Karin drove with Zo to the John Radcliffe mid-morning. Reeking of sweet-and-sour hand-wash, they went into the ward.

'How long could Brendan be unconscious?'

She blurted out the question before she or Mr Howard had even sat down in his office. Mr Howard, lean and considered, paused beside his chair, one hand cupped over the back of it.

'Prognoses like these are never easy. Impossible this early.' He gestured to her to sit and swivelled his own chair into a position where he could face her. 'The preliminary CT scan shows swelling and evidence of bleeding into his brain. In the circumstances such results are hardly unexpected. Nevertheless the pressure is still giving us cause for concern.' He chewed his lower lip. 'At the moment all we can do is ventilate him hard, keep on with the drugs and try to bring down the swelling.'

'But he'll pull through?'

'Ms Shilan,' he said slowly, 'we hope he'll pull through. However, given the traumatic nature of your husband's injuries, I'm afraid you would be wise at least to prepare yourself for the possibility that he might not. I'm very sorry.'

Her head dropped forward, and her breathing took on the deep, mechanical rapidity of a sprinter. She focused her attention on the back of her hand and tracked her other thumb hard up and down the tendons.

'Please, I'd be failing in my duty if I were to bolster you with false hopes.' Mr Howard inclined his head and caught her eye. 'We'll do everything we can.'

'If he doesn't die, will he have brain damage?'

'Not necessarily.'

'But?'

'From what we can see at the moment the injuries are diffuse. There's no obvious surgery we can do.' He exhaled heavily through his nose. 'It – is a possibility.'

When Karin entered the relatives' room fifteen minutes later, she closed the door quietly and leaned her back to it, her fingers still resting on the handle. Zo wriggled her buttocks to the edge of the easy-chair, leaned forward and with a little grunt poked her magazine back into the fan of papers on the coffee table.

'Any news?'

'No new news. It's serious.' Karin let her arm fall carelessly to her side and tipped her head back against the door. 'Still serious.'

Her lips pulled downwards.

'Oh, Kar...'

Zo helped her to the seats and sat her down. She shoved the coffee table to one side and knelt in the space on the floor. Karin clenched a fist to her chest and squeezed her other hand so hard inside it that her fingers began to turn purple.

'What if -? Zo, what if I they ask me to -?'

Tears began to run from her closed eyes and streaked over

her chin.

*

Zo encouraged Karin into the town centre later on the grounds of needing an outfit for a Christening service.

'I wouldn't bother if they didn't keep making me godmother,' she called to Karin through the apricot curtain of a changing cubicle. 'I don't believe in God. I think children are best confined to the consulting-room, preferably when the door is locked and I'm the other side. And I don't run courses or bind people to eighteen-month treatment contracts, so I'm not even likely to end up rich. Can't think why they choose me.'

'Kids adore you.'

'Yeah. Right.' She threw back the curtain and posed in a blue velvet dress, her chin high, her arms tossed skyward with the arrogant grace of a Russian dancer. She turned sideways and examined herself in the full-length mirror. 'God, a phantom pregnancy. Can't I just wear my black leggings and a posh blouse? My legs are my best asset.'

'You live in leggings. What about a two-piece with a loose top or a jacket?'

'Or a spinnaker,' Zo grumbled, swathing herself in the curtain.

She settled for a navy dress and long jacket in peacock blues and greens, and mid-afternoon they sought respite from the sales at The Nosebag. Zo ordered a Colombian coffee and slab of iced carrot cake, and Karin a pot of lapsang souchong. Zo poured a steady stream of milk from the small pottery jug into her cup, and watched the blackness explode in fluid puffs of tan.

'Thinking about the Irish conference this year?'

'God, a lot has to happen between now and the summer.' Karin held her cup below her chin and pensively inhaled the smoky coils of steam. 'In a way I'd rather do a few festivals with the Travelling Homœopaths. Brendan says if these people didn't let their kids eat mud and run amok with no knickers they wouldn't get ill in the first place. I think he's afraid I'll drop out and end up roving Albion in a beaten-up bus.'

'At least you get to hear some good music.'

'I'll try converting him.'

Zo emptied two sachets of brown sugar into the coffee and stirred it with slow, deliberate circulations of the spoon.

'Remember that quote writ large on the walls of my hall?'

"Whatever you do −"'

"What you can do,"' Zo corrected, *"or dream you can, begin it. Boldness has genius, power and magic in it. Begin it now."* Goethe. Don't forget it.'

Karin bundled her two carriers of food shopping over the threshold and went through to the kitchen. Six tins of cat food clacked on to the refectory table.

'Another message on your answer-phone,' Zo called, leaning her bags against the legs of the hall table.

'Play it back, would you?'

Zo stood over the machine. *'Karin, hi. It's Craig. Call me. I really need to meet up with you soon.'*

'And who,' Zo inquired, riffling through a pile of papers beside the phone, 'is Craig?'

'I've just started supervising him. The one I told you about, remember? The man with the voice.'

'No wonder Brendan's jealous.'

Karin put her head round the door. 'He's a social worker, married to a social worker. They've got three kids under five, and he just about comes up to my shoulder.' She disappeared back into the kitchen. 'Having said that, I could listen to him from dawn to dusk.'

'I believe you.' Zo trailed her through the doorway, tapping her fingertips on the bundle of papers. 'Reams of scrawl in the margins. You've been busy. What a diligent marker. Bad luck getting Silica, though.'

'I was meant to be taking those to Tavistock. I'll have to post them now Finn's put my lectures back. Anyway,' said Karin, screwing up the empty bags and stuffing them into a drawer, 'spaghetti and salad okay? Bottle of Jacob's Creek?'

Zo beamed. 'For Jacob's Creek, worms.'

*

As she was about to leave next morning, Zo turned on the doorstep and pointed a finger at Karin.

'Photos, nearly forgot.' She put down her carriers, dropped her long, bottle-green rucksack on to the coir doormat and unbuckled the top. She slid her arm inside and felt around with the frowning concentration of a vet about to extract a calf. 'There they are.'

She slapped the paper wallet into Karin's waiting hand, and Karin gave her a hug.

'Thanks. And just – thanks for being here.' She took a step back, still holding Zo by the shoulders. 'You know we didn't buy a Christening present?'

'Ah well, a Bible or some pointless piece of silver. I've got all week.'

'I was beginning to suspect –' Karin cleared her throat with a little cough '– that this Christening was just a timely diversion. An invention, perhaps.'

Zo stared. 'It's next Sunday. In Wells. As for your photos, I thought I'd have another flip through them Friday afternoon. Twenty-two of them. It goes against the grain, but call it intuition. I checked the negatives to see what you'd lost. Twenty-six of them. No obvious disasters, so I ran the extras through my scanner.'

Karin's lips parted.

'Oh yes, the homœopath is just a glorified Plod, Karin. The holistic supersleuth perceives the case yet again. And my Christening is as much an invention as the man in the four photographs you've removed from that packet. I think there's something you haven't told me...'

10

Inspector Jim Straker squared the car on the tarmac hard-standing in front of the garage. He cut the engine, but let the music play on, drifting the sensual rhythms of Duke Ellington through the window into the crisp Oxford morning. He began tapping the heel of his right trainer in the foot-well to the plucking of the double bass, took up the saxophones with his fingers on the steering-wheel and emitted a pressurised, nasal sound between his lips in rendition of a train siren.

By the end of *Everything Goes*, his whole body was fluid with the language of jazz, his right knee jerking time, his elbows working like those of an old, drunken drummer. The music lifted to a shrill climax, faded to a satisfying purr, and the Pink Pantheresque introduction to *Bird of Paradise* struck up. He pulled a face. On the short toots of the saxophone he imagined a villain tiptoeing away from the scene of the crime, peering, louche-eyed, over his shoulder on the long notes. The first few bars gave way to a little indulgence for the solo saxophone, but it was an up-and-down whirl of disappointingly ignorable background music more suited to a television advert or cocktail party.

He switched off the music and returned the CD to its box. He wound up the window, picked his wind-cheater and paper off the passenger seat and got out of the car. Upstairs, the two sets of closed curtains had not moved since his departure for Frilford Heath just after eight. They looked like pallid, dozy eyelids in the brickwork, which was appropriate when each room contained one of his pallid, torpefied teenagers.

He opened the boot of the estate, picked out his spiked shoes and swung the bag of golf clubs over his shoulder. And then he saw it, in the laburnum tree by the front wall: a magpie, the first he'd seen there in the six months since they'd moved house. The bird looked at him with an insolent eye. Straker spat over his right shoulder. His spittle landed on a hebe in the border beside the drive, a variegated hebe, he noted with satisfaction, where the bubbling, glairy mess did not show. The bird defecated, unabashed, and flew off in the direction of the wood behind the houses.

He opened the double garage to stow his golf things. Hilary's car was inside. He laid the bag and shoes on the concrete, and hurried to the front door. He pressed the bell and began whistling through his teeth the introduction to *Bird of Paradise*. The door opened.

'Hilary!'

'Hello, Jim.'

She kept hold of the catch with one hand, regarded him in her slightly ironic way and disappeared into the lounge. He shook his head.

'I was under the impression,' he called from the hall as he untied his trainers, 'that you weren't due home till tomorrow.'

'I got Social Services sorted out, thank God, but mum's such hard work. I thought I'd come back a bit early. Catch up here.'

There was a reverberating clump. Ironing, and she disliked ironing at the best of times.

He padded quietly into the lounge, the Sunday paper under his arm. She was standing at the ironing-board in the dining-room, through the open connecting-doors. On the table in front of her sat several slumping piles of sweat-shirts and pullovers, and the bevelled-glass doors were curtained with shirts.

From the back garden behind her the sun streamed in and stabbed, white and glaring, at his eyes when he tried to look at her. He settled into an armchair in the shadows of the lounge, shook out his paper and laid it on his knees.

'You'll never believe the hit-and-run we had on Friday.'

Hilary banged the iron on to the ironing-board and sighed into the steam. 'When it comes to what happens to you at work, nothing surprises me, no matter how incredible.' She laid into a police shirt with a sweep of the iron and ran a knife-edged crease into the sleeve. 'You're home early yourself. It's not even twelve-thirty. No session in the club bar to console yourself?'

Straker detected an optimistic change of subject; his wife

was casting about for some new channel down which to discharge her vast reservoir of spleen.

'Actually,' he said, staring at the open paper, 'I won.'

'Were you playing Jane?'

'I walked off the last green with ten over par.'

'Spurred on, no doubt, by the adoring eyes, the train of fatuous compliments and feigned helplessness requiring repeated demonstration by you.'

'Christ, Hilary, the woman's husband has walked out. She's down. Anyway,' he said in a louder voice, 'I've told her I shan't be playing next week because I'm on days.'

'Oh dear.' Hilary specialised in delivering stock phrases of sympathy with contempt. She swept across to hang another shirt on the door. 'Still, I don't suppose she'll be too bothered by the moratorium. From what I've heard, she has plenty of other irons in her golf bag.'

'You misjudge her.'

'No more than any of the others.'

Straker felt in no mood to tolerate another pillorying. Nor was he inclined to engage in the futile business of reassuring his wife of his continence while she stood close by wielding a very hot, very heavy lump of metal. He muttered 'Sod it!' under his breath and went out to the kitchen. He knew she would narrow her eyes and track him through the door with that nasty graduate amusement of hers.

'I did use the breadboard,' he said, when he entered five minutes later with a tray. He watched her eyeing his two grossly sawn slices of toast and honey. 'I put the breadboard away. I wiped up the crumbs. And if the score marks on the work-top are what's bothering you, I should have a quiet word with Anyta.'

He put his tray at the far end of the dining-table. He set a mug of coffee for her on a coaster between two piles of T-shirts, and she made a grunt of acknowledgement. The iron chuffed away into the silence.

Any other day he would have taken the snack and escaped into the garden to feel angry there instead, but after hovering for a moment with his plate of toast he pulled up a dining chair.

'This hit-and-run,' he said, perching eagerly opposite the ironing-board, 'there was a distinct whiff of dog's breakfast about it right from the start. We had a 999 call on a mobile: hysterical woman screaming for an ambulance in South Parks Road. A couple of minutes later, similar call, different mobile: a man garbling a registration number and saying a woman in a blue car had just driven off after hitting someone. The first mobile gives us a woman with no previous, but she owns a blue car. The second is some scrote from Blackbird Leys who claims a man borrowed his phone when he was driving down South Parks Road. No, he'd never seen him before, no, he wouldn't recognise him again – do they ever? And inquiries from the University departments overlooking the road turn up precisely diddly-squat.'

'So?'

'Either...' He incised the air with his toast. 'Either we had a serious hit-and-run with two reluctant witnesses. Or, one reluctant witness plus a woman driver who failed to stop at the scene, but did, in a manner, report it. With possible sundry motoring offences. The next of kin turns out to be some alternative medicine practitioner we can't locate for hours, and the male witness still hasn't come forward by the time we interview the woman driver.'

'We?'

'The section was short. I took the new sprog along, Fiona Kingston. Calves like ostrich drumsticks. Interesting case for her second day.' He bit into his toast and softened it with a mouthful of coffee. 'As for the driver, she was in a wretched state from the moment she opened the door. I caution her and she bursts into tears and turns tail, leaving me and Fiona peering into this blazing orange hall. We found her curled up in a ball in an armchair.'

Hilary stood the iron on its end and rested both fists on the metallised ironing-board cover, her arms rigid.

'And did she have calves like ostrich drumsticks?'

Straker ignored her. 'She admitted hitting the guy, though

she maintained he stepped off the pavement straight in the path of the car. She slammed on the anchors. He bowled over the bonnet, and when he didn't move she assumed he must be dead. She panicked and called the ambulance as she drove away.'

Hilary flicked the last item, a rumpled T-towel, out of the laundry basket and on to the ironing-board.

'And you believed her?'

'Strange as it may seem. Fiona suggested she might have been drunk at the time of the accident, because there was wine on the table. Recall the position of the skid marks, I said, straight as a die. I stuck her on for failing to stop and failing to report. And when we get back to the station, in strolls the witness, with impeccable timing, and confirms everything to the letter.'

'Another road traffic mystery successfully sewn up.'

He watched his wife collapse the ironing-board with a clang.

'Yes,' he said thoughtfully. 'I suppose.'

He carried the ironing things through the kitchen to the utility room, which was cramped and dark and stank of fabric conditioner. He returned to the dining-room and sat in a wicker throne in a pool of sunshine by the patio windows. He could just see Hilary in the kitchen, counting out mini-pizzas on to a baking-tray.

Shading his eyes, he scanned the back garden. It was unusually large, even for a corner plot, and backed on to fields and an area of mature, mixed woodland.

He picked up the binoculars from the carpet beside the chair and trained them on the bird-table. Three sparrows picked through the leftovers of the morning offering, and a great tit was swinging from the feeder.

'Bird-table?' Hilary had exclaimed, when she had discovered him hammering away in the garage days after they had moved in. 'The children's bedrooms need painting. What about some prioritising?'

He had prioritised. He had slipped Daniel and Anyta thirty

quid each to decorate their own rooms and spent his next day off constructing an owl box.

A small darting movement caught his eye from the back hedge. His mouth half-open, he adjusted the focus of the binoculars: a yellowhammer. It had probably dropped down from the wood. Though the underparts looked very pale for a yellowhammer. Possibly a first winter female. Or -

'Oh my God... *Hilary!*' He swung his left arm towards the kitchen door, agitating his extended hand in his urgency. 'Hilary, this you will not believe,' he murmured, his hand still reaching for her as the door flew open. 'I think we've got a pine bunting...'

The door closed.

A pine bunting in Marcham, in his own back garden. His throat seemed to constrict with excitement. This rare vagrant made for an exceptional sighting in Oxfordshire. He would have to report it. He could see her beak working, nibbling delicately on some morsel. Never again would he complain about Hilary's five-seed loaves.

A brown smudge, a robin, crossed his field of view. The bunting crouched, momentarily startled, and launched itself from the hedge in a brisk, undulating flight. Straker jumped to his feet, making clumsy, desperate sweeps with his binoculars, but the bird had disappeared into the wood.

On the feeding table the robin curtsied, cocked its tail and froze warily, as though sensing Straker's disappointment. It darted forward, paused, snatched up a shred of crust, paused again and bolted for the hedge opposite.

He sat down again with a pleasurable, reflective shake of his head. Sparrows, tits, robins. And a pine bunting. His brow clouded. The last visitor they wanted in the garden was a magpie. According to his mother, a thoroughbred county Anglican, and therefore both pious and superstitious in equal measure, the pynot was black and white because it refused to go into full mourning like the other birds at the Crucifixion. Adaptable and intelligent, it would bully and terrorise the magnificent little birds he had spent the last few months cultivating with such quiet pleasure. Still, he had seen only the one.

A pine bunting. He put down the binoculars and rubbed his hands.

*

After lunch, he loaded the dish-washer while Hilary scrubbed the baking sheets with a scourer. He suggested they might go swimming, but she declined.

'It's my bad time coming up, and I've a bit of a stomach-ache. I'm going to lie down.'

'I could rub it for you, if you like. The kids are out.'

'Jim, I'm tired.'

'I won't do anything.'

'No.'

If the subject touched upon sexual tension, no matter whose or how remotely, discussion became impossible and argument futile; he lost on every occasion and ended up more aroused than before the spat. In fact, it seemed to him of late that he could win only by committing a criminal offence. Marital sex was a vicious circle these days: he paced its impenetrable perimeter, and Hilary sat inside it looking smug.

He drifted into the lounge and sat down. Much of the furniture in the house had been bought new and it would stay new, never belonging or merging with the whole. Expensive reproduction nesting tables, side-board, telly- and video-cabinet: fake style that lacked the energy to make an apology, let alone a statement. The leafy potted plants were real, but they never put out flowers, or grew, or even died. The three-piece suite was real, too. Leather. Forgiving, apparently, but cold. Hilary had chosen it.

He leaned forward and rested his elbows on his knees, his fingers just touching as though casually at prayer. Between his right thumb and forefinger he squeezed his wedding band and worked the ring between them. After eighteen years he could still twist it just enough to remove.

Hilary's footsteps sounded on the stairs, as slow and burdened as those of her arthritic mother. She had looked tired at dinner-time. Her grey eyes had the slight, unfocused convergence he associated with long-term spectacle-wearers like himself, yet she had never worn glasses in her life. He imagined her slightly overweight, but not irredeemable body laid out on the beige bedspread in her ecru kimono. His magnolia wife.

He raised his head and looked round the lounge. He had a magnolia wife and a magnolia house. Whatever overblown names the paint companies alighted on to promote their dingiest and most lack-lustre colours, they had them all: bland boletus, faded fustian, restful rusk. To ring the changes she had painted the new kitchen grey – a different shade of dull. The only bold colours were in the children's rooms, but only because Hilary had not chosen them. Anyta's was scarlet, Daniel's, black. Straker smiled to himself. Anyta was about as unlikely to join the army as Daniel the priesthood, judging by her weight and his conversation.

His thoughts turned to Nadine Stone's house in Norwood Gardens, a little seventies' semi with a replacement front-door and a flat-roofed garage. Inside this unprepossessing house he had found the décor exuberant and stylish, the whole place a vibrant palette of colour. The lounge walls had been colour-washed terracotta, and through another door he had spotted, with momentary alarm, a carmine kitchen. The floors were varnished wood laid with thick, gaudy rugs, and the lounge furniture was heavy, with a strong flavour of Mexico or India. A huge vase of curly twigs stood on the floor in front of the curtains, and on the hearth he'd noted an enormous earthenware onion mounted on a wrought-iron stand. The flames of a small wood fire flickered through a hole in the front.

'You can cook on it,' she'd told him after the business had come to a close. 'I noticed you looking at it earlier. I had to put that copper cowl over and get the whole fireplace modified. It's a chimnea. From Mexico.'

He had admired it, faintly embarrassed, and glanced round the rest of the room.

'You like it, don't you,' she said. 'Everybody likes my house.'

Nadine Stone had been crying when they left that night, and crying when they arrived. He'd known she would be in the moment Fiona swept into Norwood Gardens. She would be sitting on the sofa, waiting for the bell, her knees clenched, levelling herself with a chain of cigarettes or, preferably, a glass of scented white wine. Nadine. The name resonated with refinement, sensitivity, the exotic. Completely hysterical, according to the woman operative who had received the 999 call. He encountered plenty such women in his line of work. They were putty in the hands of Fate.

Dark, he reckoned, when Fiona pulled up outside number ten. He depressed the doorbell and peered through the glass into the yellow light of the hall. Slender. Made-up. Smart. Dark.

He didn't get a good look at her until they reached the lounge. The black bob had slewed forward into her hands, which were stuffed with peach-coloured tissues from a box on the floor beside her chair. Her reversion to the foetal position disarmed him somewhat; curled knee to chest in her powder blue cashmere jumper, her bare feet sunk into the cushion, she looked small and fragile.

The colours of the room pumped him with adrenaline. On the back of his neck the hairs prickled with a mixture of pleasure, embarrassment and dread as he ascertained her details and verified her ownership of the car. She cried the whole time, occasionally blowing her nose between her index fingers and thumbs.

He indicated the wine-glass on the coffee table.

'Had you been drinking at the time of the accident?'

'Drinking?' She dabbed her eyes with a disintegrating ball of tissue. Her mascara and eyeliner had smudged and the tissues came away black. She regarded them, her bottom lip curled, and threw them on to the gabbeh in front of the fire. 'I hadn't been drinking. I'd just been made redundant.'

His solar plexus tightened and his palms began to sweat.

'I adore this place,' she sniffed. 'You know those uninspiring old roadside houses you see in a French village? Get past the front door and you discover an Aladdin's cave. That's what I wanted to create here: a sort of *trompe l'oeil*. This is my first house. Like your first love affair, you invest a fortune in it. But I've no mortgage protection, and if I don't find another job -'

She began weeping again. He could feel Fiona's eyes on him, but his own gaze never wavered.

'Perhaps,' he suggested, 'my colleague can make you a cup of tea.'

'I'm sorry, okay, and I wouldn't, under normal circumstances, have sent you out.' He had tossed his flat hat into the back seat of the police car and slammed the door as loudly as Fiona. 'You heard it all from the kitchen anyway. And I've stuck her on. Failing to stop and report are about as much as we can prove at this point in time.'

Fiona said nothing, but Straker sensed the pins.

He'd had no choice but to send her out. Nadine Stone compelled him. Her self-absorbed anguish, supplemented by the central heating and the spicy colours of cayenne, chilli and ginger, ran his blood hot and pounding. She was in distress and manifested it exquisitely. Her defencelessness underscored his power, conjured up the little tell-tale vein that bulged as it meandered down his forehead. And he could do nothing about it except get rid of Kingston.

When she walked out he followed her, pushed the door to and then took up her place at the other end of the sofa, nearer Nadine Stone.

'I was only there five months,' she wailed. 'We bought this house on the strength of it. A new firm, you know the sort of thing, all confidence and glitzy brochures and image. I was suckered in by them like I was suckered in by Darren. Bastard.'

He dealt with the rest of his police business between her waves of weeping. What he really wanted to do was make love to her on that rug in front of the onion in the fireplace. He wanted her to sink into the thick, yellow pile and dig her fingernails into the ginger stick men and scream.

He became aware that he had ceased breathing. Tension fed

on tension. He exhaled a slow and controlled breath, the heat of it rising over his upper lip. He sat forward, slowly, like a hunting animal, and let his left hand float across the divide and settle on the terracotta arm of her chair, as close to her leg as he dared without actually making contact. Neither of them spoke.

The fabric of her trousers stretched tight over her legs. He wanted to stroke that smooth navy skin, run his hand up the tapering thigh and cup her knee. He wanted to cup her breast, diffuse the static of that soft cashmere and feel the thrill of the electricity.

The door swung open and Fiona came in. His viscera convulsed. He snatched his hand back to the armrest of the sofa and tapped on it nervously. Had Fiona seen? Maybe he should not have reacted so fast. But she'd said nothing since, nor been at the station long enough to hear rumours. Either way she had broken the spell with her tray of steaming mugs. And what about Nadine? Had she seen? And if she had not seen, had she sensed the mood? He wondered.

His susceptibility to tears... He preferred to call it a susceptibility, which suggested merely a heightened sensitivity to a normal stimulus. Or did he have a fetish? Peccadillo sounded Spanish and, therefore, all the more sinful. A perversion ranked more serious still than a peccadillo and would lay the tacky onus of sin firmly at his door. Whatever name he gave it, it was a problem, and it was his. Hilary knew. He had been making an effort to deal with it this past year. She knew that, too.

'But there's only so much forgiveness,' she'd told him after the last time. 'And then it's called stupidity.'

Hilary could not be described as a woman to tolerate foolishness in anyone, least of all herself. And then he would end up alone in some frowsty bedsit, or worse, as the disgraceful veteran in single-men's quarters.

'You used to be nice before you went in the police,' she'd added.

He'd never forgotten those words; they would have stung

even if they had been untrue. You rubbed shoulders with low-life and eventually you joined them. The same, only different: hypocritical. Nevertheless, a distraught woman did acquire some special quality, something delicate and irresistible. He savoured her red-eyed docility, the sensation of her sweet, tearful proximity, when he might squeeze a compliant hand, or shoulder, or knee as he divined how far she might yield. There had been that mother a year ago in the incest case down the Iffley Road.

He went out to the garage via the door in the hall. On the ground at the back, in a wire bicycle basket, was a stack of old newspapers. He upturned the basket on to the floor, retrieved a magazine from the bottom of the pile and took it into the lounge.

He'd seen *Erotic Forum* advertised in the back of one of the Sunday magazines just before Christmas, a promotional copy free. He wasn't really into sex magazines, especially erudite ones which still had adverts for Belgian chocolate willies. He'd read part of it, felt titillated by the sexual excess and then nauseous for the same reason, and hidden it. Until now, when his little weakness needed to be put into the perspective it deserved.

He sat down, flipped idly through a few pages and skimmed an article on the *partouzes* of Paris. And then he saw it: at the bottom of the page, a row of three cartoons entitled *Funny Peculiar*. The middle one showed a sobbing woman and a be-suited man seated either side of a large desk. The caption read, *Dacryphilia – sexual arousal from the sight of crying*. It was only then that he noticed the unusual tilt on the desk.

He slapped the magazine shut and threw it on the carpet. Yes, and afterwards would follow the guilt, and then the rebound chastity. And then it would all begin again, this susceptibility, this joke that raised more than a laugh.

He took the magazine outside and hid it under the front seat of his car to dump at the paper bank. He went indoors again and into the cloakroom, and unzipped his trousers. The urine gushed forth in a healthy stream, and then stopped. He stared miserably into the ivory toilet bowl and waited. His bladder indicated pressure. He strained a few times. Now, even a pee seemed beyond him.

He glanced sideways into the mirror over the hand-basin. Prostate trouble at forty-two? Yet his hair was still naturally dark, and long and thick enough to fall over his spectacle frames. His boyish looks had not quite deserted him. He peered closer. Behind his square, silver-rimmed glasses his brown eyes had always been a little too intense. A few lines here and there, and his skin had coarsened, emphasising an appearance that was already slightly doggish. Hilary had changed, too, and not only physically. He was married to a magnolia armadillo who could turn on him with the most biting cynicism he had ever known. No wonder they seldom made love.

'But I do love you,' he'd told her after the incest. 'More now than I've ever done.'

'The more you hurt me, the more you love me,' Hilary murmured, 'is that it? Aren't you confusing love with guilt?'

He took the point. 'They can both cause pain. But if you lose your sense of guilt, the pain vanishes. If you leave me, Hil, or throw me out, that hurt will never fade.'

'Try wounded pride, Jim. Try a pricked ego.'

There was a spattering in the toilet pan; the urine reappeared in a series of slow drops. He relaxed a little and watched his water splashing like chips of peridot off the ceramic. The flow ceased, revelling in its own idiosyncrasy. He strained hard and relaxed again. If it wasn't sex, it was waterworks. His bladder now seemed to be lobbying for self-rule as ruthlessly as his dick.

The pee surged back out of its own accord. He watched himself pissing with a sickened curiosity, slowly at first, until the urine flowed in a great, satisfying cataract and his bladder was empty.

He rearranged himself, washed his hands and went back to the lounge. Little enough in life could be taken for granted anyway; he at least expected to be able to pee when he felt the urge. And if he wanted to save his marriage, he also had to address the matter of his – yes, his dacryphilia.

*

'I've decided,' he announced to Hilary that night, 'that I need to approach someone about my – difficulties.'

Hilary, poring over a primary science text, laid down her pen. 'Who will you see?' she said softly. 'The police doctor?'

'Are you joking? I don't need them knowing anything they even vaguely suspect. I'll be relegated to some station in the sticks, making cups of tea. If I'm lucky.'

'Isn't there some sort of Stress-line? Something anonymous?'

'Stress?' He smoothed his lips with his fingers. 'I tried counselling before, remember? A protracted waste of money. This is beyond counsellors anyway.'

'The family GP, then.'

'Protracted waste of time,' he said sullenly. 'I don't want to see any psychiatrists or psychotherapists either. It's one of the first signs of madness.'

'Oh, Jim.'

Hilary slid her book to the floor. She knelt in front of her husband and took his face in her hands, and he thought how much younger she looked.

'I would come with you, if you wanted. If you're serious.'

He enclosed her wrists in his fingers and smiled. 'Do you know someone called Karin Shilan?'

Hilary frowned and turned away.

'I thought you might have heard the name, that's all.'

She considered. The name sounded familiar, she told him, but she couldn't place it.

'She's a homœopath.'

'Yes! Esther went to her evening class last term, Esther from year six.' She nodded in excitement. 'Homœopathy and First Aid. Esther's full of it. The class are trying to persuade her to carry on this spring.'

'Do you know anything about it, then?'

Hilary shrugged. 'Something to do with herbs? I've no idea. Esther's the one to ask. Why, do you want to try a homœopath?'

Maybe, he told her. He would think about it. He hadn't

ruled it out.

He prepared their supper in the kitchen while Hilary watched the end of some women's drama on video. He switched on the kettle and went through the mindless but pleasant ritual of setting the tray as he thought back to the journey from Karin Shilan's house to the hospital. She was a statuesque woman with incredibly dishevelled black hair, and she wore a long raincoat, which, with a touch of ironing, might have been smart. She hadn't cried much, but the tears had been waiting. That never passed him by.

'I appreciate you must have been asked a thousand times,' he'd ventured, partly out of curiosity and partly to defuse the inexpressible tension in the car, 'but what *is* homœopathy?'

She hadn't minded. It was a holistic healthcare system, she'd told him. 'Speak to ten people with a cold and you'll find they all experience it in different ways. Some take to bed, others can keep going. Some are thirsty, some not, some always get chest infections afterwards. So we look at the whole person, the mind and emotions as well as the body, and we find a remedy which will gently stimulate people to heal themselves.'

It made sense. It made far more sense than batting the same pills at everybody who crawled over the doctor's threshold.

He jiggled the tea-bag in his wife's mug, expressed the last few drops between his fingers and left the semi-solid brown lump on the edge of the sink. Brain and bladder. Dick and dacryphilia. Maybe that was the answer: he could go with prostate trouble, mention the other, and they would conveniently fuse into one issue. It would be discreet. It would be confidential. It would be perfect.

*

'I'm off to bed,' Hilary said after supper. 'Don't forget the cat.'

He crackled noisily through a few more pages of the paper. He was lucky, really, that that witness had come forward. Someone should have informed Ms Stone that Cooper had presented himself and backed up her story. Her neat, oval face, her neediness and receptivity, her glowing chimnea and luxurious rug... He should have told her yesterday. It would have been out of courtesy rather than duty, but that made the stuff of good public relations. The gesture might also have allayed a few of her worries. God knows, she seemed to have enough of them.

He took his supper debris into the kitchen, cursing; his obsession was irresistibly renascent. He stepped into the hall and listened for the bathroom door to squeak shut. The house fell silent. He removed his wallet and mobile from the pocket of his wind-cheater in the cloakroom, and left them on the kitchen table. Then he picked up a torch from the cupboard in the utility room. From his wallet he removed Karin Shilan's business card. He checked his watch: ten thirty. He might well get an answer-phone now, which, in a way, was preferable.

He waited for the brief torrent of the toilet's economy flush before unlocking the back door. He leaned out: the bedroom curtains had already been drawn. He walked down to the end of the garden, rubbing his arms and exhaling victorious plumes of condensation into the night air. Underfoot the grass crunched, grey and brittle.

He stopped near the back hedge and tugged the card, torch and mobile from his trouser pockets. Squatting, he lit the torch, keeping it pointed downwards. *Karin Shilan RSHom, Homœopath*, the card said. The choice was his now. Adrenaline coursed a queasy weakness through his muscles.

He turned the card over, tapped out the number scribbled there and reached the answer-phone. After the beep, he took a deep, icy breath and left a message: 'This is Inspector Straker speaking, Jim Straker. I wonder if I might call in tomorrow evening, around six. Perhaps you would leave a message at the station before then if it's inconvenient. Thanks.'

He hurried indoors and tidied away the torch, phone and wallet. Orpheus appeared round his ankles, tail expectant. Straker frightened him out of the cat flap, locked it and went upstairs to use the bathroom.

He had made his decision. He had called Nadine Stone.

11

Karin stood at the back door, contemplating the garden through the imperfections of the old glass. Another hard frost had bleached the landscape, and sun glistened on the rime at the bottom of the garden. Nothing stirred to break the ethereal perfection.

She remembered it was dustbin day.

The number of practicalities seemed unreal. Her life had slid to a halt on Friday afternoon, and yet the outside world marched on, dragging her with it like a hostage on the end of a rope. The diary was peppered with appointments and commitments. Clients would be arriving, expectant, at her door that very morning. The room needed heating. And the dustbin waited at the bottom of the kitchen steps. Brendan usually carried it round. He did the bin. She cleared up cat vomit and any vestiges of Ruskin's nocturnal menu. She trapped and released those specimens fortunate enough to be discovered intact, and Brendan dispatched with a brick any that the cat had crippled beyond hope of recovery. It was never discussed.

She checked the kitchen clock, which was numbered back to front and ran anti-clockwise, and worked out the time: in half an hour, at eight twenty-five, a lorry from the Oxford City Council cleansing department would crawl past, heralded by its whining hydraulics and the hollow thud of bins.

She went upstairs, tugged on yesterday's pullover and jeans, slipped Brendan's dressing-gown on top and went back downstairs. She put her head round the door of her office. The sun already spilled through the bay window overlooking the drive, yet the room did not feel quite warm enough for patients to sit talking for an hour or so.

The sunlight glanced off a flat, shiny object on her desk: the photographs. Opening the wallet, she drew out the zigzag pack of negatives and held each length up to the light until she had located the four frames. She filed the remainder away and took the two strips out to the kitchen. She turned up the boiler thermostat, then removed the kitchen scissors from the drawer, placed the negatives one on top of the other and made three longitudenal cuts down them to within a finger's width of the edge. Holding them by the uncut end, she snipped crossways through the glossy plastic fingers so that showers of little brown squares fell into the open top of the swing bin. Goodbye forever. Anyway, it made a fitting end. She had cut him out of her life; now she was cutting him up, sprinkling the past like ashes on to the oxidised peelings from last night's dinner. He could not contact her, she would certainly not contact him, and with nothing to refresh her memory he would fade like an after-image until he no longer impinged at all.

'Aren't you going to tell me his name?' Zo had pressed on the doorstep before she left. She'd made her disgusting, one-sided smile. 'At least tell me his name.'

'There's no point.'

'Karin, if you want to jet off to Tenerife on your own at a couple of days' notice, I'm more than happy to locum. God knows, I owe you enough favours after India. But you can't come back with photos like that and pretend nothing happened.'

'Photos like what? A couple of snaps volunteered by some old dear on a sightseeing trip? What was I supposed to do - turn her down? You couldn't get anything more innocent.'

'So innocent, they've got to be guilty.'

'It meant nothing.'

'Then why get rid of the photos? Friendship is nothing to hide. It's certainly not a crime. Anyway, given the circumstances I'm surprised you cared. Especially with a guy like that. I'd have been boasting if we'd got as far as a cup of coffee.' Zo narrowed her eyes. 'Or have you just hidden them?'

'No! I ripped them up and threw them out. I didn't want Brendan jumping to conclusions, surely that's obvious. In the event he hasn't seen any of them yet. I judged it politic to wait a while after I got back, and then –' Karin nodded gravely to herself, as though absorbing the counsel of some internal mentor. 'And you think he's good–looking?'

'Don't you?'

'I didn't to begin with.'

'Then all of a sudden you looked at him and thought, "O my God?"'

Karin stared at her friend with disconcerted admiration.

'Karin, that's the worst scenario imaginable. When you find a man attractive straight away, part of you is already on guard. But when your subconscious clocks him first, you end up kidding yourself it's ordained by powers and dominions. Of all the ways to fall for a man, that's the pits. And you land on concrete.'

'Zo, I haven't fallen anywhere.'

'Did you sleep with him?'

Karin made no reply.

Zo dug her bottom incisors into her lip. 'Do you mean you didn't make love, or that you were too engrossed to doze off?'

'I mean I don't want to talk about it.'

'Point taken.' Zo had picked up her bags and backed down the steps. 'Oh, and good luck with the kid-from-hell tomorrow.'

Ten o'clock, Monday morning, at home with Jordan Cleaveley and his attention deficit. Karin sighed. She left the scissors on the work-top, pulled the liner from the swing-bin and stepped outside wearing Brendan's crusted gardening boots. The air caught in her throat as she shut the kitchen door behind her, and her lungs tightened. The steps were mossed and dark, slippery even on a dry day, and she gripped the old iron handrail as she made her way down.

A plaque of ice filled the bin's indented lid. She tugged the lid off and flexed it so that the disc jumped from its mould and exploded with a crack on the concrete. She dumped the rubbish inside, replaced the lid and carried the bin round the side path, ducking to avoid the lilac. She left the bin by the gate and returned to the back garden.

The brick path that wound down the lawn was too uneven to be slippery, but she preferred the sensation and sound of the grass snapping underfoot, like a self-conscious guest eating toast. Brendan said that walking on frosty grass damaged it, but she didn't care. She crossed to the first patch of sunlight by the wall and inspected the japonica's early flush of red flowers. She bent briefly to examine one, its stamens spangled, every petal hemmed with ice. As for the swing, ten summers had passed. Ten winters above a blowsy sea of elephants' ears. The chains glinted, white and wet, where the sun caught them, though delicate spicules of ice prickled the seat.

She glanced round the garden. The swing, too, seemed to be gripped by this unnatural stillness, an active, intractable rigidity infecting it from the frozen landscape. She walked over, grasped one of the chains and shook it until it clanked and droplets of water spun off, and the spell was broken. She sniffed her fingers; they smelled of metal, just as they did after making love there, raw and sharp, like sweat.

She left the swing fidgeting to and fro. Inside, the kitchen already seemed warmer. Upstairs she sprinkled some of Brendan's herbal crystals into the bath, started the water running and went along the landing to his study.

Habitually she avoided the print next to the ball photo. She'd never liked it. She perused his CDs and the grey, scoured cassette boxes lined up against the wall behind his desk, and pulled out the tape of *Tattoo You*. Then she picked through his extensive collection of LPs. But the picture was hanging in her mind as clearly as the night Brendan had brought it home.

Turning the cassette over and over in her hands, she forced her eyes to the great antique gilt frame. He'd thrown its brown paper wrappings on the sitting-room carpet in his excitement, and she'd found herself eyeing this gossamer-gowned gentlewoman kicking her slipper into the air from an improbably small foot, watched by a statue of Cupid and some voyeuristic dandy in a bush.

'Good God! Hardly your taste, is it?'

'Nostalgia is no respecter of taste. It's *The Swing*. Fragonard. I saw it in a poster shop. I couldn't resist having it framed.'

He held the picture at arm's length and tested it at a distance against the four walls of the sitting-room.

'You're not thinking of it for here?' she demanded. 'It's

hideous.'

'It's perfect. But I'll hang it in my room where I can gaze on those stockings and frothy underskirts and dream of you.'

'I seem to recall I revealed more than peach petticoats and a calf-length of silk.'

Brendan had capitulated. 'But then, Fragonard would never have got as far as painting your portrait.'

And he'd disappeared from the room, cradling the print triumphantly in the crook of his arms.

She found an unopened cassette, ripped away the packaging and set one of his early Queen LPs to record on his hi-fi in the corner.

*

'I want to go,' Jordan intoned again from the cheese plant.

The Cleaveleys had been there all of ten minutes, and in that time he had rooted out every toy from the box, played with each, briefly, and systematically discarded them about the room. Joanna Cleaveley, pretty but prematurely greying, sat on a chair facing Karin and bounced her eleven-month-old daughter on her knees.

'We won't be too much longer. We've just got to tell Karin the important things she wants to know about you, haven't we.'

Jordan made no reply, but selected another pencil crayon from the heap beside him. He curled back over the sheet of cartridge paper on the carpet, his wispy blond hair falling into spikes across his forehead. Soon there came the sound of shading, a regular, energetic sound like a steam train travelling at excessive speed down an incline.

Karin inquired about his behaviour at school.

'Easily distracted.' Joanna Cleaveley set the baby on the floor at her feet and she crawled off in the direction of a jointed caterpillar. 'He can't concentrate on anything for more than two minutes. When they diagnosed him they described it as a failure of his brain to exclude "background noise." He has to attend to everything new the second it enters his field of awareness, can't get on with anything on his own. And if his teacher tries to make him, he plays up.'

'By?'

'Trashing his neighbours' work is not an unusual complaint.' She inclined her head slightly to check over her shoulder. 'And the more he's admonished, the more intractable he gets. With individual attention he's all right. Revels in it.'

Jordan appeared again beside his mother, a glimmer of mild curiosity pointing up his elvin features. He was a spindly, almost translucent little boy with long blond lashes, his prettiness marred by thickened red eyelids coated in grease.

He sidled round the back of his mother's chair and sat cross-legged on the floor. He had mastered his interest, and was now displaying an effective mixture of boredom and disdain. He pulled down her right hand while she carried on talking. He began tracing round her cuticles with a red crayon, then insinuated the point of it under her thumb nail.

'Ow!' Joanna Cleaveley retracted her hand sharply. 'Jordan, that hurt.'

'You can show me what you've drawn, if you like,' Karin said.

Jordan shook his head, stabbing the tip of the crayon into the fleshy mound of his own thumb.

'Well, you'd better put all those crayons back in the pencil-case anyway.' His mother cast around for a motivating bribe. 'Or we won't be ready to go.'

The child jumped up and ran back to his corner. He knelt with his back to them and they heard a musical chinking of wood against wood.

She asked Joanna Cleaveley how her son slept.

'Very much like he is now: always on the go. He gets very hot. He throws the duvet off. Oh, and he grinds his teeth. It's hard to believe he's got a stump of enamel left in his head.'

Karin scribbled notes in large, untidy writing, and when she raised her eyes again, Jordan had his arms laced round his mother's neck.

'Will you bring the drawing things over here, please?' Joanna Cleaveley said.

No reply.

'We'll do that at the end, shall we?' said Karin. 'So, what's your best food, Jordan?'

'Chips.'

'We hardly ever have chips,' said his mother, reddening.

'I like milk.'

'But that makes your eczema worse.'

'I don't like that soya yuk.'

Karin smiled. 'And what gets you really angry?'

Opposition, his mother mouthed.

'Charlotte taking my things,' he said.

'And what do you do when you get cross?'

Jordan opened his mouth very wide and rolled his eyes conspiratorially towards his mother. He drew his right hand to his shoulder. He clawed his fingers round an invisible missile and propelled it with considerable force at his mother's face, his fingertips almost meeting her eyeballs. Joanna Cleaveley, keyed in to some unknown source of fortitude, looked straight at Karin and didn't flinch.

'When he was a baby,' she said, coming to life again, 'he used to dash his forehead on the floor if he didn't get his own way. Didn't you?'

He dropped to his knees and gave an energetic demonstration on the carpet before rocking back on to his haunches.

'That was when I was little, because head-banging's for babies like Charlie.'

Charlotte lay on her stomach, her maroon corduroy dress rumpled on to her back revealing a huge padded rear stretched over with scarlet tights. She was fingering the lids of a farmyard jack-in-the-box.

'No, like this is how you do it.' He yanked the toy closer and slapped one of the coloured plastic buttons. A lid flipped up, quickly followed by a stylised Friesian cow. He grabbed his sister's adipose hand and pressed her fingers against another button to release a pop-up pig. 'Like that.'

'Tell me about the pregnancy,' Karin said, 'and the birth.'

Jordan smacked open the horse and sheep boxes, slammed the lids shut one after the other, then slapped his hands down again on all four buttons so that the boxes flew open in a succession of rapid and noisy clacks. He repeated this procedure three more times, apparently engrossed.

His mother broke off her son's prenatal history. 'Hush, Jordan.'

'Can we go home?'

'Soon. Why don't you help Charlie work that again?'

Joanna Cleaveley resumed her account. Moments later, out of the corner of her eye, Karin became aware of him holding the jack-in-the-box at arm's length in front of him. As she turned, he loosed his grip either end and let the toy drop on his sister's head. It landed on the base of her skull, tipped sideways and slid off her neck. The baby released a sustained and deathly shriek. Both women leapt to their feet. Joanna Cleaveley snatched the infant up in her left arm and hugged her to her chest, while grabbing the boy by the wrist and shaking him.

'I'm warning you. Don't you *ever* do that again.'

Her face was a breath from her son's, her jaw thrust forward. The boy began to howl and retreated to the door, and the piercing duet bounced off the walls. Joanna Cleaveley paced up and down between the chairs, rubbing the back of the baby's head and making noises of sympathy, but the little girl showed every sign of sharing her brother's tenacity.

'Don't think there's any lasting damage. God, I'm sorry about this. I don't think she'll settle.'

Karin swung her remedy case on to the desk, flicked the catches and took out two bottles and two small, polythene sachets with sealable tops. She unscrewed the bottles, pinched open the sachets, shook two tablets into one and four or five into the other and pressed them shut. She wrote on the opaque labelling strips, and handed both sachets to Joanna Cleaveley.

'I've seen all I need to see.' She raised her voice further against the din. 'These are for Jordan. Twelve hours apart, as per the sheet I gave you. And this is just some Arnica for Charlotte. Get her to suck one as soon as she's calmed down. It'll reduce any bruising. Oh,' she said, closing her case, 'you may find his eczema and breathing worsen for a few days. Stick with it, if you can. It's generally a good sign, but if you've any doubts, ring. And if you're happy I'll see you in five weeks, as arranged.'

Jordan had stopped crying and was massaging the brass doorknob and periodically leering at his inverted reflection.

'Look at this room,' said Joanna Cleaveley. 'We can't leave this mess.'

'I'll sort it this time. Jordan?'

He looked up.

'You like sweets, don't you? Well, your remedy tastes just like sweets. See how long you can make them last. Have a bet with your Mum.'

*

That afternoon she went into town and bought a personal stereo, and drove from there to Headington. Bridget, one of the nurses, hurried over to meet her.

'Progress! He's showing signs of stabilising.'

'Oh, thank God!'

'Mr Howard's just having a word with another visitor. A family friend of yours, I believe.'

Karin followed the nurse's eyes. Beside Brendan's bed Mr Howard stood in discussion with Emrys Clifford, Mr Howard reed-like in his dark suit, Emrys in navy jeans and sports jumper. However casual his clothes, they always looked as though it were the first day he had worn them. From time to time the consultant turned his head slightly, raised his chin and made a series of small nods.

'Mr Clifford brought in a beautiful flower arrangement,' said Bridget. 'The relatives' room is beginning to look like a nursery. We've even had some with a card from America. Mr Clifford,' she said, returning to the nursing station as Emrys came over, 'I was just admiring your flowers.'

'My wife has a bit of a talent, yes. Hello, Karin. The poor lad's in a bad way, dreadful to see it. Still, it's early days.' He waved to the nurse, acknowledged the consultant as he passed, and began edging towards the door. 'The meter's on the point of expiring, you see. Oh, and Liz thought the first of March for the retirement do. Spring, I suspect. Something metaphorical. Plenty of time to think about that, anyway.' He backed away with more resolution. 'Must be going. She sends her love.'

Karin stared after him. 'How long has he been here?'

'Maybe he's been visiting someone else as well.' Bridget leaned over the desk. 'Nice old boy, though. He was in here Saturday.'

*

Not quite time to try taking him off the ventilator yet, Mr Howard considered, though the signs were promising.

She shifted the chair into a suitable position beside the bed and leaned over Brendan's face. The swelling had lessened now. His face had assumed a more normal colour, and his own features were at last beginning to form through the mask.

She pulled, tentatively at first, on the tucked edges of the bedcovers, and eased back a triangle of sheet and blanket to expose his upper chest. He was still as naked as all the rest, stripped of vitality and left with nothing but the pink-skinned vulnerability of the neonate. And the wires still clung parasitically to his chest. The bank of machinery at the bedside seemed more alive than his body. They could have been preparing him for a passage to the far reaches of the universe. Somewhere there would be a hermetically sealed capsule for him with as many dials and gauges as an aircraft cockpit. Her husband, the spaceman.

She laid the sheet and blanket over him again.

'Hello, Bren.' Her voice sounded louder than usual, louder and forced. 'You're going to be fine. *We* are.'

Suddenly she noticed that the tube from his nostril was now white and opaque. Her eyes traced the tube to a bottle on the wall. The bottle contained a milky substance and the tube was taking it right into his nose. The sight made her recoil, almost gag, but she bit her lip and quickly pulled herself together.

'Look, I've brought some music for you.'

She picked up her bag from the floor, drew out the personal stereo and cassettes and laid them on the blanket. With the headphones over her own ears, she clicked in *Tattoo You* and set the tape running. She adjusted the volume, and transferred the headphones to her husband to mine for some deep vein of good times, some memories worth living for. The music jingled and hissed into his secret world, taking its rebellions of adolescence and the reminiscences of old sex, drugs and rock'n'roll that might rekindle youthful energy and love and, maybe, hope.

She was happy to let the music play awhile; addressing her unconscious husband still unsettled her deeply. At times she had found herself almost rehearsing before she spoke, considering her words far more than normal when they had possibly never mattered less. Talking to him compared with being in a play and taking all the roles: she asked the questions and then she gave herself the answers. Talking to a baby or a cat would have been easier; at least they responded visibly. And why should Emrys be in such a hurry to get away from her? He'd scarcely met her eye in the ward. One of the last of the gentlemen solicitors, he refused on principle to rush anywhere outside the tennis court. Maybe he just found the situation hard to cope with. Maybe he had a hospital phobia, or a pressing engagement. Or maybe she was imagining things.

She switched off the tape and removed the headphones. Talk normally, that was what they said. Normally.

'Brendan, I want us to try again. Things were better the last few days. Weren't they?' She lifted the covers again and found his hand. She rubbed the skin of his palm with her fingertips, curled his fingers over and rolled them up inside hers. 'I've decided I'm re-decorating the sitting-room wall, getting rid of the Louis XIII. Call it a bit of spring-cleaning of the heart. Wish me luck.' She squeezed his fingers and shook them. 'I love you, Bren. If you hear nothing else, hear that.'

12

The stain damage affected only one panel of wall-paper, but she had to re-decorate the whole recess to the window-side of the fireplace. She swept across the area with graceful, criss-crossing arcs of the Stanley knife, first from the floor, then from the top half of the step-ladder, scoring up what was mostly perfect paper. The wall looked a mess, gashed and wounded, at the end of it. Had she done this three weeks ago, she would have held the knife, blade down, in her fist, borne her weight on to it and struck the wall long and repeated blows, ripping through the plaster to the brick. How could she forget when bitterness was such a potent preservative; it seemed more like days, a week at most.

The paper was handmade, white, with a large but subtle design of pendulous pale blue flowers. The stain, the colour of tobacco taint on a low pub ceiling, ran in divergent streaks from a point two-thirds up the wall. If the paper had been bold, or any shade of cream, yellow or orange the mark would not have shown. Most people didn't notice it anyway. To her, it ruined the room.

She fetched a bucket of hot water and an old sponge and began soaking the paper nearest the chimney-breast. When the panel was finished top to bottom she rasped with a scraper at the bruised, softened paper until it began coming away in tatters like the peel of a gigantic fruit. The stain went with it. Not many people could boast a Louis XIII stain on the sitting-room wall. Not many could boast a bottle of Louis XIII, and most that could treated the cognac with the reverence inspired by its price-tag, and did not spray it over the sitting-room wall.

The rehydrated glue stuck the paper to her slippers and the dust sheet. As it dried, the paper crackled and curled and caught around her ankles. She sanded the plaster lightly, removed the dust with a damp sponge, then made up a bucket of thin paste and sized the wall. She fetched a bin liner and cleared away the debris of wall-paper shreds and the paste and tools, then she remembered that Jordan's case needed writing up, and his litter of toys still awaited across the hall. Anything to occupy her. Anything.

In her office she picked her way through the garish chunks of plastic, most of which she had acquired secondhand at car boot sales, and drew the long, lemon curtains across the bay window. She planted the toy box in the epicentre of the chaos, tossed the toys in, one by one, and towed the full box back to the corner of the room near the bay. Then she spotted the drawing things by the back wall. He had folded his work of art in half. She picked it up and opened it: he had drawn, in red crayon, a figure with angle-iron legs and feet, a triangular body and raised stick arms. The head had a dome of long, black hair draped over it, and the triangle appeared, on closer scrutiny, to be a dress, patchily shaded in dark blue... with a long and forcefully drawn arrow poking into the apex. Karin looked down at herself. Dark blue dress. She brought the creation closer to her face. Above the hair was a narrow, light blue cap, resembling a halo. And that day she was wearing a sky-blue alice band.

She carried the drawing in both hands to her desk and slipped it into a cardboard folder that contained his case notes. Ten seconds before, she could have screwed the picture into a tight ball and sent it arching into the waste-paper basket.

She fetched the drawing board and the crayon case, slid the board down by the wall, and opened the desk drawer for the crayons. Then she laid the case on the desk-top, unzipped it and folded it open. The whole of one side was empty: ten crayons missing.

She cupped her chin in one hand and hugged her other arm round her solar plexus. Think child, a child endowed with the intelligence that went with cunning, and a five-year-old's desire to manipulate, deceive and punish. Where would a mind such as that conceal a bunch of crayons? Not in the toy box, she knew already. She crossed to the large rectangular rag rug at the back of the room and hauled it up, corner by corner. Nothing.

Her gaze alighted on the plant in the corner. He'd been working near that, a sprawling, dusty cheese plant she'd bought from the small-ads in the Oxford Times. She had re-potted it a fortnight ago into this great orange and amber glazed planter.

She lowered herself on to her stomach, crawled forward and felt around in the corner behind the pot. Nothing. She glanced up amongst the leaves, then sat up and peered into the pot. A small, red eye stared up at her from the compost, a red pupil with a brown iris. She stuck her thumb and index finger into the soil either side of it and extracted a scarlet crayon, dusty with plant fibre. Little wretch! She pushed her fingers, two joints deep, into the soil, and raked through it until she met more resistance. Over the next two minutes she recovered every one of the crayons. Each had been inserted vertically into the compost and depressed, she suspected, to the limits of a five-year-old finger.

She took the crayons into the kitchen, wiped them with a damp piece of tissue, and made herself a cup of tea. A break was definitely in order before she returned to her desk.

On the top-sheet of Jordan's file she recorded the date and the remedy she'd prescribed: Tuberculinum 1M. Two, twelve hours apart. Two, in case he spat out the first or decided to eat half a tube of toothpaste after it.

The form that Joanna Cleaveley had completed on behalf of her son showed him to be glaringly tubercular; they had a marked family history of allergies. The paternal grandfather had suffered from TB, and the child looked to be a walking bag of keynotes. In Mind, he had:

Malicious (3)
Anger, throws things away
Restlessness, children, in (2)
Precocity
Striking, himself, knocking his head against wall and things (3)
Obstinate, children (3)
In Teeth: *grinding, sleep, during (3)*
In the Generals section:

Food, milk, desire (2), as well as Skin: *Allergy, milk, to (3)*

And it went on. Even Eye: *eruption, lids, on, eczema, margins of lids* - the only symptom she'd had any uncertainty about when she'd tapped the rubric into her laptop – had turned up Tuberculinum, and it was a classic remedy for attention deficit.

She jotted down a clutch of rubrics for future reference, and returned his file to the cabinet.

When she got into bed that night, her mind was still picking over the case. Did that make her a good homœopath, or a bad wife? And soon, the eczema on Jordan Cleaveley's lower legs would probably flare and his eyes would end up like overblown tomatoes. All hell would be unleashed in that household. But it wouldn't last. A good homœopathic aggravation echoed a crisis in a relationship; the situation had to get worse before it improved. Because if Jordan's remedy was the simillimum, chances were that, over the next few weeks, the entire Cleaveley family would be transformed. The simillimum stirred up muck, then washed it clean away - like cured like. And she and Brendan would get their second chance.

13

During the lunch-break Jim Straker put on a civvy pullover and a mackintosh against the rain, left St Aldate's police station and went shopping. He returned with a stuffed carrier, the top discreetly folded over, and hid it under his desk.

He spent the rest of Monday afternoon report writing, breaking periodically from the computer to consult his watch or the clock on the office wall: Nadine Stone did not call.

Just after five he quit the station and caught the Park & Ride to Red Bridge. Before joining the rush-hour traffic he bundled his mackintosh into the carrier with his clip-on tie and swapped it for the new fleece, a flamboyant affair in shades of red and orange, with diamonds and runic squiggles in dark red, amber and black. He switched on the courtesy light and studied himself in the rear-view mirror. For the devotee of murk it represented a startling fashion departure, and yet the effect was not unappealing.

She was wearing black jeans and a black roll-necked jumper: her contract-killer clothes. They suited her. She could murder him anytime, preferably slowly and at point-blank range.

'I suppose you'd better come in,' she said.

He lingered behind her while she shut the door and arranged an orange and black tie-dye curtain over it. He gazed round the hall, awaiting direction, and peered up the stairs, which were carpeted with some knobbly door matting.

When no invitations materialised he clenched his fists and made for the living-room. She followed without a word. She did not invite him to sit down either, so he remained standing. A strange smell hung on the air, a smell which, though not pleasant, struck him as distantly familiar: cow carcasses at the butcher's, cow carcasses queuing for the cold-room.

She folded her arms. 'What is it this time? Did you forget to arrest me?'

He explained about the witness.

'On the point of blame, Inspector, my mind was at rest, as you put it, before you ever set foot in the house.' She pushed her sleeves further up her forearms. 'Did you really come here to tell me what I already know?'

The house seemed very warm all of a sudden. Inside the fleece, his back became moist.

'Miss Stone, the Fates were obviously conspiring against you last Friday. I thought one less worry might lighten the load.'

'Did you. Would you excuse me one moment?'

She went through the orange connecting-door to the kitchen, pulling it hard enough to catch in the frame. Another door squeaked open beyond. With a dull reverberation the same door slammed shut. A fridge, maybe. Metal pulled over metal: a saucepan on the hob. Maybe there was a cup of coffee in the offing. Then came a slow, metallic tinkling. A bin lid thudding shut. The fridge door opening and closing again.

He refused to sit. On the side-table by the far armchair lay a collection of papers. He bent to examine them: nothing personal, bank statements, an old mortgage letter from a building society. He re-positioned the papers and turned to the bookcase. On the top shelf, in a plain glass mount, was a photograph of Nadine and a benign-looking human gorilla in a white T-shirt. Straker picked it up. They had their backs to some railings overlooking the sea, and the gorilla appeared to be toasting the photographer with a can of Export lager. He also had his arm round Nadine Stone.

Straker glanced about the dim, atmospheric room. He tilted the frame towards an opaque white wall uplighter, the closest source of illumination, and brought the picture to his face. She was smiling, but surely this smile had been caught on the wane. Either the sun had dazzled her, or the photographer was dithering. Or Nadine Stone had wearied of her partner's ebullience and felt just a little bored.

Something rustled against the kitchen door. He just managed to replace the photograph and take a side-step from the bookcase before she arrived back. Her lips remained unrelentingly puckered and there was neither sight nor suggestion of liquid refreshment.

She assumed a mannish stance in front of the chimnea, her thumbs hooked into the pockets of her jeans.

'Nice jacket.'

'I've just come off duty.'

'More fun than the magpie kit.'

'I don't like magpies,' he said. He inserted his fingers into his shirt collar and peeled it away from his neck. 'Look, would you mind if I took this nice jacket off?'

She gestured to the nearest armchair. He wasn't sure whether he was supposed to deposit the jacket there, or whether he was now permitted to sit, or both, or whether the gesture had been a mere shrug of indifference. He removed the jacket nevertheless and arranged it round the back of the armchair.

'I can't say magpies hold much appeal for me either,' she

said. 'But they're the perfect embodiment of our times: smart, nosey. Overbearing, destructive. Loud. Popping up everywhere. Gosh, just like the police.'

'You want me to go –'

'I let you take your coat off.'

'But, until advised otherwise, I'll assume the chairs are just for decoration.'

'Won't you sit down?'

He chose the armchair near the window and sat in it like a Great Dane on a throne. She turned her back to him and from a tall, carved cabinet she took two wine-glasses. She walked dismissively past him to the connecting-door.

'Drink?'

'No, thank you.'

She swivelled to face him, the glasses pressed to her chest. 'You're off-duty. One glass won't do any harm.' She fixed him with a condescending smirk. 'There's tea or coffee, if you prefer. Or cranberry juice.'

Wine, he told her.

She held the glasses in one hand so that the stems crossed, and closed the door behind her. Excluding him. From the kitchen came the irritable squealing of a cork being eased from an opened bottle, followed by the plash of wine into glass, two clunks from the fridge and the intriguing sound of the saucepan.

He crossed to the door, depressed the handle and opened the door just wide enough to see beyond. The wine-glasses and bottle stood on the end of a multi-coloured, tiled work-top straight ahead. Newspaper masked the rest of the work-top, in the middle of which she had a small, shallow, green plastic tray. She was hunched over it, pouring into it a stream of clear, yellow fluid from a saucepan lined with foil.

He opened the door wider. 'Shall I take the wine?'

She straightened, the empty pan raised at an angle in her hand. Her bob swung back with the movement and then resumed its perfect, sculpted form round her face. She clanked the pan back on the hob, giving no indication of having heard him, and wiped her fingers on a loosely scrunched piece of paper towel.

He ventured in and picked up the glasses. 'What are you doing?'

'Bird cake.'

She walked past him and left him in the kitchen. Glasses in hand, he peered at the confection. He could make out at least three strata of fat and seeds apart from the oil she had just poured in.

'Quite a work of art.'

'If you do it any other way, the seeds float on top of a blodge of lard.' She flopped into the armchair by the bookcase and watched him through the doorway. 'After each layer I put the tray in the freezer compartment. It sets quicker.'

He joined her and held out her glass, which she took in two hands without thanking him. He resumed his place in the other armchair.

'You like birds, then?'

'No, my hobby is rendering down lard.'

'Do you get a decent number here?'

'Not bad for an estate.' She took a couple of mouthfuls of wine. 'We back on to woodland. At the moment.'

She picked up the bundle of papers from the side-table and slid one or two over the others. He noticed her black-varnished fingernails, and her heavy eye-liner gave her the exotic allure of an Egyptian aristocrat perusing her papyrus.

'I've just been going through my standing orders,' she murmured, 'seeing what I can cancel. A couple of home magazine subscriptions... that's no hardship. But the Wildlife Trust will have to go, and the RSPB. And *British Birds*, and *Bird Watching*. God...'

He laced his fingers round the wine-glass as though it were a crystal ball. 'How are things? Honestly?'

'Honestly? Better for being believed.'

'Look, I'm sorry, okay? In our line you file your ideals and whack on the good old breast-plate of cynicism. It's the only way you get the job done.'

'Any jobs going?'

He stared at her. 'Maybe something in the canteen.'

'Don't think that would satisfy the mortgagees.' She emptied her glass and put it on an olive-wood coaster. 'Am I still reported for whatever it was?'

'As things stand. But what looked to begin with like a juicy hit-and-run now turns out to be not much more than human foibles. Personally I'd like to see the whole thing written off.'

She shifted in her seat and sat up a little. 'Is that possible?'

He could guarantee nothing, he told her. 'But I'll see what I can do. The witness says McDonald was daydreaming, and his wife seems to have no issue with that.'

'Has he come round yet?'

'No.'

She jerked forward suddenly, stretched out her legs and leaned over, rubbing her shins with extended fingers. She wore just one ring, an undistinguished sapphire and diamond on the third finger of her right hand.

'I keep seeing his face.' She cupped her hand over her nose and began to sob. 'Inspector, his eyes –'

The words trailed away as her shoulders quivered and the tears began to run. Poor woman. Frightened and confused. Accused. Alone.

He left his armchair, put his glass on the bookcase and knelt beside her chair. She looked at him then. Her eyes were bloodshot. They could have been resentful or accusatory; they were not. Not now. The frame of hair round her face had lost its perfection where she had repeatedly raked her nails through it. Strands had separated, single black hairs stuck to her cheeks.

He removed her right hand from her thigh and pressed it to the arm of the chair. Her eyes flickered all round his. And then it happened.

Inside his chest arose the discordant pulses of desire, fear and exultation.

'The images,' he said vaguely, 'they'll fade. With time they will.'

With the slightest dip of her head, she assented. He patted

her hand, got to his feet and reclaimed his wine-glass from the shelf.

'I ah – I take it,' he said, indicating the photograph with a finger uncurled from his glass, 'that must be Darren the Bastard?'

Her eyes followed his finger and returned to his face, quizzical for a moment before she opened her mouth and her eyes widened. She sank her head back against the cushion and roared with laughter, a throaty braying that seemed wildly but endearingly at odds with her appearance.

'Darren the Bastard,' she grinned. 'I've got to write to him suggesting that since he's seen fit to walk out, how about contributing half the mortgage payments till I get myself sorted?' She paused. 'I thought I'd end up throwing myself into the decorating to take my mind off him.' She got up, addressing no one in particular, and smoothed her palms one across the other. 'Maybe we didn't have enough in common.'

'Well,' said Straker, retrieving the jacket and heaving his arms into the new, stiff sleeves. 'On that note you might be interested to hear that, despite being a policeman, I also happen to be a member of the RSPB and the local Wildlife Trust and Ornithological Society. If things are slow to work out, I could pass on the events diaries. And magazines. You know, just till you're back on your feet.'

'I wouldn't want to put you out.'

'It's on my journey home.' He shouldered his way out to the front door and let himself on to the step. 'Oh, and if I hear anything else –'

'You can drop round,' she said, 'and let me know.'

14

The news came two days later.

The mist had gathered thickly across the Oxford plain. She'd had a clinic at the Natural Health Centre that morning:

three follow-up cases, starting at ten. It was the first time since the accident that she'd needed to drive to east Oxford. Banbury Road, Parks Road, South Parks; the first stretch of her route took her through the heart of the University's science area. She seldom passed without thinking of Brendan at work there, maybe lecturing in the Department of Anatomy, maybe in the Physiology labs, or in the Radcliffe library, at whose long dark tables she had used to sit when researching for her MSc.

As she turned into South Parks Road she switched up the heater; it seemed so cold. Yet there wouldn't be blood on the road, or twisted car wreckage. And Brendan was alive.

She saw Le Gros Clark Place, the access into the science area where Leon and Maggie had parked up. There was no traffic behind her. She decelerated.

The road had generous proportions, with the imposing Dyson Perrins Organic Chemistry Department behind stripped winter trees on one side, and a row of pale brick-built University buildings opposite. Yellow lines bordered the road, which had no bends, no slopes, bollards or crossings, no external distractions of note. The pavements were broad. Even crossing the brilliant green cycle lanes would take at least two paces. And there, the other side of the road, she spotted the only testament to the collision: tyre marks, long scars, far longer than she had expected, starting almost straight down the centre of the lane and tailing towards the dotted lines. They were nothing, details that belied the destruction. They looked like someone had painted them.

A horn sounded from behind. In her rear-view mirror she saw a blue Transit van crawling towards her back bumper. The driver raised his hands at her. She accelerated away.

St Cross Road, Longwall Lane, High Street. Magdalen Bridge. Cowley Road. Grey tyre marks on grey tarmac in grey mist. Nothing else remained, as though the whole event had skidded through a portal into a parallel universe.

She parked in the rear access lane and walked round the corner to the Natural Health Centre.

'Oh, there was an inquiry for your clinic.' Anthea, the

receptionist, scraped over the next few sheets of the register. She ran a finger down the page, pausing to switch a couple of stray dreadlocks over her shoulder. 'Friday. First-timer.'

Karin thanked her, scribbled the details in her notebook and went upstairs to room 1. The upper floor comprised three therapy rooms, shared by a traditional Chinese acupuncturist, an osteopath, a cranial osteopath, a counsellor and a hypnotherapist. The pictures, exhibited for free by members of some local art society, had changed again. The seascapes, ignorable but pleasant, had been replaced by three takes on phosphorescent dryads in a dark forest, which were not nearly so ignorable.

She opened her laptop, unpacked the files, laid out her books and settled down to refresh her memory about the morning's cases.

The third client left at twelve-thirty. She followed him downstairs and saw him out.

'Message,' Anthea said. 'Mr Howard for you, and could you ring back as soon as possible?'

She made the call from the phone in the osteopath's room. She burst straight into tears when he told her, and then she rang Zo in Banbury.

'Zo,' she announced, her voice high-pitched and shaky, 'they've taken him off the ventilator.'

'Oh God —'

'No, he's all right! They made the switch this morning, but Mr Howard wanted to make absolutely sure before he called. And I can see Brendan as soon as I want!'

*

What had she expected? She had not anticipated the tracheostomy still gouged into his throat, a brash blue plastic disc with a stump of tube protruding from it. Neither had she imagined that he would still be hitched up to the feeding tube. Off the ventilator meant approaching physical normality, being stripped of sensors and wires and other artificial devices. And somehow the image of unaided breathing also brought with it the imminence of self-awareness. She had not expected to find him sitting up in bed with a cup of tea. Eyelids flickering would have been more than enough, but when she saw her husband he still looked like he was deeply asleep. At best asleep.

'It's a brain injury,' Zo whispered, when she arrived at six that evening. 'Progress will be slow. Hope. Just don't hope for too much too soon. Anyway, are you ready?'

Karin twisted the clasp of her shoulder bag and took out the bottle of Opium 50M she had prepared at the clinic by crushing and dissolving a tablet in distilled water. She untucked the blanket towards his feet, unscrewed the bottle top, moistened some cotton-wool and applied the solution to the finer, hairless skin behind his knee.

'How long do you reckon before changing the remedy?'

Zo shrugged. 'How often does a situation like this arise? Twenty-four hours? No idea.'

Not a transformation then, but it was a change for the better. She drove home, singing to the Rolling Stones cassette, and ate the whole of a ready-made lasagna for two.

While the kettle heated she went out to the laundry room and prepared a bucket of wall-paper paste. She stirred the porridgy mass smooth with a handful of wooden barbecue skewers and carried the bucket through to the sitting-room. She erected the trestle-table and cut the requisite lengths of lining-paper, then returned to the kitchen to pour her tea. The dent on the side of the chrome kettle marred its perfect, shiny curve and seemed to suck in and warp the other reflections from the kitchen. It was a bruise that would never heal, an everlasting reminder of Brendan's desperation.

She took the tea into the sitting-room and began slapping glue, like grey jam, on to the first length of paper already weighted on the trestle.

Would she have made the same decisions now, she wondered, the same mistakes? Probably. In a professional therapeutic situation, distance had to be maintained. On that walk through a patient's history, you walked with them, side by side, not hand in hand. You listened, experiencing their world, absorbing it, but never entering it. Observers too close to the situation could never be without prejudice. They became drawn in. They saw, at best, a warped reality. New Year's Day had brought her a warped reality. And yet, it seemed no more warped than the reality she was living now. Just different.

At last she trimmed the top edge of the final strip of lining-paper. She pushed it home under the picture-rail, and expressed the air bubbles from the wet, lumpy paper, sliding them out with her fingers. She rollered the seams and the edges, and when the job was finished, it still looked uneven and awful.

She switched off the radiators in the room and tidied away. By the time she was ready to retire, some of the paper had already paled and dried. She pressed her body to the wall, raised her arms above her head and swept her hands across the paper as though she were greeting the sun. The paper was already flatter, tightening itself to the plaster. It felt good to the touch, cool and not quite smooth, like the skin of a man.

15

When she went to the hospital late Thursday afternoon, the Opium had achieved nothing. Maybe he had moved on now, left Opium's sphere of action behind.

She re-took his case. His blood pressure registered slightly lower than normal, according to his records. She timed his pulse, and touched the back of her hand to his forehead, then to his chest, his hand, his foot: evenly warm, no unusual perspiration or skin colour. Very little with which to make a prescription, when inside his skull seethed a chemical volcano.

She leaned over his face, close enough to give, or receive a kiss.

'I need more, something to go on. Help me!'

The only reply was his breathing.

She entered the rubrics into the laptop she had open on the chair next to her:

Respiration, deep
Respiration, slow
Respiration, sighing
Mind, unconsciousness
Generals, pulse, weak
Generals, pulse, frequent
Head, inflammation of brain, traumatic

And Opium came out at the top of the list: Opium followed by Aconite, Lachesis and Phosphorus, then Stramonium, Belladonna, Glonoinum and Helleborus.

'But it's not Opium, is it,' she wailed at the silent, ordered table on the screen.

She went immediately to find a telephone, called the pharmacy and ordered 50M Aconite and Lachesis by overnight delivery, and Phosphorus by standard post. On the way back to the ward it occurred to her that she might first explore a different approach and administer Aurum, his constitutional remedy. He might be battered outwardly, but the inner man remained unchanged, unscathed, the same one that had gently kissed her goodbye on the lips last Friday morning.

'Aurum, then,' she whispered as she was about to leave. 'It's worth a try. Oh, and I've finished the wall. You'll be impressed when you see it.'

On Saturday she marked the difference the moment she arrived.

'Don't you think he looks more normal?'

Bridget leaned into the mattress, her stocky form supported on her knuckles. 'The nasogastric tube, perhaps?'

Karin looked back at her husband. 'It's gone!'

'Removed this morning.'

'Is that good?'

'They swapped it for a pe.g. Straight into the stomach.' Bridget pulled back the sheet and showed her the new tube. 'You have to be unconscious, so they decided they might as well do the procedure here on ICU.'

Not the Aurum, then.

'Time to turn you, Brendan. Ready? Bit of upheaval now.' Bridget tugged out the sheet, her brow furrowed with the exertion, and jerked her head at Karin. 'You can help, if you like.'

Between them they rolled and propped him on to his right side. Karin re-arranged his legs, minding the catheter as instructed, and crammed a pillow between his knees and another against his feet. Bridget flapped the sheet back, and they re-made the bed over him.

Bridget snapped on some gloves, and Karin stood back to watch as the nurse swabbed his mouth, first with a colourless solution and then a pink one which smelt of hygiene and cough sweets. She smeared on his tongue a transparent solution with the consistency of thin jam, and greased petroleum jelly over his lips. Then she stripped off the gloves and patted his head.

'You're deserting us shortly, I gather. I'll miss you. Still, I expect you could do with a change of scene.'

'Neurology?'

'Hasn't Mr Howard told you?'

'They hadn't finalised the day when we last spoke.'

Bridget collected up the bottle and dishes on her tray. 'We've done as much as we can for him here. Mr Scrivener, Brendan. First thing, Monday.'

*

Aconite went, to be followed two days later by Lachesis. Both looked promising and achieved nothing. She ordered, and administered Stramonium and then Belladonna, all 50M. Remedy after remedy after remedy, a different 50M every few days, and all to no apparent effect.

'Are you sure you're doing the right thing,' Zo queried the following Monday, 'chopping and changing like this? Hitting him with all these 50Ms?'

'What choice do I have?' she argued. 'There are simply *no* differentiating symptoms to work with. None. His face is still bruised from the accident. He just lies there. Standard rules no longer apply. What would you do?'

And when Zo could offer no more constructive suggestions,

Karin called the pharmacy and requested Glonoinum and Helleborus.

Just over a week after Brendan's arrival in Neurology, Mr Scrivener rang her at the Natural Health Centre.

'I thought you'd like to know,' he said. 'Brendan has come out of coma. He's opened his eyes.'

Her heart hammered. When at last she spoke, her voice cracked with emotion.

'After all this time... God, it's been so long. I was beginning to doubt he'd ever come back.'

'Mrs McDonald –'

'I'm so happy! But what happened? Tell me what happened.'

'Mrs McDonald, whilst we're all delighted, obviously, at the step forward, Brendan isn't conscious yet.' He paused. 'Your husband's mind is not behind his eyes.'

'Something must be going on inside for him to open his eyes?'

Mr Scrivener acquiesced with a quavering, nasal sound. 'There is a degree of reflex activity taking place, yes.'

'What made him open his eyes?'

'He was being tested for deep pain. He's also showing signs of movement, although I would stress that it's random movement at this point in time. Spontaneous, non-volitional.'

'But he's not without hope?'

'Without that,' Scrivener sighed, 'you don't tend to last too long as a neurologist. Or much else, I believe.'

He blinked. Brendan blinked, staring at the ceiling. Maybe the Belladonna she'd given him on Monday had brought about the change.

She peered greedily into his eyes, shuttered and unseen for almost three weeks. He would register and know her. At some level of consciousness, no matter how obscure, he would respond. But there was no mellowing, no melting, no tenderness, no obvious recognition at all. She could have been staring through a window into the face of a stranger's cat. The body she pored over was either unforgiving or soulless. His eyes looked as they had done after the argument, but those taut lids had softened over the next few days, and the laughter lines had been exercised once more. Now, it was as though he didn't see her, as though she wasn't there.

'It's very difficult,' she whispered, 'not to feel you're punishing me, Brendan. I can't help thinking you're only absent because I'm here.'

She passed her raised forefinger in a line before his face, and his wide-eyed gaze seemed for a moment to follow it, and then wander off elsewhere before settling on some invisible mote. She wanted to pinch his cheek. She wanted to drag him off the pillow by his shoulders and shake him, shock him conscious. Or maybe, now his body showed itself more amenable, the soul would steal back overnight. All in good time. Wanting too much came woefully easily.

She lowered the nearest cot-side and freed his right arm from the sheet. At the bottom of the bed, the blanket rose in a sharp wedge that pointed to the ceiling. They had the boots on him again.

'He's developing foot drop,' Janice had told her. One of the new nurses. He'd been undergoing intensive physiotherapy right from the beginning to minimise the contractures. Recently, however, they'd started giving him these white, moulded half-boots held in place with straps to stop his feet pointing to the end of the bed. His arms and wrists could follow in time, they'd warned her, curling protectively across his chest. His body would submit to a new and inexplicable impulse and fold itself into a semi-foetal position, but they could splint wrists and elbows too, if need be. First, the robot feet, then the unyielding arms of a toy soldier. With his unruffled blinking and dead eyes, it was not a great leap to seeing a metamorphosis in process before her. Man and medics were colluding to suck him out and re-form him into something she could only dimly recognise as her husband.

'Brendan.'

She stretched out her hand and rested it over his fingers. The fingers snapped shut.

She screamed.

16

Down the corridor someone was whistling the sunny repetitions of *Love Is In The Air*. Straker listened closer, and tapped his pen top on the memorandum he'd been reading. The liquid fluting faded and Larry appeared, framed in the open doorway. Straker laid down his pen. The office PC rarely advertised his presence; walls had ears when he was about. So did doors and, especially, keyholes. Straker always left the door open. With Larry as office PC there seemed little reason – other than bloody-mindedness – for keeping it shut.

'Hand-delivery.' Larry wagged an envelope at him. 'Red, Mister. Could be a Valentine.'

'Hah!'

'It *is* February the fourteenth.'

'Traditionally the day by which the birds have chosen their mates, Larry. That's what they say. Was it my wife?'

'No, Sir.' Larry ambled into the room. He held the envelope horizontally above Straker's in-tray and let it drop, his expression pitched with some skill between innocence and insolence. 'Nice-looking, though. Remember *Antony And Cleopatra*?'

Straker opened his mouth, but had to scrape the words from his throat. 'When did this arrive? Is she out front?'

'Left five minutes ago.'

'Was there any message?'

'She seemed rather nervous, Sir.'

Larry pried his tongue round his upper molars and fixed the envelope with stubborn intensity. Straker took up his pen and went on reading, idly following the lines of print in the margin with the tip of the ball-point.

'Thank you, Larry.'

'Thank you, Sir.'

The obtuse angle of Larry's moustache flattened to a grinning hundred-and-eighty degrees as he backed into the doorway, and the fluid whistling receded down the corridor. The tune was different this time, one Straker didn't recognise, equally melodic, yet more languid and haunting. He listened to the refrain, then, blowing a soft stream of air between his lips, copied it several times over.

He kept on writing, though invisible fingers palped at his heart. In spite of the red envelope, it couldn't be a Valentine. Not if the sender was Nadine Stone. His own wife had not given him a card last year. The Iffley Road incest had left her ill-disposed to romantic declarations. Nothing had been forthcoming that day either. Admittedly he had left the house at just past four in the morning. He had put one for Hilary on the breakfast table, a pink slice in the stainless steel toast-rack, and he had bought her a gift during his breakfast break. He had not given up all hope of receiving a card from her. It would be less a love token than an olive branch, but pax created an opportunity for love, a chink, if not an opening in her defences.

He craned his neck forwards and studied the even, rounded handwriting on the envelope, almost every letter heavily pregnant. Care had been exercised. It might have been the writing of a teenaged girl with a brand new pen. He reached for the envelope. It was a wind-up.

He pushed his chair backwards, and, in the gap between his parted knees, ripped the top of the envelope apart with small, brisk thumb actions, like his mother with her old-fashioned can opener.

The card came out picture first: a rooster standing on dense green sward. A Rhode Island Red, its neck bulging in mid-crow. No sugar. No greetings. He opened it: a Thank You card from Nadine Stone, with *Kindest Regards*. Quaint. A little antiquated. Unexpected from her. *Dear Inspector Straker, The letter arrived this morning. I can hardly express my relief that this sad business is over. Heartfelt thanks for believing in me.*

Kindest Regards and *Heartfelt thanks*. He closed the card and touched its upper edge to his lapels. What had the Super said in his letter, and how deeply heartfelt were her thanks? *Heartfelt*. Emotionally registered.

He took the card straight to the front-office. Three or four faces turned simultaneously in his direction.

'For information, lads, it's a Thank You card. All right?'

The Duty Sergeant slipped into the room behind him, sallow and apologetic amongst the sniggers.

'Nice to see some appreciation for services rendered, Sir.'

'Nice to see some appreciation for anything round here,' Straker countered. 'Come on, let's hand this shower over to Inspector Greenslade.'

He left St Aldate's just after two when early turn had finished for the day. The shift had been quiet, dulled still with the hopes, efforts and good intentions of Valentine's Day. By the middle of night shift the romantic let-downs, snubs and petty jealousies would be making for a prime clutch of punch-ups and domestics. He was glad to be out of it for a year.

Hilary and the children were all at school. The gym didn't appeal. The swimming pool appealed less. What was in Nadine Stone's letter? A visit to Nadine Stone appealed a lot.

*

He blew into his fingers as he walked up her ribbed concrete path. He rang the bell and thrust his hands back into the pockets of his golf wind-cheater. He had no stylish fleece to catch her fancy that day. His hair needed a wash and hung in lank clumps, and a little run of early turns had deepened the bruise-blue shadows under his eyes. In fact he had more in common with a shabby school-kid.

Nadine Stone did not appear to notice.

'Inspector Straker – how lovely to see you!' She welcomed him in with a sweep of her arm. 'Go through. Take a seat.'

The house greeted him with warmth and the smell of herbs and freshly-baked bread. On the coffee-table was a plate of red and green lettuce topped with a round of white cheese and a few walnuts, and an elliptical roll torn lengthways and soaked inside with melted butter.

He sat on the sofa, lowering himself between his fists so that his arms arched oddly either side of him like flying buttresses.

She shut the door behind them, giving him the opportunity to take in her short dress and the figure-hugging chenille cardigan in reptilian green.

'I was just having lunch. Have you eaten? I can get you some. It's no trouble.'

'No – This is just a quick visit.' He accepted her offer of coffee nevertheless. 'Black,' he told her as she disappeared into the kitchen with her plate of food. 'Two sugars.'

He tilted his head back to meet the sofa cushion, closed his eyes and sagged into its embrace. The house, her yielding, shapeless sofa, her extremely shapely dress... The combination of material delights and effusive welcome washed round his mind on alternating tides of pleasure and tension and guilt.

When he forced his lids open again, he found himself looking at a greetings card. Groundless indignation incised through the fatigue: a Valentine's card without a shadow of a doubt, though placed to one side of the mantel. At least she had not accorded it a central position.

He was just on the point of investigating when Nadine Stone arrived back with his mug of coffee.

'Here, Inspector.'

'Please... Jim.'

'Nadine, then.'

She sat in the armchair near the window, and there followed an awkward but celebratory moment when neither spoke.

'I received your card,' he said at last. 'Thank you.'

'Thank *you*. When I didn't hear, I began to wonder what fate lay in store for me.'

'I submitted the file only a couple of days after I saw you. Almost a record,' he reflected. 'But the wheels grind ever slower as files progress up the system. Two to three weeks, I reckon, for a written response from on high. A caution, was it?'

'Failing to stop. My fingers were shaking when I opened it...'

He nodded to himself. 'I considered recommending no further action, but one has to be realistic. In practical terms, a caution amounts to little more than NFA.' He explained that he had not yet heard the decision himself. 'Despite a specific request that Mister Galt inform me -'

'Please, it was the mildest ticking-off imaginable. He obviously sympathised. Anyway, it's over, and the letter is so much ash in the bottom of the chimnea.' She let her hand drop forward from the arm of the chair, palm upturned, her fingers relaxed in space, the gesture aimed in his direction without being close enough to bridge the gap. 'I really appreciate your support.'

His cheeks began to burn. 'I must be getting home.' He drank down the remainder of the coffee, banged the mug on the table and got to his feet, the wind-cheater rustling protests. 'I see you still have at least one admirer. Would that be Darren putting in a re-appearance?'

She uttered a shrill laugh. 'No. I think it's from a guy who lives down the road.' She got up and plucked the card from the shelf. 'A pair of hippos about to bump into each other at the intersection of two pavements.' She flashed him the picture. 'And inside: "*Love is just around the corner*," and a huge, curly question mark.'

'Lucky you!'

'It can stay round the corner,' she said flatly. 'If the sender is who I think it is,' she added, though she stood the card back on the shelf.

She followed him out to the car despite his advice to stay indoors, her arms pinched across her midriff to hold her unbuttoned cardigan together.

'Roses!' she exclaimed as she bent to look through the passenger window. 'For your wife?'

He nodded with embarrassment.

'That's nice. No one's ever given me roses. All sorts of other flowers, but not roses. Actually I prefer white ones. Lighter,' she confided, 'more pure, somehow. Oh, I almost forgot, Jim. I've just had a call from a mate in the Oxford Ornithological Society. There's been a sighting of a pomarine skua at Farmoor.'

'A pomarine? What, this early? You're joking.'

She shrugged. 'Could be a juvenile, blown off-course. He

wanted me to go over this afternoon, but I've got an interview, so a group of us are heading there tomorrow. We might see it, we might not. Depends how long it graces us with its presence. Anyway, we're meeting at the amenity building at twelve. I suppose you're working, or have other arrangements?'

'I don't know what's on, to be honest,' he replied. 'Thanks all the same.'

She was right about the roses, he decided as he turned into his drive. If you lived in a house like Nadine's, the roses needed to be white.

He leaned over and lifted the three red ones off the back seat in their cone of cellophane. Up in the laburnum, a magpie sat waiting like a malevolent concièrge. He cursed it as he got out of the car and spat at the hebe, but the coffee-streaked gobbet smacked instead on to the drive. He scuffed the saliva with his shoe, took a swing at the magpie with the rose buds and watched it whirr into an acer two doors away.

He went straight to the living-room. Yes! His Valentine card to Hilary had been transferred to the mantelpiece. It was laid flat and at a careless angle so that one corner overhung the edge, but it had at least made the journey from the toast-rack. Maybe Hilary had stood it up, maybe in the centre of the shelf. Maybe the kids had nosed into one or more of its four sugary sides and tossed it down in disgust. Maybe it was incapable of standing without a prop; it was so long. He picked his card up, worked it like a harmonium a few times and set it upright in the centre of the dark wooden mantelpiece. Why had he bought such a card? The emetic pinks and roses and bears revolted him. And he'd penned exactly the same old *Darling Hil* and *All My Love* as last year and the year before that. The genius to purchase a Valentine with hippos on it had never occurred to him.

He sighed and went to consult the diary by the phone in the hall. Saturday: day off, and golf with Steve Bennallick at eleven. He picked up the handset and punched in a number.

'Hello, Beverley, it's Jim Straker. May I speak to Steve?'

'He's out, Jim.'
'Out out, or pretend out?'
'Password?'
'Golf.'
She put him through.

*

'Dad,' Daniel whined as Straker peeled off his dazzling fleece in the hall that night, 'can you stop whistling?'

'Was I?'

'You've been doing it ever since this afternoon, the same old fogey dirge over and over.'

'All right, all right,' said Straker, who had just returned from a pizza supper and cinema trip with Hilary. 'I heard it at work today. On the radio, I mean. As I drove in. I can't get the tune out of my head. I don't even know the title.'

'*My Funny Valentine*,' Hilary shouted from the kitchen.

He stared, aghast, at the kitchen door.

'I couldn't manage a card,' she told him. 'Not this year. I'm sorry. But the roses were lovely.' She climbed into her cream silk pyjamas with her back to him on the far side of the bed. 'I have bought you a little present, though.'

'For me?'

'Just a little thing. A joke really, though quite appropriate in the circumstances.'

He cupped his head in his hands against the pillow, wondering if the gift was appropriate because of the circumstances or because of the joke, or if they amounted to the same. He prepared himself to be both appreciative and disappointed.

Hilary folded open the bed covers, sat on the sheet, swung in her legs and whisked back the covers in one, slick movement. She rolled on to her left side, and he heard a drawer of her bedside table open with a hollow, cardboardy sound on its runners.

'Here.'

She passed him a small rectangular box.

'"*Love Cuffs.*" What the –?' He unpicked one end and pulled out a pair of black plastic manacles trimmed with scarlet fluff. 'Good God...'

'One's for you, the larger one. And the smaller one's for me.' She snapped hers on to her right wrist. 'See? Then I slip this on to your left... and we're hitched.' She squinted and put her face to his portion of the handcuffs. 'I can't seem to make yours fasten.'

He removed his glasses from his bedside table with his free hand and fidgeted them on to his nose.

'I think it's too small for my wrist.'

'You're hardly overweight.'

'Well, that's why it won't lock.'

'Oh.' She examined the empty, supposedly man-sized manacle swinging from her trapped wrist, while he returned his spectacles to their case and switched off his lamp. 'Oh dear. Maybe that's the point.'

'No, Hilary.' He slid his arm under her shoulders. 'It was a sweet thought. Imaginative. Perhaps they have smaller men in Taiwan.'

Maybe it was the point, though, he thought when she had turned out her lamp. Maybe she was right. He rubbed his wife's shoulder with his fingertips. The silk felt good between their skins, like a woman's welcome or the slipperiness of saliva... But why did they have to be pyjamas? And why beige? Nadine wouldn't wear beige pyjamas.

He squeezed Hilary's shoulder. In spite of the meal and the film and the roses and card, he wanted no more than a cuddle. She would be relieved. Her body felt as rigid as Orpheus' when Straker swung him outdoors by the armpits.

'Golf tomorrow,' he announced into the blackness, 'I've cancelled. Couldn't face it this weekend.'

'Oh?'

'No, there's an agenda. Jane's been lobbying me to press him for a reconciliation. Again.'

'A reconciliation between the Bennallicks would delight almost half the golf club.'

'Well, considering he left her for serial infidelity with their husbands, it's rather unlikely.' The darkness seemed to thicken and congeal round his words. 'Anyway, Steve should have time to find a guest amongst his clients by the weekend, and we'll have a re-match when Jane's being a little more realistic.'

Hilary snorted. 'What will you do instead?'

'Depends,' he said, 'on the weather.'

17

In the distance, through the windscreen wipers and specks of drizzle, Straker thought he spotted her blue car. She'd parked at the end of a line of vehicles just below the reservoir. He swung into the space alongside and got out, his pulse already starting to race. He scanned the long concrete ramp leading up the slope to the sailing club, but saw no one. Walking round her car, he touched the flat of his hand to the bonnet: still warm.

He opened the boot, changed out of his shoes and put on his wellingtons. He strung his binoculars over his head, arranged the strap under the collar of his green oil-jacket, and swung on his black mountain-cap by the peak.

After pulling out his scope, he locked the car and hurried towards the ramp. At the top the Farmoor basins came into view, adding their sombre expanse to that of the skies. No dinghies sallied forth from the slip that day and, for once, no plaintive clinking of halyards carried from the nearby boat park. The grey water shone as though vitrified, reflecting endless grey stratus. Only the drizzle peppered the water's oily stillness, hanging like a muslin pall over the reservoir; the visibility promised little. And passage migrants were fickle creatures at the best of times; maybe a day's stop-over, maybe four days. Maybe a week. A glimpse of his first pomarine skua would be nice, but not essential to his anticipated enjoyment of the outing. There was only one sighting he really wanted.

He passed the sailing club. The amenities room, another low, utilitarian, seventies' construction, stood just beyond the clubhouse at a short distance from the main path. Large and bare, the amenities room always reminded him of a school prefab, regularly used by a number of different groups, none of whom cared too much about its appearance. To one side stood tables and chairs dotted round a blackboard, which was usually covered with zigzag sketches of sailing manoeuvres or race layouts. A long notice-board took up the opposite wall, providing information about the reservoir site and advertising all manner of outdoor pursuits in the area. One section had been dedicated to the birders, where they displayed pictures of the birds common and less common to Farmoor's waters, and copies of the society's latest monthly bulletin of observations and events.

Through the glass he could already make out a small group gathered round the Sightings register on the counter below the posters, a sexless knot of people in long coats.

As he went inside, the faces turned in unison, four pale, wintry faces under dark hats. Only one smiled.

'Jim!'

Her voice cracked through the silence with such volume and delight that his heart seemed to cleave. She broke from the group, one arm outstretched.

'Hello, Nadine.'

'Glad you could make it, hi! Let me introduce you.'

He just had time to rest his scope against the wall before her hand met his back, ushering him gently towards the others. He stole a sidelong glance; between her green boots and dark brown oil-coat, he noted a length of baggy, broad-ribbed green corduroy trousers. Most of her hair had disappeared under a camouflaged cotton hat with a wide downturned brim covered in bird badges. Her face without make-up caused him to wonder why she ever bothered with it. He realised then that Nadine Stone was endowed with the gift of natural and effortless chic. She could go to a ball wearing rice sacks and still turn heads.

'Everybody?'

Her voice rose as though she were putting a question, yet rang with authority. Her three companions, two men and another woman, each took a step back to face him.

'This is Jim, who I said might be along today. Jim... Mike

and Barbara, and this is Jez.'

Mike and Barbara, a thin, intense couple in their fifties, both leaned forward and shook hands. Jez nodded and eventually offered his hand, paw-like in a green fingerless glove. Straker put him in his late thirties, a stocky specimen with golden red hair and a thick, short beard. He gripped Straker's hand for far too long.

'Nadine tells us you're a member.'

'That's right.'

'I don't recall seeing you at meetings.'

Straker pulled on his forearm, and Jez grudgingly relinquished his hold.

'I've been on a few field outings. Not the same ones as you,' Straker conceded. 'My shifts make it impossible to attend any kind of meetings on a regular basis, so I find the bulletin a good way to keep in touch with what's about. I go out on my own a fair bit. Pretty antisocial, I'm afraid, but it's one of the restrictions that goes with the job. So...' He turned to Nadine. 'Still on for the pomarine skua?'

'Still on, yes.' She pointed to an untidy entry in the Sightings book. 'Well, it was there at ten this morning on the F1 basin.'

Straker looked down the last list of birds. 'Anything else of interest?'

'An Iceland gull,' said Jez.

'Jez is a bit of an authority on gulls,' said Nadine. 'Summer plumage, winter plumage, first-, second-, third-winter juveniles. Incredible.' She called to Mike and Barbara, who were waiting in the open doorway. 'How's it looking?'

Barbara held her bare palm skywards, crinkling her nose. 'Lighter, I think.'

The rest of them collected the scopes they had propped against the wall and trooped out, one by one. They turned right and then left on to the causeway between the two reservoir basins.

'Snap!' Nadine said beside him.

He frowned and followed her finger pointing to his chest.

'Same bins,' she said.

He smiled and looked over the sloping side of the F2 basin; the usual flotsam of white feathers rimmed the water-line, a sort of ornithological scum gently bobbing against the concrete.

Silence descended over all five of them as they narrowed their eyes in concentration to survey the waters. A couple of grey and pied wagtails scuttled along the raised wall of the causeway ahead of them.

Soon Jez fell in alongside him and Nadine joined Mike and Barbara. Jez had his hood up now, the coat zippered and buttoned to the chin, his face reduced to a round white porthole inside it.

'Where is everyone?' Straker cast a glance over his shoulder. 'You know,' he went on haltingly when no response issued from the hood, 'pomarine, mid-February, Farmoor? I thought we'd be queuing back to the car park.'

The hood turned to Straker. 'A mate of mine spotted it. He wants an extension and I'm on the planning committee. He'd get his permission anyway, but he still seemed to think he owed me a favour.' The beard twitched once at the side of Jez's mouth. Whether it was a nervous tic or an attempt at a smile, Straker couldn't quite decide. 'Plus it pissed with rain yesterday afternoon, which fortuitously kept most of the locals away.'

'So, in a few hours from now...?'

'Standing room only, I wouldn't mind betting.' The hood swivelled forwards again. 'How long have you known Nadine?'

'Just a couple of weeks. She – witnessed an accident.' Straker paused. 'You?'

'Oh, years,' Jez purred inside the hood. 'Yes, we go back a long way, me and Nadine. Made any good obs of late?'

'As it happens,' Straker said, drawing himself up, 'I thought I saw a pine bunting.'

'In this area? A pine bunting?' Jez stopped in his tracks. 'Male?'

'Female. In my back garden.'

Jez gave a slight toss of his head and resumed walking. 'Yellowhammer.'

'That's what I assumed at first,' Straker said keenly. 'But

the underparts looked white, and no way were the primaries edged yellow.'

'Well, I've seen no records of pine buntings in the annual reports. Corn buntings, reed buntings, yes...'

'If they've been spotted in Dagenham –'

'But you can also miss the yellow tint on the underbelly at a distance if you're not rigorous enough with your observations.' Jez marched off after Barbara, Mike and Nadine. 'How about if we split? Say Nadine and I watch F1, and you three take F2?'

'I'll join Jim,' said Nadine, 'seeing I asked him along. We'll take F2, and Barbara and Mike can look at F1 with you, Jez.'

She opened the legs of her tripod on the spot. Straker glanced at Barbara, Mike and Jez, but followed suit before they could intervene. He set up his stand a short distance from hers and uncovered the lenses.

She already had her face to the eye-piece, her nose wrinkled and her lips twisted as she shifted the handle to scrutinise the open water. He took a second to admire her naturalness and grit, then settled down to the business of his own observations.

They saw the usual numbers of regulars, the great crested grebes, the goldeneye, the tufted ducks with their reverse quiffs and eyes as bright as pencil torchlights, and a handful of cormorants brooded malevolently on the limnological tower. A small fishing party of goosander drifted in a thin raft across the water in the distance. There were occasional mallards and a few mute swans, and a couple of great black-backed gulls paddled past not far from the causeway.

'Seen the little grebes?' she whispered. 'Near the water's edge, over there.'

He copied the angle of her scope and tracked the water-line. 'Got them. One, two... five...'

'I love their powder-puff bums,' she murmured. 'No pomarine, though. Shall we see how the others are faring?'

'No pomarine,' Jez agreed. 'Coots, thirty or so greylags. A couple of dunlin fiddling around on the shoreline. But no Iceland gull or pomarine skua so far.'

'Swap in a moment?' Nadine suggested.

'Sure.'

They had been back at their posts for only a few minutes when she suddenly seized the eye-piece of her scope.

'What is it?'

'Don't know. Not sure...' But her voice quavered with excitement. 'Jim, I think I've got it!' Her mouth stretched to a smile as she peered into her scope. 'Here!'

She shuffled back and beckoned him over. He stepped into her place and she hovered close in to his right side.

'See it?'

'The dark one?'

'It's got the skua's bill. I think it's the dark morph. They're less common than the light ones. I can't make out any barring, but it could still be a juvenile. Especially given the lousy visibility.' She patted his back. 'I'm going to tell Jez. God, he'll be so jealous.'

Straker raised his head momentarily to watch her. She walked fast, her arms swinging straight and at a wide angle from her hips, her head down. He saw her speak to Jez and thumb in Straker's direction. He ducked back to the eye-piece of her scope.

Soon all five of them were grouped round her tripod. Jez, Barbara and Mike each took their turn to look, then set up their own scopes in a line down the side of the causeway.

Ten minutes later the drizzle condensed to larger droplets and the air filled with an electrical crackle as heavy rain fizzed on to the huge surface of open water. They picked up their scopes and made, damp, but jubilant, for the car park.

He and Nadine opened the boots of their respective cars and fed in their scopes. She tossed a pair of black trainers on to the tarmac between the two vehicles.

'That guy,' Straker said, stepping on the heel of his right wellington to lever it off, 'he's still watching me.'

Jez had parked beside Barbara and Mike further down the row. Nadine looked across and waved, giggling when his hand shot up in reply. She bent over to tug off her boots, and her binoculars swung on their strap and struck her twice in the chest. She exclaimed in annoyance, lifted them over her head and laid them on the edge of his car boot while she finished pulling off her wellington.

'You and Jez,' he said, 'you know each other quite well, then.'

'He's just a mate.' She loosened the laces of her trainers and pushed her foot into one before removing her other boot. 'He's the guy who phoned me about the pomarine in the first place.'

'He doesn't like me.'

'Well, Jez invited me, and then I made damned sure I invited Barbara and Mike. And it's not a phone tree. Put it that way.'

'Territorial, is he?'

'Misguidedly,' she said, her eyes flashing. She wriggled her foot into the second trainer. 'I'm really pleased you found the time to come.'

'A day to remember,' he smiled. 'My first pomarine skua. *Dark* morph. You know your stuff.'

'And you thought I wouldn't.'

'I thought it unlikely that a decorating fanatic would be equally passionate – and knowledgeable – about bird watching. But I was wrong.'

She swung her wellingtons into the boot of her car. She flipped her hat off by the brim and threw it in after the boots. She drove her fingers through the crown of her hair, agitating it, shook her hair back and beamed him a smile so disarming that he could only stand and stare at her.

'I've got a flask in the car,' she said.

'I think –' He banged down the lid of the boot and tested the weight of the car keys in his hand. 'I think I'd better be heading back.'

*

He fidgeted the key into the lock and felt the front door give under the bundle of clothes and equipment. He became aware of his whistling only when it was drowned by the thud and buzz of Daniel's music from upstairs. He let the things slide from his arms into a heap on the carpet. Hilary was out. Anyta was at a friend's house and, to all intents and purposes, Daniel was absent as well.

He put the scope away in the cupboard under the stairs, then extracted his field guide and pad from the pile and slotted them back into the bookcase in the study. The strap of the binoculars was protruding in a loop beneath his coat. He pulled them out, restored them to their place of honour in the dining-room drinks cupboard, and returned to deal with the damp clothes. He plucked up cap and gloves and slung the crumpled coat over his arm. And there on the carpet he found himself looking at his binoculars again. In a moment's confusion he scratched his nose with the peak of his mountain-cap. Then he dropped the clothes in horror. He snatched up the binoculars and turned them over: NADINE STONE. NADINE STONE printed in what looked like orange nail-varnish down the underside of the lenses. His heart pulsed with the drum-machine. What an idiot! He had shut hers into the boot when they were loading their kit. He had a woman birder's bins in the house. Worse, Nadine's.

Straker jingled his trouser pocket to check for the car keys and let himself out not ten minutes after he had arrived.

'Jim!'

He swept the binoculars from behind his back and presented them at arm's length like a newly delivered royal baby.

'Thought you might like these.'

'Oh God, I did, didn't I...' She thanked him and, with equal reverence, scooped her lost binoculars from his hands. 'They were a twenty-first birthday present too. I've been looking everywhere for them. What a dope!' She squinted up at the flat, grey sky. 'Still damping? Quick, come in! The kettle's just boiled.'

This time he did not even get an invitation. He combed his fingers through his hair, clean but sticky with drizzle, and followed her into the small, square kitchen. Invitations required decision-making. Orders were simply to be obeyed.

'You can have hot chocolate if you prefer,' she offered,

slicing through the wrapper of a packet of cheese straws with a vegetable knife, 'or some soup. Carrot and coriander, leek and potato, or tomato.'

Tomato, he told her, would be most welcome.

Against the only spare length of kitchen wall she had a drop-leaf table with one leaf raised. Either side of it stood a chair. Nothing was ordinary: the chairs and table had all been painted red, the top with an orange, red and yellow checked pattern that resembled a permanent tablecloth. He sat down there out of the way while she skated to and fro in skinny lilac socks, casting shadows on the metallic pewter cupboard doors.

She slid the opened pack of cheese straws into the middle of the table, and finally brought across two mugs, each with a teaspoon in it.

'Help yourself.'

She sat opposite him, fetchingly unkempt. Her hair hung as stringy as his. He guessed she hadn't had time to bathe or change, though she had managed to slough a few layers. The navy top and leggings still matched. They could have been thermals. They clung like thermals.

He stirred his soup, finished the job with a cheese straw and bit the end off it. They could re-run the afternoon's birding, deconstruct her three unsuccessful job interviews, exchange life stories. All they could do was haunt the past, like benign, aimless spirits. Giving her his address or telephone number, or verbalising how much he would still have enjoyed the trip had they not seen a bird all afternoon, or suggesting another trip, that would have meant weaving her into the future. With the outing to Farmoor he had reached the limits of possibility. The police connection had been severed, and a shared pastime would become shabby if he grew keener on the birder than the birds.

With the back of his spoon he flattened the starchy orange lumps at the bottom of his mug.

'I must be on my way.'

'Of course.'

'Any chance I could use the bathroom -?'

'Top of the stairs. Straight ahead.' She sucked some carrot

soup from the bowl of her spoon. 'I haven't finished decorating up there, Jim,' she called after him 'And I haven't touched the bathroom yet so I'd close your eyes.'

The air seemed to rarefy as he ascended the stairs. It could have been his relief at saving himself from himself, for his desire to feel women like putty in his hands was tainted by the suspicion that he was also putty in theirs. Or maybe the tonal lightening of the walls provoked his slight headiness; by the time he reached the landing, the hall's vibrant colourwash of orange over yellow had completely reversed.

Five doors off the landing: bathroom, two bedrooms, box room, airing cupboard, he guessed. Four white and one red, three white ones shut, one ajar, and the red one wide open, blasting an even bolder Indian scarlet from within. Her room, it had to be.

He let himself into the bathroom and relieved himself into the yellow seventies' pan. The room was covered, wall to wall, in small white tiles with alternating rows of orange and shit-brown marbling. It ranked as his most depressing pee in months. He pulled the flush, rinsed his hands and stepped on to the landing. Time to walk down the stairs and out of her life and, for better or worse, back into his own. A red bedroom, though...

He glanced into the stairwell and trod lightly across the landing, testing the floor for creaks under its vestments of coir. Supporting his weight either side on the architrave, he leaned into the red doorway. To set foot over the threshold would set off alarm bells, in his head, and at St Aldate's and at home.

Even the ceiling was red, a vintage burgundy, even darker than the walls. The floorboards had been varnished the colour of old mahogany and brightened with zigzagging kilims. Pictures of Indian dancers in moulded gilt frames hung on the walls, and across the dressing-table lay a twisted hunk of driftwood on which draped her necklaces and bracelets. The wardrobe and dressing-table, formerly nondescript dark brown pieces of the kind that littered the sales rooms, had been heavily stencilled in black and gold and elevated from dusty auction bargains to exotica that inclined him to rifle the drawers. The most diverting feature, however, had to be the bed. It was surmounted by a gilded setting-sun bed-head, the diverging rays of which fanned almost halfway up the wall. The bed itself, no more than a humble mattress, stood raised on gold-sprayed pallets, and its burgundy and red covers rambled casually over the floorboards. Long swathes of fabric hung down the wall either side of the bed, ready to enclose it, an inner layer of transparent burgundy, and an outer of gold mesh. Beside the mattress stood a pile of magazines and a lamp, a beaten brass globe with a red shade tilted at a jaunty angle towards the mattress. This was a room to fire the imagination. It could be the set for Salome, a bed in which to lie and wait, to doze and dream, surrounded by curtains to conceal or reveal, as required. Dancing women would come with ankle bells and mischievous eyes, women with veils, weeping and distracted.

'What do you think?'

His fingers clawed round the door frame and he hung his head. 'Sorry. It was open.'

'And you couldn't resist peering in?'

'Christ, I'm really sorry –'

'You're a policeman. Why shouldn't you? It's your line of business. I've only just finished the curtains, actually. Bought the material before I lost the job, and I had time on my hands. Go in, I'll show you.'

She was blocking the stairs, and, therefore, his exit. He had overstepped the limits of innocence. She had glimpsed the sexual curiosity beneath his mask of good intent. If she wanted him to admire curtains, he would admire them.

He crossed the threshold of the Indian boudoir. His mouth felt so dry, the skin could have peeled away.

She indicated the window. 'I'm not much of a seamstress, but I'm proud of these. You pull the red ones, then they're framed by the gold drapes and swag.'

She drew one of the curtains to the centre. The daylight halved and he turned his attention, moth-like and mesmerised, to the remaining square of illumination.

'That,' she said, 'the mirror over the dressing-table, I made that, too. Twisted ivy stems sprayed gold, copper foil cut into leaves and an assortment of coloured glass beads from a junk shop.'

'You're extremely talented.'

'And jobless, and nearly broke and dumped by someone I should have dumped only he got round to it first.'

'Seriously,' he said, addressing her reflection, 'have you considered interior design as a career? You'd have people paying you a small fortune to indulge a natural gift.'

'And spend the rest of my life realising other people's visions? I want to do what *I* want.'

'Then persuade the punters they want the same as you. It's easy.'

'Is it?' She faced him and turned the image to reality. 'Then you can walk out of here right now. If you like.'

He crept home at six-thirty under the blanket of dusk, having spent just long enough at the Carpenters' Arms to pick up an irrefutable alibi of tobacco smoke and beer.

Whether it was a natural extension of his duplicity or the effects of downing Morrells too fast he did not know, but as he turned into the estate, he swore that two magpies took flight from the laburnum tree.

18

He's sitting up this afternoon,' said Janice. 'He likes the chair, don't you, Brendan? More natural than lying on your back.'

Karin inquired what she was putting into his feeding bottle.

'This? Antibiotics. He's had a bit of a temperature this last day or so, a nasty little infection.' She stood the bottle on the cabinet. 'It's the catheter. Some people are more susceptible than others. I sent a sample of his wee to the lab when his temperature went up, and now we're on antibiotics and cranberry juice.' She patted him on the shoulder. 'I know which I prefer.' She squeezed between the bed and the supporting wing of the chair and stopped to inspect the box Karin had left on the blanket. She peered through the cellophane at the cocoa-dusted balls on the lining of red serviette. 'They look delicious. Handmade?'

'Rum truffles. I'm going on to a retirement party afterwards.'

'None for us today then, Brendan. Shame.'

Karin let her pass, and pulled another chair round to face him. She rested one arm across her knees, pushed her other hand into his and waited for the squeeze.

'Purely reflex,' Mr Scrivener had told her after her first experience, 'like a newborn grasps hold of a finger, or makes treading movements when you support it upright. I know he appears to be responding - it's only natural to want to believe that - but the reaction isn't what it seems.'

She didn't care. To her it equalled recognition, a sign of greeting. His eyes opened in the morning. He blinked normally all day. At night they closed. At night he slept, as far as she was concerned, and during the day he was awake. Mr Scrivener had his interpretation of consciousness, and she had hers.

She moved into the line of his gaze.

'I'm going as your proxy this evening, Bren, I hope you appreciate that. Yes, they'd have invited me anyway, but I won't know anyone apart from Emrys and Liz. At least it's only Park House. One of the partners offered the use of his place at Boar's Hill, but Emrys was adamant. They even mooted The Randolph. I don't suppose they were too offended when he declined that offer. So Garnham & Foulkes are paying for caterers. I'm sure Liz will have "alerted" everyone, but I think I'd prefer honest gaffes to sympathy.' The sun had moved across the bed. She leaned over and pushed the truffles into the shade. 'Garnham & Foulkes are arranging the leaving present. I made a donation. Not sure what the gift is yet. Something appropriate.'

Brendan opened his mouth and made a series of loose and noisy chewing movements. She glanced back at the chocolates. His tongue hovered uncertainly between his parted lips and he began chewing again.

'*Janice!*'

Karin waved to her up the ward. The nurse left her work and came to the bedside.

'Janice, look! I moved the truffles and he started this. Is he indicating he wants food? Could he be hungry?'

'He had a big feed not twenty minutes before you came.'

'That can't be a coincidence –'

'I'm afraid he can make all kinds of unpredictable movements. They don't necessarily signal anything. Not the meaning you or I might give them, anyway. See, he's stopped.'

He had slipped from quasi-humanity back into his distant, double-glazed world.

*

'Truffles!' Liz thanked her and gave her a smooth, powdery kiss on the cheek. 'I shall have to keep these from Emrys, I can see. Lovely of you to come, Karin. Do you like mulled wine? Paul's dispensing drinks here in the hall. And Emrys is in the sitting-room.'

Emrys came straight over, wearing a grey lounge suit and rebellious turquoise tie patterned with leaping trout.

'I think,' he corrected her, 'they're meant to be salmon.' He caught her by the arm and guided her towards a couple of lean, benevolent-looking older men. 'You know Colin and Aubrey, of course, from tennis?'

She made an effort. She bore up. She ate stroganoff and tiramisu on the settee in the sitting-room next to Colin, and when he disappeared in search of seconds, Liz took his place.

'Coffee's arriving,' she said. 'Have you seen Emrys? He's been meaning to talk to you for some time, but we're off to London on Monday to spend a few days with our daughter, then we fly to Cyprus for a fortnight.' She inclined, with perfect elegance, either side of the couple standing in front of her. 'Never around when you want them. Then they retire. Ah, here come the cups.'

During coffee the guests assembled in the sitting-room.

There were about forty, the partners from Garnham & Foulkes and their wives, plus Emrys' chosen friends. The managing partner made a speech and presented Emrys with a Hardy travelling fly rod in a tube the size of a telescopic umbrella.

'Did he know?' Karin whispered during his speech of thanks.

'If you mean, is that why he's wearing the revolting fish tie, no,' Liz said amiably. 'Actually, the rod was my suggestion, but for heaven's sake don't let on or he'll think I'm trying to get rid of him.' She caught his eye as soon as the round of clapping subsided, and he excused himself and came over, clutching his rod case. 'I've told Karin.'

'Yes?'

'That you need to speak to her, Emrys.'

'Here?' He frowned. 'No, I think not, on reflection. How about tomorrow? I could call round. Is half-nine too early?'

She assured him that half-past nine would be fine, and watched him swoop off to a colleague who had been making invisible fly-casts in his direction, and was now furiously reeling him in.

*

It wasn't fine at all. Something had gone wrong. What could he have to discuss, she'd wondered in the sleepless small hours. Maybe the wills they'd made the preceding year. Why had he delayed till now if the matter was of such great import? And would he have broached it at all if Liz had not smoothed the way in her gentle but practised manner?

'It must be serious,' she said as she showed Emrys in, five minutes early, next morning. She indicated his briefcase. 'I see you've come armed.'

'Yes.' He pinched the knees of his trousers and sat on the sofa beside her. 'We need to discuss Brendan's living will.' He waited, unsmiling. 'Brendan appointed me as his health care proxy a while back. You don't remember?'

She shook her head. 'Though it wouldn't be the first time.'

'Are you quite sure you didn't discuss this? Given the nature of his wishes, I'd be surprised if you'd forgotten. It's usual, you see, for the wife to be named. Particularly when there's an age-gap. I did press, but he felt it wouldn't be beyond the bounds of possibility for you both to be involved in the same accident. Nor did he want you faced with difficult decisions when you might not be best fitted to deal with them.'

'Decisions?'

'Bear with me, Karin. Dear God, he hasn't told you, has he.' Emrys gripped his thumb and fingers across his forehead and massaged his temples. 'As Brendan's proxy, I'm responsible for ensuring his wishes are carried out in the event that he loses mental capacity, his wishes concerning his medical treatment.' He picked up the briefcase from beside the sofa, opened it on the cushion between them, laid some printed papers on his lap and lifted the case on to the carpet by his feet. 'Now, this is the document. Brendan has declared that if, for whatever reason, he becomes permanently unconscious or severely mentally impaired, he wants to be allowed to die with dignity and not be kept alive by medical treatment –'

'But he's off the ventilator now.'

Emrys raised his head. '- when treatment is also taken to include artificial, or tube-feeding and drinking.'

Seconds passed, her brain incapable of response. Her mouth opened. She did not open it, though she felt her lips part.

'Wait! Wait, I know he would have told me. Something as major as this, he would have said...'

'He *should* have told you. I thought it neither necessary nor appropriate to raise the matter earlier. I've been hoping against hope. I've already waited, what, six weeks before approaching you.'

'Weeks!' She was shaking. 'What about the hospital? Nerves can take months to heal. Years. Does the hospital know?'

'It was my duty. I've been in regular contact with Howard and Scrivener, all the medical people –'

'When did Brendan make this?'

'I – Not so very long ago, in fact.' He held the papers out to her. 'It's a copy. You can keep it. I think it's important you read the detail for yourself. There: signed and dated, the fourteenth of January.'

She grabbed the papers and turned savagely through them. 'And he just came to see you, like that, to sign his own death warrant?'

'It wasn't like that at all. He rang me to discuss his wishes and the best way of making sure they were carried out, and we arranged to meet a couple of days later to do the paperwork.'

'And how was he? You might as well know we were going through a bad patch. Whatever you might have thought, I'm sure he wasn't in his right mind.'

'He seemed fine to me. In good spirits, completely normal. And having seen Diana die of the brain tumour, as we all did, his decision wasn't quite as incomprehensible as it may seem to you now. It's a terrible tragedy. But no one has any idea what life is waiting to deal them just around the corner.'

She sniffed. 'You're talking about killing him.'

'Letting someone die with dignity, in accordance with their wishes.'

'Murder.'

'*Look* at the document, Karin. I no more dreamt I'd find myself in this position than you in yours.'

She got up, swinging her arms, the papers unread in her hand. 'What does Mr Scrivener have to say about it?'

'It's an advance directive. He can't ignore it.' Emrys shrugged. 'I'm sorry. My main concern for the moment is that you're aware of the position. Scrivener's the doctor. It would be better for both of us if you spoke to him direct. I'm hoping our time away will give you the chance to discuss the position with him and the family, maybe do some reading round the subject and consider the future in a calmer state of mind. It's not the time to make any decisions now.'

She was examining the wall-paper in the alcove to the right of the fireplace.

'Look, would you like to come home, spend a couple of hours

with Liz? I know she wouldn't mind.'

'I'm better on my own just now, thanks.'

The briefcase clicked shut. Fabric teased over fabric as he got up. A hand came to rest on her shoulder.

'Phone us, if you need. We don't leave till tomorrow morning, and at least one of us should be in. Any time. Don't hesitate.'

He let himself out. As the gravel bit under his feet, she leaned her back to the fresh, brilliant panel of paper. She sank down the wall and sat on the carpet, eyes closed and back erect, propped in position by her sharply bent knees. The fourteenth of January. Four days before her return from Tenerife, seven after her departure. Five days before the row. Ten before the accident. You didn't have to be a genius, or even a mathematician.

She curled over her knees. The wail arose from her guts, deep and inconsolable as an infant's. The cat crept in, his tail low and cautious. He sat on the hearth and watched her, his ears twisting with helpless concern.

She contacted the hospital as soon as she managed to steady her voice. Mr Scrivener was away till Monday afternoon, but someone made her an appointment. Desperate, she rang Zo, refusing to hang up until she answered.

'Suicide?' Zo paced the hearth-rug in her leggings and pyjama top. 'You wake me up and call me all the way to Oxford to tell me Brendan was attempting suicide? That's not funny, Karin. A lot of things happened at once, so what? You can find all sorts of patterns in events if you start looking for them. And I don't – can't – for a moment believe Brendan was trying to take his own life.'

'It was a deadly row,' said Karin, who was hunched on the sofa.

'Everybody has rows. If you have the good fortune to be in a relationship, you have more than the rest of us. You don't rush off and top yourself on account of an argument.' Zo stopped and her eyes darted to the ceiling. 'When did I see you that week?'

'Tuesday.'

'That's right. We had a good laugh. He didn't give the slightest impression of being emotionally crushed.'

'Be more specific.'

Zo put her fist on her hip. 'As I recall, he was very jolly. Joking, full of smiles. Very chatty for him.'

'More cheerful than usual?'

'I assumed a reconciliation was on the cards. Like you.'

'You'd never have guessed anything was wrong, in fact?'

'Shit.' Zo pushed her fingers through her hair behind her neck and then covered her nose. 'Oh, shit. His remedy's Aurum.'

'*Cheerful, death, while thinking of...* Single symptom. *Death, desires, thoughts of, joy, give him... Delusion, unfit for the world...* Et cetera.' Karin inflated her cheeks and blew into the air. 'As for how far he planned what happened —' She shrugged. 'I was in a state myself. Not fit to notice anything.'

Zo's bulk bounced on to the sofa beside her. She rested a consolatory hand on Karin's upper arm and pushed a couple of times till Karin's shoulders swayed with the pressure.

'Hey, it could still have been an accident.'

'Yeah. Yeah, I keep feeding myself that life-line. We managed to keep out of each other's way on the Saturday. Then next day... ground zero.'

Zo dug her fists into the sofa cushions. 'Time to make us a drink,' she said decisively, getting to her feet. 'I'll listen, if you want to talk. But I'm not pushing.'

From the kitchen Karin heard the gush of water filling the kettle, and the music of mugs and spoons sliding along the work-top. The cadences were immediately recognisable, the rhythms old and soothing, if slowed by Zo's lack of instant familiarity with the kitchen.

'So...' Zo said afterwards, swilling round the dregs of her hot chocolate as she paced in front of the sofa. 'Where do you think he went?'

'Christ Church Meadows, he said.'

'You don't think -?'

'No, I believed him.' Karin swallowed a mouthful of chamomile tea. 'He wasn't gone long anyway, and he came back as sulky as sin. Then after work on Monday, a transformation. Shrugged it off as though nothing had happened. He said there was nothing to forgive, and I began to think, with time –'

'And was there?'

Karin stared into her lap.

'So, in one breath you're telling me you went to Tenerife with the express aim of screwing someone, and in the next you stonewall me for querying the outcome.'

'There are holiday firms that trade on the perennial quest for a shag. Get real, Zo. People do it all the time.'

'*You* don't. Though I understand your reaction. Anyone would have felt the same. It's that pride of yours all over, in spades.' Zo stretched out her hand towards the sofa. 'God, Brendan must really love you.'

*

She occupied herself that afternoon with some cases, weeded the backlog of messages from the answering-machine and drew up a list of return calls to be made the following morning and evening. Two patients had cancelled follow-ups that week and wanted their appointments re-scheduled. There were four requests for advice for non-emergency acutes, and a call from Inspector Straker leaving a number but no message. The policeman's call worried her, and she rang back straight away. The phone was answered by a youth whose voice had not quite broken, and who gave a petulant croak for his father.

'Jim Straker speaking.'

'It's Karin Shilan. You asked me to call.'

'Yes, indeed! I'd like to make an appointment to see you.'

'About my husband?'

'On a personal matter, actually. As a homœopath.'

He inquired after Brendan.

'He's stable, Inspector.' There didn't seem much else to say. Either she told him everything, as a wretched wife, or, as the professional homœopath, she told him nothing. 'But I'm afraid my patient list is almost full at the moment, and I'm looking to create a little more time for Brendan and myself over the next few weeks. However, if the problem can't wait I'd be happy to recommend someone –'

'You come highly recommended yourself. Jungle drums...'

She thanked him. 'Though I assure you the person I have in mind is excellent. We trained at the same college, and I've known her for eight years, professionally and socially. We locum for each other. She's very down-to-earth. I think you'd get on well.' She paused, reaching for a pen. 'Should I give her your number?'

'It's an impressive testimonial...'

'Seymour is the name,' she said. 'Zoe Seymour.'

19

She glanced at the clock on the back wall of her consulting-room: nearly three-thirty. Almost finished. Almost time to leave for her interview with Mr Scrivener.

'You're chilly,' she read, looking back over her sheaf of hand-written notes, 'and you feel worse for being in the open air?'

'Yes.'

The moment she felt it coming, she pressed her lips hard together. Her lower jaw dropped at the articulation. Ligaments tensed and clicked inside her head. With considerable effort she dissipated the movement sideways in a twisting, gargoyle grimace that seemed to last forever. Yawning in the presence of a client: betrayal, nothing but betrayal. Part of her life had collapsed into the Atlantic, and the shock wave was carrying its repercussions far into space and time. Fortunately, Ms Brown, mute with misery, did not raise her eyes from her lap.

'And during your periods, how is the sadness then?'

'Better. Yes, actually. Better.'

Karin slotted her ball-point between her teeth, masking another yawn, and tapped a few rubrics into her laptop.

'Periods, heavy and very dark...'

She sent the woman away with a sachet of Cyclamen. She closed the front door after her client, yawned without covering her mouth and watched through the hall window till the woman vanished beyond the camellia.

In the kitchen she poured herself a glass of apple juice from a carton in the fridge and drank it, poured a second and sat on the bench. Cyclamen, the female Aurum. The failed Vesta, beating herself up for flunking the self-imposed duties of the domestic goddess. Ms Brown had despondency without desperation, though, sadness without suicide. She lacked Brendan's drive.

The brown liquid in the tumbler bit like cold acid into her stomach. She turned to the sink and slung the remaining half-glass in iodine-yellow streaks over the porcelain.

*

Mr Scrivener welcomed her into his office with an expansive gesture that directed her to a seat at the side of a cluttered desk. He towed his black swivel chair from the desk and turned it to face her.

'I gather,' he said, sitting down, 'that Mr Clifford has spoken to you about actioning Brendan's living will.'

'Mr Scrivener,' she flung at him, 'people with head injuries can make a spontaneous recovery after six months, can't they? Six months or more? This is six weeks! And how can you pass judgment on his cognitive abilities when he's so disabled? He can't communicate with you. Do you read his mind? Surely, with medical advances, they might be able to save him, implant cells, or stimulate his brain. Aren't they already doing that kind of thing? Who's to say what might be possible?'

He shifted on his seat. Without the white coat, his dark suit looked even longer and more funereal.

'I can't deny the rate of technological advance, Mrs McDonald, especially in neurology and related fields, and I can identify with how you must feel. But that isn't the issue here.'

'He's my husband! My husband!'

'I'm afraid your husband also has the right to make his own decisions regarding how he lives his life, and how he chooses to die. Brendan has declared his wishes, in advance, before a solicitor, and I'm obliged to give serious consideration to his instructions -'

'Even though he'll die as a result?' Her voice rose in desperation. 'You'll be acting unlawfully, Mr Scrivener, because my husband is committing suicide.'

His face froze. He blinked once. 'Brendan declined to consent to treatment that might prolong his existence. That is not suicide.'

'He wasn't in his right mind when he made the living will. Does that make a difference to your obligations?'

'Mr Clifford led me to believe he was a long-standing friend–'

'In my experience, any deceit is possible given the motivation. He's a thorough man, my husband. Nothing gets left to chance. Not even his own survival.' Her eyes smarted and a tear ran down the side of her nose. 'He stepped in front of that car to die.'

Mr Scrivener marked a lengthy pause. 'Can you substantiate this? Coroners tend not to return verdicts of suicide unless there's very clear evidence to support it. Did your husband leave a note?'

'I spent most of yesterday looking. The office, bedroom, drawers all over the house. I checked his computer. I went through his room in Pembroke College, and this morning I called one of his colleagues. They checked his room in Physiology, and the labs. But I don't need proof for what I instinctively know.'

'I see.' He pushed his hands up either side of his face and pulled them sideways to his temples, sitting for some moments with his head lowered and his eyes closed. 'And on the same basis, do you think it's in Brendan's best interests to spend the rest of his life as he is now? Because medical advances don't arrive to order, or come with any guarantees. He can't see. He can't hear, or experience pleasure or pain. He can't move. He can't communicate in any way, shape or form. He has no apparent cognitive function whatever. He's completely insensate. We did an EEG on Friday.' He twisted on his chair, picked up a file from the desk and thumbed though the papers inside. 'The traces I'm going to show you were recorded from the part of the brain called the cerebral cortex.'

As an afterthought he laid the file on his knees and picked up the crinkly, pale yellow plastic brain beside his desk-tidy.

'I know where the cortex is, Mr Scrivener.'

The brain went back on the table. He leafed through a pile of papers there and from it drew a sheet which he left beside the pile. Then he bent the file open from the top with the fingers of his left hand and held it in front of his chest. She leaned forward, her brow creasing at the sight of the rows of lines. She stretched out her hand.

'Just the general appearance will be enough,' he said. 'And for comparison...' He held up the second sheet beside the file. 'A normal EEG.'

'God...'

'Without going into details you can see the dominant rhythm is grossly subdued in Brendan's trace. There's a bit of intermittent activity here,' he said, indicating from above with his second finger hooked, 'and there are some low amplitude theta waves here, but generally it's pretty low frequency stuff.'

'At least something is happening...'

'The vegetative state is a behavioural diagnosis. We don't need to show a complete absence of cortical activity, just a lack of behaviour that would indicate a functioning mind.' He replaced the file and paper on the desk. 'Mrs McDonald, even if he doesn't die he'll never achieve independence. He'll need permanent, full-time nursing care just to keep him alive. As for his alleged suicide, I certainly lack any intent to assist in it. His own intent I can't vouch for, but his death would be caused by his injuries, not by discontinuing feeding and hydration. Without modern technology he would have died within days. Hours, more likely. To my mind, what he wants – and deserves – is to die with dignity.'

'Is that what you call it?'

'Believe me, his own choice is the most dignified of the

options.'

She shifted forward on the cushion, slumped against the chair back and lost her gaze into the glare of the lights.

'What would happen to him? I mean -?'

'Dehydration,' Scrivener said gently. 'It would upset the chemical balance of his body fluids and eventually cause the major organs to fail. It would take one to two weeks.'

'I see. And how long do you anticipate before Mr Clifford -?'

'Nothing more will happen until his return from Cyprus. At which time I'll apply to the Courts through the Trust solicitors seeking permission to go ahead. Particularly as you have reservations. We'll assemble all the medical evidence, arrange for independent assessments... Look, if we carry on as we are now, I estimate he'll be dead, from infection or general systemic failure, in three years. Almost certainly within five. My feeling is that if he survives at all, it will be an appalling existence. Think of the quality of life he's had, the job, the status, the satisfaction that go with them. Do you really think the chance of ending up just outside a vegetative state is preferable to being in it? Would that be his choice? And do you think he'd want to inflict this living millstone on you?'

She hesitated. 'I don't know.'

'What?'

'No —'

'I don't understand. What *do* you want for him?'

'Time. To buy time and pray the miracle happens.'

Two vertical furrows appeared between his eyebrows. He closed his eyes and pinched the bridge of his nose.

'Mrs McDonald, no amount of time will heal your husband. It would take the miracle. When a person is abducted and presumed murdered, the family has no peace until the body is found. Then hope is lost and replaced by certainty. A tragic, life-changing certainty, but one that allows them to say their goodbyes. They know their lives will never be the same again, but at least they can get on with them. Well, the person you love is lost too. The difference is that his body persists. Outwardly he's intact and alive, but it's an illusion, no more than an illusion of humanity. As long as he lies in that bed you'll never be able to grieve. Please, let him go. That's what he wants.'

'It cures everything, doesn't it.'

'I'm sorry?'

'Death,' she said. 'The best remedy of all.'

Sheila cut across the ward and stopped her, intercepted her before she could reach Brendan.

'I should warn you,' Sheila said, 'we think he may have a slight respiratory infection. The urine test has come back clear, but his temperature's up again and he's definitely wheezy.'

'A chest infection?' Her own breathing tightened at the thought. 'Isn't that serious?'

'We've caught it early. We've sent some sputum for analysis and put him on antibiotics. The labs should be able to track down the specific drug for us. I was just going to suck him out before getting him in his chair. Would you like to do it? Everything you need is there.' Sheila walked off down the aisle of the ward. 'I'll go and fetch the hoist.'

Karin bent over her husband's supine form. 'I know what you did.' Her teeth, her lips scarcely let the words pass. 'They might not believe me, but *I know.*' She picked up the nearest hand and gripped his fingers in hers till they criss-crossed like jack-straws. It should have hurt. She intended it to. '*Why?* Why, why, *why?*'

She yanked on his arm, and he slid sideways on the pillow. His head drooped, but still he stared straight ahead, seeming to mock her more. She pushed him upright again, laid her coat and bag on a chair and went to wash her hands.

She snapped on the sterile gloves, took the end of the catheter and fed it through the tracheostomy and down into his lungs with one hand, carefully occluding the tube with the other. When the catheter was deep enough inside him she began to retract it, rolling the tube between her fingers while releasing the pressure with her right hand so that the suction machine could do its work. She remembered watching with horror the very first time she'd seen Carla suck him out, how the choking white slime had crawled up the tube and fallen into the bottle, how she'd walked to the toilet afterwards, feeling sick. The thought was disgusting, but the deed itself turned out to be reassuring and oddly intimate.

She withdrew the catheter, dipped its end into the pot of sterile water and sucked that through to free the bore of its gelatinous contents, before snaking the tube back inside his airway and repeating the process. The secretions were thicker and more copious than usual.

'All finished?'

Sheila shoved and tugged the great hoist into position beside the bed. Karin helped her pass the straps of the sling under his back, buttocks and legs, and watched as Sheila operated the hydraulics to lift him into position above the waiting chair. She put out her hand to steady his swinging body and lowered him on to the rubber cushion. She unhitched the sling, then laid a blanket over his knees and arranged pillows under his elbows and round his neck.

'There we are,' she said, puffing as she wheeled the hoist to the end of the bed. 'I'll leave you to it.'

Karin moved her own chair just in front of his, took his hands and positioned her head so that his eyes coincided with hers.

'Brendan, were you trying to escape from me?' She softened her hold on his hands. 'Were you that desperate, or did you really hate me? Because if you did it to punish me, you've succeeded. If you wanted to dump the responsibility for your death on my doorstep, I feel responsible. But I don't want to carry it for the rest of my life.' She parted his hands and laid her forehead into the concave of his palms. 'Or were you punishing yourself? Is that it? Oh God, I'm sorry. Please come back. I just want you back.'

She buried her nose in his fingers, but he didn't smell of Brendan anymore; he smelled of laundries and hospital soap.

*

Her foot began its numb, tell-tale needling the moment she lay down in bed that night. With a sigh of grim resignation she drew up her right knee. Her foot slid across the sheet, dragging at the end of her leg like a rubber brick, dense and inert. She reached down the bed to massage it, but her sole curled and twisted involuntarily beneath her hand with a cold, drawing pain that intensified to the point of making her cry out. Gripping the front of her shin with both hands she fought to flex her foot, only for it to arch and warp again with the unseen malignant force. She gritted her teeth and persisted, alternately stretching and raising, stretching and raising her foot until the cramp and the pain began to subside. It was the only way.

She let her foot drop to the mattress and slid her leg back down the bed. The angular mound of bedcovers softened over the void. She smacked it flat with her hand, leaned over and turned out the lamp. Until her nerves wore themselves out and gave up their restless jangling, even reading would be impossible. Sleep ranked well down her body's order of priorities. She shut her eyes, but even in these warm, moist, shadowy wings, Brendan lay ready to ambush her. She rolled over and waited unoptimistically for sleep to claim her. His features seemed to her, in reality, to be growing more and more juvenile, more rounded and plastic. His dependent state had not warped her perception. He simply had the face of an infant these days, even Janice agreed.

She tried to erase him, but from the pulped features appeared the waiter. When she exiled the waiter, Roy Meredith emerged. Photographs and negatives, those could be consigned to the dustbin and incinerated, but memories could only be bricked up. Worse, the bricks were porous, the mortar weak; they could hold their secrets only for so long. Then the walls came down, and the past, dusty and pop-eyed, stared one right back in the face.

And maybe she should have taken Jim Straker on, though Philippa Cooling had brought her four new clients in the past fortnight, and she was tired. Philippa Cooling was one of the worried well. Karin used to watch her four-wheel drive describe its arduous pentacle in the gravel before crawling back on to the road. They all had four-wheel drives, the worried well, four-wheel drives with bull-bars like Victorian radiators. Anyway, Zo hadn't turned Straker down; he was a thank-you present for standing in during her trip to Tenerife. With these cramps she really needed an appointment herself...

20

The front door banged shut.

'Jim?'

'Hello.'

The mackintosh rustled across the hall and into the dining-room behind him.

'I thought you'd have left by now. What time is your appointment?'

'Six.' He turned back to the window. 'Look at them.'

Hilary joined him and surveyed the garden.

'In the blackthorn, Hil. Magpies. I'm sure they're looking for a nest site. We've got robins and blackbirds in the hedge. Between Orpheus and the magpies it'll be a blood-bath. I'll have to destroy the nest.'

'Jim, they haven't even built one yet.' Hilary shrugged off her beige coat and cuddled it in her arms. 'Anyway, it's nature. There have always been cats, and there have always been magpies.'

'Never so many of either,' he muttered.

He hunched his shoulders and caught Hilary doing one of her silent sighs. She went into the kitchen.

'Cup of tea before you go?'

'Thanks, but I'd better make a move.'

'Nervous?'

'No! Well...'

The freezer door opened and something dense and brittle banged on to a work-top. One of the magpies swooped down from the branches and landed on the lawn with a couple of hops and an upward flick of its tail. It paused for a second and stalked across the grass, its head and tail held high. In his mind, Straker spat. The bird stabbed its beak half-heartedly into the earth, then raised its head and looked directly at him. Straker made a fist to rap on the glass, then pulled back the sliding door and stepped on to the patio. The magpie crouched, uncertain, then launched itself into flight and fled with rapid, heavy wing beats into the branches of the chestnut.

He went back inside. He slid the door across, pressed it home into the frame and locked it before going to fetch his wind-cheater from the cloakroom.

'Guess what,' he called. 'Daniel walked home from school today with a girl.'

'Emma. She's his girlfriend. Sweet 'n' sour pork okay?'

He sighed, and shut the front door to the plaintive beeping of the microwave.

*

He found a parking space in one of the side-streets, and walked back to the Cowley Road. He had clocked the Natural Health Centre a number of years ago. It was the kind of place he'd noticed and then forgotten about, other than to wonder whether such a venture could possibly survive. Cowley Road was the home of the halal hot dog, a mecca for second-hand furniture only two minutes from the wealth and grandeur of Magdalen, and a battleground where bars and cafés sparred for trade with the latest paint effects. What it lacked in architecture and investment it made up with a gritty determination to survive in whatever form dictated by the need or fad of the moment, and whilst that brought a regular turnover in businesses, the Natural Health Centre remained.

In the middle of the pavement outside lay a discarded cigarette, half-smoked but intact, still burning in the breeze that hustled across the pavement. He stepped over it.

The Centre was painted in yellow and dark green. It could have been a pharmacy once. The door, a large expanse of plate glass with a brass handle, looked original. The windows either side were made a little more discreet by alternating panels of lime and turquoise bead curtains, through which he could just make out a water filter and a row of chairs.

A hand-printed note had been taped to the inside of the door: *Push Hard*. He complied, and stepped on to a coconut mat set in a brass surround. He half-expected to hear the tang of a bell overhead.

The ground-floor was decorated a softer green. It looked to have been split, with the reception desk and stairs at the front, and a door marked *Osteopathy* in the partition. On the walls hung some prints, a rack of complementary therapy brochures and a notice-board stuck with small ads and curling business cards. A couple of self-absorbed men sat limply on the seats, and a woman with a child occupied the sofa. No one spoke, but the child smiled and banged two chunky wooden animals at him.

He made himself known to the girl with dreadlocks at the reception desk, and followed her directions to the waiting area on the upstairs landing. He sat alone in the alcove of seats and took in the mural of wishy-washy angelic forms on the opposite wall. From his seat he could see four doors, two to his left and two to his right, all shut. Three were numbered and marked 'Engaged' on a sliding plaque. The fourth had a picture of a cherubic child on a potty. Low voices could be heard.

He glanced at a poster of acupuncture meridians, and another showing a buddha with blobs of coloured light down his front. He picked up a magazine from the pile on top of the pot cupboard: *Caduceus*. He turned through a few of the others. *Kindred Spirit*. His heart began to race. *The Big Issue*. *Positive News*.

'Jim Straker?'

Her face appeared round the door jamb so unexpectedly that he could only nod, his mouth pinched to nothing. The door swung wide; Zoe Seymour almost filled the frame, a large, cheerful woman with the charm and finesse of a rottweiler.

He got up. She introduced herself and extended a hand, which he eyed before managing a perfunctory response.

'Do you have your medical history with you, by any chance? I know you haven't had much time -'

He presented it from his trouser pocket.

'Marvellous! If you could just give me a couple of moments to look through...'

She disappeared back into room 1. He sat down and got straight up again, ostensibly to make a closer inspection of the acupuncture meridians. The figure reminded him of Spider Man, a New Age Spider Man far more sinister, somehow, than the original. The other side of that hung a poster entitled 'Healing Foods In Chinese Medicine.' Foods to increase heat, foods to cool. Foods to clear damp and phlegm. Disgusting. He thought with fondness of the sweet and sour pork waiting for him at home.

'Mr Straker, Jim. Do come in.'

Spider Woman. No escape. Off to the Interview Room where, for the first time, he would not be the one putting the questions.

He swallowed and entered the room like a self-conscious stork. The walls were unobtrusive enough, the colour of rind on clotted cream. There was an old sash window at the far end with a café net curtain filtering in the last of the evening light. He raised himself on his toes: it overlooked a long, narrow yard sprawling with ivy and elder. To the side of the window stood a desk. Apart from that there were three chairs, a therapy couch with a roll of hand towel and a box of tissues on it, a plastic box of toys, a bin, a rubber plant and some pictures.

'Please, sit down.'

There was a choice of two seats, side by side. He looked from one to the other: a hard-back with a padded cushion, and a dark green director's chair.

'Either,' she said, settling on to her seat by the desk. 'It's not a test.' She cocked an ankle over her other knee and laid a clipboard across the triangle. 'Now, some questions you'll be expecting, others might surprise you. All I'm trying to do is build up an accurate picture for the purposes of prescription. Also, if I'm not looking at you, don't worry; I'm taking notes, not ignoring you.'

She started with his main symptoms, for which he happily furnished the details.

'And have you seen the doctor about your prostate?'

He nodded. 'Not that it's especially painful. Or consistent. Sometimes it hurts when I pee, sometimes afterwards. Other times not at all.'

She wanted to know what kind of pain he experienced. 'Is it cutting, for example, or pressing? Throbbing, dull, stabbing...?'

'Pressing, I'd say, pressing.'

'And is there any position that relieves the symptoms when you urinate?'

He stared at her. 'I can't say I change position once I start. I've only ever tried standing.'

'When did the symptoms begin?'

'About a year ago.'

The pen swept with a dry scraping sound across the paper.

'Anything major happening in your life around that time?'

'Nope. Not that I can recall.'

'Tell me about yourself, Jim, what kind of person you are.'

He felt his eyebrows rising. 'Well, I always discharge my police duties to the best of my ability. I think I can say I'm pretty good at it. I'm quite orderly, I suppose. I can keep my cool when the situation demands. The job does make you cynical, though. Hard. And I find difficulty taking anybody or anything at face value any more. But everyone ends up like it. After a while you stop noticing.' He paused. 'I'm a bit of a loner. I enjoy golf. I like bird watching. It's not that I mind other people being about. As long as they don't bother me.'

'Family?'

'Two kids. Anyta, sixteen. Dan, fourteen. "The Lodger," they call me.' He made a small, ironic laugh. 'I guess it's a case of survival till retirement. There's not a lot else I'm qualified for. Not forgetting they're off to college in a couple of years.'

'Do you have a partner?'

'Hilary. My wife.' He studied the ceiling and massaged his throat. 'Rather like with the kids. You know, I work, she works. We don't see enough of each other, but then, most families are like that these days, aren't they.'

She offered no corroboration. He watched her pen scuttle across the page.

'Mr Straker,' she said suddenly, 'please could you tell me something about your physical relationship with your wife?'

'It's fine, thanks.'

'Your libido?'

'Fine. As it ever was.'

'All right.' She paused. 'Anything else?'

'I don't think so, no.'

He made a point of assessing the nearest picture, which appeared to show wishy-washy angelic forms in a dark forest. There was the sound of lines being drawn, like whiplashes, on the page. How could she be putting down so much? Was she writing in Chinese?

He shifted his weight and fiddled with his fingers. The idea of the director's chair had appealed more than the reality of being suspended by the backside on a canvas belt.

'Tell me about your childhood.'

'Father was a pharmacist, I have two older brothers and a younger sister. My mother didn't work.'

'What sort of memories do you have?'

'Of my childhood?' He considered. 'I was a boy by default really. Eric got away with it because he was the firstborn. Julian turned out to be gifted: chess for fun, Mensa for fun, little round glasses due to excess fun. Professorship at Durham. And I was the daughter my father had always wanted. Apparently my mother dowsed me with her wedding ring. The pink shawl was at the ready. I was a bit of a let-down. I didn't have the novelty value of being the first. I didn't have a brain the size of Wales. I was practical rather than intellectual. I was a waste of space, and not even female.'

Zoe Seymour watched him very intently. 'How did you get on with your sister?'

'Angela?' He chuckled. 'I used to torture her. Oh, nothing serious, just teasing, tweaking her hair. Anything to make her cry. She looked really ugly then. Her mouth used to go like an elastic band. Needless to say, we aren't close.'

'And your father?'

'He wasn't the first misguided parent in the world, and he won't be the last. I get on best with Eric, not that we see a great deal of each other because he lives in Sheffield. Weddings, Christenings, funerals. Landmark anniversaries. You know the kind of thing.'

She waited for a while. It seemed a satisfied silence. 'I note from your medical history you had gonorrhoea when you were twenty.'

'Well,' he said, 'yes. I horsed round a bit as a teenager. You play, you pay, don't you.'

'Tell me all about it,' said Hilary, setting his dinner on the place-mat on the dining-room table. 'Has she given you a remedy?'

'She's posting it. She wants to work on my case.' He screwed the head of the salt-mill back and forth over the steam of his sweet and sour pork. 'It's weird, talking in such depth to a complete stranger. Liberating, in a way.' He forked in a chunk of meat, then opened his mouth and panted out a couple of puffs of searing air. 'Every fart, belch and rumble, she wanted to know about it. My preferences in food and drink... My appetite. That woman knows more about my call to stool than any other person alive. Sleep. Dreams.' He stood the end of his fork on the place-mat. 'What makes me feel better or worse... They're big on that. Fears...'

'You don't have any,' said Hilary. 'Do you?'

*

When he arrived back from making love to Nadine after early turn on Wednesday, there was a lumpy brown envelope waiting on the kitchen table. He picked up the envelope to open it, but someone – Hilary - had already done the honours. He fished out a cigar of bubble-wrapping and a compliment slip: *Remedy enclosed – one daily, 24 hours apart, sucked under the tongue. Avoid taking it near meal-times or tooth-brushing, and don't forget to cut down the coffee for a few days afterwards. Best wishes, Zo Seymour.*

He picked the sticky tape undone, unrolled the bubble-wrap and inside it found a tiny plastic sachet with his name printed on the label strip. Inside that were two small, crumbly-looking white tablets. Was that it? Hours of talk distilled into two little pills?

The cooker clock showed just gone four. That would do. He pinched either side of the sachet to snap the seal, and tapped it against his hand until one of the tablets slid out. Cupping his hand near his mouth, he pressed the tip of his tongue to the tablet and flipped it inside. He stared out of the kitchen window, concentrating, while the tablet softened and moistened to a paste in his saliva.

He half-expected something momentous, a wave of unconditional love for his father, a loss of desire for Nadine, or an urge to pee which he would be able to execute in a strong and uninterrupted stream. He expected witchcraft, but it seemed no more exciting than paracetamol. He would have to wait.

21

'I'm going to Matthew's tomorrow.'

'This is a first,' Joanna Cleaveley confided as she wiped her shoes on the front mat. 'He can't wait.'

Jordan nodded gravely and stepped, with the presence of a laird, into the hallway.

By the time the women entered the consulting-room, he had already arranged his coat on the back of one of the patients' chairs and installed himself on the seat, his feet swinging in gentle unison back and forth above the carpet. His mother sat down next to him. Karin picked up her clipboard.

'So, who is Matthew?'

'My friend from school.' The legs began to swing harder and

faster. 'I'm having tea at his house. He's got a train set. And if I get two more stars, I get a gold one and Mrs Watts lets you pick a sweet from the jar in her secret cupboard.'

'She rang me up, actually,' said Joanna Cleaveley. 'He was getting on so much better with the other children. In fact, she wanted to know if he was on medication because the improvement in his work was quite marked.'

'Wow! Mrs Watts rang your Mum?'

Teeth began to show through Jordan's smile.

'The eczema's resolved now,' said Joanna Cleaveley, 'and we're sleeping better. I mean, we're all sleeping better, even Charlie. I'm not saying things are perfect. We still have our moments, but things are definitely moving in the right direction. He's much less aggressive these days, more focused. The whole family seems calmer, and tranquillity is not a word that springs naturally to mind in our household. Two little pills... Amazing.' Creases appeared between Joanna Cleaveley's eyebrows. 'This improvement, how long might we expect it to last?'

Karin finished writing. 'The more balanced and stable life is for him, at school and at home, the longer I'd expect the remedy to hold. Two to four months? It depends. Then you might begin to notice a return of some of his old behaviour, in which case I'll repeat the remedy. But for the moment...' Karin gestured to the boy as though presenting a conductor to a theatre audience. 'I'd say Jordan's doing brilliantly. That's it. And I'll see you again in five weeks unless you notice any deterioration.' She picked up her diary and flapped through the pages. 'How about same day, same time, April the ninth?'

Joanna Cleaveley agreed the appointment. Karin jotted it in the diary and copied the details on the back of one of her business cards, which she handed over.

'That should be just before you break up for Easter, Jordan. Do you reckon you'll get your gold star before Easter?'

His lips disappeared into his mouth and he nodded vigorous approval. 'I'll have five gold stars before Easter. No, this many.' He jumped off the chair and indicated as far above his head as he could reach. 'A hundred.'

She showed his mother to the consulting-room door. Jordan snatched his coat from the back of the chair and made a quick detour to the cheese plant. He inclined slightly and inspected the compost, then skipped past his mother into the hall.

'Oh,' said Joanna Cleaveley, pausing in the doorway, 'I was wondering whether you could see my grandfather sometime. He's well into his seventies, but Jordan's response is so encouraging...'

'Of course.' Karin went back for her diary. 'Would you like to make the appointment now? I'd be happy to arrange a home visit –'

'God, no! Let him come by bus. He goes everywhere by bus. Likes to manage for himself, you know, even when he can't, leaving me tactfully picking up the pieces while he denies all knowledge. I must confess I haven't actually suggested the homœopathy yet. I think it could do him a lot of good, but he'll have to chew it over for a while and get used to the idea.'

'I can see him on a donation basis, if that will help...'

'Thanks, but I'll pay. He'll take a home visit as an insult, but he can't resist a freebie. His cupboards are stuffed with all manner of disgusting samples he's squirrelled away and never used.'

Karin saw them out. Halfway down the steps, Jordan stopped and turned.

'At Matthew's house,' he shouted, 'we're having chips. And dinosaur feet. And chips!'

*

It had been a nice, short follow-up, and left her just enough time to repertorise Brendan's case before Zo arrived for supper. He'd been on the Belladonna for three weeks. In any event, she saw no harm in re-assessing the case. Zo would furnish her opinion, invited or not.

She took a piece of scrap paper and began scribbling down the symptoms she needed to cover. The range was expanding without a doubt, but, for a prescriber who set great store by the mentals and emotionals, Brendan's totality still looked bald and threadbare.

Finally she called up his file on the laptop, copied over the rubrics still pertinent to the picture, and added the list of new ones:

Face: *chewing motion of the jaw*
Mouth: *motion, tongue, lapping to and fro*
Mind: *gestures, makes: involuntary motions*
Extremities: *contraction of muscles and tendons*
Eye: *staring*
Mind: *grunting*
Mind: *moaning*
Mind: *grimaces*

'Show us, then,' Zo ordered, nosing over Karin's shoulder, her after-dinner coffee still in hand but precariously ignored. 'What did you come up with? Anything interesting?'

Karin recalled the case for the second time that evening and let Zo peruse the grid of remedies thrown up by the programme.

'They're pretty similar to the last lot, aren't they? No Glonoinum. Lycopodium instead, I see. I've just given your policeman Lycopodium.'

'Already?'

'I had a cancellation last night. It matched his shift. Why wait?'

Karin blew loudly and returned her attention to the screen. 'And how was "my policeman?"'

'Out of his depth, but not unamenable. Looks like a strong case.' Zo finished her mugful of coffee in steady, snorting gulps. 'I notice Belladonna heads the cast. Interesting, in view of what's been happening this past few weeks.'

Karin wrinkled her nose.

'Oh? Don't you think you're on the right track?'

'Not sure. The progress seems to have ground to a halt. I was hoping for a clear change of remedy, but I suppose on this basis I could repeat the Belladonna.' Karin hesitated. 'I don't know that he's up to a CM.'

'So, repeat the 50M. Easy.' Zo leaned forward. 'What else

have we got?'

'A clear corner in the Solanaceae... Belladonna, Stramonium, Hyoscyamus. Phosphorus second, mind. Those four are the only ones that cover both the contractures and the involuntary movement, the symptoms central to the case. The next five score about the same, but Helleborus lacks the contractures. Aconite, Opium and Lycopodium don't have the movement. Lachesis has neither.' Karin dropped her elbows on to her knees and put her face in her hands. 'I need more time.'

'You can't blame Scrivener -'

'Yeah, Zo, I forgot: he's just doing his job.' Karin chopped with both hands at the air. 'He honestly believes it's the right decision. He's already got a scan and EEG lined up for the hearing.'

'I see.' Zo ran her tongue between her upper gum and lips. 'You're not thinking of opposing the hospital's application?'

'I don't know.'

'They're doing what Brendan wants.'

'I don't *know*.'

Zo pulled one of the chairs closer to the desk and sat down, her knees parted and her fingers laced round the empty mug.

'Karin, it's possible Brendan's going to die anyway, whatever we do. You've got to face up to it.'

'Not their way.'

'But what grounds will you object on?'

'It's not an objection in principle. If we can carry on treating him and exhaust the possibilities at least I can give up with the satisfaction of knowing we did our best. If I can buy nine months, even six months, I know I'll feel more confident about his chances. Either way. This is just too quick. Wouldn't you feel the same?'

'If...' Zo slid her mug on to the desk, hooked her fingers round the edge of the seat between her legs and began to rock. 'If, by the time the hearing came round, he was still showing no signs of improvement, I would –' Her eyes drifted up the lemon folds of curtain and settled on the pelmet '- I think I'd want to set him free.' There was a long silence. 'It doesn't mean I won't support you, whatever you decide. When the coin spins on its edge you always see both sides. But it has to fall one way or the other in the end.' She nodded to the glowing grid on the screen of the laptop. 'How much time have we got?'

'Nearly three weeks. Scrivener wasn't sure how long it would take to get a court hearing after that. He thought weeks rather than months. Still, at least we have that window.'

'Maybe the situation will have changed by then,' said Zo, 'who knows? Go on, tomorrow. Repeat the Belladonna.'

22

She'd repeated the Belladonna a month ago. Now came the turn of Hyoscyamus.

Brendan was propped up in the chair on pillows, with the hoist taking up most of the spare space. He moved his right hand and idly scratched his flank through his pyjamas, his head unmoving, his eyes transfixed. Mr Scrivener never saw scratching, choosing instead to witness 'fragments of unco-ordinated movement.' The scratching stopped. All fragments of movement stopped, but for his blinking and the rise and fall of his chest.

She pulled aside the blanket covering his knees, eased up his pyjama leg, and in the crook of his knee she rubbed a little of the solution of Hyoscyamus 50M. Brendan might have lost his mentals and emotionals, but if the memory of them remained behind, like an energetic imprint, maybe Hyoscyamus would key into it.

Atropa Belladonna, Datura Stramonium, Hyoscyamus Niger. Deadly nightshade, thorn-apple and henbane: three poisonous plants of the order *Solanaceae*, and some of the wildest remedies in the homœopathic materia medica. And she was dosing Brendan with the lot, one after the other.

She'd lectured on them not ten days earlier at college: Belladonna with the first years, three hours of comparative work with the third years.

'The more poisonous the plant, the more evocative its common names tend to be,' she told the first years.

She asked whether they knew any of deadly nightshade's synonyms. The students, sitting in a sociable semicircle of chairs, floor cushions and meditation stools, knew none.

'Well, there's black cherry and great morel... The divale and dwayberry, both from the Old Norse *dvali*, meaning delay or sleep. Naughty man's cherries...' That caused a ripple of amusement. 'And tradition has it that the devil tends this plant with meritorious diligence, save for Walpurgis night, when the witches' sabbat makes a greater claim on his presence. The generic name comes from the Greek Fate, Atropos, old Atropos poised with her shears to snip the thread of human life.'

Atropa Belladonna had done nothing for him at all. She had followed it with more Stramonium. Stinkweed. The devil's trumpet, the devil's apple. *De rigueur* in the company of witches, it worked no magic for Brendan.

She entertained high hopes for Hyoscyamus, another sorceror's weed and the crown of the dead in Hades. Hog's-bean. Jupiter's-bean, though Culpeper argued a case for Saturn on the grounds that the herb grew in refuse dumps and cemeteries.

Belladonna was a cauldron of trouble brewing. In Stramonium, the disaster was imminent, and, with Hyoscyamus, it had struck, leaving the patient beaten, cast down and scorned, the patient who felt he was rubbish – or rubbished: *Delusion, wife is faithless* (though Stramonium had that too). *Delusion, deserted, forsaken is; Delusion, sold, being* and *Fear, betrayed, of being* (both mental symptoms unique to Hyoscyamus).

She heard the rapid, efficient squeak of Janice's soles behind her. Brendan's eyes flicked momentarily left and then right again as though he had lost interest, or switched his attention to someone arriving from the opposite end of the ward. She had seen him do it before; his eyes would rove for a time, but never long enough towards a stimulus for her to ascribe any intent.

'Another remedy?' Janice said. 'What is it this time?'

Karin told her.

'Fancy names, aren't they?' Janice leaned over the bed, one foot rising from the floor as she took her weight on her hand and tugged back the top sheet. 'I'm just getting him into bed again. Then I'll freshen your hands and face, Brendan, make you feel better.'

She installed him back in the bed. Karin tucked in the sheets round him and raised the far cot-side while Janice fetched a towel and a dish containing a hot flannel.

'May I do it?' Karin asked.

'Go right ahead.'

Washing his face and teeth, helping with his physiotherapy, aspirating the mucus from his lungs, that much she could do for him. Interaction, even if limited to meeting his basic needs, was still possible. Grooming him and maintaining his airways had been elevated beyond acts of compassion to expressions of love now that kisses had lost their meaning. If the medics were to be believed.

She dropped the flannel back into the dish on the cabinet and patted him dry with the towel. Janice was sucking out a patient a couple of beds down the ward.

'Janice?'

'Nope, I definitely wasn't there.'

'No please, when you've finished I need you to tell me something.'

Janice came over afterwards and pulled up another chair.

'It's just –' Karin began. 'Do you ever see any signs of awareness in patients like Brendan? I mean, I know you're not supposed to. But do you?'

Janice took a breath to speak but released it again without words. 'Well... When you turn them, they tend to move a little... move their limbs, that is, as though they're in some sort of discomfort. And their breathing can change. You're in close proximity, don't forget, when you turn a patient. It's something you do on a regular basis, and you hear things. The changes are subtle. I doubt the doctors would notice. The physios or OTs might. And when I turn the sheets, they can open their eyes like they're looking round, even though they can't see. They do seem to respond to a calming voice, and that's not text-book.' She patted her knees and got up. 'I'd better clear these things before Professor Isherwood arrives.'

'Isherwood?'

'Oh, one of Mr Scrivener's contemporaries. From the University of Glasgow, I think, the Institute of Neurological Science.' Janice paused. 'He's come to make his assessment for the hearing.'

'What?' Karin leapt to her feet. 'I was told it was Friday.'

'Something came up. Mr Scrivener was ringing you this morning –'

'Oh God! I started playing back the messages, but everyone wanted remedy advice for the 'flu, and after a morning seeing patients I couldn't face it. Oh God!'

'Well,' said Janice, flustered, 'I'm sorry - But he's very nice. That's him now.'

Karin followed the nurse's eyes down the corridor and saw beside Mr Scrivener a greying, thick-set man with as much beard as hair. He wore the regulation dark suit, and carried a white coat over one arm.

A pain swelled in her throat, as though she had swallowed a bubble of acrid air. 'It's okay. I can disappear to the restaurant.'

'Oh, but he'll want to meet you. I'm sure he'll want to talk. Look, he's coming over.'

Janice made the introductions and Karin shook his hand with a tense nod.

'Mrs McDonald, I hope it hasn't inconvenienced you too much,' said the Professor, 'changing my schedule like this? Tiresome but unavoidable, I'm afraid.'

'Not at all. I was just leaving.'

'Oh?'

'I'm due to be seeing some clients.'

Her tongue seemed to trip round every syllable, and she left without kissing Brendan goodbye.

The moment she reached for the door a string of loud and wild groans shattered the silence of the ward behind her. She turned part way before stopping herself. She touched both hands to the fingerplates and stepped in so close that her nose almost grazed the glass. She closed her eyes, bounced the door violently off her hands and walked straight out.

She arrived at the restaurant. She didn't recall getting there. She bought a hot chocolate, not that she wanted one, and nursed it at the nearest table. She didn't even like hot chocolate, but it was warm and sweet and resembled food and brought with it memories of marshmallows by the fire with Netta.

A man was assessing Brendan for court, a man she'd never met before, assessing her husband's best interests and his quality of life. The lump choked up her throat again as she tried to swallow. To the ear of anyone, anyone but a doctor, that haunting groan told, more eloquently than rhetoric, of distress and despair. And fear.

She removed her fingers from the cup and swung a hand up to her throat. And suddenly a brown river washed away across the table, flooding her tray with a lake of chocolate.

23

'I'm sorry.'

Jim Straker rolled on to his back and flung out his left arm so that his fingers rested just above the floorboards. They both stared at the constellations of gilt stars on the ceiling. A ball of heat and moisture hung over them.

'It's me, isn't it.' Nadine's voice was barely a whisper, but the quaver in the last two words did not escape him. 'It is, isn't it.'

'No! No, not you. I promise.'

'But it was never like this at the beginning. I don't turn you on any more, do I.'

'God!' He rolled on to his right flank to face her. He supported his head on one hand and pressed the other across his chest. 'Nadine Stone, I can say, with hand on heart, that you are the most beautiful woman I have met, ever, and the last two months have been the best and most exhilarating weeks of my life. Truth, whole truth and nothing but.'

Her hair made a scuffing sound as she shifted her head on the pillow, and her mouth widened into a small but indulgent smile.

'In the beginning - Well, it was, wasn't it.' She glanced out of the corner of her eyes at his limp penis, but casually enough not to emasculate him any more than he had already done for himself. 'I just don't see what's changed. At least I could understand it if you were bored.'

'Not likely.' He traced a circle with his little finger round her more accessible nipple. 'If anything, I'd say I was more confident of my feelings for you, and I can assure you your sexual magnetism is every bit as formidable as it ever was.'

'Formidable. Not irresistible.'

'Both! I'm potty about you. If they counted up the number of times a day I thought about making love with you, I'd be arrested. Castrated. My spirit's falling over itself to be your sex-slave while the flesh...' - he flicked disconsolately at his penis - 'is forcemeat.'

'Hilary?'

'I wondered.' He re-arranged the sheet over their cooling bodies, then lay back on the pillows and supported her head on his shoulder. 'Guilt eating insidiously away at me from the inside... Wife and two kids at home while I'm entwined in scarlet bed sheets with you.'

'And do you feel guilty?'

'I should. I have in the past. I can't say I'm aware of it now. Maybe it's age. Maybe it's desperation. The kids have mutated into two cynical teenagers who treat me like shit. My relationship with Hil is a cycle of meals and ironing and taxiing our offspring through the unending whirl of their social lives. House maintenance, child maintenance, car maintenance. Cat maintenance. Everything's so functional. She keeps all the balls in the air. She can't risk dropping them because they might bounce out of control and have to be retrieved, which would mean stopping everything and actually looking at life for a few seconds. Christ, it must be guilt. A honeymoon of total oblivion, then the debt collector comes calling.'

'Do you want us to finish?'

'You know I don't!'

He picked up his damp, miserable member and let it drop back on to his belly.

'Jim, how about those tablets you took?'

'What, this?'

'The dates match. And they've done nothing else for you, as far as I can tell...'

He considered. He'd taken them at the beginning of March, and the problem had started about a fortnight later. Thirteen days later, to be precise. A bit of legitimate overtime after a late-turn, then a bit of illegitimate and failed overtime at Nadine's.

'I suppose it's not impossible,' he said. 'I'm seeing her next Monday. I'll ask.'

'What were they anyway?'

'She didn't say, and I can't say I'm bothered as long as I get better.'

'Now, what would really make *me* feel better...'

He waited with flaccid dread.

'... is a lovely mug of that new coffee and some chocolate biscuits.'

'That,' he said, sliding off the mattress, 'I can manage.'

He slunk, naked, out to the bathroom and retrieved Darren's towelling robe from the back of the door. He watched his lean, spidery legs as they pumped down the stairs. Sometime he would have to invest in a robe of his own; Darren's was ridiculously, almost obscenely short on him.

He set out the mugs and shook a few biscuits on to a plate, then wandered into the living-room while he waited for the kettle to heat.

It had been a quiet late-turn. Hilary had gone to spend the night at her mother's, and the kids were at mass sleep-overs somewhere. It was to have been his and Nadine's first ever night together, a night of unhurried and repeated love-making. Instead it would be a night of unhurried coffee-drinking, fraternal cuddles and fretful sleep as he pondered the ego-crunching reality of impotence. Still, at least the photograph of Darren had disappeared now. In its place on the bookcase stood a clock, a black, electronic device under a clear plastic cover, that she had moved downstairs from the guest-room.

He watched a bearing plop down from the top, trundle along a sloping groove and stick in a slot calibrated into minutes. Twelve hours plus one five-minute bearing plus three one-minute bearings: nearly ten past midnight. Eye-catching enough, but it took forever to tell the time.

The end of an envelope was protruding behind the clock. Checking over his shoulder, Straker lifted it out. Official. *Nadine Stone and Darren Mulvaney.* He raised the flap and drew out the letter: *Oxford & Central Building Society.* April the third. Four days ago.

He scanned the contents and a ripple of pains shot though his chest. He took the letter out to the hall and copied down a few details on to her memo block by the telephone, writing lightly enough to avoid denting the paper below. He tore off the sheet, put it in the pocket of his robe, replaced the letter behind the clock and finished preparing the coffee.

'Spoken to Darren recently?' he inquired as he rattled in with the tray.

'He never returns my calls.' Nadine's eyes closed, but her breasts still stared, pert and cool, at the ceiling. 'I'm sick of him.'

'Did you find out where he's living?'

'I winkled it out of my Valentine. Somewhere down the Iffley Road.'

He put the tray on the floor near the mattress and knelt beside it.

'Only you said you were going to write to him about forking out his share of the mortgage. I just wondered if you'd come to some arrangement.'

'I wrote. He didn't.'

'When?'

'Ages ago. February?'

He depressed the plunger on the cafetière. 'Would you like me to go round and see him?'

'No! No...' She sat up, crossed her legs and folded her arms. 'In any case, I've already tried twice. His landlord says he's never there.'

'Is the lender aware? They do know, don't they.'

'I can't say I'm falling over myself to tell them I've lost my job, no.'

'That's mad! How many months do you owe? Nadine...' He crawled across the bed on his knees and sat cross-legged in front of her. 'I'm sure you could reach some financial agreement if you spoke to them. Because these people don't mess around. You're just a number working its way through the system. Three or four months, and they'll kick you out.'

'Why? I got away with January, I cancelled my holiday. Lost the deposit, but paid the mortgage. Anyway, since when do waitressing and a bit of bar-work make for an acceptable financial agreement?' Her head drooped. 'My bloody car loan's secured on the house. I've been paying that. It's not even a very wonderful car. I can't manage everything.' She sobbed and folded forwards, hugging herself and rocking. 'Fuck Darren. Fuck him!'

'Give me his address.'

'My financial affairs are none of your business.'

'Your sexual affairs are, I take it, governed by a different set of rules?'

'Yes! No...'

She wailed and beat her fists on the coverlet. Amorous and expectant, he picked her up by the wrists, but all the little man downstairs could manage was a half-hearted twitch. He leaned his forehead against hers in a shared, but different sort of despair, and stroked her shoulders.

'Promise me you'll write to him again – today. If there's no response ten days from now, you give me his address. Is that fair?'

She nodded, sniffing. 'Then you can pulp his face.'
'Attagirl,' he said.

*

'How have I been?' Straker echoed, a little tersely. 'Unchanged. In fact, I have more problems now than I came with.'

She motioned him to continue. It was five-thirty, and he had just finished a day's reports. He wrung his hands.

'I seem to be having more emissions of prostatic fluid. I assume it's prostatic fluid. Even in the absence of an erection, though it's more pronounced during sexual contact. Or when I have... thoughts...'

'And this is new?'

'Absolutely.'

'Did you experience any change at all in your original complaint after the remedy? No matter how brief - improvement or deterioration?'

'I don't think so.'

'What about your general energy levels?'

'Much as before. Work I get on with, though concentration is more difficult these days. At home I'm brassed off. I try not to show it. I just don't feel I belong. I hardly merit the title of lodger any more. I've turned into a virtual lodger; even when I'm there, I'm not, you know?'

'Where are you instead?'

He looked past the side of her head at a flower design in the net curtain. Time spread like treacle round the therapy room. His heart thudded inside his chest, but inside his skull every cell seemed paralysed. The homœopath sat as immobile as himself and, like himself, did nothing and said nothing, threw him not even a crumb of a word to grasp at. She offered nothing but a soundless, galactic void, and he filled it with tension so unbearable that it seemed to twang in rhythm with his heart.

'I have a thing...' His voice trailed away. It sounded so loud and harsh. 'Women. There's no shortfall in the libido department, don't get me wrong. When they cry.'

Silence.

'The sexual element just seems to well up. I want to rush over. I want to comfort them. They're so fragile, like salty-faced dolls. A head nuzzling into my shoulder, arms flung round my neck... I know it's ridiculous.'

'How long -?'

'Even before we were married. The intensity waxes and wanes. At the moment it's not too bad, but I've put my job in jeopardy that many times...'

'Can you describe how you feel, when you say you want to rush in and comfort these women?'

'Oh, heroic. Heroic, powerful. Remember when you were a child and you grazed your knee, and your mother said she'd kiss it better? I want to kiss it all better. That's what I want to do.'

'And are these feelings that you experience solely at the time?'

'No.' He squeezed each pad of his fingertips between the thumb and index of his other hand. 'I might run through them again afterwards. Outside work.'

'Do you ever become involved with these women? Socially? Sexually?'

'I ah – I've had the occasional affair. Nothing of note. They were meant to console, not to last. Thank God no one ever complained. I'd have ended up in security, vegetating away in a Portakabin on some industrial estate.'

'Was Hilary aware of your affairs?'

'Some. Not all, but the worst thing -' He nipped the tip of his tongue between his teeth. 'The worst thing is that I can't follow through any more.'

'Follow through?'

'Wood!' he said, angling both hands towards his crotch. 'A major deficit in the wood department, ranging from an apology to total hibernation. Sometimes I seem to go off the boil at the crucial moment, even though in my head – Not to mention the humiliation and the disappointment. And since it started in mid-March, I need to know if it could be the remedy you gave me. I really need to know.'

Zoe Seymour pulled a face. 'It's not impossible, Jim, though in this case I very much doubt it. Did you follow the instructions?'

'I cut down the coffee.'

'How much did you say you drank per day?'

'Six, seven cups.'

Zoe Seymour stared at her page for a moment, then arched her right arm over her head and scratched her left temple.

'Okay, I'm going to give you a remedy to take with you now. Only I want you to stay right off the coffee this time.'

'None at all?'

'Decaff's acceptable. And buy yourself some mint-free toothpaste. Can you manage that?'

'With a sex-life like mine,' he said, 'anything.'

*

'Have you seen the eggs?' Hilary demanded when he went into the kitchen that night. 'I'm going to complain to the milkman. There, on the table.'

She watched him lift the unfastened lid. One of the six brown eggs was smashed on top, the mingled yolk and white congealed and the carton soaked dark grey around it.

'Bit of a mess,' he said drily. 'The lid's not damaged though. Was it shut when you took the box off the doorstep?'

'Not properly.'

'Could be a magpie. Especially if the box wasn't fastened.'

'Oh, don't be ridiculous,' said Hilary, flitting back with the egg-box to a frying pan on the hob.

He stuffed his hands in his pockets and drifted across to the kitchen window. In the distant blackthorn, a fibrous, elliptical dome was taking shape, and both birds were flouncing round in the branches.

'Two for joy,' Hilary said, 'isn't that how it goes?'

'That egg,' he muttered, 'is nothing compared to the havoc they'll wreak in the blackbirds' nest.'

'I'm sure Orpheus will keep them in order.' She cracked four eggs, one after the other, into the pan. 'How many do magpies lay?'

'Five, six, seven. Eight, maybe. We could end up with seven of them massacring the local bird life. Ten, even.'

'Seven for a secret never to be told,' said Hilary, easing a fish-slice under one of the eggs. 'I don't know the rest.'

'Eight for a wish. Nine for a kiss.'

'That's nice.'

'Ten's slipped my mind.'

He let himself into the dining-room and stood looking out at the magpies. *Ten for a marriage never to grow old.*

24

'To be quite frank, we ticked along very nicely till my wife died.' Mr Wilson, still wearing his hat, hugged himself deeper into his stained tweed overcoat. 'Our daughter hitched up with a frog, lives in Grenoble. Joanna came home, mind, our granddaughter. Married an accountant. I don't go much on him. Always coming round, she is. She thinks she's helping, but by the time you get to my age you have your own way of carrying on.'

'Give me an example of something she does differently,' said Karin.

Mr Wilson pondered. 'She buys me soup. Bread and soup hit me in the gut like two-pound boilies. And she says she salts the veg, but I don't get through salt like I used to. She can't take criticism. No respect, brought up in France. As for Jordan, I'd have given him a damned good hiding. Still, I must say he's been more tolerable of late…'

He rumbled through a fit of racking coughs, and, at the back of his throat, made the snarling of a werewolf resisting metamorphosis. Karin grabbed the box of paper tissues from the desk and held them out to him. He waved the box away, slewed sideways on the chair and reached into his coat pocket. He drew out a rigid ball of fabric the colour of whelk eggs. With his eyes fixed at the cornice, he retched twice and emptied on to the handkerchief a clod of guacamole mucus. He examined this with some interest before crackling the fabric into a new ball around it and returning the handkerchief to his pocket.

'We've talked about your stiff neck and hands,' said Karin, 'but what about this cough? How long have you had that?'

'Not long. Everybody's got it.'

'Not everyone's out and about on the buses.'

'Best not to give in to it. Born and bred in Osney, in the same house I'm living now, and if I'm not up to catching a bus and walking a few yards at the end then it's a poor show.'

She asked what time of day his cough was worst.

'Three in the morning,' he said, jutting his chin forward. 'I can answer that one to the minute. When you sleep as bad as me, there's plenty of time to clock-watch.'

'Any reason for not sleeping?'

'Beats me if there is. I get off all right. I just wake in the small hours and that's it for the night.'

'How do you feel during the day? Some people tolerate the lack of sleep better than others.'

'Let's say I'm one of the ones as doesn't, in that case.'

Pause.

'What sort of things frighten you, Mr Wilson?'

'That little devil,' he said, clasping his hands over his stomach, 'leaping out at me behind doors.'

'Are you in discomfort?'

He poked himself under the sternum. 'That's where it gets me. He's shocked years off me, that child. I reckon I'd live far longer if she left him at home.'

She wrote at a furious pace on her pad.

'Nice place,' he nodded to himself, gazing round the room. 'Difficult to heat, I imagine, with the high ceilings and sash-windows.'

'Built-in ventilation,' she smiled.

'Built-in gales,' he muttered. 'I'm double-glazed.'

*

She cut out the card that evening from a piece of thick, hand-made paper. Taking down her ancient Synthesis Repertory from the shelf in her consulting-room, she thumbed through until the pages separated at a sheet of blotting paper. The paper ticked as she unfolded it and it parted company from the sprig of heather inside.

She glued the heather to the front of the card. Its flowers were tinged brown, not quite as white as the day she'd snipped them from the garden last year, but the blue paper seemed to brighten the colour. She stood the card on the desk to dry and rang Zo.

'I finally saw him,' she said. 'Eleven on the dot: the reluctant grandpa. He'd have made a brilliant teaching video, but it's taken a month to get him here even with someone else footing the bill. I decided movie stardom wouldn't do much for his case on balance.'

'The boy?'

'Yes, not bad. I repeated the remedy last week.'

Zo snorted. 'Your inspector's keeping me on my toes. Not only does he fail to respond, he presents with new symptoms. Every time that man opens his mouth, the more he looks like Lycopodium. The dominance and power aspect, his personal life, generals, physicals, even the hierarchy and the job. Everything. If I suspected he was Lycopodium the first time, the second time I was positive. I can only conclude he antidoted somehow. I've banned coffee, increased the potency to 10M and crossed my fingers.'

'What else came up?'

'Nux, Thuja. He's not hidden enough for Thuja. And Conium came high, but he just doesn't fit the picture.' Zo hesitated. 'So, where are you staying?'

'Staying?'

'London, Karin. Hotel. Have you booked somewhere?'

'Oh.' The note of her voice dropped. 'Brendan's uncle is putting me up. He's too frail to make the hearing, but at least it'll be more homely than subsisting in a concrete cube.'

'What about his sisters?'

'Not feasible, really. They're both younger. They've got families. It's too far.'

'The offer still stands...'

'Thanks,' said Karin. 'I'll be fine.'

After the call she went out to the kitchen, slopped a can of game soup into a saucepan on the Alpha and made a mug of elderflower and lemon tea, dunking the tea-bag aimlessly on its string until the pan began to hiss.

She ate the soup with a leathery pitta bread, the final slice from a pack of six which had sat in the bread bin for a week. With Brendan around it would have lasted two days at the most. Bread and tinned soup. Dinner. The preparation of vegetables for one seemed far too energy intensive these days. Maybe tomorrow she would eat out, something vegetarian or a huge salad. And she would eat on her own, like one of the sad, staring folk who took forever over their meal on a table for four, or else eked out the time with a newspaper or, worse still, a novel they had brought along expressly for the purpose.

She came to and found her eyes on the engagement calendar, where Renoir's gay April Parisians fought for space on the hook alongside her apron. The squares from the seventh to the thirteenth were marked through with crosses. The hearing date had arrived on her doorstep only a week after Mr Scrivener's application. Wasn't the judiciary committed, by tradition if nothing else, to delay? Yet everything was happening so fast.

Pushing her bowl aside, she took up the black biro dangling on string from the hanging loop of the calendar and drew a cross into the fourteenth. Tuesday the fifteenth, the afternoon she travelled to London for the High Court hearing, she had not marked; only entertainment and unavoidable social duties and the abundant trivia of bills and expiry dates needed reminders. The most major events never needed signalling; they burned straight into the calendar of the brain.

In her consulting-room she sat down and opened the card flat on the desk. No familiar rubrics could guide her now, no thesaurus could field the words. She picked up her pen.

25

'This is for you. See, I didn't forget. And you remember me when I'm away.'

On Tuesday morning she had seen three clients at home before driving to hospital. Brendan was lying on his side in bed. She held the card in front of his eyes, stood it on the side-table and sat down.

'Jack sends his love. I've never quite understood what he means by airing the room. I suspect it's opening the window to let out the smell of mould. Remember those sheets? I've packed a hot-water bottle this time. I'll plead poor circulation.' She reached over and touched his shoulder. 'The bed's cold without you, Brendan. I've let you down, haven't I. Emrys says it's daunting, the High Court. A grand entrance hall, old panelled rooms. I keep imagining the shoes echoing up the corridors.'

Janice had just started changing the sheets of the neighbouring bed.

'Good luck in London. We'll be thinking of you.'

'Do you think I'm wasting my time?'

'People who stand up for what they believe in are never wasting their time. That's the way I look at it.'

Janice worked along one length of the mattress and then the other, lifting and pushing, tugging and smoothing, as if it mattered.

'What will happen, if they go ahead?'

'If -?'

'The judge makes the order they want?'

Janice's knuckles radiated creases like stars across the top sheet. 'I have seen it. But not recently.'

'Tell me what it's like.' Karin sucked her lips inside her mouth. The first thought of a tear was pricking at her eyes. 'Please. I don't want this to happen, but if it does, I don't want to witness it cold.'

Janice left her bed-making and came round. She cupped a warm, veiny hand over Karin's, and Karin clutched at the nurse's wrist.

'I'm not afraid to hear. Mr Scrivener... either it hasn't crossed his mind, or he's too frightened to say. The last three months have been nothing but uncertainty. Knowing what to expect will be a relief, believe me, a relief.'

'No one's ever asked me before,' Janice said slowly. 'Look, shall we go to the relatives' room?'

'No.' Karin pressed the heel of her hand into her right eye, smeared away the dampness and blinked her vision clear again. 'I'm all right.'

Janice sat on the edge of the bed, staring at her shoes. The toes, flat and broad, bent upward off the floor and the leather was creased and dull. Not patent.

'Everything,' Karin said.

'Well... They dry out. Everywhere, they dry out. But the physical appearance and the discomfort we can treat –'

'Discomfort! How can there be any discomfort?'

'It's us, Karin, *our* discomfort. Humanity is something we can't help hanging on to. It's a mark of respect.' Janice nodded her head over her shoulder. 'Some people's skin is a lot drier than others anyway. You know when I make Freddie's bed or turn his sheets, I whip up a cloud of skin flakes? That's how it goes.'

'How long?'

'Five days? Less than a week. And the mucous membranes can split. The lining of the nose and gums might bleed, the lips and mouth become caked. The tongue swells. That can crack too. The eyes pull into their sockets. The eyes themselves we moisten with saline, and we can moisten the mouth and moisturise the skin. The respiratory tract dehydrates. The secretions can actually plug the lungs and cause death. Their temperature rises. They might vomit blood, or go into convulsions. And as time goes on they begin to look emaciated. If their blood pressure drops far enough, they might slip into a coma. Or the sleep-wake cycle can persist until they die, but Mr Scrivener would put him on a morphine driver well before then.'

'There's no need to be kind,' said Karin, staring at the card.

'That's to finish him off, isn't it.'

'To keep him comfortable. Maybe for our benefit as well as his. And there's another thing - during his last few days of life, this baby-like swelling of his face would disappear and return to normal, so that –'

'When he dies I know it's really him.'

'I think it's nicer that way.'

'Easier to say goodbye. *I don't want to say goodbye...*'

Janice sank to her haunches and took each of Karin's hands in hers. 'Nothing I can say will deaden the pain. It will be worst for you, of course it will, but you won't be alone.'

'It's very easy to feel alone.' Karin shook the nurse's hand through her tears. 'But what about you? You've spent far longer with him, had far more contact than I have. Investment of time always costs. This must be awful for you too.'

'The courts can say what they like, yes, but withholding treatment is instinctively far more acceptable than withdrawing it. So...' Janice got up. 'How are you for time?'

'Okay. I arranged for a taxi to pick me up from the house later.'

'That's pretty,' Janice said, pointing to the card. 'May I?'

Karin watched Janice's eyes as she opened up the card. There was not a flicker, neither her brows nor her lips betrayed the slightest surprise.

Janice replaced the card on the table.

'Written on your heart, eh?' She put the back of her hand to Brendan's forehead and withdrew it, her fingers in a fist. 'Well, I'll leave you to it. My shifts are one to nine Thursday and Friday. Maybe I'll see you then.'

When Janice had finished with Freddie's blankets and gone down the ward, Karin slipped off the chair and crouched by the side of the bed. Brendan's eyes were shining, the sclera clear and bright, his pupils dilated in the shadow of his own body.

'Your eyes look beautiful today.' She raised herself a little, turned her head sideways and touched her lips to his. Then she took his head between her hands, turned it towards her face and kissed again his soft, curious, unresponsive lips. 'Goodbye,

Brendan. Love you.'

The words had always been written on her heart, smudged by tears at one point, but never washed away.

26

'This train will shortly be arriving at Oxford. The next station stop will be Oxford.'

People were already folding up newspapers and stuffing paperbacks into their bags. Briefcases snapped shut.

Karin took a taxi home. She leaned her temple against the passenger window and let the engine vibration drill into the sound reel and images, frame after frame of images that streamed through her mind.

A terrible tragedy... Of paramountcy in this case is Brendan McDonald's right of self-determination. The decision, whether rational or irrational, to accept or reject medical treatment is his and his alone. By making an advance directive or "living will," Professor McDonald has provided the Court with clear evidence of his anticipatory choice...

Sir James Greville had called them back that morning at ten o'clock to deliver his judgement, during which he peered at them from time to time over thick, black-rimmed glasses.

...and formed the opinion that he was unlikely ever to recover his capacity for rational existence... ...does not wish to be subjected to any medical intervention or treatment with a view to sustaining or prolonging his life...

A tickle irritated her throat, advancing up it with spidery feet.

The views of Professor McDonald's family should be considered with the greatest respect...

She broke into a string of dry coughs that made her eyes sting. She reached for the bottle in her handbag and swallowed down a few sips of water.

'All right?' said the taxi driver. 'Lot of it about.'

She'd already rung Jack, Brendan's two sisters, Leon, and her mother who, during the call, had burned the dinner. She would even have been entitled to her own legal representation, Emrys said, as an interested party, but no amount of barristerial voices speaking on her behalf would have changed the message.

...Mrs McDonald is of the opinion that another six months... Mrs McDonald and Professor McDonald's uncle have pledged significant funds to help offset the financial burden on the hospital... ...whilst acknowledging that cost is not at issue here... ...motivated by the best of intentions... ...cases where remarkable recoveries have obtained... ...nevertheless the Court has heard that, in the considered clinical judgement of Doctor Scrivener, Professor Isherwood and Doctor Tate... ...I am persuaded... ...the Court feels enormous sympathy for the family, and for the distress of his wife in particular. Whilst I acknowledge... ...the Court is nonetheless obliged to address the issue with all possible dispassion and objectivity. Dispassion and objectivity... Swayed by the overwhelming weight of medical opinion...

In the distance buildings passed by with cinematic serenity, but her thoughts inhabited the blur of foreground, the clattering disintegration of form, substance and detail.

...and I therefore declare that the plaintiffs and the physicians in whose care Professor McDonald finds himself, may henceforth lawfully discontinue may henceforth lawfully discontinue all treatment intended to sustain him in his vegetative existence... ...not administer any medication nor further supply it but for the purposes of

'Killing him quietly.'

She sensed the taxi driver's head turn, but he said nothing.

Professor Isherwood and Doctor Tate had left after giving their reports. Scrivener stayed overnight to hear the judgment, as did Emrys; she sat next to him. He touched her arm when Sir James Greville began his declaration. Her head dropped forward as though someone had struck her a blow to the back of the neck, and Emrys squeezed her hand. He was Brendan's friend after all. And then they stood for the judge and Sir Greville disappeared and Scrivener came shuffling over.

'Monday,' he said. 'Mrs McDonald? We'll say Monday. I'm very sorry.'

It needn't have been Monday. One quick phone call would have brought on the first protesting contractions of his stomach that very afternoon. He'd elected Monday as an act of kindness, a last period of nurture before nature was loosed on his unsuspecting body. She had three days to adjust and kiss goodbye to the ephemera of hope and happiness. Three days in which to shake Death by the hand, to learn to look him full in the eye without flinching and invite him with good grace over the threshold. She had three days to achieve where she had failed for three months.

*

Ruskin emerged to greet her from the foot of the camellia, the fading red flowers now littering the gravel like discarded wax seals. He kissed her legs with his tail, followed her into the house and sat by the kitchen door.

'No,' she croaked, setting down her overnight case and handbag in the hall. 'I'm sure Mary's given you plenty.'

Thumping herself on the chest, she inspected the answering-machine: twenty-five messages. Twenty-five! She made a cup of tea instead, appeased Ruskin with a handful of biscuits and drove to the Radcliffe.

'Karin, thank goodness!' Janice took her aside as soon as she set foot in the ward. 'You got my message?'

'No, I've only just arrived back.'

'You're here, that's the main thing.' Janice set off at a brisk pace down the ward, speaking over her shoulder. 'Brendan's poorly again. I called you, twice.'

Janice stopped in the central aisle. Brendan was supported on pillows, the head of the bed angled so that his eyes fixed the ceiling in meditative supplication. His skin appeared white, almost luminous, his eyes dark and glassy and ringed a malevolent shade of violet.

'My God...' Karin ran to him and touched his forehead. She looked with accusation at the nurse. 'How long has he been like this?'

'I had my suspicions Tuesday evening, but the fever really set in yesterday.'

'Is he not responding then? Listen to him! Maybe you need a different antibiotic. Are the results of the sample not back from the lab?'

'No –'

'Well, tell them to hurry!'

For a while the two women simply looked at each other.

'I see.' Karin crossed one arm over her chest, gripping her biceps, and caressed her lips with her thumbnail. 'Is he on antibiotics?'

'No, Karin, he isn't.'

'You've heard.'

'Mr Scrivener rang just after eleven.'

Karin raised her chin above her hand. 'Did he have any yesterday?'

Janice gave a slow, half-shake of her head. Karin bent forward and picked up Brendan's papers.

'His temperature hasn't been read since yesterday lunch-time. The line just stops!' She let the file fall on to the bed. 'You haven't treated him.'

Janice reached for her, but Karin shrugged her away.

'It could be a blessing – We're letting him take his chance. If you wanted to try your homœopathy, maybe that would help him now? It's kinder this way -'

'Kinder than the alternative waiting on Monday?' Karin turned on the nurse. 'Brendan stopped wanting to live months ago. If he's determined to die, nothing can bring him back. No one. It doesn't matter what you know, or how much you love someone. Or how hard you pray.'

Zo came straight over after Karin's call that evening.

'I won't get in your way,' she said. 'I'll pick up shopping, I'll fix the meals. Spend all the time you want with Brendan.'

When Karin arrived at his bedside next morning Dr

Gilmour was listening to his chest. She moved the stethoscope from one patch to another and frowned.

Karin leaned forward. 'Well?'

'I can't pretend it's good.' The doctor eased the arms of the stethoscope from her ears and let the instrument settle down her front like a necklace. 'I'm afraid there's not a lot of air entering his lower lungs at the moment.'

'Compared with yesterday?'

'Compared with yesterday,' the doctor murmured, patting Brendan's shoulder, 'a little worse.'

'Brendan, your hands,' Karin said, pressing them between hers when Dr Gilmour had left, 'how can they be so cold under the sheets?'

She sucked out his airways three times during the first hour of sitting with him. The wheezing sounded almost musical, squeezing from his lungs like an attempt at communication.

She took their album of wedding photographs from her bag and opened it on his lap.

'Remember that?' she said, pointing to a small flurry of grey on a background of grass. 'Everyone else was snapping photos of us outside the chapel, but Leon has to get a hawk eating a sparrow at the far end of the Quad. And there's your dad, look. That's the only photo he smiled for all day. What a lovely smile...' He was gone now. 'And there's that Annabelle Pilkington. *Doctor*. She fancied you. She did. I was so nice to her. I hated her guts. Well, her eyes are too confident. Still, a rebound fling with Leon soon sent her packing. He has his uses.'

'Sorry to interrupt,' said Janice, appearing at Karin's elbow. 'Time to turn Brendan. Can you give me a hand with the sheets?'

Karin set the thick white album on the chair. Working together, they rolled back the blanket and top sheet.

'Oh my God!'

The skin of his feet and part of his calves was mottled purple. Karin touched the top of his foot.

'He's freezing.'

'It's because he's ill,' Janice said. 'I'll fetch another blanket.'

'I could have given this to him,' Karin sighed over supper. 'I've obviously got some throat bug.'

'Don't talk rubbish!'

'I could have! Half my patients have either got or had some respiratory infection.'

'So it could have come from just about anywhere. Hospital's the worst place for picking up infections, and right now Brendan's highly susceptible. Anyway, I forgot your wedding anniversary.'

'That hardly matters.'

'As maid of honour...' Zo patted herself on the cheek. 'As maid of honour, I take a close interest in you both. It's the first year I've missed.'

Karin rinsed her plate and cutlery under the tap and slotted them into the dish-washer.

'I forgive you.'

She awoke with such violence she thought someone had shaken her, twisting and then dropping her like a wave on the beach. Her guts were rigid with adrenaline. In the distance she heard a resonating clack, the third and last in the normal sequence of the cat flap below her window: Ruskin.

She relaxed back into the pillow. And then, over the tap of her heart rose a muted but insistent metallic toning. Her heart thumped: Zo had disconnected the answering-machine.

She checked her watch by the lamp: two-thirty. Immediately she ploughed from the bed, almost overbalancing, and ran down the stairs with Brendan's unfastened shirt cuffs flapping over her fingers. She slapped the hall light switch and shook the cuff up her arm before grabbing the receiver.

'Mrs McDonald?'

'Yes?'

'It's Marion. I'm afraid Brendan's deteriorating. Can you come in?'

Her arm sank under the deadweight of the receiver.

'Mrs McDonald? Mrs McDonald?'

The voice twittered distantly. She brought the receiver to her cheek again.

'I'm on my way.'

Hanging up was impossible. Hanging up meant acceptance, demanded response.

Zo was huddled in her dressing-gown at the top of the stairs. Karin made a single, jerky nod to her, still clutching the phone.

'Would you like me to come with you?'

Another nod.

Staring through the spindles, she finally put back the receiver. It slipped from its cradle and she clattered it back into place.

'We think it's pneumonia,' said Marion. 'His lungs are consolidating. The effort of breathing is exhausting him.'

They had moved him into a side ward on his own. Though they had positioned him almost upright, his rasping breaths were audible from the foot of the bed. His eyes were shut; she had expected them to be open in such distress, staring as his chest laboured for survival. Even with his lids closed, the eyeballs of flesh seemed shrunken into their sockets.

'Will he make morning? He looks blue.'

'Karin, he's dying.'

Marion left her sitting by the bed, holding his hand. As the minutes went by, the heaving and the violence subsided and the movements diminished, accepting of his clogged and useless lungs. She watched him with such intensity that it hurt, until the sheet over his chest made no tell-tale crease to coincide with his breath. In panic she leaned over him, her own breathing silenced. She heard a brief, loaded sigh. Dazed, she stared back at his chest. The sheet did not move. He was as still as a photograph.

'Brendan?' She agitated his hand. 'Oh Brendan, *no!*' She threw herself against him. 'Brendan, don't go! Oh God, don't go!'

She gathered him into her arms and rocked him, her eyes squeezed shut. She wept until her own lungs seemed to collapse for lack of air, leaving her scarcely the strength to draw breath. Against her cheek his hair was wet with her tears, and her heart pounded in the warmth between their bodies. There should have been a reply, the reassuring bubble of mismatched beats, the occasional solid synchrony. But only one pulse kicked, hard and insistent against her shirt, one pulse beating wildly enough for them both.

How long she held him she did not know, but only when the crying had exhausted her could she lay him down. She unfastened three buttons of his blue pyjama top and parted the fabric. Curiously she trailed her fingertips across the springy, greying hairs of this chest she loved, this man she loved and had not touched for so long with the reverence of a lover. She smoothed the hairs twice with the flat of her hand and brought her head to rest gently on his chest. Only then, when there were no more tears, could she bear the sound of his silent heart.

*

'What about a bath?' Zo suggested. 'It'll help you relax.'

It was late on Easter Saturday after a day of telephone calls and funeral arrangements.

'I think I will,' she said.

As the water drained away afterwards through the steam, Karin opened the cabinet. She reached for his deodorant and rolled the wetness, his essence, under her arms until the bathroom smelled so strongly of him that he could almost have been standing behind her. But there was no one.

From his wardrobe she selected a green checked shirt, one of the favourites he wore to work. She wrapped herself round with his dressing-gown and went to fetch a glass of water. Halfway down the staircase, a noise stopped her. Someone was in the kitchen. She listened, holding her breath. The sound came in bursts of soft, rapid movement. Something muffled struck the leg of the bench or table, and then the front cover of the boiler.

She hurried down, flung open the door and switched on all the lights at once. Ruskin emerged from under the table, his tail erect with pride.

'What is it, Rus? What have you got?'

The cat sat down beside the boiler, his head lowered, his ears pricked and pointing almost to the floorboards. She lifted the bench away from the table and peered underneath. On the floor lay a small rodent with a short tail.

'Another vole. Oh dear, is it –?'

The animal made an intense scrabbling with its hind paws and rolled, anti-clockwise, round the floor in a perfect circle. After a few seconds, with near frantic urgency, it repeated the sequence. Ruskin's tail twitched with fascination.

'My God, what have you done?'

She tore the cardboard front from a cereal packet on the table, slotted it under the vole and placed it on the kitchen table for closer examination: mice were safe to handle, Brendan said, but shrews and voles could bite.

There was no sign of bleeding or torn flesh, except for a mark over one of its eyes, and the paws were contorted, the back ones pedalling the air. Suddenly the vole rolled off the cardboard and on to the table. She put out a finger to stop it, but only succeeded in turning it in another direction as it pivoted round her finger.

'This is sick.' She peered with morbid curiosity at the round, furry, belligerent little face, half-wanting the animal to roll, half-wanting it to lie still and die. 'Jesus...'

The vole whirred away again. The cat leapt on to the bench, his eyes black, his tail lashing.

'Maybe I should let you have it. No, I can't. Oh God.'

She bit her fist and opened one of the wall cupboards. She removed the inner sachets from a new box of tea-bags, poked the vole back on to the cardboard, squeezed the cardboard between her fingers and poured the animal gently inside the box. From the sitting-room she fetched an old broadsheet, opened the back door and carried the vole down the steps, its claws still making hollow scraping sounds inside the box. The mossy slime on the steps seeped between her bare toes.

She folded two sheets of newspaper twice and placed them

on the concrete at the bottom of the steps. Crouching, she shook the vole on to the layer of paper. The animal suddenly looked so small, so distant. She could have been looking at it through a prism.

She folded two more sheets and laid them over the animal. From the side of the steps she picked up a broken piece of edging tile and felt for the vole, rustling under the paper. She raised the tile in both hands, its broad surface parallel to the ground. At first she lowered it without conviction, then raised it once more in front of her face. The second time she brought it down with all her force through a cry of pain and triumph.

As she picked her way back up the steps that Easter Saturday night, she noticed the stars were out, clear and abundant. Some had burned up so long ago, and yet the memory of their light shone still, far into a distant time and place.

27

'You've got through the day brilliantly,' said Zo, patting Karin's arm as she loaded the dish-washer.

'It's not over yet.'

'True. In which case, are you sure you're up to working tomorrow?'

'Three afternoon follow-ups,' said Karin, sliding sherry schooners one after the other into the glass-rack. 'Nothing too heavy. And then it's the weekend. Anyway, I want to keep occupied, get my life back into some sort of routine. I'm going swimming again.'

'Good!'

'And I've decided to run that homœopathy class.'

A large round serving plate hung, dripping froth, from Zo's hand. 'Isn't this a bit sudden? You know, a bit late? Term starts again next week.'

'I'll hire a room.' Karin began feeding in side-plates, brushing crumbs and cocktail sticks and celery leaves into a crumpled piece of foil on the work-top. 'The Ferry Centre or one of the schools would do, provided I can drum up enough support to cover the hire charges. At least eight are interested. And I've signed up for a couple of festivals with the Travelling Homœopaths. You've done your training day now. You could join me.'

'Grieving takes time too, you know,' Zo said quietly.

'I know.' The energy and verve vanished. She began folding the foil round the rubbish with the absorption of a child wrapping its first parcel. 'Yes, I know. Only to me, he's died a hundred times since the accident. Every time I left the hospital. He'd been dying since the early hours of New Year's Day. It wasn't like a heart attack.' She creased the foil with two strokes of her thumbnail and folded the end of the package into a neat triangle. 'I don't know which is worse,' she added. 'Anyway, what I need right now is structure, a bit of order to shore me up. A quietly busy existence, Zo, and no insurmountable challenges. That's what I'm aiming for.'

The funeral service had taken place in Pembroke College chapel, where they'd been married. The same chaplain who had joined them was nine years later to part them. Many of the faces were the same, the expressions lengthened this time with age and sombre restraint, the clothes as muted the second time as they had been bright the first. Emrys and Liz were there, Scrivener, three or four neighbours, Leon. Marion, Janice and Bridget. Brendan's sisters and brothers-in-law, but no children and no uncle Jack. Inspector Straker arrived with an elegant woman in a dark suit. A policewoman, she thought. The Master and his wife attended, with a good showing from the Department and from College. And a large party of respectful and complimentary academics she didn't know at all.

They buried him with his parents in the churchyard of St Michael's at Cumnor. She stood the little blue anniversary card on the coffin before the bearers returned him to the earth. The breeze sent it skimming along the shining wood and threatened to cast it on to the grass, so she laid it flat. The middle was still blank. The words were still written on her heart, though the message was different now.

'You want a break,' said Zo.

Karin picked up her foil parcel and dropped it with an air of finality into the swing-bin. 'Tenerife, remember?'

'There's always the Irish conference in June. Soon enough to look forward to, far enough ahead to organise your appointments. Distant enough to pass for abroad.'

'Wet enough to give it away.' Karin rattled the top basket back inside the dish-washer. 'I'll think about it.'

'Well,' said Zo, wiping the last slops of washing-up water from the sink and drainer, 'your band of willing helpers has all but restored the kitchen to order. That's a start, isn't it? And when Kath and Marianne have gone, I vote we crash in the sitting-room with a drink.'

Marianne, Brendan's younger sister, appeared round the kitchen door.

'We're on our way. Gareth's turning the car.'

In silence she and Karin hugged each other, their eyes tight shut. Zo pinched the fingertips of her kitchen gloves, peeled them off, tossed them like yellow sea-slugs into the sink and followed the women to the front door.

A horn sounded below. Kath's hand emerged through the passenger window as Phil pulled out of the drive. From the top step, Karin waved.

In the space created by their departure the last car swung round, chewing up the gravel, and braked at the foot of the steps. Marianne got in, revealing a sleek, navy calf. She lowered the window and smiled up at them.

'Take care, Karin. We'll give you a call at the weekend.'

They watched the car out of sight.

'She's the image of him,' said Zo. 'When she looked up just then – Do you find it disturbing?'

'No,' said Karin, speaking out across the drive. 'Yes and no. It would be more testing, I think, if she were his brother.' She turned to Zo. 'That's it. Immediate karma.'

28

'No, that is *not* it,' Straker said into the phone, his eyes on the wall opposite the open door of his office. 'Nadine, don't give up. I'll try again this evening.'

'And he'll be out again, Jim. Nothing changes.'

'Trust me.'

The line became silent.

'You won't beat him up?'

'I'd love to beat him up. Not at the expense of your mortgage, but rest assured he'll cough up his dues. Oh, Nadine?'

'Yes?'

'I miss you.'

She laughed. She didn't mirror the compliment, she laughed and hung up. Unexpected, wonderful, wicked laughter.

Did he miss her because he loved her, he debated? Did he miss Hilary? He could scarcely describe being in Hilary's presence as a state of blissful togetherness, therefore the impact of her absence was correspondingly dulled. The house grew untidier during her periodic visits to her mother, and smelled less of her vaporising toiletries. Food was no longer conjured out of thin air. Balanced meals ceased. He noted the evidence of her absence, certainly, but did he miss her presence?

He recalled the gradual passing of his grandparents, and his yearning for these loving and familiar human fixtures in the world of his youth. He would miss Larry with his retirement because the station walls would lose their ears, and he would miss Pinke because Pinke was a darned good copper. Were Orpheus to croak, Straker knew he would note even the cat's demise with regret. One could miss, he concluded, anything that engaged one emotionally or intellectually. But did he miss what made Hilary Hilary as opposed to Larry, or Sergeant Pinke, or Orpheus? Had there not been a time when the little root of yearning he associated with Nadine had longed for Hilary? He closed his eyes and a light sweat broke on his forehead. Once, that had been the case.

Once upon a time. Now Hilary's departure stirred milder emotions overshadowed by the dread of pending domestic disruption. Being apart from Nadine, on the other hand, provoked in him a nagging pain beyond functionality or regard, or fondness.

He rubbed the moisture from his brow with his knuckle. It was already time for his lunch-break. He opened the bottom desk drawer, took out a red, long-sleeved T-shirt, ironed and folded, and pulled it on over his police shirt. His clip-on tie went back into the drawer, which he rolled shut with his foot.

He walked into town, dodging the tourists and squinting against the sun on the walls of Christ Church. The city hummed, bright and busy, the voices cosmopolitan on the air. It was one of those perfect, fresh days of late spring before the Council hustled in summer with baskets of candy-striped petunias and trailing lobelia.

He wouldn't see Darren that night; he wouldn't even try. He hadn't wanted to knock on that peeling door in Regent Street after work a week ago either. One visit, fortunately, had sufficed. He'd rapped on the knocker under the letter-box, taken a step back on to the small frontage, and then banged harder. Under the bay window, a couple of split bin-liners disgorged beer cans into a lush growth of weeds, and the wheel-less remains of a postman's bicycle lay like a skinny old drunk on the concrete beside them. Had the curtains been open he would have taken a look in. They could have been drawn against the glaring evening sunset, though in this mixed territory of flats and student bedsits they were equally likely to have remained shut all day.

Just as he was about to turn back, the door opened. A shadowy youth wearing jeans and a blue, grease-spotted T-shirt appeared in the gap between the door and a stack of mountain bikes.

'Yeah?'

'Darren,' said Straker, sliding his hands into his trouser pockets. 'I need a little chat.'

'Don't we all, mate. Let me guess – owes you, does he?' A white smile broke through the lad's stubble. 'Yeah, can't think of anyone who's not looking for Darren right now. He owes the landlord three months' rent. He owes me seventy quid. I spend half my time answering the door to Darren Mulvaney's creditors.'

'Where is he, then?'

'We have a card...'

The youth disappeared into the gloom of a passage lined with cream and burgundy flock-paper. Presently he returned, waving a postcard. Straker took it. He glanced at the paradisic beach, turned the card over and read in silence the short message pencilled on the back:- *Goin' sloa in Goa. Lifestyle ace, but weary of laying the backpackers. Off to Thailand for change of scene. Don't work too hard. D*

He shifted his thumbs either side of the postmark.

'Too smudged,' said the youth. 'It arrived about a fortnight ago.'

'And he left here -?'

'What, middle of Feb? Having told us nothing of the proposed itinerary, or we'd have lynched the bastard before he hit Magdalen Bridge.' He'd plucked the card back from Straker and eyed up the door. 'Perhaps I could stick this up for the next caller. You wouldn't be heading Thailand way, by any chance?'

Straker opened the door of the building society and stepped into its commercial plushness. Thailand seemed to him an excellent destination for Darren. A stilt-house on an Indian beach was just as good. Either made his situation with Nadine agreeably neat. And, it transpired, Darren really was a bastard. Straker smiled to himself as he laid his passbook on the counter; he'd known Darren was a bastard the moment he'd set eyes on the photograph. Hilary had called him one on several occasions. Maybe it took a bastard to recognise bastardy in others. He had his faults. But he would never jet Nadine off to Thailand when Hilary's car needed replacing. He was a bastard with magnanimity. Therefore he counted himself less of a bastard than Darren.

'I'd like to make a withdrawal, please,' he said, patting the passbook. 'Cash.'

*

Next morning, Saturday, he left Marcham before nine.

'Where are you going?' Hilary ran after the reversing car and rapped on the driver's window. 'You're not on till lunch-time, are you?'

'It's a surprise.'

'For whom?'

'You'll see.'

He fed the steering-wheel between his hands, working them with firmness and precision up and down the wheel while the car swept into the turning-circle. No crossing of arms for him, no sloppiness. Perfect control.

He parked near the Westgate, collected the book he had ordered, then walked to the building society. As there was no queue he went straight to the desk, flinching as he caught sight of himself sliding across the security television screen overhead.

From the breast pocket of his jacket he removed the envelope, put it on the counter, then picked out a small piece of paper from the same pocket, unfolded it and laid it on the envelope.

'I'd like it paid into this account, please,' he said, tapping a finger on the paper.

The girl took the paper and envelope, and pattered the account number into the computer. She removed the notes from the envelope and slapped through them with ring-laden fingers while Straker jingled a handful of loose change from his trouser pocket and picked through it, setting some coins on the counter. The girl's red nails flashed as she skidded them one at a time into her hand.

'Perfect. I'll just give you a receipt, Mr – Mulvaney?'

'Tah-nah!'

Straker swung the carrier from behind his back and dangled it over Hilary's coffee mug on the kitchen table. She made a little gasp. Her mouth fell open and the gasp spread into a smile.

'It's something for me!'

'A book. Nothing outrageously expensive,' he said gruffly, proffering the bag, 'but I hope you find it useful.'

'Useful?'

'Not boring or utilitarian, I promise. No gardening, cakes or craft ideas for kiddies.'

She slid her hand into the bag. 'Oh! Miranda Castro's *Complete Handbook of Homeopathy*! Oh, Jim...' She flicked through the pages. 'This is such a good book. How on earth did you know what to buy?'

'I rang your friend Esther, so it stands or falls by her recommendation. Well, I thought, with your new course starting soon... An excellent introduction, was her opinion, and a solid book for the family reference library. To me it looks like a sorceror's herbal.'

'Oh, I wish you'd asked which remedies Zoe Seymour gave you. I could have looked them up. Not that they seem to have transformed your waterworks, mind. I should give her a ring.'

'*Mum?*'

The quavering rise in pitch denoted a distant but urgent request. Straker paused and cocked his head to one side.

'He's in the garden. It's such a lovely morning again. He was reading.'

'Christ! Is there a power-cut?'

'*Mum!*'

The tone had changed to the swooping downturn and enhanced volume of a demand.

'I'll go,' Straker suggested. 'I haven't seen him today.'

Before he reached the back door, Daniel, wearing shorts and a pair of unlaced trainers, bounced up the outside steps.

'Mu- Oh, Dad!' Daniel came inside, panting. 'Dad, you know what you said about the magpies?'

'What, exactly?'

'Like, trashing other birds' nests?' Daniel thumbed outside. 'Well, I think that's what they're doing. The nest in the high bank. I think it might have been going on for a while.'

'*Think it might?*' Straker ran into the dining-room. 'My Christ, look at it!' He hauled on the sliding doors. 'You're the saviour of the bloody universe when you're plugged into those games machines, but give you a dose of reality, Daniel, and you can't even put the wind up a bird.'

'I had the headset on –'

But Straker was already halfway across the lawn, clapping his hands over his head, and hissing.

High in the old hedge, one of the magpies sat, mildly flustered, the tip of its beak daubed with gluey yolk to which a chip of pale shell still adhered. The parent robins fluttered round in the nearby branches, bobbing and darting through the leaves. For a second they remained motionless, the air pierced with their twin, reedy alarm cries before they drove at the intruder once again.

The magpie watched Straker's own noisy display and wiped its beak either side of a twig, successfully dislodging the shard of eggshell.

'Dad!' Daniel wailed.

Straker stopped shouting. He stood for a moment, one hand on his hip, the other flat on the crown of his head. It was all too late, even the boy could see. He turned on his heel and walked back towards the house.

Orpheus, sitting like a statuette of Bastet beside the kitchen steps, looked up his long, sleek snout at Straker, his close-set eyes glinting in the sunshine.

'I don't know why we bother with that cat,' Straker muttered, crossing the patio. He scuffed his shoes on the doormat. 'Never around when he's wanted. Everywhere you look when he's not.'

'He's frightened of magpies,' said Daniel.

'Is he,' said Straker. 'Is he indeed?'

'I went back before leaving for work,' he said, cradling Nadine's head in the crook of his right arm as they lay in bed together on Sunday afternoon. 'The robins had deserted the nest by then. They built it in the top of the bank where an old tree stump has rotted, a loose affair of moss and dead leaves lined with horse-hair and wool. What craft, everything so neatly executed, so well-fitted to their needs. And it was full of smashed shells stuck together with albumen and yolk, small white eggs with ginger freckles...'

Nadine lay on her side, watching him unburden himself to the stars. 'They might try again.'

'They might. Whether they risk the same nesting site, I don't know. I put on some plastic gloves and cleared out the mess as best I could. It must be devastating for them, though. All their work and effort destroyed in minutes by that marauding, piratical opportunist.'

'Just one?'

'Unusually. The female must be incubating.' He paused for a while, then rolled on to his side to face her. 'I do have some good news, though. Two pieces, in fact. The first concerns your ex.'

'You saw him? You spoke to Darren?'

'Put it this way: your mortgage arrears should be discharged any day now. The lot. You can ring up tomorrow morning and check.'

Nadine made a little gasp. Her mouth fell open and the gasp spread to a smile as she clapped her hands to his cheeks and kissed him with a hard smack on the lips.

'Oh, Jim!' She kissed him again. 'How was he? Oh, I must go round and thank him!'

'You silly woman...'

'Am I?'

'Very. In any case he's away a fair bit,' said Straker. 'I should write. Plus, Hilary's starting a homœopathy evening class. Seven-thirty to nine-thirty on Wednesdays, confirmed last night.'

'Is that good?'

'Well, Daniel will be having after-school cricket practice then and staying for tea at his mate's. Anyta's fallen in love and wants to get in touch with her femininity all of a sudden, so she's signing up for a belly-dancing class which coincides with Hilary's. Hil takes Anyta with her, and she collects Daniel on her way home. And so, except when I'm on Lates -'

'We'll have the best part of two hours all to ourselves?'

'Every Wednesday for the next six weeks. Maybe longer if they're keen.'

'Oh!'

She rolled him on to his back and lay across his chest, gazing down at him, her lips soft and her eyes flickering round his face with admiration and ardour. His mind buzzed in excitement. Without touching her, he slid his left hand over his thigh. He pressed, and met with half-committed, half-inflated sponginess. He squeezed again, first in hope, then pinched himself with harsh, almost painful desperation.

'What is it?'

'Nothing!'

She shifted herself forward, and one of her nipples brushed against his. She closed her eyes, and her mouth floated down to his face. He held himself rigid and began to groan.

'Jim, what's the matter?'

'Nothing. I've come,' he muttered. 'I don't bloody believe it! I've never felt so turned on, and yet I can't even get a rise. Next minute, the finale's over before the curtain's gone up. I'm cursed.'

'Cursed? You're adored. And didn't that Zoe woman tell you to call if nothing happened? This homœopathy, let's face it, Jim, it's doing you no favours.'

He pursed his lips.

'Well, what's the point of waiting another four weeks? If nothing's happened yet, it never will. You come out with all these threats against your magpies and how you're going to do for them, but what about you?'

'It takes a long time to get ill,' he said thoughtfully. 'It can take a long time to get well. It makes perfect sense.'

'Is that what she told you? It's sop. *Ring* her.' She pressed her hands over his ears and her forehead against his. Her eyes loomed above him, black and fuzzy and huge as plates. 'I want to make love with you properly. I don't believe in curses. That's another you, a different life. I care about this one here, now. Us. Don't you?'

*

'I'm surprised you didn't find any benefit from the last remedy,' said Zo Seymour. 'I think I'm going to have to re-take your case. Many patients present with similar symptoms, you see. What matters is the route they travelled to get there. Do you follow? The details a patient considers irrelevant are very often the ones that guide us to the right remedy. So if you can think of anything you haven't told me because you forgot, or because it didn't seem important at the time –'

Straker studied the distorted golden rectangle of sunlight on the wall to his left. He'd called Zoe Seymour the day after the last fiasco with Nadine, but he'd had to endure another long, dismal week before an appointment that suited his shifts.

Within the outline of the window frame, the net curtains across the lower sash projected complex, web-like shadows, and the flowers sat amongst the threads like fat spiders.

'Well,' he said, 'I made the enlightening discovery last week that I can only pee standing up, if that helps. I forced so hard I broke out in a sweat and wound up with a headache.'

Zo Seymour looked up from her pad.

Flashing, he told her, indicating his forehead. 'Right across here.'

When she finished writing, her pen hovered pointedly above the paper. He cleared his throat.

'The fantasies I told you about?'

'Yes?'

'It's more like an obsession. When I have one it colours my whole existence. It's like an enchanted treasure chest that draws me back, and back again for the pleasure of picking over what's inside. I know it's petty and adolescent, and I know I should be able to let them go, but I can't.'

'When did you last have one of these – obsessions?'

'Between January the twenty-fourth and February the fifteenth.'

There was a harsh whirring sound from the paper; she had ringed the dates.

'Can you tell me a little more about your relationship with Hilary?'

'I think,' he said, 'you need to know about my relationship with Nadine.'

*

By the time he had finished, Zoe Seymour had written three-quarters of a side of notes.

'So there's been no physical relationship with Hilary for about eighteen months?'

'I deserved it,' he said. 'I didn't hightail it elsewhere, or give up hope. Not for a long time.'

'And now?'

'Nadine has this little-girl frailty, yet sometimes she can be utterly outrageous. One minute she slips through my fingers. The next, she's as solid and real as that desk. It was only when I fell in love with her –' He paused '- that I realised how long Hilary and I had been kidding ourselves we had a marriage in anything but name.'

'Does she know?'

'When you work irregular shifts and unpredictable hours, conducting a clandestine relationship is not as difficult as you might think. The funny thing is that my relationship with Hilary is better now than it's been for years. She's less tense, I'm happier... At least I was, until I was struck down with impotence. It's like a punishment. Nemesis.'

'You believe in nemesis?'

'Oh, I don't know. I believe in bad luck.'

'What were the tablets you gave me last time?' he inquired as he prepared to leave. It was almost eight o'clock. 'Only Hilary's just started an evening class with your friend, and she's curious.'

Zoe Seymour slid his file between the books in her briefcase. 'I gave you Lycopodium, Jim, which is made from the club moss, *Lycopodium clavatum*. It's one of our polycrests, our major remedies. Not an uncommon prescription as remedies go, put it that way. But it's not your remedy. What did Hilary think of her first session?'

'Fascinating. She's ordering a remedy kit, and on the look-out for victims. So,' he ventured, 'do you have a better idea now what my remedy might be?'

'I have a couple in mind, but I'll need to work in more detail on your case to be certain. I'll call you.'

She unlocked the door of the Centre, let him out and locked up again behind her. He heard the heels of her ankle boots nipping the pavement, and as he turned into the side-road where he'd parked, he glanced over his shoulder. She carried on advancing in the same direction, her upper body rocking like a metronome between her briefcase and the laptop bouncing on her opposite hip. Then she followed him into the side-road.

He took out his keys, depressed the handset and made a third, uneasy glance back.

'It's all right,' she called cheerfully, 'I'm not trailing you. One of my friends is away and she's letting me use her parking space.'

He just wanted to get in the car; confessions with a homœopath behind the consulting-room door were one thing, conversations with them on street corners somehow frayed the neat seams of acceptability.

'Like rabbits, do you?'

He froze, one foot on the sill.

'Or is it for your children?' She jabbed a stubby finger at the rear passenger window. 'The hutch.'

'It's not a hutch, actually.'

She thudded the briefcase on the kerb and put her face up to the glass. She had small feet, he remarked, for a woman her height, small feet and a large backside.

'It looks like a hutch.'

'It's a Larsen trap.'

Zoe Seymour straightened and looked at him out of the corner of her eyes. 'To catch thieves, right?'

'To catch magpies,' he corrected. 'A gamekeeper friend of mine owed me a favour. I picked it up just this afternoon.'

'Larsen trap... Never heard of that before. And how does it work, Jim, this trap?' She paused. 'You have a problem with magpies, I take it?'

He raised the boot of the estate, leaned inside, grasped the trap and, with both hands, dragged it across the sheets of newspaper covering the floor of the boot. Grunting, he lifted the trap clear and set it on the pavement for her inspection.

It was a square, shallow cage with a wooden frame, the bottom open and the other sides closed with chicken wire. Internally, wire partitions split the space into four equal chambers, each given access by a separate door in the cage roof.

'It's a double trap,' he explained, 'so you can capture two at a time. This –' he depressed one of the doors '- is fixed on a sprung hinge.'

He removed his fingers and let the door flip upwards again, then he took two short, identical cylinders of wood from the boot.

She frowned at them. 'They look like bits of broom-handle.'

'That's exactly what they are. You push them end to end, press the trap door right down like I showed you, and fit the reformed stick between the vertical side of the trap door and the side of the cage, so that the force of the spring holds the stick horizontal.'

He demonstrated.

'Like a perch?'

'You've got it. The magpie lands. The "perch" collapses, releasing the lid, the lid flies up and bingo!'

He put his fists thumb to thumb and twisted them in opposite directions.

'I presume they don't have a death-wish?'

'Eggs,' he said bitterly, 'they're partial to eggs. But a decoy is better.' He reached into the corner of the boot and produced a plastic magpie. 'Best of all is the real thing. You put a foreign magpie in the neighbouring cage with a twig perch and a bowl of cat-food, and down come the locals to beat up the intruder. Then your first catch becomes somebody else's decoy for the rest of the season. My mate caught fifty-eight last year.'

'But what about buzzards?'

'They're less of a problem,' he said, tossing the magpie back into the boot. 'And any bird-lover who's ever witnessed a magpie systematically devouring songbirds' eggs and nestlings, one after the other, would do just the same. They're a scourge, magpies, a plague on the face of the earth. Remember the saying, a cat would look at a king? A magpie would eyeball God Almighty. Evil, they are.'

'Do you walk under ladders?'

'Ladders? No, always round them.' He reached over the trap and bundled it back inside his car. 'Common sense, isn't it.'

'I think I know your remedy,' said Zo Seymour.

29

Karin read over Mr Wilson's case, her chair turned to the windows. Plumes of wistaria flowers hung in a lilac curtain either side, exotic yet gracious in the bursting light. Everywhere spring was prising open the tight buds, expanding the coils and infolds of winter with an explosion of vibrant green. All round her spring uncurled, leaving her in autumn, inwardly fading, contracting and drying.

She'd kept herself busy; her night-class students professed to be as keen after the third session as before the first. The swimming had improved her fitness, and the patients kept coming. If that was what they called coping, she was coping.

She could take a lodger, she considered, putting Mr Wilson's file on the desk. The house had too many rooms: Brendan's office had not been used in five months, any more than the dining-room had seen entertaining. Her life revolved round the kitchen, her office and the bedroom, their bedroom. And the rooms all seemed as large as temples. The last time she'd watched television, she'd crept from the sofa on to the hearth rug and levered herself, on her buttocks, closer and closer to the screen and away from the cold space breathing on her shoulders. Maybe she could take several lodgers. She could move. No, the house *was* Brendan now. Before his death, she'd lived so long with the idea that he might return. Sometimes, when the knocker sounded – But part of him had never left. He carried on in the rows of cassettes and CDs, in the pile of back issues of *Nature*, in the bottle of peaty Laphroaig no one else would touch, in *The Swing*. That was where he lived now, in the high ceilings and marble fireplaces and the spaces.

The knocker sounded.

'To summarise...' With her pen Karin indicated different sections of her notes. 'Your cough is almost resolved. You have greater mobility in your fingers and neck, and you're sleeping longer and more restfully.'

'Not as well as a week ago,' countered Mr Wilson. 'I'm starting to wake up again, I tell you. And my fingers aren't as good.' He directed his palms at her face and slowly curved his fingers and thumbs. 'See, that's the best I can do now. And my neck...' He rotated it to the right. 'I'm not expecting you to turn me into an owl, but that's a definite deterioration.'

'Well, the indications are that the remedy's been working, Mr Wilson, so I'm going to repeat it. If it doesn't pick up where it left off, or the situation improves and then relapses, ring me and I'll send you a higher dose. How does that sound?'

'All right, I suppose. I wouldn't have come back at all, you know, if I hadn't improved so much.'

'I was lucky then,' she smiled. 'We don't always hit the jackpot first time.'

'No, I mean I don't approve of how some women carry on these days.'

'In what sense?'

'Your other job.'

'My teaching?'

'And with that look in your eye.' He leaned forward. 'See, I thought I recognised you the other day. I was sat on the bus, and I knew I'd seen you before, but I couldn't quite remember where. Not surprisingly.'

'Mr Wilson, you've lost me.'

'Down the railway station,' he whispered with a nod, 'by the mainroad. You have a look.'

He was old, she thought as she saw him to the door. Youthful confidence had fused with the failing perceptions of senescence. He was old and refused to elaborate. He had *Confusion of mind;*

Delusions, faces, sees; Memory, weakness of. Remedies like his experienced in their dreams the riots they could not permit themselves in reality. They dreamed of masks because, metaphorically, they wore them. Quick to moral outrage, he had seen something risqué and given it her face.

She returned to her office to update his prescription details on the laptop, but closed the file without amendments and fetched her car keys from the kitchen. Maybe she would take a look anyway. He was her last client of the day. She had set the afternoon aside for repertorisation, and her concentration vacillated enough without distractions to trip her up before she began.

She left the car at the station and walked over to the main road. *Down the railway station...* Somewhere along Hythe Bridge Street, then, or the start of the Botley Road. Soon enough she saw it, just across the road from the railway station – And disbelief was a short-lived refuge. Her heart rapidly thudded through that flimsy stockade into the bald fact that Mr Wilson's observations were as acute as anyone else's. The whole picture, but for a sporty red four-wheel drive, was printed in a hazy and slightly distorted black and white, creating an illusion of unreality for all eyes but her own. It was her. Her on a billboard, naked but for a spear, her skin bone white against a sweep of charcoal sky. Her eyes, now as black as the sky and hauntingly alien, pierced the humming space of the road. Karin and her image stared at each other, transfixed. For some reason, her warrior double appeared to be assessing the vehicle as it bounced a trail of dust away across the plain. In the curled lips and the eyes Karin saw the sidelong revelation of interest veiled, but only thinly veiled, with disdain. *The new Yamamoto Shen*, read the caption in the bottom left corner. *The new Yamamoto Shen - The hunt is on.*

The cars tore past, slowed to a crawl, accelerated again. Their roar echoed under the railway bridge as she stood motionless in the middle of the pavement.

'How could you?' she murmured. 'How could you do this?'

There was as much of him in the picture as herself. It was

the Penthesilea sequence. In her head she heard him still: '*Who are you?*' And he had merged her with a Japanese car and sold her into the bondage of advertising.

Drivers began to stare. Heads inclined to discover the object of her interest. She backed away, began the return walk to the station car park. Every step seemed to reverberate through fragile bone and muscle. The bending of her knees, the arc of her arms found her limbs leaden. Surely an offence had been committed, but she had no proof. She needed evidence, she needed legal advice. The cars slid around like building blocks in her tears.

'I liked you.' She beat her hand on the steering-wheel when she arrived at the first set of traffic lights. 'I trusted you. I *trusted* you.'

*

She returned home for her camera. She photographed the poster on half a roll of new film, left the film with a one-hour processor in the town centre and walked to the Westgate. She bought a cup of tea in a café and drank it too fast, perching on a high thin stool at a counter not much wider than a paperback. Another cup followed. An hour's waiting! A consultation twice that length seemed brief in comparison.

'I'm afraid,' said Miss Jeffs, 'that principles come with a hefty price-tag these days. Whilst this initial consultation is free, justice, unfortunately, is not always affordable. We have a duty to make our clients aware –'

'Whatever it takes,' said Karin.

St Aldate's boasted several solicitors' offices, and she had walked into the first she'd seen. She'd waited twenty minutes in the Reception of Handley Myers with the traffic shushing through the double-glazing and folds of net curtain, and now she had progressed to an even blander interview room.

She recounted the story, and Miss Jeffs, a young, well-groomed woman in a short-sleeved white blouse and bottle-green skirt, quizzed her about her acquaintance with Roy Meredith.

'And do you have any idea where he lives or works?'

'Somewhere in Southampton. And he is – or was till

recently – a solicitor.'

Miss Jeffs boxed the fact with four firm strokes of her pen. 'So,' she said, reading back over her notes, 'you requested the photographs and – correct me if I'm wrong – told him you'd pay. Did he ever ask you to sign anything?'

'Never. I offered to pay. It seemed only fair.'

'You would have sent the money on receiving the photos at home in England, and he took that on trust?'

'Of course.'

'But during the last day or so of the holiday you felt Mr Meredith was becoming too attentive, and, given your marital difficulties, you avoided him and then forgot about the photos.' Miss Jeffs spread them into a fan across the table. 'This may seem a strange question, Ms Shilan, but I must ask you the basis of your objection to the poster.'

'Objection? My objection,' Karin said heatedly, 'is that I'm a homœopath here, I'm a course tutor! This was a private business arrangement. It was never intended for the public eye.' She skimmed the nearest picture with the back of her nails. 'Look at it! It compromises my career. It's a slur on my reputation. Thanks to Mr Meredith I almost lost a client this morning.'

'I see.' Miss Jeffs kept her eyes on her writing. 'And what would you be looking to gain, should the case go ahead?'

'I want any posters withdrawn and taken down. That's all I want.'

'Compensation?'

Karin considered. 'No, I'm not out to make a killing. An apology would be nice.'

Miss Jeffs finished her notes and closed the cover of her pad. 'Well, Ms Shilan, I'm optimistic. Copyright law is quite complicated but, on the basis of what you've told me, I think you should have a case. I'll pass the file to my boss and write within the next couple of days, enclosing our terms and conditions. If those are acceptable, Mr Bennallick's secretary will contact you to arrange an appointment, by which time he'll have the relevant facts at his fingertips and be able to discuss how best to proceed.'

Karin thanked her. 'What is he like, Mr -?'

'Bennallick, Steve Bennallick. Very good.' Miss Jeffs studied the ceiling light of white globes and brass. 'I'd rather have him acting for me than against. But he's good.'

*

By the time Karin drove west on Friday evening, she had an appointment for the following Thursday with Steven Bennallick.

She spent the night at her usual Bed and Breakfast in Tavistock. The college weekend was well timed, she thought, as she ate her full English breakfast next morning. There would be the company of thirty second- and third-year students of all ages, the intellectual demands of teaching and the stimulation of lively questions, all in the setting of Tweenaway House, Finn's beautiful, rambling home on the outskirts of Tavistock. This physical and mental oasis fitted the bill perfectly, well away from Oxford and the contentions and plottings of law. Away from solicitors, good and bad.

The entrance was the threshold of dreams, an arched, dark red Hobbit door in a towering wall whose moist brickwork sprung with ivy. Next to the door, the morning sun was beginning to catch the brass plate engraved *The West Devon School of Homœopathy*.

Beyond the gate, a gravel path beckoned through shrubbery into the secret, vernal world of Finn's garden. A few students sat, cross-legged, on the edge of the distant lawn. Others basked in the sun on the faded grey wooden benches and seats either side of the porch. She greeted them, slipped off her sandals in the quarry-tiled hall and wandered into the kitchen. She set down her rucksack and took out a basin of coleslaw, a Stilton quiche and a carrier of fruit.

She took the third-years for Causticum that morning, and they ate their Dutch lunch outside, sitting in lazy, sociable, barefooted groups on the lawn. Karin lay on her side, peeling an orange. One of the second years knelt beside her.

'Have you got a sister?'

'I have a sister, Kira, yes.'

'Does she look like you?'

Karin dug too deeply into the flesh of the orange and an ellipsis of juice spurted across her purple skirt.

'Not the Yamamoto Shen?'

'Hey, you know it. Yeah, I was looking through the landlady's *Telegraph* magazine after breakfast - I said it was!' she yelled to the group on the nearest bench. 'Are you a model, then?'

'And pop star. Autographs can be provided at tea-break. Have you studied Palladium yet?'

Heads turned to the laughter and expressions of admiration. She picked her orange peel, piece by piece, out of the grass, and the sounds blurred round her into the buzzing of bees in the Californian lilac. With the bitter rinds in her hand, she went in search of Finn and found him photocopying a case study in his admin room upstairs.

'God, this is awful,' she said. She leaned against the wall and shut her eyes. 'And I had no idea it would find its way into the Press.'

'*Telegraph* today, *Times* tomorrow?' Finn grinned into his beard as he swapped the master in the photocopier. 'Did you stop at the Services on your way down?'

'Taunton. I'm really sorry.'

'On your return journey, try Exeter.'

'What?'

'Saw it earlier in the week, Karin, on the hoardings. A doppel-ganger, I assumed. I looked three times, I must confess. Twice to check, and the third because I was so impressed. It's a very nice picture,' he said, stapling his two piles of copies into pairs. 'Don't you think? I'm sure Yamamoto are delighted.'

'It's without permission.'

'Ah.' Finn paused and bounced the ends of the stapler together, making nipping sounds. 'In that case somebody -'

'Somebody has. But you're not bothered?'

'For an up-and-coming homœopath, yes, it's somewhat unconventional, but I don't think I'll be requesting your resignation. As for what your clients will make of it —'

He shrugged, stapler still in hand.

*

Just after she arrived home on Sunday night, Zo rang.

'Good weekend?' she inquired.

'Tweenaway at its best! Everything in bloom, the clematis, my favourite horse chestnuts, the magnolias...Gorgeous! Causticum seemed well received. Oh, and Finn and Anna asked to be remembered to you.'

'Thanks. Karin, I was reading the paper today –'

'And you saw an advert for the Yamamoto Shen?'

'Wow!'

'I can tell,' Karin said, 'from your voice.'

30

'It's an intriguing case, Ms Shilan. And you do have a case, subject to me checking a couple of points raised by my colleague.'

Steven Bennallick reached for the wallet of photographs, set in a neat square of desk surrounded by clutter. The desk, which seemed to fill half the room, was a grand affair in Victorian mahogany, marred by a utilitarian burden of plastic office hardware and eel-like nests of cables.

Her eyes wandered across the dimly lit, sage green walls: a large plain calendar, a couple of framed certificates, several washed-out prints of Oxford. To the left of the desk stood three chipped grey filing cabinets, on top of which sat a stack of orange cardboard files and a couple of plants. One had purplish leaves that hung in limp, hairy ribbons down the side of the cabinet. Beside it, in a plastic pot still bearing a faded price label, a crispy fern more brown than green clung bravely to life. And boxed in a brass frame just in front of the plants was a photo of Steven Bennallick head-to-head with a close-cropped blonde.

Steven Bennallick opened the flap of the photograph wallet, pulled the bundle halfway out, shuffled it back in and closed the flap. He laid the wallet flat, then picked it up again by its short sides and tapped its long edge on the desk-top.

'*The hunt is on.* Clever, these advertisers. Man hunts girl by baiting with nice red car, girl hunts car but switches affections to man on basis of his exquisite good taste. Fork out for the Yamamoto Shen and you get irresistibility to beautiful women thrown in with the air-bags. Wonderful.' He tapped the photos again, laid them on the desk and leaned back hard in his chair. 'Now, your case comes under the Copyright, Designs and Patents Act, a section of which grants certain rights of privacy – what we call moral rights – to those who commission, and only to those who commission photographs for private and domestic purposes. This includes the right not to have your photo, or copies of it exhibited in, or issued to the public.'

'But don't I own the copyright?' she inquired. 'The photographs are of me, after all. The rights of the individual, Mr Bennallick, aren't they the gods of the New Age?'

'Ah, but as a sentient adult you can determine only what happens to your body, not images of it. Copyright rests with the photographer or, in the case of a picture, the artist. Unless there's a written assignment of copyright governing the creation of that work, which, in your case, doesn't apply. The key issue here, without which we can't proceed, is that you commissioned the photos.'

'I decided everything,' she said. 'The location, the costume, the props. The whole thing was my idea.'

'Good.' He took a pen from a blue plastic desk-tidy by the phone and made a few jottings in a pad beside the photos. 'But you've never consented to their use, either verbally or in writing?'

'No!'

'Do you ever go by another name?'

'McDonald, I used to use McDonald sometimes. My late husband's name.'

'Are you sure Roy Meredith never asked you to sign a model release? Because I've been doing a bit of phoning this past couple of days. Nothing of consequence with Yamamoto, but it appears that Sanderson Keayes, the ad agency who put the image together, were shown a model release for you before accepting Meredith's photo. Here...' He extracted a white sheet of paper from a sheaf in a paper clip and held it out to her. 'Faxed to me this morning.'

She perused the page. 'Impossible. This isn't me,' she said, jabbing the paper. 'Look, it says Karin Crossport. I didn't sign that. It's a forgery. That's not my address, it's not even my name! And what's this? *Absolute right and permission to publish* -? *Having received the sum of* –? I've never received a penny from anyone.'

'Date and location?'

'They're the only entries that are accurate.'

Bennallick got up and paced along the windows. His shirt flashed with the fingers of sunlight that insinuated themselves through the slats of the vertical blinds. She shifted on her worn leather seat to watch him. SM Bennallick BA (Cantab). She'd noted from the list on Miss Jeff's letter that he was also a Partner. His hair should have been grey, or at least seriously receding. No, he was too young, she thought. She wanted a tubby old patriarchal greybeard, a legal teddy-bear who would exude compassion, offer her coffee and set her at ease. This one was too young, too slim, too tall, and the sleeves of his blue and white striped shirt were rolled unprofessionally above the elbow.

'You see,' he said, pausing to adjust one of the blinds, 'Bodystock International, the picture library where Meredith placed his photos, didn't require sight of a model release before accepting them. It's implicit within their terms and conditions that photographers have all the requisite clearances. But when Sanderson Keayes came along they wanted to see the document for themselves...' He shook his head. 'So, we go for Yamamoto, and Yamamoto can pursue the rest of the chain as they see fit. We want an undertaking to remove any images already on display, an undertaking not to display them further, a written apology, payment of costs and token damages for your distress if you're not seeking full compensation.' He stroked his dark blue and magenta tie. 'However, in order for me to be able to tackle your case with absolute confidence, I do want to clarify, for my own peace of mind, your relationship with this photographer. How often did you see him?'

She swallowed. 'He gave me a lift once. We met to discuss the possibility of doing the photos, then there was the day of shooting. That's it.'

Steven Bennallick sat down on his great black office chair. He placed his elbows on the desk, pressed his hands palm to palm as though in prayer, and ran one hand alternately down the other so that his bare forearms swung side to side. Finally he snapped the fingers of his right hand shut over the left.

'I'm going to infer you got on well with Mr Meredith.'

'I wouldn't dispute that.'

'Ms Shilan, this is somewhat delicate. You see, just as you feel your professional reputation is at stake over these posters, so I put my professional reputation on the line every time I accept a case and, therefore, commit to fight a client's corner. Now, before I go in with all guns blazing on your account, which I'm more than happy to do, I do need to know whether your involvement with Mr Meredith moved at any time beyond friendship.'

'No!'

'I also need to be aware of any emotional undercurrents that might be thrown back in my face at a later date. Once bitten, I'm afraid.'

'Mr Bennallick, there was nothing.'

'Right. And yet you avoided Mr Meredith the day before you left because he was becoming –' he leafed through the sheets of Miss Jeff's handwriting '- "too keen?"' His voice rose inquiringly.

'I didn't want to get involved. My husband –'

'Who wasn't there with you at the time?'

'No – I even lied about the name of my hotel.'

'But if you lied about your hotel, you must have done so from the very beginning. Before Mr Meredith became "too keen?"'

'I didn't want to take any chances. I never told him my surname either, any surname.'

'In other words, Roy Meredith couldn't have got in touch with you, even if he'd wanted, because you'd made yourself untraceable.' He took a breath through his nose and held it captive for some moments before releasing it in a thoughtful rush. 'I must say, for a woman travelling alone, especially one who doesn't want to take any chances, being photographed nude seems a rather compromising course of action. Would the marital difficulties have any bearing?'

'I did it to boost my confidence.'

'Which I'm sure it must have done, given the position in which you now find yourself. Not a great surprise, was it, when Meredith became over-attentive?' He chuckled good-humouredly to himself. 'Well, I appreciate your candidness, Ms Shilan. Is there anything else I should know?'

'Nothing.'

He drew a line across his page of notes and flung his biro on to the desk. He reclined against his chair, put one hand on the back of his head and with the other swept his hair from his forehead.

'Of course, you'll also have to decide whether you wish to make a professional complaint against Mr Meredith.'

'Professional?'

'To the Law Society. Selling private photographs, without consent, for profit... Putting your name into disrepute... Making false declarations, forging a document. Not what I would call conduct befitting an Officer of the Supreme Court. My personal view, for what it's worth, is that disciplinary proceedings might be warranted. However, that's a separate issue here and the final decision is up to you. Think it over. In the meantime, should I -?'

'Yes, yes. Please, you go ahead.'

'Excellent.' He picked up the discarded pen and dropped it, from a pincered finger and thumb, into the desk-tidy. 'I gather from Miss Jeffs that you're a homœopath. I suffer from crashing headaches. Migraines really, not helped by that direct sun in the mornings. Hence the blinds. I've tried everything, tablets, diet, cranial osteopath. Never homœopathy, though. Perhaps you'd consider a consultation some time?'

'I'd be glad to.'

'No hurry, of course,' he said amiably, getting up. 'Just a thought.' He took her downstairs and showed her out. 'I don't know whether I should tell you this,' he said, the front door of Handley Myers half open on to the landing. 'But at Sanderson Keayes, word has it that the Shen, spear-headed by your good self, is heading for an early sales record. Must be the eyes.'

She stepped out into the white mid-morning light and rubbed her arms, squeezing her cold skin in the sunshine. She glanced up to the third storey. After thirty minutes in the cool, semi-shuttered world of Steven Bennallick, she, too, was pleased he was working for rather than against her.

She examined the back of her hand, half-expecting it to be shaking. Walking out of Handley Myers felt like leaving an examination hall after a paper that had deviated from the syllabus.

She returned to the car park. At one point her cheeks had begun to warm with annoyance over his personal probings, but somehow he'd undermined and crushed her irritation with his hail of quick-fire questions. He scarcely let her recover from one before he drew his next incisive conclusion and hurled that back at her too. He took his cases and she took hers; the techniques just never coincided. He made her feel as though she were an innocent stooge set up for a magician. At any time he might have leaned over that desk, ripped off her blouse intact from under her waistcoat, and, before she'd protested, trussed her up and suspended her from the ceiling in a net.

She collected the car and drove back to the house. Still, he made it his business to machete through the jungle of dross and home in on the information he needed, and that was just what she had given him. She'd told no lies. She'd not told him the complete truth either, but the omissions had no bearing on the facts of the case. Had he swallowed her partial truth? Or did he have his suspicions? How much weight did he accord her assurance? Her version had painted no one black, though in truth, one deserved painting blacker than the other. She could still see Roy's face when she'd suggested the second shoot.

'Are you serious?' he'd said. He'd studied her with large,

unsettled eyes. 'I mean, I didn't anticipate studio work. Holiday, and all that. I didn't come equipped.'

'Do your best with what you have.'

'I couldn't guarantee the quality -'

She shrugged, smiling, her hands in her lap.

They walked, side by side, close but not touching, along the paved path back to his room. It seemed a perfect beginning to the night, strolling round the pool with its illuminated shrub and cacti borders and long, spiked shadows. The gardens created a dense weave of textures through which jewel-green and brilliant white lamps flared from the earth and faded to darkness. It was inevitable that she and Roy would end up in bed.

He chatted about the photographic equipment he had and what he lacked, and how he might incorporate the existing light sources. She heard herself responding remotely to his conversation and laughter. She recalled little of what he was saying, or what she was replying, as though the details had been etched away by the *vino blanco*. Her nervousness had burrowed so deep inside her that it had metamorphosed into confidence. The air seemed to fizz round her, and she flaunted the adrenaline like a ball-gown.

Roy unlocked the door and let her inside. He switched on all the wall-lights and closed the curtains.

'Nice room.'

'Not a bad floor,' he said. 'Nice pale marble.' He looked upward, his mouth open. 'The ceiling's pale, that long wall's pale. I could bounce a bit of light off those. Feel free to thrash an armchair while I sort myself out. And don't undress; you'll get cold.'

She took off her sandals and curled up in the corner of the settee by the curtains. He lifted a hold-all into the centre of the floor, knelt beside it with one knee raised and rummaged inside. His jeans were stained with the reddish dust from the caldera, the sleeves of his blue and white striped shirt still unevenly rolled above the elbow. He looked dishevelled and busy and youthful.

A reel of masking tape appeared on the floor, followed by

elastic bands, hair grips, a camera flash, a rectangle of black card, some cable and a crumpled ball of muslin that expanded out of his fist to smother everything else.

He got up and dug inside a storage cupboard, from which he produced a folded sheet in each hand, one white and one mottled grey-blue.

'I thought you were short on equipment.'

'These are just odds and ends. You know, trusty penknife, piece of string, half-sucked bull's eye. It's going to be make-do-and-mend photography tonight, but it should be fun. How do you like ironing?'

'Not at all. Steam facility!' she exclaimed, when he handed her his travel iron. 'Sheets will take forever with this. It's the size of a teaspoon.'

'Ah, but creased back-cloths are the height of photographic naff. When you see your unrumpled backdrop...'

'Yeah, Roy. To die for.'

He thanked her effusively when she'd finished and sent her in search of some flowers. By the time she arrived back, he'd pushed the settee against the end of the beds, its back facing the opposite wall. The white sheet was draped lengthways across the floor and halfway up the wall, where he had fixed it in place with masking tape.

He took the sheet they had used in the mountains, shook it out and arranged it along the back of the settee.

'You can undress now. Maybe a hint of eye make-up?'

'Hair?'

'Just brushed.'

He took the first shots with her lying on her back, her legs crossed and feet up the wall, and her hair spread in all directions on the floor round her head. He stood by the wall, on the TV table, peering down at her with the camera tilted on its tripod. In his right hand he held the flash aimed at the lower part of the sheet to the left of her body.

Just when she thought he might begin to shoot, he got down again, went to the bathroom and came back with the toothbrush glass.

'Otherwise we get a stunning nostril shot,' he said. 'Lift your head.'

He slid the glass, inverted, under the back of her skull. Making love seemed a long way off at that point.

'Your right hand,' he said, climbing back on the table, 'try it on your right thigh, and the left just below your left shoulder. Great! Now, this is more soft glamour, but I think it'll work well here. Make some eye contact. Fabulous! Hold still.'

The motor drive whirred and clicked, and the flash seemed like a succession of flares popping above her.

Afterwards she put up her hair in the bathroom. By the time she emerged, the set had changed: the settee had returned to the corner, minus a cushion which lay on the floor. The white sheet had been replaced by the dark blue one, and the flash was balanced on the dressing-table.

'What's that black thing stuck to it?' she inquired.

'In a previous incarnation it was part of a cereal packet. Now it's a shield to keep the flash light out of my camera lens, because I want to do some oblique shots of your back. Not full-length, so we can cheat a bit, and you'll have the luxury of kneeling on a cushion. Do you have the flowers?'

She pointed to the cream Bougainvillaeas on the dressing-table. He made a circling motion with his index finger, and she obediently turned her back to him. Standing naked in the semi-darkness with a handsome man tucking flowers in her hair, taking the initiative was going to be easy. In the palms of her hands she held both power and vulnerability. All she had to do was choose the moment.

'Very elegant,' he said. 'Beautiful. Oh! Don't move.'

She heard rustling.

'I'd like to refresh the baby oil, if I may. Trust me. Just to enhance these lovely, sweeping curves.'

She held her breath. He didn't hurry. At first he used just his right hand, but the one-sided pressure made her body twist and after a time he laid his free hand on her opposite shoulder to steady her.

He made long passes down her spine, working outwards to

her flank, then mirrored his efforts the other side. She let her head drop forward, patiently receiving his attentions and relishing the contact and the heavy tracking of his fingers over her skin. Neither spoke. The sound of his fingers filled the silence, like waves lapping the beach through half-sleeping ears. She wanted to turn and kiss him, but icy air seemed to fill her mouth. She lifted her arm and, turning it, saw the shadows of gooseflesh.

He leaned over her shoulder. 'You can slip on my robe for a few minutes, if you're chilly.'

No need, she told him.

'Here, take the last flowers,' he said, when she knelt on the cushion. 'You can use them as a prop. The side of your face nearest us will be cast in deep shadow, so you can almost imagine you're unwatched. You're in a very private, very special place and you're beautiful, perhaps you're in love. Let your body tell us a secret.'

Afterwards he moved the back-cloth to the apricot wall opposite, next to the beds. He taped it lengthwise, a third of the way up the wall, with the remainder spread on the floor.

'Last set.'

'You haven't used the bed.'

'Cliché,' he said, putting his hands on his hips. 'Hackneyed, white-on-white bed scenes. No thanks. But I've got a small piece of candle in my bag. I'm trying something by candle-light.'

He made her lie on her left flank, and extinguished all but the nearest bedside light and the lamp in the seating area. Then he fetched two dark shirts from the hanging cupboard and draped them with great care round the lampshades.

'That one,' he said, pointing to the seating area, 'is to give a bit of modelling to your body. The one above is to stop your hair disappearing into the back-cloth.' He lit the candle with a match. 'Try supporting your head on your left hand, and steady the candle on the floor with your right. Good.' He dragged the stool nearer, angled it towards her face and flapped the grubby, white sheet over the seat. 'Better. These are going to be long exposures. Several seconds, so don't move a muscle. Don't even laugh.'

She laughed immediately.

When they had finished and he was putting his camera away, she carried the candle to the seating area and stuck it with a little wax to the glass ash-tray, which she transferred to the bedside table.

'Hey!' She slipped her hands into his. 'Thank you.'

She raised herself on tiptoe and planted a quick kiss on his lips. She drew back, her eyes flickering in anxiety over his, but he inclined his face to hers. His hands pulled free of hers, and met round her back, and they embraced slowly and hard.

'Make love with me, Roy.'

He pressed his palms to her cheeks. 'I think a shower could be in order, certainly for me.'

'Together?'

He laughed. 'The bath's lethal. We'd end up in a heap, knocked out.'

'Then you go first. All I've done this past few hours is stare, naked, into the middle-distance, let's face it. I'll tidy up a bit. And I'll order a few beers from room service, shall I?'

Persuaded, he disappeared into the bathroom, and soon she heard him singing. She tidied what she could and put the camera and its accessories in a pile on the dressing-table.

He reappeared in minutes, one white towel round his waist, and rubbing his hair with another. As they passed each other she touched a finger to his breast-bone.

'Nice chest. About time I saw yours.'

Under the shower she soaped away the dust and the baby oil and the doubts. She was minutes away from making love with him. It wasn't that difficult after all. She could not have found a more suitable lover; he was perfect.

After spending the best part of the day naked before him, she went out with a towel wrapped round her and tucked under her arms. This time reality called. This time he would have to expose her nakedness for himself.

One of the bed covers had been folded back and on the bedside table a tray of bottles and glasses waited, but he was nowhere to be seen.

'Roy?' She opened the garden door and stepped outside, gripping the overlap of the bath towel. 'Roy?' She went back inside and pressed the door shut behind her. As she turned, a white flash exploded in her face. 'Shit! Oh! That was so mean...'

He laughed. 'Just finishing the roll. I have to finish the roll, don't I?'

'God, you frightened me...'

'So I see.' He packed the camera back in its case at the dressing-table. 'But I won't frighten you any more tonight, I give you my word. That will be an interesting shot.'

'Roy,' she said, climbing under the bedclothes, 'it'll be crap.'

But somehow it did make getting into bed with each other much easier.

'Well,' she said, as he shed his towel discreetly on the side of the bed and slid under the sheets, 'I should be photographing you now.'

'I'm very unphotogenic. Certain people the camera loves. I stick to them.'

'I think you're beautiful.'

She reached for him and pulled him on to his side. One kiss, two kisses and he was heaving the breaths of fading self-control.

'Karin...' He paused, and then pulled back. 'You don't want to, do you.'

'I do. I do! Don't you?'

'Remember what you asked me?' He felt for her hand and brought it to his groin. 'There's your proof; a distinct lack of immunity to my model in this case. Of course I want to,' he said. 'But I saw -'

'What?'

'I don't know, something. What I photographed just now. Fear? Doubt? But that's okay; I've never ended up feeling any better for this kind of experience either. I didn't know the women. It was pointless and – afterwards – it was sordid.'

'You know me a little.' She could hear her heart at that point, and the skin below her sternum visibly twitched with each beat. 'Doesn't that make a difference?'

'Yes,' he said, 'it does. Because I like you, very much.'

'I like you too.'

'Which is why we don't have to do this. Time doesn't stop this Saturday, and just because other people jump into bed the second they meet doesn't oblige us. Desire is not the problem.' He flung himself on to his back, both arms wide. 'God, I must be crazy! Crazy or old.' He turned his face to her. 'I'm offering you a bit of space, a bit of respect, unfashionable though it may be these days. I don't want to jeopardise our albeit brief friendship by trying to run too soon, that's all.'

She stared at the sheet between them and scratched at the cotton with a fingernail.

'Say something, Karin.

'Do you hate me?'

'Hate? I like you more. The superficiality bit leaves me cold.' He slid his arm under her. 'I'll still be there in the morning, and I'd be honoured if you'd spend the night with me – any which way – in this staggeringly narrow bed.'

He slept, she slept, a deep, unthreatened sleep stuck together with body heat and tight hotel sheets.

When she awoke, the candle had burned out, but in the little lobby the light was still on. His left arm had curled with casual propriety over her. For a moment she didn't move, but his breathing sighed, soft and regular. Pushing herself up on her elbows, she watched until his sleeping form took shape out of the half-light. She raised the back of her hand towards his face, almost touching him.

She swallowed. This feeling, this pain, like someone had taken a giant hole-punch to her heart... She remembered it, distantly, and it was more than nerves, more than lust. She had started to fall in love, and she was married to someone else. She had fallen out of love with Brendan enough to be falling in love with Roy. Oh God... How could love enter the equation so soon and so surely?

She retracted her fingers; he might sense them there, sense

her thoughts. She slid out of bed and crept across the floor to the bathroom. Her rucksack still leaned against the bathroom wall, and her watch, laid on top of it, showed just gone three o'clock. Her dress was crumpled on the bathroom floor, and when she buttoned it up it felt soiled, more soiled than could ever have resulted from grime.

She tiptoed to the garden door and picked up her sandals, pausing to watch him a while longer. Should she have left a note? And said what? He'd treated her with courtesy and respect, and his reward was going to be a slap in the face from an invisible hand in an empty bed. There was no other way. Better he despise her for leaving than for lying. His hatred she could endure better than his contempt. It was the way of least pain for both of them.

She'd let herself out into the thin, night air.

31

Jim Straker watched, in loving fascination, as his urine linked him to the toilet with a bow of yellow light. He took a step back; the pee pattered against the front interior of the pan. Then he shifted forward so that the flow moved with noisy plashings across the water, returning to its former pianissimo tinniness up the back of the ceramic. Not so long ago the stream would have drooped without warning and caught him unawares, or ceased to a depressing drizzle of drips, but now it quivered and sparkled with mercurial vitality, and maintained its proud arc until he sensed the deep, visceral satisfaction of a bladder truly emptied.

'Remarkable.'

He closed the cloakroom door behind him and tightened the belt of his dressing-gown as he went back into the kitchen. Peeing was a dream, a childhood pleasure re-discovered after interminable months of dysfunction.

Daniel and Anyta, slumped over teen magazines and toast,

ignored him, but Hilary looked up.

'I think I'll give Zoe Seymour a ring,' he announced. 'Let her know how I'm progressing.'

'Not before time. Anyhow, Jim, I daresay she'll be pleased. And don't forget -'

'The remedy. Yes, I know.'

He picked up his mug from the breakfast-table and padded back to the hall, his mules flapping stickily against his bare feet. He sat on the built-in stool of the phone-table, slid his back into a more comfortable position down the wall and tapped out the number. While the phone rang he sipped his coffee.

'*Hello, you have reached the number of Zoe Seymour, homœopath. If you wish to make an* – Hello?' Zoe Seymour's voice cleaved through the measured business recording. 'Hello?'

'It's Straker.'

'Jim! How are you doing?'

'Well, I thought I'd never pee again for the first couple of days, but since then I've not looked back. I might have to get up once during the night; that I can live with. The plumbing and hydraulics are functioning practically a hundred per cent. It's almost worth sinking so low just for the buzz of recovering. In the afternoons they're saying I'm almost human. I stand converted, I tell you. People are complaining about me singing.'

'Can't give you a remedy for a crap voice, I'm afraid,' said Zoe. 'But I'm delighted. You want to know what the remedy was? It's called Conium.'

'C-o-n-i-u-m M-a-c-u-l-a-t-u-m,' he read back after she had spelt it out. 'Sounds faintly botanical. Any advance?'

'That's for me to know and Hilary to find out. I'm sure she'll enjoy a bit of research. And I'll see you at the end of June.'

He passed the paper straight to Hilary.

'Conium... Well, it's not one of the commoner remedies. Not one I've heard of, anyway. I'll look it up for you. How exciting! Oh, and Jim, you've caught a magpie in your trap. Daniel noticed while you were on the phone.'

He hurried to the dining-room window. Sure enough, a small white shape was bouncing around amongst the dark, distant struts and mesh. He shook his fist.

'Got the bugger!'

He unlocked the sliding door and plunged outside with Daniel in pursuit, half-running, half-walking, their pyjama trousers wicking up the dew.

The bird cowered at their approach, its bill slightly open and the tip of its metallic green tail bent and frayed against the chicken wire. Daniel crouched and peered at the captive.

Straker looked round. 'I need a stick.'

'To beat its brains in?'

'No, Daniel,' said Straker, walking across to the hedge, 'not to beat its brains in. At least, not yet. It's going to be a decoy. I need a perch.'

'What for?'

'Because it's a perching bird.'

'Why bother when you're going to waste it?'

'Because,' said Straker, 'they have to have a stick.' He tugged on a piece of branch protruding from the hedge, fed the branch into the chicken wire of the empty cage behind the magpie, and poked it through the other side. 'Now, I'll get the bird. You open the door of the other cage.'

He depressed the edge of the trap door, the wire snagging threads from the sleeve of his dressing-gown as he inserted his hands. The magpie beat its wings and began emitting a string of harsh sounds like a key being forced in a rusty old mortice lock. He stretched out his fingers and tried to corner the bird, who jumped and tried to scramble over his wrists to the other end of the cage.

'Is it going for you, Dad?'

'Shut up!' said Straker. 'It's just frightened.'

Slowly he brought his hands together, one from below and the other from the roof of the cage.

The magpie backed further and further into the corner until its tail was almost vertical. It lunged as his hands closed over its breast and back, squawking and flapping. A glob of guano shot on to the grass.

'Got it?'

'Just about.'

He lifted the bird through the trap door.

'Let's have a dekko! Hey, it blinked. Cool...'

'Look,' Straker said flatly, 'just open that door, would you?'

He lowered the bird inside the second cage, rapped the door shut and fastened it with the two wooden clips.

'It's not on the perch, Dad.'

Straker ignored him. 'All we need now is water and food. What about the old rabbit bowls under the sink in the utility room?'

'Don't ask me.'

'Well, you don't exactly wear your fingers to the bone with housework, Daniel. I thought maybe you'd like to feed it as one of your chores.'

'What?'

'Swap it for loading the dish-washer, then.' Straker moved in closer. 'I'll pay.'

'Oh, no way!' said Daniel, storming off. 'You caught the thing. *You* look after it.'

He watched the green- and white-striped figure of his son billowing off towards the house. Bitterly he cast a glance back at the bird and let some spittle drop, in a string of white beads, to the ground between his slippers.

32

The letter arrived just over a week later. Karin was in the hall when the large white envelope dropped into the wire basket on the back of the door.

The envelope bore the red ink stamp of Handley Myers. She drew out the unfolded sheet of white paper and let the envelope fall to the carpet: a couple of lines of type. Scarcely a note: *Dear Ms Shilan, I enclose a letter obviously intended for your eyes. If there is anything you need to discuss, don't hesitate to call. Yours sincerely.*

She dropped Steven Bennallick's letter, snatched up the envelope and looked inside: a letter within a letter. She took out the slim white envelope. It had been addressed by hand, in slanting print: *Karin (Yamamoto), c/o Steven Bennallick Esq, Handley Myers* etc. *Please forward.*

She took it into her office, carrying it by the edges, like a salver, across to the window. Her breakfast churned in her stomach as she opened the envelope with slow, clumsy-fingered dread. She unfolded the flaps of the letter and slid the two sheets apart: Roy Meredith. A letter by the Trojan technique. Bennallick must have known. He must at least have suspected.

Dear Karin,

Who are you? You said yourself I knew you a little, and then left me to find out that this 'little' amounted to nothing. The staff of the San Felipe had no recollection of you. I described you at Reception that morning and again that evening. I assailed waiters, who assured me – and I believed them – that they would have remembered any woman matching your description. Nothing.

If only you'd given me a reason, even an irrational one. What I couldn't understand, I could at least have tried to accept. Most days I find myself going back to look at the photographs, even at the expense of reliving the moment of waking and finding you gone. I do it to reassure myself that somewhere out there, you still exist. Do you have any idea how that feels? Perhaps you don't care. Perhaps that's your modus operandi.

You aren't the first woman to disappear from my life in less than a week. The main difference, however, is that the others changed nothing. In fact my life was improved by their departure. The second difference is that they managed to discuss parting beforehand. In your case I've not survived unscathed, nor has time obliged with much healing.

What was I to do with the photos? Put a "Desperately seeking" ad in a national daily you'd never see? Consign them to a drawer? They were too good. I'm sorry you find the picture offensive. I prefer it without the 4x4, but to me it's still a work of art. I've earned something from its outing, I admit, but if you hear nothing else of what I'm saying, I know you'll understand how little the money matters to me. I've also attracted some professional recognition for taking a great shot of a beautiful woman, but have no doubt my moment of fame will turn all too soon to infamy. I tell myself there's never any loss without gain, a fortunate philosophy in one who stands to lose a considerable amount personally as well as financially.

'*Please get in touch*,' read Zo, pacing in circles round Karin's kitchen table that evening. '*Ring, or perhaps a letter would be preferable given the events of the past few weeks. Tell me you went by the name of Carl six months ago, and you've some adjusting to do. Tell me you loathed the smell of my sweat. Tell me something. Tell me anything. I would very much like to see you again. Yours, Roy.* Oh my God! Well, you'd better do as the man asks, hadn't you.'

Karin was leaning against the sink, her arms folded and one ankle crossed over the other.

'I can't. When I rang Mr Bennallick, he advised me, given the nature of the case and the state of proceedings, to avoid any contact.'

'Solicitors are just machines with eyes and bank accounts, Karin. When are you going to learn? Get in touch with him!'

'He also said he had a call from Yamamoto's solicitors first thing. They want to buy me off.'

'For?'

'A not insubstantial sum.'

Zo screwed up her nose. 'What did your friendly hyena have to say about that? You're not strapped for cash. Let's face it, what galls you is the principle. Or is it the poster-sized reminder of your guilt, slapped up across the country for all to see? And the thought of the tens of thousands of pointing fingers rolling off those printing presses? Guilt's a double-edged sword here, isn't it. You hate yourself for falling in love with Roy when Brendan's counting the days to your home-coming. You hate yourself for walking out on a decent, innocent man without so much as a goodbye. Whichever way you move, you get cut, so you'd rather just keep the lid on the whole business.' Zo held the letter up by the bottom corner and smacked it with the back of her hand. 'You didn't even make love with this guy. You didn't even shag, and this is the impact you've made. It's almost a love letter. I don't blame him one iota for what he's done. I think you've treated him outrageously.'

'I wasn't asking for a judgement.'

'I'm sorry. Did you expect me to condone what you're doing now you've finally come clean?' Zo let the pages float down on to the table. 'Maybe he shouldn't have flogged the pictures, but in my opinion – for the little it's worth – the offence doesn't merit your pack of lawyers nailing him to the wall. It's fine for you to go looking for trouble, but when it comes knocking on *your* door afterwards, you don't like it, do you. You mess up your marriage because you can't swallow your pride. You let yourself fall for that man and, worse still, you let him fall in love with you. And now you won't even ride out a transitory advertising campaign. A few weeks, a couple of months at the most and they'll be on the look-out for the next new image and the next darling. Swallowing your pride doesn't choke you, Karin. Christ, you're in your mid-thirties, and men look at that ad with their tongues hanging out like school ties. I'd be flogging copies on street corners. I'd do signings at poster shops. And how come you find all the nice guys anyway? I'd ask you to introduce us, only I know he'd still want you. Even after all this. They make me sick.'

Karin unfolded her arms and gripped the edge of the Belfast sink. 'Finished?'

'No! And I've changed my mind. You unleash your solicitor on him. Having read Roy's letter, maybe it's better he sees you for what you really are.'

'Zo, stop it!' Karin pushed herself off the sink, grabbed two fistfuls of her hair and walked up the kitchen with her hands on top of her head. 'I haven't committed myself either way. All right? I rejected the money, but as far as Roy's concerned I told Mr Bennallick I'd bear his advice in mind and sleep on it. Not that I shall sleep much.'

'Is it any surprise?' said Zo. 'With this on your conscience you don't deserve to sleep at all. Now for God's sake, write Roy a letter before I draft one for you.'

33

Jim Straker printed in his third answer to the cryptic crossword, the newspaper balanced on the steering-wheel. The third always proved a watershed. The confidence with which he filled in the first three clues was invariably shattered by his inability to complete any more. He rattled the pen between his teeth and caught sight of Steven Bennallick's jewel-blue TVR sailing into his rear-view mirror. It swung to a sharp halt in the neighbouring parking-space.

Straker turned the crossword face down on the passenger seat, put the pen in the pocket of his wind-cheater and got out. Steven already had the boot up.

'Ready for a tanking?'

'Straight into gamesmanship, Steve! Good morning to you too.' Straker opened his boot and took out his golf shoes and a small hold-all. 'Are you ever going to get yourself a decent motor? I was under the impression men bought for performance.' He patted the roof of Bennallick's car. 'What colour *is* this?'

'Hyacinth macaw. Metallic. Christ knows, I forget. Something like that.' Steven Bennallick removed his sunglasses. He held them up to the light, frowned at them and pushed them back on to his nose. 'Come on, locker room. Why are you policemen always so slow?'

They strolled over to the club-house. Straker trotted down the outside steps and followed Bennallick into the locker room. Bennallick slid his sunglasses on top of his head as they went inside.

'No sign of Jane,' he said crisply. 'You seen her? Word has it she's hanging round with an estate agent. Julian Pople?'

'I wouldn't know,' Straker lied.

Steven Bennallick smacked on a locker door with the flat of his hand. 'So much for the reconciliation. Shit, she's after cheap-rate commission. Yet another well-intentioned, deeply thought-out rebound between paramours. How's the bird?'

'Which one?'

Steven Bennallick's head jerked back. 'Are you serious? Hey, is there something you haven't told me?'

'Magpies,' said Straker, evening out the laces on a golf shoe. 'As of this morning I have two. I took down the food and water, and there it was.'

'Didn't you kill it?'

'I was on my way out. I didn't have time.' He put his outdoor shoes and hold-all in the bottom of the locker and hung up his jacket. 'Maybe I should give my gamekeeper friend another call, see if he knows anyone else who needs a decoy. With any luck we'll be able to swap again.'

'Right. Two down and – ?'

'Four.'

'Make good pets, do they?'

'They're responsive enough. When I take the cat food down he becomes quite animated. He recognises the sound of my voice, I'm sure of it.' Straker shut the locker door. 'But I suspect they're more intelligent than some humans. Not good pets, on balance.'

They returned to the cars, fetched out their golf clubs and fitted them on to the trolleys. Bennallick went for some score-cards and they set off for the first tee of the Green course. The fairways were already busy and the distant crack of golf balls carried on the air.

'Magpies apart,' said Bennallick, 'how are things? You seem in grand form, quietly buzzing. Haven't seen you for weeks.'

Straker smiled into his chest. 'Life's just great. You?'

'Oh, busy. You know, squash, football. Tennis now. And golf, of course. Sometimes I wonder why I bother with the flat. Bed and Breakfast would do me. I suppose a trip to a nightclub could be in order, but any single woman anywhere near my age would be as sad a bastard as I am. Besides, I'm sick of pulling. You can't even do it for revenge when they're queuing up.'

'The legacy of the good-looking, my God! Sexual *ennui* isn't something I've ever been in a position to suffer, sad to say.'

'Ah, but you're not, are you,' Bennallick said quietly. 'You're not sad.' He stopped and looked Straker up and down. He raised his sunglasses and squinted. 'Something's changed.'

Straker opened his arms and stared down at himself in mock horror.

'Don't bullshit, Jim.'

'Okay! Okay! Yes, since my last trip to the homœopath I feel fantastic. Like I'm twenty-five again. For the first few days after the remedy I was so high Hil asked if I'd had a brush with Drugs. You should try a consultation. In fact I've got my homœopath's number in my wallet. I'll let you have it.'

'I've already got one,' said Bennallick, raising himself on his toes. 'Well, potentially. A new client of mine. Very good, by all accounts. Not unattractive either. So, Jim, what are you on?'

'Hemlock.' Straker took a coin from his jacket pocket, tossed it and slapped it on the back of his hand. 'Heads or tails?'

There was a pause.

'Hemlock's deadly poison.'

'Socrates, yes, judicial and criminal homicide. The Romans weren't averse either. First the legs grow heavy and stiff, followed by progressive ascending paralysis until you die, completely conscious, of asphyxia from failure of the muscles of respiration.'

'Christ!'

'That's what I said when Hilary told me. I rang Zoe Seymour to demand why she'd prescribed tablets that could have killed me and she told me there was nothing in them. They dilute the original substance out of existence, apparently, but with each dilution they shake it. Somehow that's supposed to preserve the "memory" of the substance and its therapeutic benefits even though it's no longer present physically. Something like that. Dilution and succussion. Hil tried to explain. Anyway, if nothing worked for me, so be it. Heads or tails?'

'Christ,' Bennallick said again. 'Tails.'

'Heads.'

Straker drew a tee from the holder on his golf bag, pressed it with reverence into the earth and balanced a ball on it. He pulled his driver from the bag and took up his stance, rocking between his feet as he addressed the ball.

'Of course, the acid test is the effect on your golf, isn't it,' said Bennallick. 'Going for a birdie?'

'Anything but a magpie,' murmured Straker, eyeing up the fairway.

His mouth dropped open. He shook his shoulders, bounced a few times, absorbing the movement in his knees before settling and coiling his energy. He swung, struck.

Faintly, over the whipped air, Steven Bennallick said, 'Fuck...'

34

The car surprised her far less than the speed at which it swung into the drive. She checked the clock - one minute to one – and hung back against the curtain. Steven Bennallick got out. That was where the consultation started, down there in the garden. In fact the process began the moment the clients opened their mouth to make the appointment. They stepped on stage well before they put themselves on display.

He slammed the car door and flung his arm behind him to lock it with the handset as he walked towards the steps. He wore a white shirt and navy trousers; standard office uniform. The sleeves were rolled up again, and this time he'd shed the tie. He was already taking in the façade. And instantaneously, he picked her out from the shadows. The unexpected eye contact flashed through her like an electrocution. She stepped into the window and waved.

'I heard the car,' she told him at the door. 'Come in.'

Straight away he set about observing, the cornices, the furniture, the paintings, and she imagined she could feel his eyes on her back as she led him through to the consulting-room.

'Your case,' he said, accepting the seat. 'Could we deal with that first?'

She gestured to him to continue.

'Well, after increasing their offer twice further, Yamamoto are finally facing the facts. A client ambivalent about financial gain is a quite a novelty, I must say. When I turn down bloodmoney it's usually with a view to cranking up the stakes. It's all a big game, you see, a lot of posturing and horse-trading, and all of a sudden I'm not playing by the rules. They're chewing over their quandary, but they'll cede.' He sat up straighter and patted his hands on his thighs. 'Now, Meredith. I trust you're agreeable to me instigating disciplinary proceedings?'

'I'm not sure. What would happen to him?'

'Is the penalty an issue?'

'No –'

'If you want to know whether he'll be struck off, the answer is I very much doubt it. The breaches weren't committed in the course of his legal practice. The action is civil, not criminal. An official reprimand? A fine, maybe? I can't say.' He inclined his head towards her. 'You do acknowledge that some form of discipline is in order?' He paused. 'Perhaps you think he should be allowed to walk away, free as air?'

'No –'

'How about if I write to him, *my client is considering* etc? Just a little warning shot across the bows? I know the firm. Decent, quite high-profile. It would be entirely personal and confidential, of course.'

'Just a warning?'

'We can act on it – or not – as you see fit.'

He sounded so reasonable.

She questioned him first about his migraines. 'All right, Steven. Now tell me your pet hates.'

'Pet hates? Oh, dawdlers, being held up by dawdlers in the street. That I loathe. I work fast, I dictate fast. My tapes sound like a foreign language. I expect everybody else to keep up with me. And a lot of people don't seem able to,' he added, almost with a note of surprise. 'I go to work, and that's it. I'm very efficient, not afraid of pushing myself. I also have a rare talent for upsetting people.'

'How?'

He bounced his legs from the balls of his feet. 'Oh, they think I ask too much of them, when I only ask of others what I demand from myself. People forget that. Or can't accept it. But if I were less efficient the job wouldn't get done. I hate that feeling. If I have deadlines, I meet them. It's vicious out there if you don't cover your back.'

She let her writing arm dangle to the side of her seat and flexed her fingers a few times.

'How do you feel about people who are less efficient than you?'

Bennallick laughed. 'I cannot, in all honesty, say I'm the most tolerant person in the world. I'm quite bright, I suppose, quick with words. I've met very few people who can out-argue me, but in this line of work, they always try. It sounds awful, but I'm almost always right and I get annoyed when they waste my time in order to prove what I knew all along. They think I'm arrogant, a lot of them. But there's someone like me in every office.'

'You said you sometimes get annoyed with people. How does that show?'

'It doesn't always. I can take a fair amount before I blow. I don't tend to lash out physically, but neither do I forget. Sometimes...' He crossed one leg over the other and jiggled his raised foot. 'Sometimes, I think people are frightened of me.'

'Yes?'

'I suppose I shouldn't feel good about it, but if they're frightened because they discover they're intellectually inferior, so be it. When it's business and they've got the knives out, I have to make my mark the same way they're endeavouring to make theirs.'

'What makes you angry?'

'Jumped-up, pompous people. Slowness. Inefficiency.

Ignorant people.' He got up, walked across to the far wall, his hands in his pockets, and looked at her posters. 'And my wife. Most of all, my wife.' He thumbed up the room. 'Does it bother you if I walk round?'

'Feel free.'

He paced up to the cheese plant, across to the door and back down to her desk. She surreptitiously stretched her fingers on her writing pad.

'You see, Karin, my wife and I – how can I put this – we had pretty active sex lives before we got together. We'd both had lots of partners. But when we tied the knot – and we've been married six years – the deal was that the fooling around stopped. We didn't have to get married after all, and we were making vows. I didn't take those lightly. No other women, I told her. Forsaking all others, you know? We didn't make three years: someone she worked with. For all I know we didn't make six months. I assumed because we'd been both been promiscuous, and because I could live with the sacrifice, she could do the same. I don't think the word fidelity exists in her vocabulary.'

He returned to his chair.

'Is she the woman in the photograph?'

'I should get rid of it, shouldn't I. She's the kind of woman men flock to, always has been. Five minutes after arriving at a party I'd have to excise her from a ring of admirers. She's not a stunner, but she makes up for it with that PR personality men pick up like pheromones. I was used to steam-rollering the competition, but for Jane I had to make an effort. I was even flattered when she chose me. Anyway, we tried again. With a background like ours forgiveness came without too much resistance. And perhaps because she knew she could count on it, she abused it. Someone high up in sales, a string of soft touches from the golf club... Even when they know what she's like, they're queuing up. And so –' He pushed himself off the chair and drifted across to the window '- just before Christmas, I walked out. So antisocial at that time of year. You should try finding a flat. Of course, people think I'm a bastard for leaving her. God knows what they'd have said if I'd kicked her out on the streets, though the way she behaves she should be quite at home there.'

He lapsed into silence, apparently staring down at his car. She enclosed her pen in her fist and rested it on the paper.

'Do you still love her?'

'I hate her. So maybe it's love.'

'And there's no one else in your life at the moment?'

He half-turned, his hands still in his pockets. 'Since last Christmas there's been a whole string of no one elses, believe you me. A whole string, hand-picked. The worst thing is that I was so in love with a total bitch.' He shook his head. 'She came crawling back after the first time with her apologies and tears and how it had all been a terrible mistake. I had declarations of undying love, promises that it would never happen again. Cliché after cliché and I swallowed the lot. That's how much I wanted to believe her.'

The oppression in Karin's throat radiated to her chest, and from the oppression arose a raw pain that tightened like fingers about her neck.

'You see,' he said, 'if Jane had kept that promise, we could have started over. I'd have been happy, stupidly happy.'

Her sobs broke through with great, whooping gasps. She inclined over her knees and hugged herself as though the pressure of her arms might silence the ugly sounds. The notepad and pen fell to the carpet and he appeared in a blur on his knees in front of her, pawing at the air between them. The box of tissues swam into her vision and she shook her head and waved it away.

'I'll be all right in a minute.'

'Are you sure? Shall I fetch you a glass of water?'

She nodded, her hand over her mouth.

He was gone for a long time. It seemed long. She blew her nose and opened the three lower sash-windows, their pulleys shrieking and the windows clonking in their frames. The cool air entered in a raft and eddied round her chair. She bent down and picked up her pad and pen, and put them on the desk.

He returned with a glass of water in each hand. 'Here.'

'Thank you.'

He sat on the edge of his seat and leaned over his parted legs, the glass cradled in both hands.

'Your house has a lot in common with ours. My old house, I mean, *The Cedars*. I miss it actually.' He took a mouthful of water and rocked the glass in his fingers. 'Sure you're okay now?'

She sniffed.

'Look, this is a bad time. I'll go.'

'No! I'm just a bit under the weather, I think. A summer cold.'

'It happened to you too, didn't it.'

She swirled the water inside her glass. 'Once.'

'Once. And that's why you went to Tenerife.'

'You're very perceptive.'

'Sensitive, let's say, around the issue of adultery. Was he sorry?'

'I think he truly was. He swore it would never happen again.'

'Did you believe him?'

'He was a man of his word.'

'Once,' he said again. He scraped his teeth over his upper lip. 'Hell, once I would have forgiven at the drop of a hat. And you knew he'd keep his promise. I'd have thought myself barely a cuckold for that. He threw himself on your mercy, offered you a clean slate, and you didn't want to know.'

'It's not a decision I'm proud of.'

His eyebrows lowered and he shook his head, a slight, uneasy jarring. 'Even I couldn't do that. I know I'm a bastard. I tread on everybody's toes, but I couldn't do that to my wife if I believed her. Not if I loved her.'

She couldn't meet his eyes. Instead she turned to her pad, took up her pen and scored a line across the bottom of the notes.

'I'm sorry, Mr Bennallick. Steven,' she said, forcing a little brightness. 'You're right. Perhaps we should finish another time. At no extra charge, of course, and it shouldn't take too long. I have a fair idea of your remedy.'

He agreed, but not without some reluctance.

'By the way,' he said at the door, 'animal, vegetable or mineral?'

'I think,' she replied, 'animal.'

'Thank God!' she exclaimed, when Zo answered the mobile. 'I thought you'd be with a client.'

'Who's running twenty minutes late,' said Zo. 'What's up? You sound awful.'

'I've just blown it. I've blown it.' She resumed her pacing in front of the hall table, her strides longer and faster. 'I think I ought to stop practising for a while, have a break. Take stock.'

'Wait a minute! What are you talking about, "stop practising?" Karin, what is going on?'

'I lost it.' She came to an abrupt halt, her voice trembling. 'My professional etiquette went to hell. Completely lost it, distance, boundaries, objectivity crashing round my ears. I broke just about every rule in the book. God knows what the client thinks of me. Even when I knew it was happening I couldn't haul myself out of it.'

'Hey, who's impervious to life? We've all done it.'

'*Not* as badly as this.'

Zo considered. 'Maybe this might be an appropriate time to see Finn. Don't get me wrong, Kar, but I'm in too deep. And he thinks the world of you, you know that.'

'God!' Karin raked her hand through her hair. 'It's just I've got clients tomorrow afternoon. My confidence has upped stakes. And I feel like shit!'

'Tomorrow will be fine,' said Zo. 'The chance of the same thing repeating twice in two days is negligible.' There was a pause. 'Got to go. My lady's here. Look, make yourself a cuppa, get out and have a walk and clear your head. I'm out tonight so I'll ring you tomorrow. Okay?'

She made a lemon tea, dropped a couple of ice-cubes into the glass and put it in the fridge. While the drink chilled she went outside to the back garden and lay on the lawn, gazing at the sky and ripping up clover leaves with both hands. The grass was long; it needed cutting again already. And the clouds seemed to topple towards her, one after the other, like buildings.

She lay there till her dress became sticky beneath her back. When she went inside to fetch her tea, someone was rapping at the front door. She ran through the hall, smoothing her hair, and was greeted on the doorstep with a dazzling display of white and yellow flowers.

'Miss Shilan?'

'Oh my God! Yes. Is there a card?'

The delivery boy indicated the miniature envelope, and thrust the crackling bundle of blooms and cellophane towards her. She thanked him and carried the bouquet through to the kitchen. Who would send flowers? Clients paid, they offered their thanks. They made recommendations by word of mouth. But they didn't send flowers.

She laid them on the table and took out the card: <u>*Sorry*</u>. She turned it over. Nothing else. No name. Could it be Roy? Roy... Handley Myers might forward letters; they were unlikely to re-direct bouquets.

She fetched her tea and stood sipping it by the table, her eyes tracing over the flowers: white and lemon carnations, alstroemeria, roses and lilies, asters, eucalyptus, asparagus fern. It was a beautiful bouquet, an expensive, ostentatious apology.

She put the glass on the table, stripped away the looping yellow ribbons and the wrappings and took the flowers, shedding leaves and tiny fern needles, into the laundry room. She filled a bucket with cold water, stood the flowers in it on the drainer, put out the light and closed the door.

*

The phone call that evening surprised her even more than the bouquet.

'Karin?'

'Mr Bennallick! I –' Heat flared into her cheeks. 'The flowers... thank you. You shouldn't have.'

'Please,' he said, sounding uncharacteristically awkward, 'Steven. And forgive me if I beg to disagree. I said a lot of things way out of turn. I'm not a very nice person to know at the moment.'

'Forget it. People bring us their pathology, the baggage, not the high-days and holidays. I should never have let my past impinge on your consultation.'

'Now, I'd find that far easier to forgive over dinner. Karin?' He hesitated. 'Are you still there?'

'Dinner... I don't usually –'

'Think of it as a more convenient and enjoyable way of rounding off my consultation. What about Friday?'

'Friday week?'

'Friday tomorrow,' he said, his speech recovering its customary pace. 'If you're still under the weather, no problem. Let me know by mid-afternoon, say, and I'll cancel. Simple as that. Try a few hot toddies. My mother recommends them for everything on the basis that if you can't beat the bugs, you can at least get them drunk.' He paused for breath. 'Great! In the meantime I'll send up burnt offerings and hope to see you tomorrow at eight?'

35

At seven o'clock the next evening, she opened the wardrobe and squeaked the hangers along the rail. The red dress would be too overpowering, the black too wintry, the beige, dull. She took down a sleeveless blue one and held it to herself in the mirror. It was a mixture of blues, a palette of feathery, intermingling blues, the cut bold and simple with a deep V neck, slim shoulder straps and a long zipper that drew the fabric to a sleek fit. Brendan loved it.

She hung the dress back in the wardrobe, closed the door and sat on the end of the bed before jumping up a second later and taking it out again; demons had to be faced. That very afternoon at the Natural Health Centre she'd faced three; they'd turned out to be an old woman with vertigo, a trainee hair-stylist and an eight-year-old boy. Zo had been right. And now she had to square up to Steven Bennallick.

She massaged her throat. That morning she'd awoken scarcely able to croak out her phone calls. Cancelling the meal would have been perfectly legitimate. In her cold she had an excuse, and yet in her behaviour the previous afternoon, she had none. The date was a consultation, the conclusion of a business transaction, expiation for her weakness. He was just another demon.

She threw the dress on to the bed and sat on the dressing-table stool before the mirror. Perhaps she judged him too hard. He was witty and clever and good-looking, and she hadn't walked out in male company since Tenerife. With the exception of a trip to the Playhouse with Leon and Zo a few weeks before, and that didn't count. Despite his sexual past, Steven Bennallick had made good. He had striven for ideals, and his failure to realise them had come at the hands of another. She sighed. He deserved for her to make an effort. Hadn't he already apologised for his mistake? Hadn't he sent her flowers? She groaned. The flowers…

She hurried down to the kitchen and into the laundry room. In the bucket on the drainer, his flowers still languished on their long stems. She grabbed a large tulip-shaped glass vase from one of the cupboards, banged it down on the work-top and fetched some scissors from the kitchen. Stalk by stalk she sifted through the flowers, plucking out whatever came first to hand, snipping it to a more manageable length and tearing off the lower leaves before poking it into the vase. An apology did not require such a profusion of stems. It didn't need looping ribbons or delivery vans and a delivery boy whose face she had never seen before in her life. A small bunch of flowers – five or six freesias delivered in person - or a handful of something – anything – he had picked himself would already have been on the kitchen table by now, or the desk of her office.

She snipped and tore, snipped and tore until the bucket was

empty and the drainer had disappeared under a mound of surplus greenery. She pushed two or three blooms into more aesthetically pleasing positions, swung the mixer-tap over the vase and filled it with water. She wiped the bottom of the vase and carried it to the kitchen table, pausing afterwards to sniff her fingers: a tell-tale stink of eucalyptus and carnation stalks. Some scented hand-cream would be required.

In the moment's stillness vague protests arose from her hips and knees, fluttering pains that vanished and re-appeared like sunlight on water. Her defences were failing her, and she had no time to repertorise. Instead she fetched a vial each of Ferrum Phos and Silica from her office, and popped a Ferrum Phos tablet into her mouth as she mounted the stairs.

She put the vials on her dressing-table and picked up the hand-mirror: blue-ringed, parroty eyes stared back at her from a pallid face. Serious make-up was in order. She really should have cancelled.

*

'My God...' Steven Bennallick cleared his throat and looked her up and down. 'Karin, fantastic...'

'Thanks. I'm just about ready. Come in.'

She glanced at the taxi idling in the turning-area, then disappeared into her consulting-room and came back with her black bag.

'Satchel?'

'Your case-notes, actually. Damn!' She slung the bag at the base of the newel and ran upstairs just as the phone began to ring. 'Ignore it, Steven! The machine's on.'

She slammed the dressing-table drawer open and shut, then raked through the tights inside the drawer of her bedside table, dragging them out like handfuls of spaghetti and dumping them on the floor. At the bottom of the drawer she glimpsed the brassy glint of the little pill-box that had belonged to Brendan's mother. She took it to the dressing-table, abandoning the tights in a pile on the floor, and tapped a couple of Silica tablets inside.

As she left the room Zoe's voice greeted her. She crossed the landing and stopped to listen, resting her hand on the banister.

'...and also, have you done anything about Roy yet? Remember the photos? You might like to know I've kept a copy if you want to refresh your memory. Call over the weekend. Bye!'

Karin closed her eyes and tightened her grip round the rail. She descended the first few stairs, her feet rocking on the heels of her sandals, and leaned over to assess Steven's reaction: he was nowhere to be seen. She found him hovering on the front step. He proffered a multi-coloured golf umbrella.

'Drizzle,' he said. 'Didn't want you to get wet.'

What was their destination, she asked.

'Shut your eyes,' he told her as the taxi pulled out of the drive. 'Maybe you can work it out.'

'All right! Left turn...' she murmured, her body veering in space. 'Another left... Banbury Road. Oh... left again. Straight on for a while.' She opened her eyes wide. 'Cherwell Boathouse? Oh, I love it!'

'Good. Not a million miles from home, I'm afraid, and it's a pity about the weather. We could have sat outside and enjoyed the river. But I was lucky to get the cancellation.'

'I was rather hoping for a ride in the Batmobile.'

His eyebrows arched. 'Not only beautiful and untainted by money, but daring too... Though there's more sense of occasion, don't you think, when you travel by taxi?'

The restaurant soon filled up. The waitress moved unobtrusively between the tables, and soft jazz played in the background.

'Karin, RSHom,' he mused as they studied their menus, 'what have I chosen?'

'Starter? Not sure, maybe the asparagus. Then the vegetarian option. What about me?'

Steven Bennallick blinked hard. 'Ditto the vegetarian option?'

'Salmon.'

'I thought you people were all environmentally friendly, planet-loving fruitarian types. Are you psychic?'

'No! Not as sensitive as you. I just observe. What other food do you like?'

'Mexican, Indian, anything with a bit of flair. Salads. You tell me!'

The waitress appeared, a pen ready pressed to her notebook.

'Wine?' Steven asked.

'I don't usually. Oh, what the hell! It's been a lousy week, and I can't feel much worse. It'll make up for the hot toddies I've missed.'

He ordered a bottle of Muscadet-sur-Lie. She took the pill-box from her bag and slipped a tablet into her mouth. It was Silica, she told him.

'I've been alternating Silica and Ferrum Phos this afternoon in the hope of suppressing the cold. I shouldn't. I'll still suffer, just later rather than sooner. But tell me what else you like, Steven.'

'Music. And dancing, I love dancing.' He lifted his hands in a gesture of inquiry. 'Is it permissible to admit to this?'

'It's permissible to admit to anything. What kind of music?'

'All sorts. Sometimes to uplift me. Sometimes, if I'm feeling particularly self-pitying, I'll put on something I can wallow in. I don't suppose you're on for a spot of dancing later?'

She pulled a face.

'Not well enough, huh? Another time, maybe?'

'Maybe.'

'And I love the colour blue. I love your dress.'

'So you never feel blue?'

'Not blue. Black.'

They ate their starters, asparagus tips with a buttery sauce and small, home-made brown rolls, still warm and moist from the baking.

Within minutes of drinking the first glass of Muscadet her legs began to tingle. When she shifted her foot, the whole limb, sluggish and heavy, resisted the movement. He recharged her glass. The main courses arrived and were cleared.

'How do you sleep?' she inquired.

'My, you're asking all the right questions.' He leaned one arm along the edge of the table and rotated the base of his wine glass. 'I've always been a poor sleeper. I toss, I turn. Even when I'm worn out. The slightest noise wakes me, traffic, the radiator ticking as the temperature drops. I was prescribed sleeping tablets for a long time, maybe longer than I should have been. I'm off them now. But if you can improve my sleep, free legal advice is a distinct possibility.' He poured her third glass of wine. 'You look radiant.'

'You look nice too.'

She sipped from her glass. Her heart thudded inconsiderately hard, and in her groin she became aware of the second heart-beat and the teasing warmth of arousal.

He moved his hand to the centre of the table. 'Karin –?'

He seemed to be sitting in a kind of mist. She looked over her shoulder. The candles had golden coronas and for some reason everyone, including Steven, was whispering. She giggled and leaned forward on her elbows.

'What?'

'I'm fed up with talking about me. Can I ask you something?'

'Of course. I'm pretty sure of your remedy.'

'Are you in love with Roy Meredith?'

She sat up, hitting her spine against the chair back.

'You see, I thought you said you weren't going to get in contact with him.'

'I'm not.'

'That's not what your friend seems to think. Tell me about him.'

'Oh, he's tall,' she said sullenly. 'His face looks lived-in.'

'Slept in?'

'Lived-in, I said. He's funny, gentle. True to himself. And he gave me confidence at a time when confidence was sorely wanting.'

His hand lifted back to rest on his other arm. 'I didn't really want to bring up business. I was going to save it for later, as a sort of celebration, but I might as well tell you now – Yamamoto withdrew the image today. Here and worldwide.'

He spoke in a voice so flat. After all his work she heard no triumph, no excitement, no subliminal prod for congratulation. Maybe the alcohol had impaired her perception more than she thought. She smiled and supported her head on the palm of her hand and felt its weight.

'That's great! Really, thank you.'

'It's my job. Pudding? Not even that death-by-chocolate? Coffee then, what about joining me for an Irish coffee?'

'Not that I dislike coffee, it just doesn't like me.' She eased her chair from under her and it screeched over the floor. 'But provided I can blame you if I regret it, yes, I'll join you. Excuse me.'

Her heels wobbled far below her, high heels she seldom wore. In fact, all her joints and appendages seemed to function with rather more independence than was their habit, but she doubted anyone else would notice the intense concentration it took her to cross the boathouse.

She used the lavatory and freshened her face with splashes of cold water. And she'd used too much make-up; the mirror reflected the bride of some satanic lord.

The coffees were on the table by the time she arrived back. He watched her all the way, his face neutral, the fingertips of both hands resting apart on the edge of the table.

'Is something the matter?' she asked.

'Why should there be? Great company, lovely meal. Let's have this coffee.'

It slipped down, thick, warming and luxurious. How much whisky the glass contained she had no idea, but by the end of it, the extra shot of alcohol was dancing tarantellas inside her head.

'I'm awfully sorry.' She landed the glass on the table with a bump. 'I'm coming over so light-headed. I should have stuck to cordial.' She yawned. 'Oh dear.'

'Maybe the cold's making you more susceptible. Or that tablet-?'

'The Silica wouldn't react.' Her mouth gaped again and she just managed to clap her hand over it. 'I'm sorry, Steven. I think

I need to go home.'

The word 'taxi,' she heard the word 'taxi.' Steven's blue shirt drifted up like a carrier bag rising on the breeze, and then she felt her own body ride on unseen currents and float from one moon-face and one candle to another and into darkness that raced its cold tongue down her throat.

*

She became aware, fleetingly aware of consciousness, and gave herself up once again to the irresistible lure of sleep. Undisturbed by alarm clocks or the concerns of a working day, she melted into the immovable weight of her body, sinking through it to a place without thought. She washed back into her head and away again, and back to awareness.

She opened and closed her mouth a couple of times, the soft skin pressing, sealing and parting with a wet, snapping sound. Her mouth, her lips, her tongue, she brought her attention to each in turn. Breathing like Brendan's came to her ears, only her own ribs matched the rhythm, and from her right nostril, a faint whistle emanated on the outbreath.

She opened her eyes and glimpsed a split-second of semi-darkness before her lids imposed their blackout. She slid her right arm across the sheet until her hand touched her hip, then shifted her legs and wriggled her toes. She sighed a creaking sigh, testing out a note and letting it lose pitch and ebb to silence. Everything was dull and heavy but functional. She opened, closed and re-opened her eyes, refusing to accept any longer this local insurrection. With each effort they remained open a little longer. At last she managed to raise her head.

'Hello.'

Her head jolted backwards and struck the iron bedstead, making it rattle against the wall. A cap of pain throbbed in her skull and trickled down to her neck. She found herself staring at Steven Bennallick, sitting astride the dressing-table stool. Her hands snatched the sheet up to her neck.

'Hey, Sleeping Beauty, no worries. You're fully clothed.'

Pouting her lower lip, she peeked under the edge of the

sheet: the blue dress. And then, yes, she discerned the unpleasant sense of confinement and grubbiness that accompanied the wearing of day clothes in bed.

'How did you get in?' she demanded. 'Have you been here all night?'

He raised one hand. 'No to the second. And I got in using the door-key from your handbag, having had to return you home last night rather the worse for wear.'

'Oh...God...' She sank back down the bed and let the sheet fall over her face. 'I feel like hell. Almost as bad as last night. I remember the taxi rumbling away. And my legs mutinied.' She paused. 'How did I get here?'

'In bed? I put you there. There was no other way you were going to make it, believe me. The taxi-driver helped me get you into the house and waited outside while I carried you up and tucked you into bed. I propped you on your side with those pillows so there was no way you could roll on to your back, and I stayed a while till I was satisfied you weren't going to throw up. Then he took me home. I came back twice earlier on, and I rang.'

'I didn't hear.'

'I gathered. I've been here about half an hour. Your key, by the way, is under the bay tree beside the front door.'

'God,' she mumbled under the sheet, 'I am so ashamed. Was I sick?'

'No.' The sheet lifted off her face. 'Would you like something to drink?'

'Don't!' she said, her eyes fast shut. 'I don't want to see you. You to see me.'

'You need to flush out your system. Cup of tea? A glass of water? Water would be better.'

'All right.' She opened her eyes. 'You look disapproving.'

'Amazingly,' he said, 'in spite of the panda eyes, you still look beautiful.'

She should get up, she thought, as the door pulled softly to behind him, get up, show him her physical competence had returned and claw back a little human dignity. She paddled her legs over the side of the bed and levered herself into a sitting position using her arms as props. She might have been sitting on the bunk of a ship; the room swirled for every tiny movement of her head and eyes. She lay down on her side from her sitting position, dragged her legs back into bed and pulled up the quilt.

The door opened and Steven Bennallick brought in a tray.

'The flowers look nice, Karin.'

'Mmm.'

'I've brought you two glasses. Alcohol dries you out.' He picked his way over the scattered pile of tights, set the glasses on her side-table and returned to the stool with the tray. 'Shall I open the curtains? It's half one.'

'God! Yes, please. The accumulative effects of stress, alcohol and the cold, I suppose. I skipped lunch yesterday.'

'Tut tut.' He drew the curtains. 'Lovely day. I've been for a run.'

She grunted, reached for the nearest glass and sipped at it, regarding him over the rim. He'd changed; he was wearing faded jeans now, and a sleeveless burgundy top. He sat down, hoisted his right trainer on to his left knee and gripped his raised shin, his head forward.

'Please don't look at me.'

'Why?'

'I feel loathsome and despicable. Don't look!'

He laughed, but his lips didn't move and he didn't look away. 'Why are you so upset? Put it down to experience and forget about it. If some people don't spend the entire weekend, every weekend, in your state, they reckon they've been diddled of a good night out.'

'I feel so grimy and horrible. I need a bath.'

He got up. 'I'll run it for you.'

'No! I mean, I can manage now. Thank you for all your help, and the lovely meal. You must think so badly of me.'

'I just think you're human. But as you wish. I've scribbled my home address and phone number on the pad in the hall if you need anything.'

He stepped back across the tights towards her. A one-sided smile tugged at his mouth, and he seemed taller. The faint, salt-sharp odour of sweat reached her nostrils. He stretched out his hand and, with his index finger, traced a line from her right eye almost to her cheek, pressing just hard enough to pull her skin with it.

'Sweet,' he said.

She emptied the first glass of water, and lay back on the pillow. She had no reason to get out of bed. Steven had gone. She regretted banishing him. Why had she sent him away?

She pushed off the duvet. She looked like a long, blue fish. She must take the bath, make it her first goal of the day, or she risked daytime merging with dusk and finding her still a sluggabed.

She stumbled to the bathroom on limbs as frail as straws, and with every other step her head pounded. She leaned over the side of the bath to the taps. Her brain kicked harder still inside her skull, and the babbling of water swelled to a full roar. Bath towel... The one she'd used yesterday evening draped down the rail. She scrunched up a handful in her fist: it would do. She picked up Brendan's box of bath salts and tilted it over the gush of steaming water. A few crystals sprinkled out, the green dust vaporising immediately. She touched a finger to her nose and instead put the box on the floor by the radiator.

She laid her watch on the back of the sink, unzipped her dress and let it fall in a whipped-up ring round her. She pushed her pants down to the knee and marched her feet until the garment dropped. She pinned it to the floor with her toes and stepped out of it while she felt behind her back to unhook her bra. With her fingers and thumbs she pulled the two ends of the fastening towards each other to release the hooks. She tried again, and a third time.

'Bloody *hell*!'

Habit rendered the fastening and unfastening of a bra a slickly executed sequence of events, performed without a second thought. Maybe one of the hooks had bent shut. She ran her fingers round the strap. To her addled brain it felt all wrong: between her two index fingers she could detect a tag, a tail. On the outside. She released it, doubting herself, and felt again. No, it was on the outside. Maybe the strap was twisted. She inserted both thumbs under the straps and ran them round to her armpits, but both straps felt perfectly smooth. How frustrating, how stupid. And her arms were beginning to ache. She sighed. Crossing her arms over her chest, she grasped the fabric under each arm and raised the bra straight over her head. She brought the fastening up to her face, inspected it both sides: it was normal. With a shake of her head she hurled the bra to the floor.

She dipped a foot in the bath water, lowered herself to a sitting position and lay back. The water rose over her shoulders before she turned off the taps. She broke the water surface with her fingers, closed her eyes and let the drips plink through the glassy stillness.

*

She awoke, miserably cold. Her watch was too far away to discover how long she'd been asleep. With her foot she hooked up the plug chain, drained the bath a hand's depth and refilled it with scalding water. She submerged her head to the ears, shampooed her wet hair and plunged back to rinse it in the clean water. She massaged in some conditioner and began to wash while the conditioner did its work. Bit by bit she soaped herself, splashing to rinse away the lather.

When her fingers pushed between her legs she winced. She touched herself again, probing gently until her fingers met bone. Sore, she felt sore. Her brow crumpled. Maybe her underwear had made her overhot during the night. Maybe the sweat had irritated her skin.

She knelt up, testing her balance, and got to her feet. With the shower attachment she sluiced away the conditioner and soap suds, and climbed out on to the duck-board. She dried herself with rough, clumsy passes of the towel and stepped on to the lino. Kicking aside her dirty clothes, she parted her feet and bent to inspect herself: the skin was soft and dark after its lengthy immersion in the hot tub, but there was no hint of swelling, no rash or irritation.

Clutching the damp towel she fetched her dressing-gown from the bedroom. Afterwards she picked up a clean towel from the airing-cupboard on the landing and wrapped it round her head as she went downstairs. Immediately came the sound of scraping from the other side of the kitchen door.

'Oh my God, Ruskin!'

The moment the door opened, the cat yowled. He raised his head to be stroked and paraded an enthusiastic figure of eight round her legs.

'Almost your tea-time, isn't it, and I haven't even given you your breakfast. You poor animal.'

Ruskin planted himself by the cupboard where his dry food was stored, his front paws padding earnestly. She went to the fridge. Stuck to the door, under a pig fridge magnet, was a note in fluent, spiky writing: *I have fed the cat. Steve.*

She turned to the cat. 'I forgot you, but Steve didn't, did he. You little fibber.'

She prepared a slice of toast, smeared it with butter and yeast spread, poured herself another glass of water and carried them into the sitting-room. She switched on the television, turned up the volume, put the tray on the floor and flopped on to the sofa, jarring her head.

Outside, the leaves on the neighbour's tree glowed almost yellow in the warm, westerly light, making the sitting-room cold and dingy. The bright colours and yawning smiles and laughter from the television could not match the fine June evening. Students and tourists would be punting back to Folly Bridge now, the floors of the boats rolling with bottles and strewn with strawberry stalks.

Light, above all she needed light and warmth. She took pity on the cat in the kitchen and fed him, then sat outside on the top step to finish her meal and dazzle her brain to silence. She dozed for a while there, leaning against the wall, till the sun tucked itself behind the chestnut and the light faded to a cool white.

She rang Zo, but Zo was out. She picked up Steven

Bennallick's number and tapped in the first two digits before replacing the receiver. She went back upstairs and put on an old, unrestricting dress. The room still had Steven's eyes. Who would fail to mock her after her sluttish display anyway? How could she not fall in the estimation of a decent person?

Sitting on the edge of the bed made her wince. Again. She returned to the bathroom and squared up to the mirror. All that remained of her dark red lipstick was a thin demarcation round the margins of her mouth. The line he had traced with his finger turned out to be a particularly clear streak of smudged mascara, and the inner canthi of her eyes were spotted with black mucus. Risible, the face of a clown.

She took her make-up remover pads from the cabinet, pressed a succession of oily discs to her eyes and lips, and tossed the crumpled, blackened pads one by one into the bin under the sink. A couple fell on the floor. She picked them up afterwards and dropped them into the bin. The bra lay nearby, sprawled on the lino like a black widow. She examined it. It was damp. Perfect, not twisted, not inside out.

She stretched out the back of it, still fastened, then turned it over. That particular hook fastening, the tightest, left a tab of two unused pairs of eyes. Like a tail. But this tail was on the inside. What she had felt had been on the outside.

She re-arranged the bra so that the tab flapped free, loose and available for discovery from the outside. In order for it to be in that position, she had to have been wearing the bra inside out. It seemed to leap from her hands then, and she reeled backwards, striking her hip on the towel rail.

Did anger really surpass doubt as the more damaging emotion? She sat on the bottom stair, her head in her hands. Where anger gathered itself to a focus, doubt diffused. Anger looked outward for its object, whereas doubt doubled back on the doubter. Anger was more likely to precipitate action. Doubt, by its very nature, failed to commit, undermining foundations of rock and replacing them with sand. Untreated, it festered, grew insidiously and ate one away from the inside out. Doubt grew like a cancer.

She owed it to herself to piece together every available fact.

'The waitress yesterday evening?' the male voice repeated over the phone. 'That would have been Vanessa. She's in now.'

There followed a muffled exchange, and a woman came on the line. Karin explained who she was.

'Look, I'm awfully sorry, but I've mislaid an earring.'

'Nothing's been picked up here.'

'Maybe the taxi. I don't suppose you remember which firm you called?'

'Mercury. Your friend was settling up and he had their card in his wallet.'

Karin thanked her. She depressed the button in the cradle, released it and moved the directory closer to the phone. Its pages were already open at the taxi listings. She replaced the receiver, her heart pounding. The moment those two lines made their connection, she called Steven Bennallick a liar.

On three occasions that evening she almost made the call, but by the time she had summoned the courage to let the phone ring, she realised that trade would already be brisk. Steven Bennallick's character could remain unblemished that night. But she changed the bed-linen.

*

She called Mercury early next morning.

'The person on the radio Friday night? Yeah, you're speaking to him. What can I do you for?'

'One of your cars,' she said, 'picked up a couple from Cherwell Boathouse, acquaintances of mine. I wonder if you could tell me where they were dropped?'

'Data protection, miss. Sorry.'

'Oh please, I need to contact them very urgently. *Please.*' She hesitated. 'Bardwell Road, Northmoor Road maybe?'

There was a smacking of lips and a laboured sigh. 'You didn't hear this from me, okay, but yeah, I remember. I had another fare lined up at Summertown and the driver radioed back to say no can do: the guy wanted him to wait and then drop him elsewhere.'

She picked up the details Steven Bennallick had left by the phone. 'An Iffley address?'

'Iffley, I think it was, yes.'

'How long did your driver have to wait?'

'That I'd have to check, and I can only give an approximate time. I seem to recall he said five, ten minutes. You know, not that long, but long enough for me to have to send out another car. Can you give me a name for the computer?'

'Bennallick.'

'Bennallick... Friday... There it is. Pick-up time, drop-off...' He made a series of soft, regular blowing sounds between his lips. 'Yeah, that adds up. Can't have been any more than ten minutes.'

Steven had been telling the truth.

*

She stopped paddling her feet and let herself glide on outstretched arms till her fingertips touched the end of the pool. Panting, she lifted her face, water pattering from her lips and nose. She grabbed the wall and touched a knuckle to her cheek: burning. Fifteen lengths instead of the customary thirty, and her subdued body was calling time. She dipped her face back into the water and let the cool wavelets lap her skin.

With her first few steps away from the pool ladder her head sang, and she veered briefly sideways as she walked back towards the changing rooms.

The shower water lashed her hair into a lank curtain, peppering her with tiny blows and hissing on the shower floor, but nothing could muffle the theorizing inside her head. He had told the truth. Or was it an abridged and expurgated version; the truth, but not the whole truth?

The water cut off above her and the dregs trickled down her back. When the taxi had dropped him off at Iffley, had Steven Bennallick brushed his teeth and crept into bed? Or was there more?

*

'Let me get this straight,' Zo said in a pained tone. She had been in bed when Karin had pounded on her door at eleven-thirty that Sunday morning, and she had crawled back there to hold court while Karin paced up and down at the end of it. 'You think the guy you went out with on Friday drove back to your place, molested you while you were semi-conscious, drove home again and visited you in the morning as though nothing had happened.'

'I don't think,' said Karin. 'I *know*.'

'Know, and yet don't remember.' Zo turned her two pillows on their end, shoved them lengthways up the headboard and hauled herself into a sitting position. 'I really think you need to see Finn. I'll make the appointment. Hey, I'll even drive you down if it'll help.'

'Zo, I am not losing it. Everything I've told you is true.'

'How much had you drunk? Three wines, one indirect whisky... I could manage a small slam on that, but it's a lot for a borderline teetotaller. And you were poorly.'

'Poorly, yes. Run down, probably. Drunk, yes, a little. Okay?' Karin sat on the bottom corner of the double bed, and it gave under her like marshmallow. 'But drunk enough to forget everything between stepping into the taxi and waking next lunch-time? Bruised in the nether regions when I've not made love for almost six months? My bra inside out?'

'Your bra?' Zo spat air between her teeth and laughed, and under her nightshirt her breasts quivered like great balls of dough. 'Twisted perception, twisted bra. Was he drunk too? Or is he just blind, or stupid?'

'I swear! He put it on me inside out. I'll prove it.'

Karin bent over. Her wet hair fell forward, revealing a collar of grey damp round her white T-shirt. From her rucksack she fished a transparent blue freezer bag containing the bra. She shuffled up the edge of the bed, pulled out the bra and handed it to Zo. It was a black, underwired bra, the cups made of fine netting decorated with leaf shapes.

'The fabric's so thin it looks the same inside and out, certainly...' Zo murmured. 'You can tell by the label though. Am I allowed to finger exhibit A? Where's the label?'

'I cut them off,' Karin said with a note of triumph. 'They stick out and annoy me. None of my bras have labels.'

'Let's see the seam.'

Zo examined the join running down the centre of one of the cups.

'Not so easy, is it,' said Karin. 'With that one even I have to check. And without the label, a man could put that bra on somebody else inside out and it would look quite normal. But you try taking it off – or putting it on. Try it!'

'God, you're serious.' Zo dropped the bra and it seemed to float like a giant marine oddity on the dolphin duvet. She waved a finger at a tump of clothes in the corner. 'Well, come on! I'm hardly going to make it into yours.'

Karin picked up a raspberry T-shirt and a pair of jeans.

'No, in the T-shirt, *in* the T-shirt.'

Karin stuck her hand inside and reeled out a white brassière of daunting proportions. She threw it on the bed. Zo grunted, knelt up and dragged off her nightie. She wove her arms into the shoulder straps of her bra, leaned forward to ensnare her great, straying breasts and reached behind her back.

'Here goes.' She pursed her lips and made fidgety movements with her elbows. 'Come on, come on... Bugger... Well, I can see what you - Oh, hang on. Is that it? I think I'm in business...' Her eyes flitted across the ceiling. 'Done it!'

'But you'd have checked long before now, wouldn't you. Now try taking it off.'

A light sweat began to bead Zo's forehead and she collapsed face down on the bed.

'Convinced?'

'Yes! Oh, fuck this, Karin. You do it. And chuck me the jeans and T-shirt, would you?'

Karin unfastened the hooks, threw the clothes on the bed and lowered herself into the diminished laundry pile masking the armchair.

'Who was he?' Zo demanded, her head bursting through the hole of the T-shirt.

'I can't tell you.'

'You tell me everything.'

'I just can't. But he's a client, and it was part of his consultation.'

'Cherwell Boathouse? A client? Bad move.' Zo wrestled with her jeans on the side of the bed. 'Dishy?'

'I still wouldn't have slept with him.'

'And he couldn't wait?'

'He had his own agenda.'

Zo raked her fingers through her hair into a mirror almost obliterated by the photographs and postcards tucked into the frame. Suddenly she stopped, her hands buried in hair.

'Look,' she said. 'Is it possible you were drugged?'

'Who would know for sure?' Karin repeated, her voice dull. 'Leon. His first degree's in pharmacology.'

'Shall I call him?'

'No.'

Karin left the kitchen and Zo crept after her into the sitting-room, fingering her tension round her coffee mug.

'He might be out –'

'He's home,' said Karin over the receiver as she entered the number. 'If anyone likes his day of rest, it's Leon. Some girl will be concocting him a roast while he's in the garden reading the papers over a Pernod. Yes, could I speak to Leon, please?' She met Zo's eyes with a brief, neutral glance. 'Oh hello, Leon. Leon, a favour.'

'Excellent! We can trade.'

'I have a client who thinks she may have been drug-raped.'

The line fell silent. 'Okay,' he said wearily, 'trading on hold. Administered how? Spiked drink? That's the usual.'

'I think so.'

'Then?'

'Merry to begin with. Muddle-headed, dizzy. She became sleepy, lost her co-ordination. She assumed she'd drunk too much. And when she came to, she'd lost hours she can't account for.'

'Anterograde amnesia.' He sniffed. 'Could well be. What you've described, some kind of sedative, maybe? Anxiolytic, sedative, muscle relaxant, psychomotor performance right up the creek. Hypnotic, causes amnesia. Basically a nervous system depressant with the effects amplified by alcohol. Something like a benzodiazepine? Though other drugs can cause similar symptoms. A definite possibility, I'd say. When was it? Has she been tested?'

'No.'

'Well, in the absence of other proof, she's pushing it if she wants to make a formal complaint. These things don't hang around forever.'

'How long?'

'Depends on the dose and the individual. A day, maybe less? Thirty-six hours maximum, I reckon. So, Karin. You and me, Saturday. I was just thinking about you, wondering whether you'd like to join me for an afternoon's punting – without chaperone? Bottle of Pimms, strawberry-flavoured mineral water, your call.'

'No, Leo. You wind me up.'

'I'll be the perfect gentleman.'

'*No!* Oh God, I'm sorry...'

'If Zoe came, would you?'

'If Zoe came.'

'Then ask her and let me know.' He paused. 'I'd rather see you with company than not at all.'

She brought the receiver in front of her chest and stared for a while into the mouthpiece. Then she hung up, her back to Zo and her hand not moving from the receiver.

'Thirty-six hours,' Zo mused. 'And yes to the punting, the bastard. What are you going to do?'

'Ring Inspector Straker.'

'You're reporting it?'

'I don't know. I want to know what it – what would –'

'I'll speak to him, if you like. If you prefer. We're on

good terms.'

Karin made no reply.

'I'll find you the number then.'

Straker was about to go off duty, but someone called him back.

'I see,' he said, when Karin had recreated the client scenario. 'Well, she'd be allocated a victim liaison officer, a WPC, and she'd really need to be examined as soon as possible by the force medical examiner – female, of course. They'd have a urine sample for analysis, take swabs and so forth. It's handled with much more sensitivity these days, tell her, much more orientated to the concerns and feelings of the victim. Do urge her to come forward. I can give you a direct number.'

She thanked him and let him read it out.

'Though nothing,' she said levelly, 'can make up for what he did. He deserves to die.'

'What?' said Straker.

'He deserves to die.'

Zo strode across the room, pressed the button and cut the call. Karin stood there with the receiver to her ear. Zo eased it from her hand. Karin's eyes were swollen. Tears lay like glycerine along her lower lids. Zo put her arm round Karin's shoulders, guided her to an armchair and sat her down.

Karin's eyes widened. 'He *does* deserve to.'

'But the Plod doesn't need to hear about it, right?' Zo bounced down to her haunches in front of Karin, balancing on the balls of her bare, fleshy feet. 'So, have you decided?'

36

People stepped aside for her as she walked down Cornmarket Street towards Handley Myers that Monday afternoon. Men, women and children, irrespective of nationality, the crowds parted. Heads turned. Was it the bold purple of her outfit, the careless bohemian flow of the skirt? Perhaps the set of her shoulders, or the bold mask of make-up? Or maybe it was the eyes that attracted the oblique glances from the women. Maybe they attracted the men. Or was it the anger that suffused every forceful step, muted just enough for them to confuse it with desirability?

She shook her head and the warm breeze fingered her hair. If they had seen through to her core, they would not have stepped aside; they would have run. The anger knotted inside her, pulsing to send blood round her body. It glowed to keep her warm. It glowered under its burden like a toad under a stone, exuding poison through its skin. Let Bennallick caress that. Clients had come and gone that day, but he remained, the unremembered memory, buried inside her.

'Bennallick,' she told the receptionist, 'I want to see him. Karin Shilan.'

'Do you have an appointment?'

'He'll see me.'

She endured the hiatus while the receptionist's eyes lingered on her. The receptionist smoothed the pocket of her short avocado jacket, and with her other hand reached for the phone.

'Mr Bennallick?' The receptionist angled her body slightly from the desk as though the adjustment might render her inaudible and invisible. 'Ms Shilan is here to see you.'

'Is she indeed?' The response carried to perfection. 'Well, send her up. She knows the way.'

She mounted the stairs and moved silently down the carpeted corridor. The unavoidable forewarning would give him a breathing-space, preparation time. Before she reached that office, what remained of his misgivings would have been polished away to expose a veneer of gleaming self-possession.

The door stayed shut until she was but a couple of steps away, when the handle rattled and the door opened sharply.

'Karin, what an unexpected pleasure! Come in, come in.'

He supported the door against his back, but left a gap scarcely wide enough for her to pass. She could have deflected her shoulders, as she might avoid a stranger in a narrow corridor, but if he saw her defending herself against him she only confirmed and reinforced her intimidation.

She squeezed by with her shoulders turned towards his, pausing to look him straight in the eye.

'Well... I wish I had a camera.' He shut the door, but remained holding the brass knob. 'You look great! I like the skirt.'

'Purple,' she said, facing the window. 'For repentance.' She turned. 'I know what you did.'

'I'm sorry?'

'Oh, I wasn't expecting anything other than a denial, don't worry. But neither am I going to indulge you with an explanation for what you already know.'

She paced across the far end of the room. He moved to the front of the desk and raised a hand with an air of benign benediction.

'You know I haven't the faintest idea what you're talking about?'

'Of course.'

'What am I accused of denying? Finding you attractive? Show any man that poster.' He supported his weight on his hands and hoisted himself on to the desk. 'I don't deny I wanted to take you out either. Your trial by alcohol was unfortunate...' His eyes drifted at a leisurely pace down her body and back to her eyes. 'That aside, I don't mind saying how much I'd like to – repeat - the experience.'

The choice of words and the slowness of his delivery flickered over her like tongues, savouring the memories she had lost. She took a step in retreat under the pressure of his gaze.

'Oh, and good news, Karin: the headaches are gone. I haven't had one since last Wednesday. For me that's a record. Not a twinge in almost a week.'

'Oh, don't give me that! If you ever had them in the first place. Or were they a fabrication too?'

He jumped off the desk and strode out of the room, leaving

the door to swing behind him. She heard a single knock followed by another door opening. Presently a dumpy woman with curly, strawberry-blonde hair followed him in on tiny black court shoes like hoofs.

'Karin, meet Beverley, my secretary,' he said, waving from one woman to the other. 'Bev, do I or do I not suffer with headaches?'

Beverley ackowledged with a nod and turned her pale, exophthalmic eyes to her boss.

'And? Please tell Miss Shilan.'

'He gets very ratty with them.' Uncertain, Beverley looked from one to the other, her glossed lips parted. 'He always used to be after my painkillers. I got so fed up, I bought him a box of his own.'

Bennallick raised a school-masterly finger, opened a drawer of his desk and held up a packet of tablets for inspection.

'And this week?'

'Well, this past week you've been quite nice.'

'Thank you, Beverley.' He snapped open his fingers, let the painkillers drop into the drawer and shut it hard. 'See?' he smiled, when Beverley had backed into the corridor. 'No deception there. I'm glad you came actually. You've saved me a job.'

He picked a thick brown manilla envelope off the desk and took it over to her. He stood so close that there was little more than the envelope's width between them. She fixed her eyes on it, but made no move. He agitated it.

'Go on. You'll be pleased. It's another dispatch from David Bailey.'

She had to force her hands to accept the envelope. His proximity seemed to immobilise every muscle except her heart.

He turned on his heel and wandered to the desk, his hands in his pockets.

'Photos this time,' he said. 'Meredith's sent them back.'

'What?' She turned the packet over. 'It's open. You've opened a package addressed to me!'

'Yeah. Sorry about that. But addressed to you care of *me*...'

Bennallick sat on his office chair. 'Look, it came in my post this morning, a pile almost up to my chin. Little envelopes, big ones, chunky ones, thin ones, I just opened it. I didn't check. It happens. Don't get so aerated. It's one of those self-adhesive types, so if I'd wanted to make a clandestine raid on your mail, I'd have re-sealed it, wouldn't I, not ripped it like that. I'm sorry.'

He took a sheaf of stapled papers off the desk and began reading them with great concentration. From the envelope she pulled a pile of prints out part way, sandwiched either side between sheets of sturdy card. She tucked them all back in and crossed to the desk.

'You've looked at them.'

'I have.'

'You bastard!'

'An honest one, though, and that's what's important here, isn't it.' He tossed the papers on the table. 'Once I'd seen the first, checking what I'd opened, I couldn't resist the rest. Who would? You should see the horrors that got passed round Med. Neg. from time to time. The candle shots are my personal favourites. Though it galls me to say it, the guy has talent. If things go very well for him, he'll end up broke but exceptionally happy.'

She drew out a sheet of white paper that was protruding between the photographs and one slat of card, and unfolded it:

Dear Karin, I must suppose, not having heard from you, that forgiveness is too much to ask. I am therefore enclosing the negatives, contact sheets and prints as a gesture of goodwill. I've kept one to remind me of you, but would be happy to return it. In photographic terms the shot has little merit, but, of all the frames I took, this one has captured you as I feel you really are.

I gather Yamamoto's solicitors are still debating whether to hang, draw and quarter me, or merely write me off as a bad debt. A word from you would restore some much needed perspective. All best wishes, Roy.

'It appears he's kept one,' Bennallick mused, not looking up from his papers. 'I wonder which that was?'

'You shit!'

She stalked behind the desk and swung the envelope over

her head. He launched himself backwards on the swivel chair, laughing, and crossed his arms over his face.

'Hey!'

'I wasn't the first, was I? But I don't suppose you need to dope the little tarts at the nightclubs. They'd be flattered enough by your attentions to open their legs for you round the back of the fire-escape. Nothing wrong with a little throwaway screw to wind up the evening. Give them what they deserve, do you? But the problem is, not all women are slags like Jane. We're the ones you love to hate, aren't we. My mistake gets punished at the altar of your sad little vendetta. It's us that bug you, isn't it, Steve, because women are all the same.'

'I was wrong about you,' he said, folding his arms. 'I'm beginning to think you're disturbed.'

'Do you get a kick out of screwing unconscious women? Do you?' She struck her hand to her forehead. 'Oh, but I forgot! We're not unconscious, are we. Just separated from our inhibitions, conscious but parted from our soul. I played right into your hands, didn't I. I hope the thrill is worth the risk.'

'Well, well, I didn't know you were so fiery. The dash of temper is quite becoming. Though I have to say I'm concerned about you. I haven't done anything to hurt you. I give you my word.'

'There's no appealing to honour, Bennallick, where the purveyor of justice is the perpetrator of the crime.'

He got to his feet. 'I think you'd better leave before you say something actionable. You need help. You need to see someone.' He clapped his hands. 'What about a homœopath? I had an excellent… initiation…'

'You bastard!' she flung at him. 'You've seen nothing. See someone? Actually, yes, I have done. I've had a urine sample taken, and in a week's time it's going to wing its way back to the police doctor contaminated with whatever poison you fed me. I don't want to report Roy to the Law Society, by the way. Maybe he does deserve a reprimand, but that's nothing compared to what they're going to do to you. You'll have a criminal conviction. I think that ranks as conduct unbefitting, don't you? I think they might strike you off.'

'Listen to yourself!'

He came towards her, his arms outstretched. She shrugged violently and lashed out with the envelope.

'*Don't* touch me! To think I could have felt something. Look at your face in the mirror, and then take a good look at your heart and see which is in the better state. Be as arrogant as you like, but don't think the guilt won't get you. It'll eat you away from the inside till your body's as empty a husk as your soul.'

'Very lyrical,' he said as she took hold of the door handle. 'And the test will prove nothing but your paranoia.'

She clutched the packet to her chest, her breath clouding the sheen on the white glossed paint-work.

'Nevertheless, Steven, I'm waiting for that day. And till then, rest assured you're never far from my thoughts.'

37

Steven Bennallick gave the door of his TVR a shove, then caught the top of it with his hand. He took his weight on it and swung his feet slowly on to the tarmac, but failed to get up from the golden leather seat.

'Good God!' Straker murmured, hovering beside the long, sculpted door. '*Old man!* What happened? A pasting on the squash courts? Ricked a hamstring?' He paused. 'Too much sex?'

'No amount of sex ever made me feel this rough.' Bennallick gripped his hands on his thighs, his elbows forward and his fingers facing each other. 'Stress, mate, I think, too much stress. It's been a heavy week, several days in Court. I've come straight from the office as it is.'

'Saturday afternoon?'

Bennallick pushed himself up. 'Sad, isn't it.'

He took out his clubs in silence. He pressed the boot shut, peered at his reflection in the side window and pressed his fingers to his cheek.

'Grey,' said Straker. 'I kid you not. If I didn't know better I'd say the morning after a near-lethal night before. At the risk of unaccustomed altruism, are you up to eighteen?'

'I stayed in and didn't touch a drop. How depressing.' Bennallick managed a pinched smile. 'I'm sure I'll be all right after a bit of fresh air and exercise. I'll rally the moment your ball hits sand.'

Straker collected a couple of score cards from the Pro Shop while Bennallick waited, disguising yawns behind his hand.

'To die for!' he exclaimed, when Straker cracked another text-book drive off the first tee. 'This is art, man, this is possession. You can't put it all down to the same little pill.'

Straker followed the ball, his mouth full open, the corners taut with a curl of smug anticipation.

'I've never thought of my present state of mind as possession,' he said, watching the ball touch down and bound energetically along the fairway. 'Some might well describe it as that. I suppose it is a kind of madness at this stage.'

'Contagious?'

'Happily not.'

Straker moved aside and slotted his club back into the bag with a triumphant swoop of his arm. Bennallick stabbed a red tee into the ground and took up position. He whirled the driver and struck.

'Hooked,' he growled, as the ball slewed off to the left. 'Oh, straight in the bloody rough.'

'Time to play a provisional?'

'Can't be assed. I'll take my chance. Plus...' Bennallick picked up again as they towed their trolleys side by side on to the fairway. 'I'm detecting definite but inexplicable euphoria at work here. This madness... It wouldn't be the breasted kind, would it?'

Straker made no response but to squint at a buzzard wheeling on a distant thermal. Bennallick stopped.

'It is, isn't it. You've got a woman.'

'This one,' said Straker, striding on, 'has a name.'

'Yes. Hilary.'

'I'm not proud. Hilary doesn't know. At least, I haven't told her.' Straker turned, dragging his trolley in front of himself while he walked backwards with careless, swinging steps. 'The name's Nadine.'

Bennallick tugged on his trolley. 'More pickings from the rich pastures of the domestic dispute? Or could she be another casualty of Oxford's criminal underbelly?'

'Neither. She's a fellow bird watcher, and she's in telesales. Well, she's between jobs, to be precise. She hates telesales, but the pay's not bad.'

'And she's obviously very persuasive.'

Straker shot him a glance.

'I imagine your bird baiting must really grab her. Or have you consigned the two little corpses to the dustbin?'

'Three,' said Straker, further slowing his pace for Bennallick to catch up, 'and no.'

'Shouldn't you be stringing them up on barbed-wire by now? They'll be tame at this rate. Stick to budgerigars like normal folk if you can't go through with it.'

Straker made a clicking sound with his tongue. 'It's the way they look at you. I tried dispatching one and found that after three decades of antipathy, it just didn't bother me any more. I don't want them in my garden, but neither can I kill them, so there they stay. When God knows how many I picked off with an air-rifle as a kid.'

'Ah, women make you soft in the head, Jim.' Bennallick exhaled loudly. 'So, is the latest sentence destined to run concurrently?'

'No. No, I don't think it can, not much longer.'

'Good.'

'I'm thinking of splitting up with Hilary.'

'Oh no...' Bennallick rounded on Straker and pushed his fingers against Straker's chest, preventing his advance. 'You've stuck this marriage out so long. I thought things were on the mend? Is it really worth throwing everything away for the latest in a long line of tear-jerkers? Can't you just let this die an amicable death?'

'Not deteriorating is not equivalent to an improvement,'

said Straker. 'Anyway, that stuff doesn't plague me like it used to. I've changed. I told you.'

'Then I'm sorry. I'm really sorry.'

Bennallick bundled his trolley aside and walked off towards the longer grass at the edge of the fairway. Straker could hear him panting.

'Hey!'

'I'm looking for my ball.'

'Didn't it land further on?'

Bennallick raised his left arm and flicked his hand.

'Hey!' Straker shouted after him. 'Don't you see yourself falling in love again? Loads of well-intentioned people screw-up first time round.'

Bennallick halted. His upper body seemed to cave over his chest, but he quickly straightened. Straker took a couple of angry steps after him.

'Did you hear what I said? What's the big deal? You're lucky. You're as good as single. And while we're at it, Karin Shilan. Did you ask her out in the end?'

Bennallick put his hands on his hips, breathing deeply, and his eyes tracked left and right over the grass.

'We went out, yes.'

'And?'

'It was okay. I don't think we'll be seeing each other again, if that's what you mean. Mutual, fortunately. Inimical chemistry.'

'I'd have thought she was just your type. She having lost her husband –' Straker chewed his lip. 'Can't see that ball, can you?' He waited for Bennallick to join him. 'When was the date?'

'Yesterday week. Why, do you want to ask her next?'

'Just my insatiable nosiness.' Straker resumed striding up the fairway. 'How are you finding your remedy? Your illness could be an aggravation, you know. Did she tell you? I had one, couldn't piss for hours. But it's a sure sign that the remedy's acting. A couple of days at the most and this should subside. She could give you something -'

Bennallick swivelled away, turning his back to Straker. His

left hand still rested on his hip, his head drooped.

'Do you mind if we stop talking about her?'

The voice sounded as though he were holding his breath. Straker grabbed his elbow and wheeled Bennallick round to face him. He had his right arm crossed over his chest, the flat of his hand on his collarbone.

'What's wrong? Are you in pain?'

'Sort of.' Bennallick didn't look up. He paced a few steps to and fro. 'I almost cried off. I hoped it would fade.'

He sucked some air between chattering teeth. Straker touched his forehead.

'You're sweating.'

'I'm freezing.'

'Are you all right to walk?'

'Not to the club.'

'Sit, then,' said Straker. 'Wait!' He ran for his trolley, lifted out his golf bag and laid it on the grass. 'Lean against this.'

'I can't! Got to stand.'

Straker turned and patted his back trouser pockets for his mobile. 'Steve? Have you got your phone?'

'Car.'

Bennallick stooped forward, binding his chest with both arms.

'Shit...' Straker backed away. He started to run. At the first tee a foursome waited, two close in discussion, two glowering down the fairway at him with arms akimbo. He broke into a sprint towards them, waving his hands over his head as he ran across the fairway. 'Please! I need assistance here!'

Behind him came a distant cough as Bennallick retched.

38

Jim Straker deliberately dug into the gravel with his heels and sent the golden peas sputtering up behind, like water in boiling fat.

He let his eyes travel up the façade of Karin Shilan's house. Five months had passed, just over five months since his first visit. On that January evening everything had merged into wet, trembling blackness, everything was low and heavy and dripping with bad news. Now, the walls were a mosaic of Virginia creeper, dotted with the errant yellow flowers of a climbing rose, and the dead, ugly root by the steps had turned into a tree.

He paused to shuffle the stones with the toe of his right shoe, enjoying the sound and textures, the yielding solidity, shifting like pennies underfoot. He'd always wanted a gravel drive, a house with a proper gravel drive, not a hard-standing of sooty tarmac or Nadine's concrete ramps with their in-fill of hard-core. Nadine could perhaps create for him a Japanese garden in front of the house, and he could crunch therapeutically round the acers and cairns with his rake. Compromise was almost halfway to a dream.

He climbed the steps and rapped four times on the knocker. The door opened.

'Hi!' said Zoe Seymour. 'Come in.'

She held the consulting-room door wide and waved him inside. He sat down, taking his time, exploring and assessing the room with the curiosity of a house-buyer on a viewing.

'Bit different from the Natural Health Centre.'

'Not bad, is it?' she said. 'Given peace and quiet you can take a case almost anywhere, but this...' She indicated the space with upturned, reverential hands as she took her place at the desk. 'My Abingdon practice is much the same as the Natural Health Centre, and at home I work from a box-room not even the estate-agents dared call bedroom three. Locuming here is like a holiday.'

'When is Karin back?'

'Tomorrow afternoon. It was a last-minute decision. I'm just dealing with her phone calls and acutes, and picking up a few appointments she couldn't re-arrange. You know, folk who work away and visit her every so often when they're back in town. And feeding the cat. So it's more convenient to see my clients here for a couple of days.' She was already riffling through his case-notes. 'How have you been? It looks to me like we might be getting somewhere at last.'

'Well, I sleep,' he said. 'My mood is less erratic, and the sexual problems have evaporated. The peeing remains much improved. And I'm still getting on better with Hilary.' His eyes scudded across the ceiling. 'In fact, it's only now I realise the extent of the deterioration, the insidiousness.'

'Have you experienced any indications yet that the remedy isn't acting as strongly as when you first took it?'

'None.'

'Then it's holding,' she said with clear satisfaction. 'I think you can carry on as you are until you notice any change for the worse. Anything else?'

'Yes. I was in town with Hilary the other day and I walked underneath a ladder without a second thought. A ladder halfway across the pavement, propped up against a first-floor window. I've been making detours round ladders for as long as I can remember. And I'm stockpiling magpies. I've always hated them and yet, after a few weeks, I'm starting to see their characters. I'm even getting to like them. This –' He made an exhalation like a cough '- is a complete departure. It can't be the remedy?'

Zo linked her hands behind her head. 'A well-selected remedy is quite capable of altering the way patients view things. It changes their perspective, let's say. If there's a particular block in someone's life, maybe they don't perceive it as a block anymore, or they see a way round it. Homœopathy is like a knife gradually cutting away the bonds we've learned to tie ourselves down with. But it doesn't dictate the answers. Maybe your superstitions were just part of your pathology.'

He hesitated. 'I've told Hilary about Nadine. I told her

yesterday.' His eyes stung behind his glasses. 'She cried. A bit, not a lot. She wasn't surprised. I felt a complete bastard. She was very calm about the whole thing. She's agreed to a separation. There was no screaming, no fuss. She didn't make to hit me. She didn't even throw anything.'

'The future?'

'Sometime, yes, I'll move in with Nadine. When we think the kids have had a chance to come to terms with the change. It's not as though I'll be severing all links. Nadine's happy for me to be round there. I'm more than pleased to offer financial support, fix things in the house. And I think Hil realises I'm not just trading her in for a younger model. In fact she told me she's been considering a change in direction for some time. After the summer holidays she's reducing her hours to part-time. She wants to train as a homœopath, actually. She's applying to your old college.'

'Fantastic!'

'She's ringing the principal this afternoon. She seems quite excited.' He paused and puckered his lips. 'I didn't expect her to adjust quite this fast.'

'Unhappiness is a two-way thing, Jim. A catalyst for one party has to be a catalyst for the other. And she'll be so busy with course-work, I doubt she'll have time to miss you.'

'I said I'd help out with the tuition fees –'

'In that case she definitely won't miss you! Does Karin know yet?'

'I don't think so.'

'May I tell her?'

'Of course.' He brushed a speck of lint off his thigh with the flat of his hand. 'Look, I have to ask you: can homœopathy kill?'

'Ask the scientists. There's nothing in our tablets.' She burst into a peal of horsy laughter, then got up and went over to Karin's bookcase. '*Can homœopathy kill?*' she mused, her head at an angle as she read the titles on the spines. She pressed a fingertip on top of a book and pulled out a slim, pale green paperback. She inspected its rather bent cover, then held it up to face him: the *Organon of Medicine*. 'This,' she said, returning to her seat, 'is our Bible. Ever heard of Hahnemann, Samuel Hahnemann?'

'I think Hilary's mentioned the name.'

'He's the granddaddy of classical homœopathy, and author of this noble work. He's not without his faults,' she added, flicking through the pages. 'Chronic verbosity for one, and sentences even longer than those in the letters of Saint Paul. However, he does lay down the basis of all our homœopathic philosophy and practice. This is aphorism 1, fortuitously the shortest in the book.' She held up the text. ' *"The physician's high and only mission is to restore the sick to health, to cure, as it is termed."*' She closed the covers. 'We don't tend to consider ourselves in the killing business.'

'But can it?' he pressed. 'I know homœopathy is billed as safe and gentle and effective, but is it possible to harm people?'

'Most things, when abused or taken to excess can cause harm. We don't reject electricity. We use it in a controlled way. You'd die if you ate nothing but carrots. Similarly, if you take too much of a remedy over time, even an acute remedy in low potency, you can prove it.' She rolled her eyes in self-chastisement. 'I mean that even a healthy person would start to experience the symptoms associated with that remedy. And if a sick person keeps dosing themselves with a potentised remedy after seeing an improvement, they just might end up with worse symptoms than before. A lot of well-intentioned pharmacists fall down there.'

'Could that kill?'

'With the symptoms they're most likely to be treating, I doubt it. But you could if you prescribed a high enough potency to a vulnerable person. If, for example, I prescribed CM Digitalis – which obviously has a strong affinity with the heart – to a frail old man suffering from a heart complaint within Digitalis' sphere of action, then yes, the remedy could be too much for him. What's more,' she said, warming to the subject, 'it would be completely untraceable: no material substance to analyse. The victim is just an old chap carried off by a fatal heart attack. A perfect murder, Inspector. But it's not something a professional homœopath would do – deliberately or accidentally. We prescribe potencies which will stimulate a patient's vital energy, not overcome it and snuff it out.'

'But it's possible?'

'In theory.'

He drummed two fingers on his lower lip for a moment. 'I'd like you to call up Steven Bennallick's file.'

'Bennallick... He's not one of my clients.'

'I know.'

'And our files are confidential.'

He got to his feet and paced across to the window, his arms folded. 'I'm asking you,' he said, staring out of the glass, 'as a police officer.'

For some time she made no reply, but behind him the quietness bristled.

'I consider that request,' she said at last, her enunciation suddenly clipped and precise, 'as an abuse of our relationship. *Inspector*. Since Mr Bennallick is Karin's client, I suggest you broach the matter with her. I can't assist.'

He stuck his hands in his trouser pockets with a casual, almost shrugging movement, and carried on addressing the glass.

'Look, I'm doing her a favour. You can show me the file informally. In all probability there's nothing untoward anyway. You keep mum, Karin's spared the embarrassment, everybody forgets about it. But a suspicion can formalise everything...'

'All right. Jesus!'

The words, snappish and resentful, flew at him like missiles. He nodded to himself, but only when he heard the laptop open and the patter of keys did he turn back to the room. He moved without a sound to Zoe Seymour's shoulder. There was one very marked click as her nail jabbed a key, and the screen changed.

'For what it's worth,' she said.

He placed both hands on his knees and peered at the scant details: name, address, telephone numbers...

'She saw him here on Thursday the nineteenth,' Zoe muttered. 'That's it, the whole entry. No record of a remedy. Shall I look at her notes?' She jumped up from the chair, forcing him to step aside. She grabbed open the top drawer of the filing cabinet, sifted through the coloured files and pulled one out. She slammed the drawer shut and drifted back towards her chair, leafing through the contents of the file. 'Registration form, duly completed... Case-notes, dated the nineteenth...' She turned over a couple of sheets. 'That's odd.'

'What?'

'Well, the notes look unfinished, incomplete.' Zoe looked back at the previous page and returned to the last sheet. 'There's stuff missing here, details I know she would have asked for. And there's no summary, no outline of her assessment, no chosen remedy or potency. Nothing, as far as I can see. It doesn't look like she gave him a remedy at all.' She closed the file, her lips pulled into a wide, taut smile, and banged the file into his waiting hand. 'Why the fascination?'

'Because,' he said, opening the file again, 'Steven Bennallick almost died on Saturday, of a heart attack.'

Straker sat in the chair, his knees parted, his ankles crossed, perusing the file.

'Mr Bennallick's paternal grandfather died of a heart attack at the age of fifty-nine.'

'Genetic predisposition then,' Zo said lightly from the desk. 'What about the parents?'

'Mother... still living. She's got diabetes. Father... he died in a car accident when Mr Bennallick was twelve.'

'Could be the missing link. Though I didn't see any mention of heart problems in the notes, or Bennallick's medical history.'

'What's this?' He rotated the file and indicated a drawing in the margin of the second page. 'Does that mean anything to you?'

Zo scrunched her lips and shook her head. 'A scribble. She's a doodler.'

He grunted. 'Did Karin ever mention a client who thought she might have been drug-raped?'

'A client? No.'

'What about Steven Bennallick? Did she ever say anything about him?'

'Of course. He's her solicitor.'

'That she went out with him socially?'

'Jim, I'm her locum in a professional capacity only,' said Zo, fixing him with an implacable gaze. 'If you want the social low-down, *as a police officer*, you'll have to speak to her yourself.'

39

'Good, Karin. Great! I'm glad you had a brilliant time in Galway,' Zoe echoed drily across the reception of the Natural Health Centre the following evening.

Karin stopped short, one foot still on the bottom stair, a hand supporting herself against the wall.

'What's wrong?'

Zo twitched her hand disparagingly and turned to the reception desk. 'Is anyone using room 1?'

Anthea, the only other person in reception, pulled on her bottom lip. 'All yours.'

'Good. You and I,' said Zo, advancing on the stairs, 'need a chat.'

Karin pressed herself to the wall. She let Zo stamp past and followed her up the stairs.

'*What's wrong*,' Zo said, when she had closed the door of the therapy room behind them, 'is Bennallick's case-notes.' She left Karin bewildered in the middle of the room, strode to the desk and sat on it. With her toes she hooked the chair towards her and planted her feet on the cushion. 'Plus, I suppose, the fact that Bennallick's had a coronary, that Jim Straker seems to think we go round bumping off clients at will, that Straker demands to see Bennallick's file and, oh yes, he's fishing for what went on between you two.' She jabbed an index finger towards the floor. 'I'd say that's quite a lot of what's wrong, wouldn't you?'

'Coronary?'

'He's survived, thank Christ. Look, you may find Straker on your doorstep. That's all I'm saying. I did what I could to dissuade him. Grandad's heart attack pacified him somewhat; previous convictions in Bennallick's genome, that he could relate to.' The volume of her voice rose as though she had caught herself relaxing prematurely. 'He also picked up the drawing in the margin, but I managed to pass it off as a doodle. One of your more stylised efforts, I'm glad to say. You knew his remedy all along, didn't you. And what a nice bundle of heart symptoms it has.'

'A coronary?'

'Yes, yes. Coronary thrombosis, myocardial infarction, heart attack. Now, the remedy?'

'He never had the remedy,' Karin said slowly. 'I knew what it was the first time I met him. Well, I was pretty sure. And he never mentioned heart trouble.'

'Family history?'

'Despite the possible family history. It's not the sort of problem that would slip your mind, is it? And he's one of these lean, fit, sporty types, always pounding some court or the other. I even took the remedy to the Boathouse, but by the end of the evening I was hardly in a state to hand it over.'

'So you just wished him dead.'

'Too damned right!'

'Oh, for God's sake,' said Zo. 'Bad thoughts wing their way back to the thinker with reinforcements. That's what they say, isn't it? Everything has its pay-back? You should know.'

'On this occasion I can't say I'm falling over myself to care.' Karin pulled the director's chair round and sat down facing Zo. 'When you're suffering, it's surprisingly easy to kid yourself that a bit more pain doesn't matter. So no, hands up, I'm not gnashing my teeth and pretending to cry my eyes out at the news. In fact, I'm glad he didn't die. Let him live with the constant, beating reminder of his close shave, and the suspicion that there might be a next time.' She became aware of Zo's eyes, boring into hers. 'But it was nothing to do with me.'

'Wasn't it.'

Karin sprang up from the director's chair and strode down to the door. 'Aren't we getting a bit Orwellian all of a sudden? Forget Straker. Bring on the thought police, why don't you.' She turned, tapping on her chest with her fist. 'It's stress, Zo. Doctors, lawyers, any other Tom, Dick or Harry who's overworked and overpaid. It's part of the package. Ask him. The stress of overwork combined, I hope, with a generous measure of conscience and some good old anticipatory anxiety. Equals heart attack. A death wish hardly qualifies me for attempted murder.' She walked back up the room, bundled the director's chair out of the way against the wall and jabbed an accusatorial finger at Zo. 'You're the one who says no tablet, no effect. Well, in this case, no tablet. You can't make a volte-face with your hard-bitten philosophy now. I didn't do anything.'

Zo grunted non-committally. She pushed the chair away with her feet and swung her legs back and forth under the desk.

'He could have died, Karin.'

She considered for a moment. 'Exactly. He could have died. But he didn't.'

*

She drained the pan over the sink that evening, sliding the lid a fraction lower to jam the four or five noodles that were making their bid for escape. She put the pan on the work-top, added a knob of butter, some salt and milled pepper, and stirred with her wooden spoon until the noodles glistened. She tipped them on to her waiting plate with some steamed green beans, poured the roasted garlic sauce on top and carried the plate to her single place setting at the kitchen table.

Did she deserve Zo's wild accusations, she reflected, impaling a bean on her fork. She hadn't done anything. Had she? Was despising someone a sufficient cause to produce an effect? Anger was certainly an emotion that revelled in action. And yet she hadn't resorted to necromancy or performed incantations. No demons had been raised. Perhaps you didn't need to do anything. But could the machinations of a distressed mind remotely influence the molecules of another human body, make its cells sticky, clot its blood, throw its heart into confusion? It was ridiculous. Hadn't she willed Brendan's recovery with all her heart, mind and soul? And all to no effect. Had Zo forgotten that?

She forked up some of the noodles, rotating the handle to coil them round the tines. But Brendan had made a conscious commitment to die. That she'd deplored and rejected his decision didn't alter the fact. Was it possible, she wondered, to use one's will as a shield? Or for it to function as a shield? Even the homœopathy couldn't slice through to him, despite the care she'd taken. And he'd always responded so well. She shook her head; this was the stuff of light sabres and Flash Gordon and Dark Lords. But who went round consciously focused on their survival, willing themselves to live as they rattled on the keyboard of their PC or sold shares, cleaned the loo or fed the cat? Or sat arrogantly in a solicitor's office, convinced they had committed a perfect crime?

She reached for the pot of Parmesan and shook the cheese, like putrid talc, over the sauce. And then she pushed the plate away.

*

He was sitting in an armchair in the day room, his head bowed over the book in his lap. He could have been reading or dozing. Either way, she had the chance to study him long before he became aware of her presence.

The air of crisp, bristling efficiency had deserted him. He was barefoot and dressed in green and red striped pyjamas. His black slippers, the toes pointed inwards, lay on the floor just in front of his feet. His hair had separated into dark columns falling, unkempt, over his forehead, and his unfastened dressing-gown seemed to have moulded itself round an indeterminate form, neither man nor chair. All the old dynamism had been scooped out of him, leaving him deflated and forlorn, like an unpopular child invited out of kindness to a sleep-over.

A couple of elderly men nodded to her. The rest, sitting in a straggly circle round the television set, stared, glassy-eyed, at the cricket.

She swallowed and moved forward, fingering the punnet of raspberries through the brown paper bag in her hands. The rustle caught his attention. Immediately his eyes widened. His lips stretched, just for a second, as though his cautious smile could not weather the uncertainty, and the light of pleasure was straight away snuffed from his eyes. He leaned his head against the back of the chair and laid down his book.

'I never expected to see you.'

For some moments they managed to hold each other's gaze. There was no daring, no bitterness, no pity, just a strange neutrality as cool and light as the breeze from the open window.

'Fruit,' she said, presenting the bag.

'Thank you! Won't you –?'

He motioned to the neighbouring chair and pushed himself up in his seat while she put the bag on the nearest table. She lowered herself beside him.

'How are you?'

'Still pretty shaken up,' he said, nodding. 'I've had all the analyses, X-rays, ECG, blood tests, and they don't seem to know what caused it, which makes survival rather more frightening than the heart attack. My cholesterol isn't high. I have a good, almost exemplary diet. I don't have angina. I don't have heart failure, and I'm already signed up with a jolly rehab gang. Even so, they've put me on enough tablets to shame a sizable rattler.'

'When do you go home?'

'Parole begins on Monday. I'm spending a fortnight with my sister and her family in Salisbury. Though that might just land me back in here.' He closed his book, a thriller so well thumbed that the edges of the cover were furred and white, and threw it on the seat of the next chair. 'Listen...' He curled his tongue over his bottom lip, and self-consciously drew away the wetness with his upper lip. 'I'm thirty-nine, not even forty. They tell me I could be on pills every day for the rest of my life, and I'm supposed to be thankful. Well, I don't want to be shored up by prophylaxis. What kind of life is that?' He exhaled hard. 'I don't suppose –?

No.' He lowered his head. 'But I meant what I said about the headaches.'

Her own heart broke into a tattoo of dread, cold and overwhelming.

'Look... I don't suppose there's any way you would still consider treating me, is there?'

She stared at him, feeling herself recoil in the seat, her spine seeking the fabric of her dress, the back of the cushion, the wall behind the chair.

'I can't. How can you even ask?' She shut her eyes and began rocking gently, almost imperceptibly, on the edge of the chair. After a few seconds she opened her eyes and let her fingers slide from her cheeks to her chin. 'It's essential,' she said, avoiding his face, 'for the practitioner to be as objective as possible, which is why you're going to have to see somebody else.'

'I want you to do it.'

'How could I?'

'I'm a mess, Karin.'

'*I'm* a mess,' she hissed. 'Grieving, sex-starved widow deludes herself that good-looking professional screws her at dead of night, poor dear. The waiting staff and taxi-driver see me apparently pissed, so pissed I can't even tell whether my knickers are in a twist. Your alibi stands to attention and salutes. I've bathed, showered, swum. The barrister would have taken me apart piece by piece, stripped the flesh from my bones to patch up your inconveniently tarnished reputation and save your ass. He'd have had a field day with me, a barrister, someone people *respect*. And you'd have let him.'

Bennallick laid his hands on his knees. 'What if the barrister were to take me to pieces instead?'

'You?'

'Whatever they rebuild has got to be better than this.'

Inside her head her teeth bit together with a soft, audible snap. Nobility was the last thing she had expected. Somehow it blunted the edge of her rawest and most trenchant thoughts.

A long time passed before she could grasp any words at all,

and he waited. She heard the fluid squeal as she swallowed her saliva.

'The potency I had in mind...' she murmured, her voice a monotone, 'will be too high for you now.'

'What?'

'LMs... We can try something called LMs. They're highly diluted and very gentle. They would be safer.'

His lips tasted the air, opening and closing round pockets of silence. 'I don't know what to say.'

'Nothing, say nothing. To anyone.'

He shook his head, his eyebrows arched. Finally he said: 'It must be pretty deadly...'

She smiled. 'Unpleasant rather than deadly. It's Tarentula. Not the fluffy, pink-kneed type. We call it Tarentula, but in reality it's *Lycosa tarentula*: the wolf spider.'

He grimaced. 'Couldn't I just have hemlock for my golf?'

'No!'

'Does Roy play?'

'I wouldn't know. I doubt it.'

He nodded sagely, his mouth downturned. 'Of course, you could always feed him to that friend of yours. She seems quite sweet on him too. What's she called, Zoe? Or have you got in first?'

'Nobody's sweet on him! And nobody's "got in," as you put it. That chapter of my romantic life is now closed. In fact the whole book is closed.'

'Well, don't relegate any novellas to the jumble sale just yet. I'm sure it offends my blood pressure to say this, but from what I saw of his letter –'

'Tarentula LM 1,' she affirmed, getting up. 'When you're back from your sister's, give me a call.'

*

'Steve!' Jim Straker exclaimed when he answered the phone on Thursday evening. 'How the devil are you? To what do I owe the pleasure? Golf re-match?'

'No shit! Jim, you offered me your homœopath's number a while back. I wondered if I might have it now? She has a practice in Banbury, doesn't she, and I know someone there who might benefit from a consultation.'

'You're not thinking of switching?'

'Any reason why I should?'

'No, no.' Straker fetched Zoe Seymour's business card from his wallet in the kitchen and read out the number. 'Guess what,' he said. 'We've booked ten days' holiday in the Shetlands in September. We're going to do a bit of island hopping, stay on Mainland and Fair Isle. Do a few boat trips, weather permitting. Maybe Unst or Noss.'

'We?'

'Nadine and I. It'll be migration time, so Fair Isle could bring us some Siberian rarities if we're lucky, a few autumn vagrants.'

'I suppose they'll make a change from Oxford's,' Bennallick said drily. 'You seem very upbeat. Is Hilary out?'

'In the kitchen,' said Straker. 'Do you want to speak to her?'

'No,' said Bennallick. 'And Jim, congratulations.'

40

The mid-morning sun was already filtering through the roof of the tent, bathing everything in a buoyant yellow light. Inside, Zo sorted the chairs into four pairs and positioned them to provide as much privacy as possible within the open consultation space. She arranged each pair in an aesthetic and psychologically acceptable proximity, checking them for stability and shifting them until they could stand on the grass without rocking.

Karin tidied her display of T-shirts in the waiting-area, then eyed up the shelves of homœopathy books and information leaflets. Zo stepped across and patted a pile of leaflets between her fingers to align the edges.

'Perfect,' said Karin. 'I think that's it.'

'Well done!' Simon called from the dispensary. 'The tent's looking great. The weather is set to last for the weekend and, most important of all, the water's boiled and we've just got time for tea and biscuits before we roll.'

They sat in a row in front of the tent, all six wearing shorts and matching Travelling Homœopaths T-shirts, and nursing mugs of tea that were far too hot to drink. The sunshine, the sudden stillness and inactivity seemed to send warm lead coursing through their limbs, and their surroundings, hitherto ignored, washed back into their consciousness on waves of fatigue and satisfaction.

The field that had been huge and bare the previous afternoon seemed to have shrunk overnight, dissected by row on row of striped canvas stalls, modern tents and display areas. Here and there drifts of wood smoke lazed on the air and, when conversation lulled, the distant clink of metal carried to their ears.

A peasant wearing a tunic and leggings and a drooping brown hood rumbled past, pulling behind him a low wooden trolley laden with spears. His short leather boots were already soaked with dew.

'For the battle,' Simon explained. 'Don't worry about them: the more serious injuries are crated straight off to the Gloucestershire Royal Hospital. Now, the public are on-site around midday and out at six. Don't expect a Glastonbury-style stampede, because we're rather unauthentic alongside the medieval herbalists. But it's a very jolly weekend, a great introduction for first-timers. And you'll find we get a stack of French and Belgians, so listen out for mangled requests for Arnica.'

He moved along the line, re-capping shifts with David, Shahnaz and Anna, and giving last-minute advice. Finally he came to Zoe and Karin. They shuffled in opposite directions and he squeezed between them, bridging the two chairs.

'Okay... Karin, eleven till one, and four till six. Zoe, three hours, one till four. Sorry I've not time-tabled you together today, but with three students here I need to spread the experience. We'll see how things go, and tomorrow I'll try to put you on together. Oh, I think we may have our first customer. Wouldn't this be worth a photo, Zo?'

Zo smirked and disappeared inside to the dispensary.

'That,' said Simon, nodding to the arrival, 'is period nobility for Tewkesbury. Except for the push-chair.'

The push-chair, a state-of-the-art three-wheeler containing a screaming baby, bore down on them, bumping over tussocks of grass. It was pushed by a plump-faced woman in a long, ultramarine dress and a pointed, pale pink steeple cap from the tip of which a sheet's worth of white veil billowed out behind.

Karin went to meet her.

'Hi!' The woman appeared almost as red-faced and fraught as the infant. 'Have you got anything for my little girl? I'm supposed to be setting up for a spinning demo. Bless her heart. I don't know which of us is more desperate.'

Karin showed them into the tent. Beside the nearest seat the woman parked the push-chair. She flopped down next to it, blew loudly, then leaned over and took the baby's hand. The baby was wearing a long cream dress and had a rumpled green and white glass-cloth draped across her shoulders.

'Teething?'

'I know she's in pain,' said the woman, 'but she's been bawling non-stop since breakfast. The only thing that pacifies her is me carrying her, but I've only just changed her wet nappy and she pooed straight in the clean one, and it's so disgusting I daren't pick her up in this dress.'

'Mind if I check the contents?'

'I would hold your breath.'

Karin eased up one side of the dress. The little girl shrieked even louder and pedalled her fat, clawed feet. Karin tugged on the elasticated leg of a distinctly non-medieval disposable napkin, which was just about stemming a tide of green slurry.

'Spinach poo, one red cheek, stroppy as hell,' she said to Zo, when the woman had been sent away inside the minute with a supply of Chamomilla. 'They don't come any easier. You'll walk it.'

The first hour turned out quiet. They sat outside, chatting, comparing colleges and the practices they ran. The students took a couple of headache cases, for which Karin confirmed the prescriptions. At midday Zo ambled off to mingle with the first members of the public, and returned just before one to start her shift.

She took off her baseball cap and wiped her forehead with the back of her thumb. 'I think I'm going to take up archery.'

'Oh?'

'Those little leather things they strap on to protect their arms, they're the fashion accessories for me. Oh, and the muscles...' She feigned a shudder. 'And the stance...'

'God,' said Karin. 'I'm off.'

'See you at four. Oh, and the blacksmith's worth a look –'

As Karin left behind the blue and yellow beacon of the Travelling Homœopaths' tent, two men carrying their offspring in aluminium-framed rucksacks stood aside for a band of soldiers. A couple wore breast-plates, the rest, padded tunics. They jingled past with their buckles and swords, helmets under their arms, noisy, purposeful, commanding. Credible. The modern age momentarily faltered and vanished before her eyes, and when it emerged again the Middle Ages still eddied, like pools of the past, wherever she looked. Linen, hemp and wool rubbed shoulders with polyester cotton and viscose and plastic. Glimpses of bare arms and backs, pale and brazen, highlighted the well-wrapped medieval modesty. There were mummers with stilt-walkers, English voices and French ones, drummers with penny whistles, and the crackle of a spit-roasting lamb turning ginger over a fire. She could have purchased her own chain-mail or a helmet, or even a complete suit of armour. Stalls sold candles and leather goods and bolts of medieval-style fabric. Some offered period garments made-to-measure. A group had formed round a juggler and fire-eater, and an even larger crowd was spilling out of the mead tent.

Her stomach groaned insistently for attention. All of a sudden a slice of sizzling, blackened lamb and a hunk of bread seemed a worthy feast. The spit, smelly and smoking, lured her back.

'Well done, please,' she asked the woman in the whimple. 'Almost burnt.'

The woman hacked off a piece of meat with a great, grey-bladed knife and took a lump of bread from a cloth-covered basket. She split the bread and closed it like jaws round the meat, handed it over and gave her fingers a cursory wipe on a grease-spotted apron.

Karin bit into the sandwich, squashing it flatter between her hands, and tore at the meat inside. Chewing, she peered at the bread, stained yellow with oil and flecked with crumbs of carbon. Fatty lamb and bread, a combination she would normally shun. There, however, with a battlefield underfoot, and the excitement of the tents and the crowds, this earthy meal was to be grasped like a privilege.

'Hello!'

She followed the voice. The noble spinner waved to her from an open-fronted, barrel-roofed tent. She was sitting on a stool, carding a cloud of wool between two broad, wooden brushes. On the grass beside her stood a small spinning wheel and two baskets of unprepared fleece with a couple of spindle whorls on top.

She motioned with a brush to the wicker tray in the shade at her feet. 'Success!'

The baby lay on her back, fast asleep on a blue woollen blanket, her arms flung either side of her head and her mouth open.

'The early life of Sleeping Beauty,' Karin smiled. 'How did you -?'

'What, get into this?' The woman laughed. 'You've heard of golf widows? Well, mine's a battle gunner. I've made quite a niche for myself on the quiet. Merchant's wife today, peasant tomorrow, the crowds love it. That Chamomilla, by the way, was a life-saver.'

Karin wandered on, content with the food and the gratitude, past a friar and a jester in brilliant red and canary yellow, past the swingboats and a jeweller's stall, a basket-weaver and a historical bookseller's. She retraced her steps. The jeweller, a large bearded man with a white, close-fitting cap, a white shirt and fox-coloured jerkin, was sitting behind his counter of wares. He held a can of beer in one hand and a packet of crisps in his lap. But her eyes settled on the parrot cage, balanced on top of a tea-chest behind the display of enamelled brooches and rings.

The bird was on the roof of the cage, standing on a modified parrot perch. She and the magpie looked at each other, their heads on opposite sides.

'He's beautiful,' she said. 'Isn't he chained?'

'No need.' The jeweller emptied the crisp crumbs into his hand and clapped it over his mouth. 'I found him flapping about on the main road not far from our house, obviously hit by a car. See how his left wing droops? The vet said he couldn't repair it well enough for him to survive again in the wild, so we kept you for our sins, didn't we,' he said, throwing the words over his shoulder in affectionate accusation. 'They're intelligent, magpies, very intelligent. Tell the lady your name.'

The magpie's head jerked to his master.

'Go on.'

'*Duke. The Duke.*'

'No!' Karin clapped her hands. 'Don't people berate you for keeping him caged?'

'Caged? He's hardly ever in it! That bird gets more freedom than I do. They're not protected anyway. And he loves trips out, all the buzz and bustle. Though he has the sense not to wander too far at shows. Anyway,' the man added, 'this is authentic, this is. They used to keep jays and magpies as pets, like parrots. And teach them to talk. I should have a wicker cage, I suppose. Not so hygienic, though. Wonderful birds. So clever,' he directed at the magpie. 'Too clever by half.'

'*Love ya!*'

She reached for her camera.

'You'll never believe what I saw,' she boasted to Zo when she arrived back just before four. 'A family of lepers. And a talking magpie.'

'What you saw, if you ask me,' said Zo, 'is too much of the inside of the mead tent. We saw a few inquiries about homœopathy, a wasp sting, two cases of hay fever, one cystitis, a sprained ankle, a depressed peasant with a bellyful of ale, a case of asthma and a hammered thumb-nail.'

'And just after you left,' said Shahnaz, joining them, 'we had a man practically crawl here, lame in the leg, and Zo piled straight on to the computer and whipped out Ammonium Muriaticum. We were so impressed. And the best bit is he walked in two minutes ago with a back like a ramrod, and bought a T-shirt!'

Zo reddened and consulted her watch. 'Time to hand over, I reckon.'

'Are you going to watch the battle?' Karin asked.

'Tomorrow. Right now I'm off to the espresso bar, aka beer tent.'

Behind them came the hollow thud of feet. A young woman in jeans and a tie-dye top ran up, panting and waving her arms.

'Your call,' said Zo.

'A man...' The girl heaved the words in great gulps out of her lungs. 'He's just collapsed down there.'

'Collapsed?'

She pointed, and Karin moved forward to follow the line of her arm.

'Between those tents. See him? There, where those people are gathering.'

'Do you know what's wrong?'

The girl shook her head.

'Hold on,' said Zo. 'I'll grab my mobile and come down with you, see what's what.'

Karin sprinted off along the avenue, her legs pumping, her ankles absorbing the unevenness of the field, her feet somehow finding a firm landing beneath her.

He was lying on his back between the guys of two white canvas tents. An old woman cradled his head and four or five onlookers stood around, gawping. He wore a full set of black leathers and a helmet. His gloved hands met over his chest, and he twisted forward in a series of small, convulsive movements.

'Not one of the re-enactors,' Karin called over her shoulder.

She threw herself on her knees next to him, shoving aside the black bag that lay in the grass. Under the tinted visor he was moaning.

'Get the helmet off!' Zo yelled, jogging up behind her. 'Or the visor. No, just get the visor up!'

Karin located the raised plastic mouldings at the bottom of the visor and it clicked jerkily upwards beneath her hands. Underneath he was wearing small sunglasses, and his cheeks were puffed against the foam lining of the helmet.

'Can you tell us what's wrong? Where does it hurt?'

He groaned and tightened his fists over his chest so that the leather made a plastic creaking.

Karin turned to Zoe. 'Get an ambulance.'

But Zo seemed frozen by the scene.

'Zo, we can't take the chance. *Do it!*'

'Oh my God... Karin, look...'

Her head snapped back to the biker. He was lying on his side now, hoisted on his right elbow with his left knee crooked to balance him. Shakily he raised his left hand. He pressed it into the open face of the helmet and covered his eyes. Groaning, he lowered his head. And then he ripped off the glasses.

For a second Karin hesitated. 'You *sods!*'

By the time she had got to her feet, Zoe was already thanking and dispersing the extras.

'How could you do this?' Karin yelled at her, flinging her arm towards Roy. 'How could you?'

'I did have a little assistance,' Zo admitted, 'and from quite an unexpected quarter. Well...' She circled her arms like a showman. 'I have a suggestion: why don't you and Roy take off? Have a wander, go into town. I can cover your shift.'

Karin glanced down at Roy. He removed his helmet and watched her with muted amusement as he heaved off his jacket.

'You've just done three hours. I can't ask you to work two more.'

'I'm offering.' Zo leaned her head close to Karin's. '*As long as you don't screw up this time round.*'

'Ha! Well, I'd better tell Simon anyway.'

'He's been in on it for the past week. We work together. Collective, remember?'

Roy got up, all the joints of the leather groaning. He was wearing a plain white T-shirt, and as he stooped to pick up his bag and helmet, Zo grinned at Karin and silently blew between her lips.

'So, balmy summer evening. Just right for a spin on the bike, Kar.'

'I don't know –'

'I brought a spare helmet,' said Roy.

'I had a go this morning,' Zo announced with triumph. 'Fabulous! Or, you could stay here for the private entertainment in the marquee later on. Rumour has it...' She touched her forefinger to her lips. 'Rumour has it that after a few flagons of ale, a handful of vanquished Lancastrians will be having their pubes shorn by buxom wenches wielding razors. Roy?'

'Can't say the prospect sends shivers of delight down my spine, no, but Karin might be interested.'

'No way! Zo, we wouldn't want to inhibit you.'

'Two go wild in Tewkesbury then,' said Zo, backing away. 'Must dash; my patients await.'

They watched her trudge off, heavy and graceless, in the direction of the homœopathy tent. They turned to each other.

'So,' he said, touching her arm, 'a homœopath. Not a librarian.'

'Not a librarian, no.'

He slid the bag from his shoulder on to the grass, unzipped it and pulled out an envelope. From the envelope he took a black and white photograph.

'Delivery for you. I said I'd be willing to return it.'

She put out her hand. 'I don't –'

'No, you should look at it.' He moved beside her, shifting his fingers down the black border of the print. 'What do you think?'

'Awful! I've got my mouth open like one of those pouty French actresses. And look at my eyes.'

'You had your precious guard down for a second. This is what was inside. What, I said to myself, is this woman so afraid of? Me? Because this is you, Karin, in black and white. Zoe tried to explain something about your homœopathy, how you match your patient's personality to the remedy with the most similar character. Well, I don't know anything about your remedies but, to me, *this is you*. The rawness is so raw it almost hurts to look at it. But I can't stop looking at it.' Without another word he returned the photo to the envelope. 'Here.'

She took it and let her hand drop to her side.

'So, there we are.' He ran his tongue over his upper lip. 'No more reminders.'

'What would it remind you of,' she said softly, 'if I let you keep it?'

'Do I have to answer that?'

'Maybe,' she said, 'you won't need a reminder one day.'

And before he could respond she kissed him, very gently, on the shadow at the corner of his mouth.

41

'Fabulous day,' said Jim Straker.

Hilary held out her empty plate and chop-sticks in separate hands. He stacked the plates and laid the four chop-sticks on top. The wok on its stand in the centre of the patio table was empty too, but for a few strands of beansprouts. He picked up the wok in his other hand and ferried everything into the kitchen.

'There's more to follow,' he called. 'And I've got a surprise.' Presently he returned with a white paper bag and two side-plates, one of which he set in front of her. 'And to round off, a very Chinese dessert...'

He opened the mouth of the bag and let her look inside.

'Jim, they're chocolate éclairs.'

'I know. I suppose I should have bought lychees, but for all the hype they taste like scented turnip.' He frowned. 'You prefer éclairs?'

'You know I do.'

'Good.' He put one on each side-plate. 'Wait! I haven't finished.'

He disappeared inside again, licking a frond of cream from

his fingers, and came back carrying a tray with an ice-bucket and a couple of flutes.

'My God!'

'Bollinger, nicely chilled.' He slid the tray on the table and twisted the wire cage off the cork. '*Et voi-là!*'

A twist of grey vapour hovered over the neck of the bottle and vanished into the warm, still air. Hilary watched him pour.

'A stir-fry cooked by your own fair hands, éclairs, nice weather,' she mused. 'Champagne. No kids...'

'Ah,' he said, raising his glass. 'Well, it's to congratulate you on securing your place at the West Devon School of Homœopathy, and to wish you much success with your course, and the whole new venture. You even have a book list; it's getting serious. Here's to you.'

Hilary made a mysterious, shy smile, and proffered her glass to his. 'To both of us.'

For a moment, just for a moment, his heart danced a little illogically inside his chest. He concentrated his gaze on the chestnut at the end of the garden until his heart fell back into its normal rhythm, ripe to be ignored.

'Fed them?'

'What? Oh, yes, they've had theirs, their Last Supper, as it were. And I gave them an egg each. I hope you don't mind. I'll buy another box. Maybe I should deal with them now, before the sun disappears. Yes, maybe I should.' He jumped up from the table. 'You come, Hilary. Bring your drink.'

They walked side by side down the lawn.

'Nice dress,' he said. 'You should wear blue more often.'

The woods were already stencilled black against the apricot sky, and the evening damp quickly crept over the soles of his sandals.

In the trap the three birds began hopping.

'Look at that, Jim.'

'They're always pleased to see me. Aren't you,' he said. He put his hands on his hips and looked about him. 'I don't really want to do this here. But it doesn't matter any more, does it. Not that much.'

'No.'

He bent down. From each of the occupied compartments he drew out the perch, agitating each branch until the magpie was jostled on to the grass beside its food and water bowl and the split eggshells.

'How are you going to do this? One at a time?'

'All together.' He paused next to the trap. 'You must think I'm stupid. Soft. Faint-hearted.'

'Folk have always been strange. You occupy your days with half of them. At times I think I work with the rest. Yes, I think you're all those.' She drained her glass. 'Though people have been loved for worse.'

Straker leaned forward over the cage and grasped it halfway along the opposite sides, causing the birds to beat their wings with anxiety. He counted to three, lifted the cage up and over them, swung it to his right and laid it down. The birds all cowered for a second in their invisible cages, then rose, one by one, drawing up their claws and whirling stiffly away into the early dusk of the wood.